D1716564

The Apollonian Clockwork

The Apollonian Clockwork

On Stravinsky

BY

LOUIS ANDRIESSEN

AND

ELMER SCHÖNBERGER

TRANSLATED FROM THE DUTCH BY

JEFF HAMBURG

Oxford New York

OXFORD UNIVERSITY PRESS

1989

Oxford University Press, Walton Street, Oxford OX2 6DP
Oxford New York Toronto
Delhi Bombay Calcutta Madras Karachi
Petaling Jaya Singapore Hong Kong Tokyo
Nairobi Dar es Salaam Cape Town
Melbourne Auckland
and associated companies in
Berlin Ibadan

Oxford is a trade mark of Oxford University Press

Published in the United States
by Oxford University Press, New York

First published in 1983 by Uitgeverij De Bezige Bij, Amsterdam
First published in English in 1989 by Oxford University Press

British Library Cataloguing in Publication Data
Andriessen, Louis.
The Apollonian clockwork: about Stravinsky.
1. American music. Stravinsky Igor 1882–1971. Critical studies
I. Title II. Schonberger, Elmer
III. Het Apollinisch uurwerk English
780'.92'4

ISBN 0–19–315461–7

Library of Congress Cataloging in Publication Data
Andriessen, Louis, 1939–
The Apollonian clockwork.
Translation of: Het apollinisch uurwerk.
Includes bibliographies and index.
1. Stravinsky, Igor, 1882–1971—Criticism and interpretation. I. Schönberger, Elmer. II. Title.
ML410.S932A6313 1989 780'.92'4 88–25543
ISBN 0–19–315461–7

Typeset by Cambrian Typesetters, Frimley, Camberley, Surrey
Printed and bound in Great Britain by
Biddles Ltd, Guildford and King's Lynn
Music engraving by N. F. Iping

For that matter, what is there to exaggerate: temperament, sensitivity, wit, humour, spontaneity, gentleness, strength, or—in the final analysis, the two characteristics of genius—naïveté and irony; all of this he already possesses.

Goethe on Haydn

Acknowledgements

Grateful acknowledgements are due to the following for permission to use copyright material.

Musical Examples

Boosey and Hawkes Music Publishers Ltd., London

Petrushka, Deux poésies de Balmont, *Le Sacre du printemps*, *Le Rossignol*, *Symphonies of Wind Instruments*, Mavra, Octet, *Concerto for Piano and Wind*, *Oedipus Rex*, *Apollon musagète*, *Le Baiser de la fée*, *Symphony of Psalms*, *Duo concertant*, Perséphone, *Three Pieces* for string quartet, *Orpheus*, *Cantata*, *Greeting Prelude*, *The Rake's Progress*, *Étude* for pianola, *Madrid*, *Agon*, *Canticum Sacrum*, *Threni*, *Variations* (Aldous Huxley in memoriam), *Concerto in D* for strings, *Requiem Canticles*, *Tres sacrae cantiones*, *La Marseillaise.*

Publishers B. Schott's Söhne, Mainz

The Firebird, *Concerto for Violin* in D, *Jeu de cartes*, *Concerto in E flat* (*Dumbarton Oaks*), *Symphony in C*, *Danses Concertantes*, *Ode*, *Sonata* for two pianos, *Symphony in Three Movements.*

J. and W. Chester/Edition Wilhelm Hansen London Ltd.

Three Easy Pieces, *Five Easy Pieces* for piano duet, *Les Noces* (1919 and 1923 versions), *L'Histoire du soldat*, *Song of the Volga Boatmen*, *Concertino* for string quartet, *Les cinq doigts.*

Rob. Forberg—P. Jurgenson Musikverlag

Le Roi des étoiles.

Mercury Music

The Star-Spangled Banner (© 1941).

Charling Music Corp.

Ebony Concerto (© 1946).

Quotations

Faber and Faber, London

I. Stravinsky and R. Craft: *Conversations with Igor Stravinsky* (1959);

Memories and Commentaries (1960); *Expositions and Developments* (1962); *Dialogues and a Diary* (1968); *Themes and Conclusions* (1972).

Hutchinson of London

V. Stravinsky and R. Craft: *Stravinsky in Pictures and Documents* (1979).

Illustrations

page

4 Photo by Hans van den Bogaard.
8 from *Igor and Vera Stravinsky: A Photograph Album* (Thames and Hudson, London, 1982).
19 'La Condition humaine' by René Magritte; collection Claude Spaak, Paris.
23 Photo Boston Police Department.
51 from V. Stravinsky and R. Craft, *Stravinsky in Pictures and Documents* (Hutchinson of London, 1979).
54 Illustration by John Tenniel (original illustration from Lewis Carroll, *Alice's Adventures in Wonderland*).
56 Gramophone jacket of first recording of *Orpheus* (HMV, 1949).
69 Photo by Dick Raaijmakers.
95 Photo collection Roland-Manuel.
118 *left:* Photo CBS; *right:* Arnold Schoenberg, self-portrait 1911, collection Arnold Schoenberg, Los Angeles.
129 from V. Stravinsky and R. Craft, *Stravinsky in Pictures and Documents* (Hutchinson of London, 1979).
143 *left:* collection Theodore Stravinsky; *right:* Jimmy Yancey, photo RCA.
148 Collection Arnold Schoenberg Institute, Los Angeles.
149 from A. Schaeffner, *Strawinsky* (Paris, 1931).
151 Photo collection Rex Lawson, London.
159 Private property Elmer Schönberger.
178 Picasso and Stravinsky, drawn by Jean Cocteau, collection A. Meyer.
185 Photo by Elmer Schönberger.
186 Photo by Elmer Schönberger.
194 *upper:* from A. Schaeffner, *Strawinsky* (Paris, 1931); *lower*: photo by Elmer Schönberger.
213 from Th. Arbeau, *Orchésographie* (Langres, 1589).
259 from Ch. Obolensky, *The Russian Empire* (Jonathan Cape, London, 1980).
260 grave of F. I. Stravinsky, photo by Elmer Schönberger.
261 grave of Dargomyzhsky, photo by Elmer Schönberger.

262 grave of Glinka, photo by Elmer Schönberger.
264 grave of Mussorgsky, photo by Elmer Schönberger.
268 grave of Tchaikovsky, photo by Elmer Schönberger.
269–70 Rimsky-Korsakov House, photo by Elmer Schönberger.
270 *lower*: grave of Rimsky-Korsakov, photo by Elmer Schönberger.

Contents

Translator's Note

Translating any book is problematic. This book was no different. The problems that arose from this translation, though, were not merely questions of style, finding the correct phrase and so on, but of catching the authors' mentality, creating the proper ambience, saying what the authors want to say in precisely the same elusive manner that they have in the original. For, as will become clear, this is not a straightforward book about Stravinsky, rather a *paradigm* of Stravinsky. To parody the authors, this book is concerned with everything and everything concerns this book.

It is precisely for this reason that I have made every attempt to keep the text as they wrote it as clear as possible. Nothing would have been easier than to footnote every allusion and reference, the effect being similar to a performance of *The Rake's Progress* in which every time a melody or harmonic sequence from musical history is referred to, the orchestra would stop, play the quoted passage, then resume performing the opera. Even such obscurely translated words as 'zoonology'—a combination of zoology and sonology, the study of sound—are left to the reader to decipher.

References are included by chapter in the List of Sources in order of their appearance in the text as a means of helping those who want to track down the sources. General works consulted, together with their abbreviations used in the text, are given at the start of the List of Sources. Where no translation of a non-English text is listed, I have translated it myself, from the original in most cases. I have attempted to use existing translations wherever possible, even when not in total agreement with them, to assist the interested reader in finding the context of the original quotation.

One problem, though, was with some text written by the authors in German. This often has a specific purpose, mainly to set off certain ways of thinking which are associated with German culture (be it Wagner or Schoenberg) against French and/or Russian. Most often, this German appears here untranslated; the *fact* that it is in German also expresses something (this German-French/Russian dichotomy is an essential part of the authors' cultural orientation and might be kept in mind while reading the book).

In general, Russian transcriptions have followed English common practice. The name of the composer has been spelled according to his own preference: Stravinsky. While some Russian remains untranslated, other Russian words are translated without the slightest clue being given as to what the original was, in accordance with the authors' intention of, not mystifying, but bringing the subject of the book closer to the reader.

Please note that $\boxed{42}$ refers to the rehearsal number in the score, $\boxed{22}_2$ to the 2nd bar of rehearsal number 22, and 25^2 to the 2nd chord of bar 25.

The translator would like to thank Louis Andriessen and Elmer Schönberger for their great assistance in this translation (one could almost call this a collaboration considering the care with which Mr Schönberger has reviewed the translation). Furthermore, he would like to thank Mrs Mary Worthington for her excellent editing of this labrythine book and Ed Harsh for his comments and criticism. And last but not least, my wife and seven-month-old daughter for their patience.

The original Dutch publication (*Het Apollinisch Uurwerk*, *Over Stravinsky*, Uitgeverij De Bezige Bij, Amsterdam, 1983) was made possible through financial support from the Prince Bernhard Funds and the Ministry of Welfare, Health and Culture.

This translation was made possible through financial support from the Prince Bernhard Funds.

J.H.

Amsterdam
Spring 1988

Preface

The most striking thing about this book is what it is *not.*

It is not a biography: not even the date of birth of the main character is given. It is most definitely not a survey, though it is about a composer whose music is easily surveyed. Survey is simplification. Nothing is wrong with that as long as it is made apparent. Since so many surveys of Stravinsky have already been written, it actually appears as if something like a survey exists, which is certainly not true. The *facts* alone are too numerous for one to write a survey with a clear conscience. A thorough investigation of the historical and musical relationship between Stravinsky and Schoneberg would supply enough material for a volume.

Stravinsky lived in an untidy period—the first half of the twentieth century. Besides, he concerned himself with everything and everything concerned him. His life as an *émigré* led him on a journey through the world; his life as a composer led him on a journey through the history of music. Both journeys, with sidetracks and detours, followed labyrinthine paths—at least to the onlooker.

The authors' decision to collaborate on this book arose not only from a shared love of Stravinsky's music, but from an agreement on a few fundamental points: that there is no essential difference between early and late Stravinsky; that the familiar division of his works into 'Russian', 'neoclassical', and 'serial' periods more often obscures rather than clarifies the music; and that the distinction commonly made between 'arrangements' and 'original compositions' is not pertinent to Stravinsky.

What they heard in the music was that all his works have been composed from an immutable musical *mentality*. It is a mentality precipitated in music that points to other music (and makes that pointing into a subject), without ever leaving a moment's doubt as to who the maker is. This is a paradox. Since paradoxes do not exist in order to be solved, it was necessary to follow in Stravinsky's path—without stepping on his footprints, without even consecutively reconstructing those footsteps, and without being concerned about following the shortest path from A to B. It became a route with access roads, sidetracks, and detours.

L.A. and E.S.

Amsterdam
17 June 1982 (5 June 1982)

I

The New Renewed

In 1981 a gramophone record appeared—Stravinsky's *Chanson russe* eight times over, nothing else. There are several reasons why this recording can be called revealing.

In 1981, things had gone so far that a fashionable bar in Amsterdam where tasteful background music (the worst kind) was played, alternated soft Thad Jones and soft Morricone with soft (but intended to be loud) fragments from Stravinsky's *Pulcinella* and soft (but intended to be loud) fragments from Steve Reich's *Four Organs*. In another five years, Webern's *Bagatelles*, and in another ten years, Schoenberg's *Pierrot lunaire* will get their turns.

Chanson russe is an arrangement of the aria sung by Parasha, the girl in love from the *opera buffa*, *Mavra*. If anything could shed light on what sweet melancholy is—of which many a poet has tasted—it is this aria. Sweet melancholy is counterfeited sorrow: to enjoy it, taste, a certain refinement, and leisure are required. In order to make this apparent, a bel canto melody, replete with sobs (however precious and well mannered) and the broad shoulders of four-in-the-bar chords (however bashful) fall short of their mark: it remains sentimental. Though these are the ingredients of Parasha's aria, something peculiar is happening. The melody wells up, but never begins to flow. Moreover, it is hindered by the accompanying voices which erect dams in the most unexpected places, even damming each other in. The bass is an ostinato in four, the middle voices are repeated chord patterns in six, and the melody consists of periods of five and a half. Together they form a mechanism that does not set anything in motion except itself. The owner of the bar in Amsterdam that played *Pulcinella* may well be ready to play *Chanson russe* once, but after eight times the clientele might realize that *Chanson russe* is more than just *Souvenir de Spa*. Russian Donizetti, but slightly too off-beat, preventing you from continuing your conversation. If once does not do it, eight times should—restore the original effect.

In the same year, 1981, the première of *Le Sacre du printemps* took place in the Amsterdam Concertgebouw: the première, that is, of an arrangement for four pianos made from the original score by Maarten Bon.[1] The public reacted as if they had just heard the *Sacre* for the first time. This was quite understandable.

[1] Maarten Bon (1933), Dutch composer and pianist [trans].

The arrangement appeared, in principle, to be one as true as possible to the notes. The effect was not merely of a reduction (as is the four-hand version by Stravinsky himself, made for purely practical reasons), but of an X-ray that, instead of showing the glittering car-body, revealed the chassis. Thus, the music became even more estranged from the tradition that made it possible—there was nothing left of 'rite' and 'spring', let alone of a semi-folkloristic ballet. Had this piece been a romantic composition brimming with filled-in harmonies and a written-out piano-pedal, this same transcription would have been a disaster; since it was the *Sacre* which was being transcribed, it created a sound which (except for a few episodes, such as the opening bassoon melody) replaced the original instead of imitating it, much as the four pianos in the definitive version of *Les Noces* replace the original symphony orchestra. And so, the source of the *Sacre*—a piano in an attic in a Swiss village—found its second destiny. We heard an enormous pianola, where eighty-eight mechanical fingers were replaced by eighty-eight live fingers, and it became clearer than ever that the distance between the *Sacre* and *Les Noces* was much less than the distance between St Petersburg and Paris. Furthermore, this arrangement succeeded in a way that virtuosic and glamorous orchestral performances rarely do any more; again we could hear that the *Sacre*, in 1913, not only reached a new limit in abstract compositional thought (the effect of which the listener can fairly easily 'play back'), but a new limit in orchestral technique, synchronization, and rhythmic exactitude. A simultaneous attack from four pianists is—because it is more difficult to realize—more simultaneous than a simultaneous orchestral attack that sounds together even if it is not.

It was just like the seven repetitions of *Chanson russe:* an original effect restored, and we sat, not in the Concertgebouw, but in the Théâtre des Champs-Elysées, albeit this time without the scandal.

And still in 1981, in the first week of April, we were reminded of the tenth anniversary of Stravinsky's death by a young Dutch composer, Cornelis de Bondt. He did not do so with words but with a piece of music, *Bint*, that the twelve-man orchestra Hoketus[2] performed for the eleventh time. The title of the work refers to a novel by Bordewijk[3], with which the music shares a certain severity, and,. of course, to the object itself—a heavy beam.[4] De Bondt's heavy beam is a piece of tramrail, or, more precisely, two pieces, as the instrumentation of Hoketus is self-mirroring. The heavy blows on these rails articulate a composition lasting fifty minutes, in which much happens even though little musical material is used and in which the listener, in spite of the process-orientated character of the music, never knows exactly where these few chords and rhythms are supposed to go. *Bint* sounds like a machine that has no other purpose than to keep itself in motion. It never becomes clear to which laws of mechanics this colossus is being subjected. It is as if two enormous cogwheels are slowly building up momentum, but because the smaller wheels that connect the big ones are partially imperceptible to the ear, the listener has no chance to disengage his attention. The gnarling in his head and the gnarling of the music on the stage form an energetic counterpoint.

Bint is a 'machine humaine'. Few things are so human as a human machine inasmuch as nothing is inherently so *un*-machinelike. In the human machine, humans must expend more effort and energy to accomplish what a machine, effortlessly, does mechanically. The musical construction of *Bint* is so finely tuned that just one moment of human inattention can be enough to throw this Swiss–precision instrument out of control.

[2] Hoketus was an ensemble formed by Louis Andriessen in 1977 to perform the composition by the same name. The ensemble, a consequence of the original composition, was based on the principle of hocket, thus being associated more with pop and folk music than with concert music. The ensemble disbanded in 1986 [trans].

[3] Bordewijk (1844–1965), Dutch author of, among other works, futuristic novels [trans].

[4] The Dutch word *bint* means heavy beam, such as a railway sleeper. The word itself has a rather hard sound. In the novel by Bordewijk, it refers to the iron discipline demanded by the schoolteacher on which the story is based [trans].

Even though the musical material is limited, the piece is by nature just as unminimal as the closing bars of Stravinsky's *Les Noces.* Quite contrary to the processes in most minimal music, those in *Bint* are irreversible. That irreversibility is a result of, among other things, vague allusions to the traditional cadence, where the value of each chord is determined by its relationship to one unchangeable fundamental chord. This chord is suggested in *Bint*, but is never heard. The music does not untangle. The knot, which is getting more and more complicated, is simply hacked through. The 'wrong' chord that determines the last minutes of the piece thrusts a spoke into the cogwheel which has been driven to its maximum velocity.

Bint resembles most the execution of a mechanical ritual. One could almost say that it begins where Stravinsky—literally, in the postlude of the *Requiem Canticles*—leaves off.

New music, at least as it sounds in Holland, takes on different shapes: strict, often process-orientated forms, with a preference for winds and keyboard instruments; simulated improvisations, written out in the most minute detail; montage-technique; neo-tonality (but no neo-romanticism and not 'back to the symphony orchestra' to be squeezed in between Brahms and Mahler, or nowadays Shostakovich). Tonality is 'played upon'—old concepts of arsis and thesis, breathing in and out, may be applied, distorted, inverted, but, in any case, are no longer ignored as they were by serial music.

What the composers of this music have in common is that they are all more orientated towards Stravinsky, Varèse, and improvised music than towards Schoenberg and Boulez. Their music reflects a conception which places serial music, as the furthest consequence of nineteenth-century music, in the mausoleum of the past perfect tense. Even so-called post-serial music experiences the same fate. When, in the winter of 1981, at a concert of new Dutch music in Amsterdam, a piano work was performed in which a cluster appeared, giggles broke out in the audience; not because the cluster was so modern and daring, but because it was so *old-fashioned.*

The true influence of Stravinsky has only just begun. It is an influence which can do without Stravinskianisms, without convulsive rhythms, without endless changes of time signatures, without pandiatonicism, without *pas-de-deux.* No neo-, post-, or -ism; rather it is the type of influence inspired by misunderstanding, the deliberate distortion, the good wrong conclusion. Real influence is a ladder that one lovingly throws behind, just out of reach.

1966—*Requiem Canticles*

On 6 April 1971 Stravinsky died in a house in New York where he had lived for a week.

On 15 April he was buried in Venice.

Before the burial, a service was performed in the basilica of Santi Giovanni e Paolo—a requiem according to the Greek Orthodox liturgy. This service began with a concert. Besides Scarlatti and Gabrieli, *Requiem Canticles* was performed—Stravinsky's last large work, dating from 1966. Unlike the *Mass*, this work is not suitable for liturgical use as only one-tenth of the liturgical text is set; it is not suitable for a church either as it does not sound good in a church. The piece needs a short reverberation time. It is chamber music: thin, pointed, articulated, tailored more to a small Italian opera theatre than to a cathedral. If the Prelude reminds us of anything, it is the music that Vivaldi played, accompanied by his girls' string orchestra in the Conservatorio dell'Ospedale della Pietà in Venice; light, repeated notes, played at the point of the bow, like the beginning of 'Winter' from the *Four Seasons*.

Requiem Canticles is the Requiem for the Requiem. After that, every composer who writes a liturgical requiem for large choir and orchestra, preferably in his old age, will seem like a taxidermist. He will be stuffing a skeleton with ersatz meat and then be putting a black top hat on it. Then he will say: here, this is a man. But he will be wrong. It is no longer possible. Stravinsky's *Requiem Canticles* is Berlioz's *Grande Messe des morts*, shrivelled to an aphorism.

The piece can be divided into seven parts, the longest not even lasting three minutes. An orchestral Prelude; then only the last line of the Introitus: 'exaudi orationem meam . . .' (thus avoiding the text 'Requiem aeternam'); then six of the nineteen couplets from the Dies irae, divided into two parts by an orchestral Interlude; the Libera me, sung in the liturgy during the absolution after the mass, here somewhat shortened, serves as the last vocal movement; and finally an orchestral Postlude. The entire work lasts for fifteen minutes and uses a symphony orchestra, two low solo voices, and a choir. (In the orchestra, some instruments are not used—oboes and clarinets. But the xylophone from *Danse macabre* is not left out in the cold, even if he only has two bars to play.) And yet, when all is said and done, it is difficult to recall if ever more than ten instruments have been playing at the same time.

As might be expected, reference is made to other Requiems from musical history. In this work too, trumpets ring out in the Tuba mirum. We hear wailing motifs, sighs, and long melismas during the Lacrimosa. But all fear is removed: in this music the Final Judgement is not a threat, there is no Resurrection of Dead Souls, who, themselves paralysed before the Heavenly Countenance, terrify mortals so, no hordes of trumpets and trombones, and certainly no Paradise à la Fauré; that was filed away long ago in the printed postcard archive. In the Tuba mirum there are only two trumpets and one trombone and by the sixth bar they petrify into held-out chords. And the bells do not toll for the Last Judgement, merely for the End of Time: it had always been evident that this bell-ringer, with his music as legal tender, belonged to the one hundred and forty-four Chosen. After such a life in the service of God, the Judgement just had to be in his favour; the Judgement need not even be feared, Death had already been celebrated too often. Death in Venice: the city is itself a celebration of death, a sinking empire of Eastern beauty, the closest Western city to Byzantium, that is the city from which the *Symphony*

of Psalms springs. The Hallelujah from the West sounds like a *Gospodi pomiluy* ['Lord have mercy']. Venice forms an image of death; the first thing that Robert Craft noticed when he came to the city to bury Stravinsky was that thousands of posters littered the city: 'The city of Venice honours the great musician Igor Stravinsky who with a gesture of exquisite friendship wanted in life to be buried in the city he loved more than any other.' Stravinsky did not die in Venice, only the ritual of the dead—the burial—occurred there. No, only 'real' composers really die in Venice, and only then do the gondolas really become *lugubre*.

Even the drums of death are merely an echo in *Requiem Canticles*. Two timpanists play four timpani to support a funeral march, the musical subject of the Interlude. They accompany a trochee rhythm (– ◡) played by four flutes and four horns that sounds like a funeral march in which the first and third beats are silent. The cortège continues, but the footsteps are inaudible. Or has the procession continued on the water? Perhaps in gondolas? The low flutes sound more transparent than trumpets. In *The Flood* as well, when the deluge begins, we hear flutes.

Once we reach the Postlude (the actual ritual of *Requiem Canticles* seems to be, in spite of the title, enacted in the three instrumental, not the vocal, movements; the instrumental movements are the corner-stones of the work, beginning, middle, and end, the caryatids on which the frame of the basilica rests), again flutes, together with piano, harp, and horn, play the long, held-out chords signalling the beginning and ending of the clock-strokes. The Postlude sounds as if it is the strictest piece that Stravinsky ever wrote. The entire movement consists of 77 beats in an extremely slow tempo (♩ = 40). These 77 beats can be divided into three sections: A, A′, and B. The two A sections consist of 22 beats each. Each section begins with a 'chord of Death' (Robert Craft): a tractatus logicus from a theory of harmony yet to be invented in which the octave is a dissonance.

The instrumentation of these chords (four flutes with horn, doubled by the piano and harp) guarantees a nasty, cold, skeleton-like sound. Then come the clock-strokes. For the first time since *Les Noces*, Stravinsky uses 'real' clock-bells (chimes sound like church bells), playing together with two instruments, one of which Stravinsky had never before used (the vibraphone) and the other only very sparingly (the celesta). Doing things one has never done before at the end of your life—ending with a beginning—that is conjuring.

Neither the great bells of St Petersburg, nor those of London or Paris are heard, they are the high, glistening bells of a small church in Venice. The clock strikes 11 times in section A, 11 times in section A′, and 11 times in section B. There are four entrances of the 'chord of Death': three times a chord of 4 beats for a total of 12 beats and the fourth and last time three chords also totalling 12 beats.

In the last bar, the strokes of the clock and the chord of Death come together for the first and last time; the 33rd beat of section B is also the 33rd stroke of the clock. The Hour of Truth? Did not somebody die at 33?

According to mystical tradition, the division 44–33–77 is related to the measurements of the cross; but one can prove anything with numbers if one counts the right things. Anyone who counts can count until some magic appears. So long as he does not miscount as Stravinsky did when he counted the number of bars in the *Symphony of Psalms* (78–88–212). In 1930 a composer did not have a pocket calculator available to balance the books in accordance with the cabbala (the correct answer is 75–100–200).

But the 77 beats of the Postlude are no coincidence, just as the division 22–22–33 is not, nor the three times 11 strokes of the clock, nor the *seven* entrances of God's horn solo.

No, the real magic is that of silence: this is the Hour of Truth. The twelve strokes that announce Shadow in *The Rake's Progress* are twelve silent strokes in *Requiem Canticles*—there are twelve beats of silence in the Postlude.

America on Sunday

San Diego, 6 August 1979

First time in the United States! No, the first time in America. Enjoying it all, without shame or reservation. To his dismay and disillusionment, this is exactly what he read in an article by a fussy columnist once home again in Holland: America is back in fashion 'not even ten years after Vietnam'. Travelling through desert nights in a Greyhound bus in which the air-conditioning consists of opening a window; trying to win the trip back in Las Vegas; visions of hostages and shoot-outs in a dubious bus station in which he (terrorized by the mere presence of a circuit of dealers and junkies maintained by whisper- and eye-contact and afraid to be taken for a plainclothes policeman) reluctantly makes that urgent phone call after hesitating for about an hour. It cannot be denied: all stories told by first-time travellers in America are identical. But each traveller is different. In all the buses between Toronto and San Diego there is only one passenger who has in his suitcase a brand-new recording of *Danses Concertantes*, bought in Sam's Record Shop in Toronto. (He did not bother to buy the *Oud-Nederlandsche Suite* by Cornelis Dopper.) When this passenger arrives in the Southern Californian university city, he is welcomed by a friend and hospitably received in an apartment in a luxurious suburb that is at his disposal. The next morning, even before he takes a swim in the nearby private pool, he places the record on the turntable, makes himself comfortable on the balcony in the sun, in the mean time enjoying the view of the Pacific and looking forward to four well-made police-action series that will be on TV between ten and two that evening, and listens. America, they said, is a new feeling. That was true, but now he realizes—he has had that feeling before.

In September 1939 Stravinsky set foot for the fourth time on American soil. Even though France had declared war on Germany just before he left, he was not planning to remain in America any longer than was necessary in order to fulfil his guest lectureship at Harvard University (*Poétique musicale*) and to complete his concert commitments. The question whether Stravinsky would have compromised himself politically if he had not gone to America (as Pierre Suvchinsky has claimed on the basis of Stravinsky's opportunistic political behaviour during the years just before the Second World War), is nevertheless academic. The composer *went* to America and stayed. In 1940 he settled in Los Angeles. 'Stravinsky was fifty-eight when he began a new life in California, yet he was to change continually and more profoundly there than ever before, both as a composer—from the very first months in Los Angeles, he was more accessible to new ideas and influences than he had been in his final years in Europe—and as a man. The metamorphosis of the man was largely due to his remarriage, but the informality and the radically different "life style" of southern California were contributing factors' (Craft, *PD*).

The difference between the French Stravinsky of the thirties and the American Stravinsky is, of course, the, well, difference between a penny-pincher who let his wife Catherine eat nail-soup ('Dr. Rist came and wanted to see me. I said that I had no means of paying for the consultations') and the philanthrope who writes in his expense-account diary: donation to a panhandler, ten cents. But it is especially the difference between monocle-frown and bespectacled grimace, between the aloofness of the *Concerto for Two Solo Pianos* and the flimflammery of *Danses Concertantes* (1942).

The well-rested bus traveller not only sits in the sun, he even hears it now. Right from the start everything is in its place: stamping in B♭ major, as many simultaneous notes from the scale as possible. The voice-leading, once examined, is often rather messy; Stravinsky's much-praised clarity is an extraordinary form of turbidity. Stravinsky at his best seems to be an extremely complicated machine that performs a very simple operation but in such a way that you cannot separate the final product from the way it is made. This is musical oxymoron. A page from *Danses Concertantes* looks at first glance as accessible as a simple Haydn symphony, but anyone who puts the score on his piano must quickly admit that even four hands will hardly be enough.

It is often said, with a little exaggeration, that it is always Sunday in the books of Vladimir Nabokov. Although the works of Stravinsky, in their totality, are more equally divided over the days of the week, it is a fact that in the music he composed in the six years before his naturalization as an American citizen (1945) and the six years thereafter, work days are minimalized. No matter what else you hear, there are few newspapers, few news bulletins, not much traffic and the telephone only rings occasionally. The world is reduced to the paradise of a backyard in which a select group of *émigrés* debate peremptorily about the necessity, yes, perhaps even the inevitability, of acculturation. Hidden behind the hedge, someone is listening. It's a surly Viennese refugee; admittedly someone who has gone through quite a lot. This conversation really is completely not about anything, he grumbles. He is most annoyed by the understanding which the company tacitly accepts: it is merely a conversation.

In the middle of the next movement, a Pas d'Action, the sunbather suddenly sits up. His lips turn into a smile, and there is not even anything to smile about. (There is nothing he hates more than 'jocular' music; he can only conjecture that the top-heavy, wordy sentences with which Zofia Lissa, in her epoch-making essay 'Über das Komische in der Musik', describes the supposed jocularity in the music of Saint-Saëns' bestiarium are a case of unintentional irony.) No, something has gone wrong in the abruptly begun *Meno mosso*. The flute and the clarinet add colour to the riffs of the four solo violins. A family that plays together stays together seems to be the motto, since the first riff sets the norm. But in the second riff, the two winds come in a quaver-beat late, and in the third one surprisingly, a quaver-beat early (Ex. 1). Something is always going wrong in this music. Of course, it is not hard to let something go wrong, but it is hard to let something go wrong in such a way that one would not ever dream of it being put right. That is more or less what he thinks in the few seconds he has until his attention is again inescapably drawn by two totally new subjects; that is: parallel seconds, and soloistic hopping in arpeggiated chords. The 'ravishing modulation to G major' (Tansman) which concludes this fragment escapes his attention. But it does not matter since someone else has heard it for him already, years ago. Still he decides to put on his sunglasses.

Ex. 1

Danses Concertantes 34

How is it possible that one can be so moved by something so unmoving, so cheerful, so superficial as *Danses Concertantes*? This music has no conflict, no rebellion, no acquiescence, no evocations of Nature, no development, no invertible counterpoint, no thematic dialectics, no *unendliche Melodie*, and between the staves of the music is only the white of the page. How can it be that music that is, more than any other music, only substance, only notes, can be the least formalistic music conceivable?

Whoever hears *Danses Concertantes* enters the characteristic, for Stravinsky's music, 'empty' state of mind. He is no longer possessed by one thought, one specific content. What becomes engraved in his memory is the movement, the richness of movement. This is not gratuitous music, however. It exists, but naked, extremely transparent. This emptiness is essential to Stravinsky's music. Only because it lacks specific content can the music become movement. One can best describe this movement as 'commotion' . . . The continuous changing structure in Stravinsky's music has an unbinding function. The consciousness of the listener unbinds itself from the music in as far as the music is expression and concentrates itself on the music in as far as it is movement. The process of becoming and—more importantly—the fixation on the substance [the content] is undermined by the rifts, the rhythmical displacements of time. (Wim Markus[1])

Just in time—since it is getting really warm—a cloud covers the sun over San Diego. Just a few notes, but exactly the right ones, whispers the happy owner of the record for the hundredth time, and for the hundredth time fully convinced that these words explain something. The trick of inventing a theme for a forty-five-page *thème varié* that is itself already a *thème varié* is nothing new. But on the other hand, the vulgar trumpet solos, especially the second one, after the buzzing, fifth-less G♭ major chord, seem to have dropped from heaven. That could never have happened three years earlier in France. A little later the final fanfare blares out of the living-room. Blinded by the rays of sun reflected in the brass, he quotes one of his favourite writers. 'Chin up. The light sparkled from my teeth.'

The truth is that at the time of its creation, *Danses Concertantes* was considered, at best, 'an attractive [piece] for anybody who likes to get sentimental about the ballet' (Virgil Thomson). Kenneth Thompson, in his *Dictionary of Twentieth Century Composers 1911–1971*, in which the œuvre of thirty-two twentieth-century composers is biographically documented opus by opus, does not mention even one article about the piece, and most of the other pieces that were written in the same period do not fare any better. Performances of *Danses Concertantes* are still infrequent. This is rather strange, considering that in no other period in his life did Stravinsky aim so obviously at the commercial market (the only thing missing from the trumpet melody in the Pas de Deux from *Scènes de ballet* are the lyrics 'Darling sweet, I love you, you're my sugar pie') and so gratefully make use of the 'thousands

[1] Wim Markus is a Dutch musicologist [trans].

of possibilities' that the new world offered him, whether it was Broadway, jazz, circus, or the film industry. Some music cannot be categorized: too light for the sophisticated, too pert for lovers of vigorous main themes and lyrical second themes. 'The music of his middle age is . . . found interesting by the intellectually cultivated but cold by the musically more enthusiastic' writes Samuel Lipman in his *Music after Modernism*.

The cloud has dissolved into strands of mist as the record reaches its end. For several minutes, a wasp manages to disturb the quietude of the balcony. After a short skirmish that draws all of his attention, the sunbather asks himself if the next piece has not already begun. Those arpeggios, is that not *Scènes de ballet*? Or is it really Tchaikovsky? And the sluggish clarinet melody, is that not *Ode*? A canon between a solo violin and a trombone clarifies things: of course, it is the Pas de Deux from *Danses Concertantes*. In that case, those shoddy bars are coming up, actually beginning with the canon itself, that just cannot seem to get off the ground. How, he desperately asks himself for the hundredth time, can he ever explain why this canon in the wrong way, and the fugato at the end of *Babel* in the right way, cannot get off the ground? The *più mosso* quickly relieves him of his despair. Never was the genre of first violins plus snappy accompaniment so sprightly. *Holiday for Strings*: Leroy Anderson certainly could have learned a thing or two. Stravinsky must have thought so too since, in the recorded version authorized by the composer, the episode was repeated almost in its entirety—something which certainly was not in the score. Another section which can be taken for *Ode* but is not and finally the Marche that started things off. That was that. Strange, after the final chord, everything disappeared—what remained was a feeling of discomfort and the desire to pat somebody a little too hard on the back. When he had put the record on, he knew (since he knew the piece): this is going to be good. But why good, how good—he still could not imagine even while the needle was falling into the groove.

Some music puts its trust in reminiscence. This is true for the late string quartets of Beethoven, for the Violin Concerto by Schoenberg, for the Second Symphony of Roussel, for *Structures I* by Boulez, and, to a lesser degree, for the *Septet* and *Threni* by Stravinsky. The reminiscence of this music weighs heavier than the listening itself: to listen is less important than to have listened. The relationship between moment and remembered moment has another extreme: the moment is everything and the reminiscence is as good as worthless. (By reminiscence is not meant recalling in the mind, but the condition that occurs at the moment that one is reminded of something.)

Danses Concertantes is an example of this extreme. To conclude that music in the category of *Danses Concertantes* has a negligible effect on the listener is premature. The reader who was brought up in a house with a piano knows that there was a moment in which—to his great surprise and satisfaction—he coaxed out his first chord. Even though the reminiscence of this moment of discovery—if it has been preserved—is merely a sheer reminiscence of a feeling as a *fact*, without this discovery this same reader would probably have had something better to do than investigate Stravinsky.

While he slips the record back into its cover, he considers how he would have reacted to this music in 1942. He can not answer this without first considering where and under what circumstances he would have found himself. Europe was out of the question, since he would not have been able to have heard the piece there. America therefore. In America as a Dutch emigrant. Would he, in fearful expectation of being drafted into the Allied army, have considered these Sunday notes 'appropriate'; or would he have felt more at home with Schoenberg's *Ode to Napoleon*, Prokofiev's *War and Peace*, or even Tippett's *A Child of our Time*, since that was the Zeitgeist. Stravinsky, as one could read in *Pictures and Documents*, was the proud Russian of Hollywood: he belonged to a committee for Russian war aid, gave benefit concerts, and was even inspired to write music for a film about the German invasion of Russia. But nothing ever came of the project. Only in the *Symphony in Three Movements* does one hear some clattering of weapons and stamping of boots; no wonder that Adorno made an exception of this work, having a good word to say about it. And there was also the Apothéose from, of all pieces, *Scènes de ballet* in which at least the composer himself heard his own jubilation about the liberation of Paris.

Amsterdam, 20 August 1980

Much unrest. At both ends of the street, barricades of stones, fences, and building materials are thrown up and the shopkeepers are busy boarding up their window-fronts. A few hours ago a police force of 2,000 men, equipped with armoured cars, bulldozers, excavators, hydraulic cranes, lifts, and water cannons drove the squatters out of the apartments on the Prins Hendrikkade. The squatters round the corner are also worried about their future. While I observe the commotion out of the window of the fourth floor, I put on *Danses Concertantes*. The warlike atmosphere becomes more bearable, but after the opening bars of the Thème varié, I decide to go out into the street. (Later that evening, everything will fizzle out.)

Ars Imitatio Artis

. . . for a code cannot be destroyed, at most 'played upon'.
Roland Barthes

Just as the heroes of Sebastian Knight's novel *The Prismatic Bezel* are neither 'inner conflict', nor 'faith in the future', nor 'rage over a lost penny', nor simply 'self-conscious first theme', neither are these the heroes of Stravinsky's music. Stravinsky's heroes are, rather, methods of composition. The frugality of this concept contrasts sharply with the excitement that it can generate. The music of Stravinsky sounds 'as if a painter said: look, here I'm going to show you not the painting of a landscape, but the painting of different ways of painting a certain landscape, and I trust their harmonious fusion will disclose the landscape as I intend you to see it' (Nabokov).

The comparison of music with painting need not be a problem provided we cleverly divest ourselves of reality. To do that we have to imagine an art of painting that has its roots in one single painting (and that is really much more similar to 'real' painting that one tends to believe). That one painting portrays the last tree and the last landscape. After the painting was finished, the tree was cut down and the landscape devastated. Since then no more trees or landscapes have been seen. Yet that one painting inspired other painters to paint trees and landscapes. The resulting paintings, in their turn, inspired a new generation of painters. This is why the present practitioners of this school paint trees and landscapes which, it must be said, in no way resemble that last tree and that last landscape.

This art of painting is similar to music. Just as tree-and-landscape paintings portray other tree-and-landscape paintings, music portrays other music and no longer the first birdsong that the first musician imitated. (As far as music is concerned, it would not matter if the bird in question was the last bird or not. Messiaen would merely have found another subject.) This 'making of portraits' must be thought of in the broader sense of the word and can be executed in many ways. Thus, the illusion can be conjured up of *no* other music being portrayed. This is exactly the illusion that many composers strive for (and the harder they work at it, the more it is in vain). These composers try to neutralize the music that has made their own music possible and thereby make that other music anonymous. Music in general lends a hand as well: it wears out after continual use. What remains is the empty husk of conventions and clichés. Some of these conventions are: brilliant scherzo for orchestra; or, pastoral oboe melody; and also, sonata fom. (Every sonata presupposes the existence of many other sonatas; but as a form, the sonata has uncoupled itself from concrete sonatas and leads an incorporeal existence, referring to no sonata in particular.)

Such anonymous portraits are extremely un-Stravinskian: they are found only in the early works of the composer (from the *Symphony in E Flat* to *The Firebird*). In these works, one can speak of influence in the most conventional sense. Stravinsky, in typical fashion, used to deny these influences, concealed them, or at least tried to minimize them. One ignores ineluctable powers.

It is ironic that in commentaries on Stravinsky's compositions that are, no matter how brilliant, primarily the product of conventional influence (such as *Two Poems of Verlaine* or the first act of *Le Rossignol*), the names of Rimsky-Korsakov, Scriabin, or Debussy, if names are mentioned at all, are mentioned only in passing; while in the descriptions of Stravinsky's later works, which have too much rather than too little personal style compared to his earlier works, teem with names varying from Machaut to Rossini and from Bach to Verdi. It would be possible to write a book about Stravinsky in the form of a history of music. The name Stravinsky would not even need to be mentioned and still the reader would always be aware of the real subject of the book. That book would be concerned with another sort of portrait-making than the sort just discussed; namely, where the portrayal and the portrayed—that is, a portrayal of the portrayed which is a different portrayal from the first portrayal—exist side by side.

'Side by side' implies all the possible relations between portrayal and portrayed. Applied to a musical composition, this means that the *fact* that it takes other music into account has become a *subject* of the composition. What makes the music of Stravinsky so typical of the twentieth century is that it is a text 'comprised of many writings, originating from several cultures, that enter into a dialogue, parody each other or disagree with one another' (Barthes); or better still, Stravinsky's music is not merely this kind of text, but (in one way or another, always differently) proclaims itself to be one.

The music of Stravinsky is a collection of variants (in sound) on Magritte's painting *La Condition humaine.*

The first variant is not a true variant as the original is no longer recognizable: it is merely the small painting 's', separated from the large painting 'S'. It is an ordinary painting, for example one entitled *Fireworks.*

(Though this is not even a real 'brilliant scherzo': one can still see part of the legs of the easel.)

The second and third variants do justice to the paradoxical nature of Magritte's painting. The painting poses the question whether realism is possible, and answers by means of realism. The painter of the small painting 's' seems like the Liar of Crete ('All Cretans are liars'), since he does not allow the viewer to see what is behind the small painting. A mirror, perhaps a black hole?

The second variant *is* Magritte's painting, the only difference being that the small painting 's' and the view out of the window (that is, according to the non-realistic tree-and-landscape art of painting, the portrayal of a painting) are in a different relationship to each other; but that is explored in greater depth in the third variant. *L'Histoire du soldat*, *Tango*, and *Ragtime* are works that are put into a frame. Here the frame is part of the piece—the woodwork and curtains. Just beyond the painting the invisible composer leans his invisible elbows very visibly on the invisible windowsill.

The third variant—the only true one—is the large painting 'S' minus the woodwork and curtains; it is, in other words, the view plus the painted view. This variant can be subdivided in several ways. These subdivisions are in regard to the relationship in size between the small painting 's' and the view (and—but the consequences of this are left to the reader—the angle between them). Sometimes 's' covers up the entire view, such as in *Les Noces*, the *Symphony of Psalms*, or *In Memoriam Dylan Thomas*. Sometimes 's' and the view are the same size (*Apollon musagète*, *Symphony in Three Movements*, *Orpheus*), and sometimes there is more view than painting (*Pulcinella*, *Le Baiser de la fée*). But these relationships are not really so important. The important points are:

1. What is the stylistic relationship between the small painting 's' and the view?'
2. What is the view of?
3. What is behind the small painting 's'?

Le Condition humaine is an extreme example of the relationship between the small painting 's' and the view: in Stravinsky's case, the view and 's' are usually less complementary (if they are in fact so complementary in the Magritte; the paradox of the painting remains that it is impossible to look behind the small painting 's').

As far as the view is concerned, that too is created by the painter of the large painting 'S'; it is just as much a painting even though it is the painting of something that was lost in the postulated tree-and-landscape art of painting. Even without having seen the (painted) 'tree' or the (painted) 'landscape' that were models (if they were in fact models) for the portrayal of the view in the small painting 's', we can still form an image of the tree and landscape. This image may agree in some ways with the real (painted) 'tree' or the real (painted) 'landscape', but it is *not* the tree or the landscape. And even if it were—and we have now come to the third question—the painting is not likely to be of a beautiful tree or an ingenious landscape, but of some simple shrubs and a couple of ordinary clouds. Did not Shakespeare's Antony, long ago, see a dragon, a lion, a bear, a tower'd citadel, a pendant rock, trees, and a horse in the clouds?

Thus the view in *Le Baiser de la fée* (based on songs and piano pieces by Tchaikovsky) is of—Tchaikovsky. There can be little doubt of that, from the first to the very last bars. In this composition, there is not merely one painting 's', but many. Example 1[1], a charming tune, is a nice view. But what do we see

[1] Transcription according to *Stravinsky: A New Appraisal of his Work*, ed. Paul Henry Lang (New York, 1963), p. 54.

Ex. 1

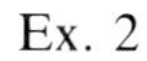

in the painting (Ex. 2)? This is where the Fairy, disguised as a gypsy, gets the Youth under her spell by means of a dance that is really a fast seductive blues (which can therefore not really be a blues), but is really really the perfect metamorphosis of Tchaikovsky's trivial *Tant triste, tant douce.*

Tchaikovsky is therefore 'Tchaikovsky'.

No Copyright Problem Here

I have already stolen much thought and knowledge from the books of others which I shall pass off as my own. It is impossible to do otherwise in our practical age.
Anton Chekhov

In 1941, having just arrived in America, Stravinsky arranged *The Star-Spangled Banner* for chorus and orchestra. The composer himself regarded this arrangement as superior to every other version that he had ever heard. However, when, after the première which had gone smoothly, he sent a manuscript to Mrs Roosevelt to be auctioned for charity, she refused the gift. According to the arranger, 'my major seventh chord in the second strain of the piece, the part patriotic ladies like best, must have embarrassed some high official'. In the setting of national anthems, major seventh chords are not allowed (Ex. 1).

Ex. 1

'My' major seventh chord was a *fingerprint* and it was almost three-quarters of a century ago that F. Galton developed a method of identification based on fingerprints in his book of the same name, and thereby fulfilled the need of the judicial powers to have a method at their disposal to determine whether the innumerable recidivists that appeared before the court were indeed recidivists and not first offenders. Because the great number of recidivists was the result of the great number of criminals and the great number of criminals was related to a new interpretation of the concept of property that the ascending bourgeoisie and the law respected since the introduction of the Napoleonic code, it should not have surprised Stravinsky that some time later, when he conducted *The Star-Spangled Banner*, a Police Commissioner announced himself, and made it clear to the composer: (i) that a law existed in Massachusetts that forbode 'tampering with national property', and (ii) that recidivisim would mean the parts being taken from the music stands by the police.

J. E. Purkyně, the founder of histology, had already discovered in 1823 that no two individuals have identical fingerprints. The fingerprint identifies (points to the owner of the finger), but, with the identification, the identity of the owner is not yet revealed; the major seventh chord in *The Star-Spangled Banner* does not do so either, no more than the piano does in Stravinsky's orchestration of Tchaikovsky's *pas-de-deux* from *Bluebird*, even though the piano could never have been from Tchaikovsky himself. Both cases concern arrangements in the traditional sense of the word, although the arranger left his marks. These marks are interesting, and not only because of who left them. They are musical 'deviations' and as slightest deviations they form material that is excellently suited to serve as a starting-point for stylistic analysis.

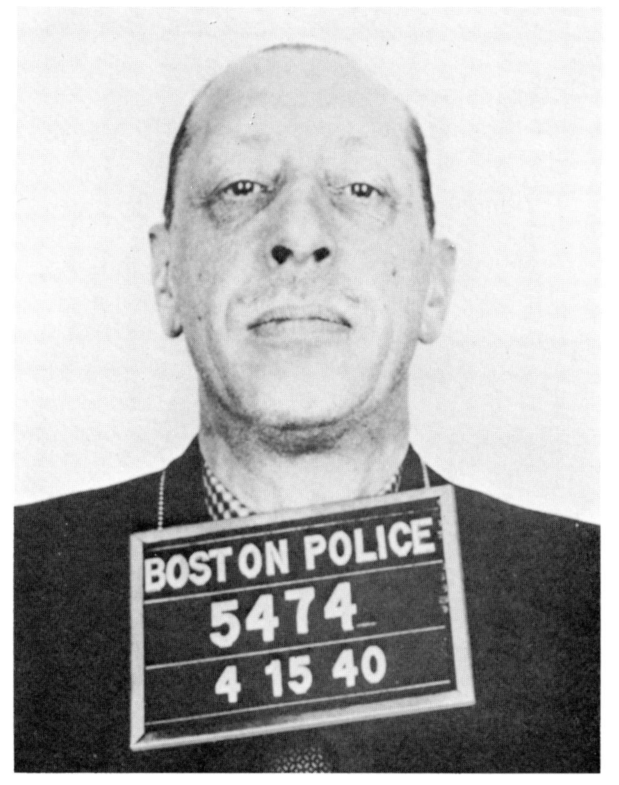

The relationship between property, theft, and fingerprint is in principle the same as in Galton's days. But the fingerprint of the composer as composer is different from that of the composer as citizen, as human being, if you will.

What is the difference between a stolen coat and a coat that is made from a stolen cow?

Are *Pulcinella* and *Le Baiser de la fée* (and why not *Petrushka*, *Jeu de cartes*, and the *Circus Polka* as well) a melodious plea for the abolition of copyright—except Stravinsky's? (Ex. 2)

Ex. 2

César Paladión, *Le Sacre du printemps*, bars 7–9

Stravinsky hardly ever made real arrangements. The ones he made are an exception to the rule that no distinction can be made in his œuvre between original compositions and arrangements. This rule also applies to *Monumentum pro Gesualdo di Venosa ad CD annum* (1960) and the *Chorale Variations on 'Vom Himmel hoch da komm' ich her'* (1956). These are homages, but framed in such a way that the one who receives the homage and the one who gives it audibly compete for the honours. The subtitle of *Monumentum* is not 'Three madrigals *arranged*', but 'Three madrigals *recomposed* for instruments'. When notes of the madrigals are changed, Gesualdo's style is taken more into account than his syntax. This is also true for 'Illumina nos', one of the three *Sacrae cantiones* for which Stravinsky composed the missing parts. If anything is reconstructed in this seven-part composition, it is not Gesualdo but rather the hypothetical case in which Gesualdo studied with a twentieth-century composer who, in spite of his great admiration for his pupil, always knew better. (According to this composer, 'Illumina nos' posed for him the problem of how 'to make Gesualdo's voice leading less arrogant' and how 'to soften certain of his *malheurs*'. (Ex. 3). As often happens, the pot calls the kettle black.)

Ex. 3

'Illumina nos' (piano reduction), conclusion

What Stravinsky did to Gesualdo, Gesualdo's predecessors did to each other in the first half of the sixteenth century. 'Paraphrasing, or otherwise reworking pre-existent material', writes Gustave Reese in his *Music in the Renaissance*, 'often rises to the status of original composition.' Examples of this can be found in such composers as Gombert, de La Rue, Lassus, de Monte, and Willaert; in Obrecht, who in *Si dedero* incorporates Agricola's three-part motet of the same name; in Josquin, who in his *Missa Mater patris* completely and almost literally quotes Brumel's three-part song-motet. But Reese's comments are just as applicable to Bach, who, in his arrangement of Vivaldi's Concerto for four violins as his Concerto for four harpsichords, paid homage to Vivaldi in the form of a 'commentary on the form-principles of the Italians' (Sir C. H. H. Parry), just as Stravinsky, in his arrangement of Bach's *Chorale Variations on 'Vom Himmel hoch'* for chorus and orchestra, gave a commentary on Bach's organ composition. Bach dramatized Vivaldi by changing Vivaldi's key-signature plan. Stravinsky dramatized Bach by changing Bach's key-signature plan. Bach brought changes on to every level of Vivaldi's composition and did not hesitate, whenever necessary, to add parts. Stravinsky brought changes on to every level of Bach's 'Canonische Veränderungen' and did not hesitate, whenever necessary, to add parts. He did that in the spirit of the music that he was working on at the time (*Agon*, *Canticum Sacrum*); one calls this music serial, although Stravinsky himself spoke initially of 'canonic writing'. Thus, a canonic voice instrumented à la Webern is added to the third variation and is the cause of the note E♭, which is alien to the harmony of the final chord (D♭ major). The thing that Bach recognized in Vivaldi is the same thing that Stravinsky recognized in Bach—himself.

The added anti-metric figures in *Vom Himmel hoch*, the doublings and filled-in harmonies in Gesualdo and the seventh chord in *The Star-Spangled Banner* bring to mind the question of what makes a composition by Stravinsky a composition by Stravinsky. Of course, this is the kind of question which can be posed for any composer; but in Stravinsky's case, the answer is special, if only because it can be found, in principle, in every bar. The reason for this is not by definition a matter of style, but of characteristics of style. Style and characteristics of style are not conditions of each other, although in the cases where this is not so it would be more proper to speak of style and mannerisms. Music can be rich in mannerisms (or poor—clever arrangers of light music create their own 'sound' using two or three mannerisms), but mannerisms (or 'sound') do not guarantee style. Style implies that the mannerisms are dictated by an aesthetic attitude; not style but *tenue* was Stravinsky's favourite term. Because his music rather has too much than too little style, it can take the liberty of making a subject out of every convention, every form, and every style (in the sense of a fixed canon of musical expression), and moreover, without the danger of becoming mannered, permit itself the luxury of being marked in every bar with mannerisms. Sometimes only one mannerism will suffice, as in the *Song of the Volga Boatmen.*

The mannerism in the *Volga Boatmen* consists of one single type of chord. All the chords that accompany the original melody of the thirty-bar song are derived from one principal chord. They are all as 'clumsily' orchestrated as possible. Rimsky-Korsakov, Stravinsky's composition teacher, would immediately have put a red pencil round the snarling thirds in the bass. One can hardly speak of a harmonization of the melody. The music is half-way between a kind of medieval polyphony (fauxbourdon) and the bungling fuss of an amateurish harmonica player, but without portraying the latter as realistic as Tchaikovsky did in his *Album for the Young* ('Farmer playing the Accordion'). The modal tendencies of the melody are blown up out of all proportion; in fact, to the extent that the entire concept of modality almost bursts. The strange system in which the two lowest voices alternately play a third and a sixth leads to a final chord that is one of the most remarkable of final chords. Above all, it is not even a chord since it has but two notes. Of course, this occurs every so often in Stravinsky's music (see, for example, the closing chords of the *Symphony of Psalms* and of *Threni*). But a chord in which the tonic is accompanied by the submediant, while that tonic actually functions as a tonic—that kind of chord opens up a far horizon where treatises on harmony prevail which provide for basses in the soprano, middle voices in the bass, and octaves as dissonances. William W. Austin, who was the very first to write something about the *Volga Boatmen* in his *Music in the 20th Century*, gains credit by his description of this chord: 'There is no theoretical name for this chord. It is simply the final tonic chord of Stravinsky's *Boatmen*. It deserves to be famous, like the *Petrushka* chord and the *Rite of Spring* chord.'

The effect of the *Volga Boatmen* is undeniable: no hot tears are spilled over the loss of Mother Russia, rather, nostalgic *émigrés* are shaken out of their dream. Seldom is such an awful cliché so effectively destroyed. Style is necessary for this to be achieved; and the instrument of that style need be but one mannerism. However that one mannerism is more than just that: it is also—and probably most of all—the audible *silencing* of all of the other mannerisms which accompany, still today, the wailing of the Volga boatmen.

What is so striking about the *Volga Boatmen* is not how much but how little the original music is changed and, at the same time, how little is left of it. The same can be said for *Le Baiser de la fée*, and even more so for *Pulcinella*. The ballet about the hero of the traditional Neapolitan *Commedia dell'arte* tells the story of boys who fall in love with girls who fall in love with Pulcinella who falls in love with Pimpinella. It is a story about disguises and exchanged identities and thereby a story about Stravinsky himself, as a stand-in for Pergolesi. (Originally the subtitle of the ballet was: Music by Pergolesi, orchestrated and arranged by Stravinsky.)

Stravinsky took the melodies and basses from Pergolesi—borrowed from trio sonatas and opera arias—almost completely intact and, along with Pergolesi's notes, also took a few eighteenth-century mannerisms, varying from the nature of the orchestra (no clarinets) to the division of the strings into a concertino and a ripieno group. 'I began by composing on the Pergolesi manuscripts themselves, as though I were correcting an old work of my own.' The method of working reminds one of Marcel Duchamp, who adorned the *Mona Lisa* with a moustache; but the effect of Stravinsky's graffiti reaches further. So far in fact that listening to the trio sonatas and arias that were used as models paradoxically means listening to an arrangement, in eighteenth-century style, of a composition by Stravinsky. Fate though, with incomparable irony, has allowed, half a century after the composition of *Pulcinella*, the discovery that part of the original material of Stravinsky's ballet music was not even by Pergolesi but by contemporaries of his, among them the Dutch composer Unico Wilhelm, count of Wassenaer.

Just as paradoxical is *Le Baiser de la fée*, an 'allegorical ballet inspired by the Muse of Tchaikovsky', and modelled, à la *Pulcinella*, on existing compositions. The real Tchaikovsky is a parody of the Tchaikovsky that Stravinsky conjures up for us and not the other way round. But the real Tchaikovsky is not Stravinsky's real Tchaikovsky. Stravinsky's real Tchaikovsky is 'the legendary composer' who attended a gala performance of Glinka's *Ruslan and Lyudmila* and in the intermission—'Igor, look, there's Tchaikovsky'—is noticed by the eleven-year-old son of one of the leading singers. Fourteen days later Tchaikovsky was dead and the eleven-year-old would save 'this image in the retina of my memory' for the rest of his life.

1919—*La Marseillaise*

On the first of January 1919, Stravinsky made an arrangement of the *Marseillaise*, for one violin. For whom or for what occasion is not known. Maybe it was, like the *Canons for Two Horns* (1917), to pay the doctor. (Because the doctor wanted it, not out of poverty. The large financial worries that tortured the composer his whole life were the worries of someone who could yet afford to travel first class.) The arrangement of the *Marseillaise* was never published. The piece has been performed—mostly as a curiosity—a couple of times in the last few years.

There is nothing amiss in the first half of the *Marseillaise*; it is only in the second half that the notes go off the rails, among other places, where the original melody takes the following turn to the minor:

Ex. 1

The harmonization of this phrase is self-evident:

Ex. 2

(*a*) is the most obvious and humbly accedes to the character of the melody; (*b*) and (*c*) are more affected due to their 'chromatic' bass.

Stravinsky does it like this:

These bars could have been the target of a remark made by Ansermet in *Les Fondements de la musique dans la conscience humaine:* 'If we had been satisfied by a melody that we had just heard and tried to reconstruct it by memory on the piano, Stravinsky could never find the proper harmonies and upholstered it with the most unexpected chords.'

This example from the *Marseillaise*, precisely because of its simplicity, clarifies something about the principle of the right wrong-note. This principle must not be confused with the principle of the wrong wrong-note. Applying that would result in the following example:

(*e*)

It would have been possible, however, to have had other right wrong-notes take the place of the seven Ds in Example 2*d*:

(*f*)

Whereas the Examples (*a*), (*b*), and (*c*) do not do anything else except make explicit what, according to the conventions of functional tonality, was already implicitly present, Example (*d*) is an interpretation of the melody. This interpretation, corroborated by the rest of the arrangement, is of a village musician playing the *Marseillaise*: folk music does not modulate and the timpani player rather prefers to play the wrong timpani (and he only has three: C, G, and D) than to have to sit with his arms crossed for two bars.

(Stravinsky's interpretation of pre-existent materials is, of course, rarely so simple. In *L'Histoire du soldat*, not a village orchestra, but seven musicians with a diploma from the conservatory who imitate a village orchestra are put on stage. That is how the music can get so stacked up, layer upon layer, which is exactly what happens: in each composition more than the preceding one. The music increasingly resembles the earth's crust. Only the geological ear knows precisely what it is listening to.)

If—to continue in the words of Ansermet—'the proper harmonies' cannot be 'found', then the implication is that they were being looked for. In other words, Stravinsky, according to Ansermet, lacked a natural feeling for harmony. This suggestion, if not proof of bad faith, is at least ridiculous since it involves the very special *dis*ability of a know-it-all who, just past his twentieth year, appeared with completely impersonal style-copies of Tchaikovsky and Glazunov (*Sonata in F sharp minor*, *Symphony in E flat*); an adept and studied disability that gradually developed irreversibly into an accomplished disability, stronger than even the born know-it-all-ability.

The jump from know-it-all to disabled can be heard in one single work, the opera *Le Rossignol*. In the first act (1908–09), the still to be composed *Firebird* is announced:

Ex. 3

Le Rossignol [5]

while in the second and third acts (1913–14), *Le Sacre du printemps*, just completed, is echoed:

Ex. 4

Le Rossignol [106]5

The leap can be seen most clearly in the form that a motif from the first act takes on in the second act (Ex. 5).

Ex. 5

Le Rossignol [26] and [81]

In (2), the harmonic origin of the motif (the Scriabinian augumented six-four-three chord) is obscured, only to become in the third act—after a complete metamorphosis—unrecognizable (Ex. 6).

Ex. 6

Le Rossignol [101]

(The jump that is made half a century later in the *Septet* is similar to the one in *Le Rossignol* with the difference that it concerns—keeping in the spirit of Ansermet—two types of disabilities, so-called neoclassicist and so-called Webernian.)

The explanation why Stravinsky, on those occasions when he openly tried to secure a place in the commercial market, was doomed to failure is concealed in the veritable art of purposeful *dis*-ability. Nothing ever came of the plan to make a version of the *Tango* for dance band, let alone a popular vocal number. Nothing could ever come of it. The tango is a *last tango.* In the instrumentation that Stravinsky later made of it, a vodka-addicted, hypochondriac balalaika tries to play the Spanish guitar. This is found on the recording made by the composer for CBS, a tempo (♩ = 64) that would sooner invite the listener to write his last will and testament than to dance.

The future of *Scènes de ballet*, music for a Broadway show, seemed at first glance somewhat more lucrative; but even here the big-band opening chords, the romantic (and for Stravinsky exceptional) accelerando, the high plink-plink à la Tchaikovsky ([42]) and the trusty mannerisms of *Symphonies of Wind Instruments* ([3]), *Capriccio* ([25]), *Jeu de cartes* ([33]), *Danses Concertantes* ([82], [90]) and the *Symphony of Psalms* ([117]) are too slick to be a sensational success. Maybe it could have been if only Stravinsky had followed the advice of the theatre manager and had authorized Robert Russell Bennett 'to retouch orchestration—stop—Bennett orchestrates even the works of Cole Porter'.

The only piece that was able to conquer the juke-box was the 'Rondo of the Princesses' from *The Firebird.* Because Leeds Music Co., who had published the third suite from *The Firebird*, could foresee a project in bridging the gap between classical and popular music, the princesses danced a slow foxtrot.

Summer Moon, you bring the end of my love story
All too soon my love and I are apart.
Summer Moon, why shine in Indian Summer glory?
Summer Moon, while I'm alone with my heart?'

Since the music, unlike the text, has been lost after all these years, we can only guess how the text was set. Was the first line of the verse a syllabic setting of the rondo theme (Ex. 7)? In that case, the spurious accent on 'my' and 'love' rival in expression the innumerable spurious accents in Stravinsky's vocal music; or to take it further, it can only be compared to the poignant fate of the lame sailor from Holland (Ex. 8).

If the lyricist John Klenner in fact did do it that way, then he certainly had taste and a feeling for style. And what about F. F. Spielman, the arranger? What did he mean when he said that using other harmonies (presumably, as in the example, added sixths and sevenths and B♭ major instead of the original B major), he still expressed the 'same feelings'? This is what Spielman testified to in front of the judge presiding over the case that Stravinsky brought against the publishers of *Summer Moon.* According to the composer, the title-page of the song ventured to state unjustly that he had lent his willing assistance. Stravinsky did not receive the $250,000 compensation that he had demanded; he did receive some serious reproaches from admirers who were not so sure whether the composer also had objections of principle against this kind of arrangement. The *Stem van Nederland* (*Voice of the Netherlands*), through the pen of Victor E. van Vriesland, let it be known that they were not angry, only sad. 'It is bitter to realize that our society crushes so much young talent to death, since this talent must do violence to their personal artistic ideals in order to make a living. Even more bitter, we might say, is that our society—its psychological foundation being based on the profit principle—is so corrupting to the character of the individual that even the greatest artists of our day, beyond any financial urgency, smother their inner voice and sell themselves as harlots. This same is true for the immortal creator of *Le Sacre du printemps*, who at one time bestowed such a radiant ecstasy on the youth of so many of my generation.'

Broadway was no success story: Hollywood just as little. Four times Stravinsky launched into a career as film-composer and four times he failed. Miklós Rózsa (who is known, among other things, as the composer who ruined the first encounter between Gregory Peck and Ingrid Bergman in *Spellbound*) recollected that when Stravinsky had arrived in Hollywood, he was invited to see Louis B. Mayer, the mogul of MGM. The composer, undoubtedly exhibiting the charming allure of 'the leader of an industrial concern', declared himself willing to write a film score, for a fee of more than six times what he received for *Le Baiser de la fée* and *Perséphone* combined, that is, $100,000 (Schoenberg, according to the *New York Times*, asked for just as much.)

Mayer: 'If you are the greatest composer in the world, then you're worth the money.'

Mayer only needed to know how much time the greatest composer in the world would need to complete one hour of music. After thinking about this for a while, the 'greatest' answered: 'One year.' Mayer stood up and said: 'Good-bye, Mr Stravinsky.'

Money was not the obstacle. They were ready to pay $100,000 merely to use the name Stravinsky—a ghost composer would write the notes. The fact that Hollywood was, literally, a music factory where rehearsal pianists, book-keepers, copyists, executives, composers, proof-readers, orchestrators, arrangers, librarians, and musicians all got in the way of each other, where sound-tracks, cut to order, were made on the conveyor belt, where the musical ideal consisted of extracts of Puccini and Richard Strauss adapted to the demands of time, the audience, the producer, and the financial director, even that was not the problem. For what one could demand from Max Steiner and Alfred Newman, one could not demand from the greatest composer in the world. No, the actual problem was that Stravinsky had a somewhat deviant view of the relationship between picture and sound.

One can draw this conclusion from the fact that, having been asked by Columbia Pictures to compose the music for *The Commandos Strike at Dawn*, he had already made sketches before the film was finished, before he had even seen one frame of it. In other words, he was a bit too literal in interpreting his 'principle of mutual independence' of picture and music.

It is true that all his theatre compositions after *L'Histoire du soldat* and *Les Noces* kept to this principle, but this independence was in fact a special case of

de-pendence where the music had the final word. *Oedipus Rex* was not a *vocalise* which Cocteau subtitled using a text by Sophocles.

The Commandos Strike at Dawn (1942) was about sabotage and the resistance in Norway. It was a real war film; just as heroic as the Royal Canadian Navy, the Royal Canadian Air Force, and the Royal Air Force, who were involved with the production, and just as realistic as the Norwegian refugees, who placed their expertise at the disposal of the producers. One cannot hear this in the music that was originally supposed to accompany the warlike activity on the screen. Only in the title of this alternative to *Begleitmusik zu einer Lichtspielszene* can one find something of the original destination: *Four Norwegian Moods.* These rarely-played pieces fulfil the same marginal position in the œuvre of Stravinsky that *The Commandos* (music by Louis Gruenberg) does in the history of the film; even though the imperturbable mumbling of the bassoons and horns in the cortège is more enticing than anything else that had been written in Hollywood up until David Raksin's *Laura.*

Neither is *Scherzo à la russe* a composition that one would think of as something that could have been, even remotely, a sound-track. (This time also for a war film, *North Star.* The film is about an idyllic Russian village that has to defend itself against the sudden invasion of the Nazis. Stravinsky's replacement, Aaron Copland, was nominated for an Oscar for his score. *North Star*, supposedly a contribution to the war effort, was one of the most controversial films of its day. The newspapers of the Hearst empire even saw

Bolshevik propaganda in the film and Lillian Hellman, the author of the original screenplay, remembered it as 'a big-time, sentimental, badly directed, badly acted mess'. It is not likely that Stravinsky made a point about the political implications of the film. He was, it is true, anti-communist in heart and soul, and right at the end of the war he already began taking offence if the Soviet Union was even mentioned; but *during* the war his patriotism was so great that he did not even shrink from listening to a radio broadcast of Shostakovich's 'Leningrad' Symphony.)

The Commandos Strike at Dawn and *North Star* (1943) were B films, just like all the films for which Hollywood attracted 'real' composers (Milhaud, Tansman, Toch). The situation of the two other films for which Stravinsky did not write the music was different, though. *The Song of Bernadette*, based on the novel by Franz Werfel, was a romantic hagiography. Yet some good did come of Stravinsky's failure to compose music for this film: Alfred Newman received an Oscar for his music and a Symphony in Two Movements became the *Symphony in Three Movements*. The fourth and last film for which another composer had to be found was judged by the Nederlands Katholieke Filmkeuring [Dutch Catholic Film Rating Board] as being 'no more than mediocre' while 'the romanticism of the subject was "extremely old-fashioned" '.

The music [of this film] is gloomy and passionate, demonstrating his complete affinity with Brontë. [The leading character] is represented by a poetic melody drawing upon modal harmonies, full of the spirit of the English countryside. A spirited orchestral accompaniment follows her across the foggy moors. For the mystery of the tower in Thornfield Hall, the fire, and the storm sequence, [he] turned to somber brass chords, thundering timpani, and an orchestra that virtually snarls and rumbles with fear and fury. The love scenes between Jane and Rochester are played against rich, romantic melodies' (Evans).

The film is *Jane Eyre* (1944). The last thing that one hears in this description is Stravinsky's *Ode*, not even the middle movement. It is not a description of *Ode* though, but the music that Bernard Herrmann composed for the film. Herrman is one of the better film composers; half the reason why Hitchcock's *Psycho* is Hitchcock's *Psycho* is thanks to the chilling strings of Herrmann. On the other hand, Herrmann's concert music is hardly worth listening to. There is justice in the world.

A Motto

The most prominent difference between the (double) fugue from the *Symphony of Psalms* and all other fugues is that bars 1–5—the fugue theme unaccompanied—are not the trigger for the following eighty-three bars of counterpoint, but rather the following eighty-three bars of counterpoint are a footnote to bars 1–5. A long, ingenious and, now and then ([17]), even a brilliant footnote, but none the less a footnote.

Ex. 1

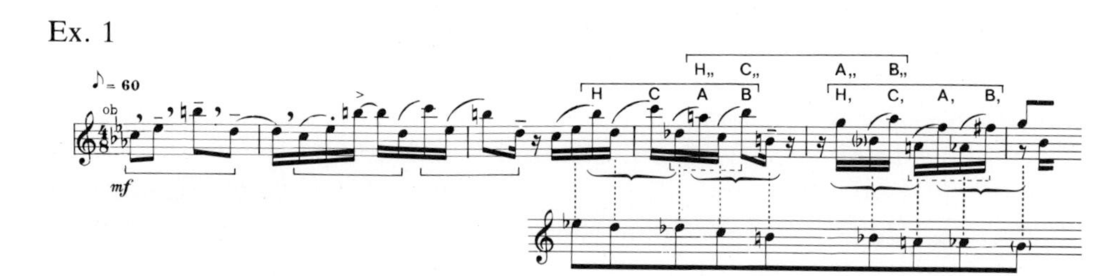

The theme can be presented as a paradigm:

1. In particular for the 'neoclassical' Stravinsky since it is a paradox in sound: it sounds like something, but primarily like itself (it reminds us of something familiar, namely itself) and thereby makes the ordinary extra-ordinary in an ordinary way. The theme does not derive its authority from the past to which it refers—it is not neoclassical but 'neoclassical' and thereby a-restorative. (Like so many other musical concepts, the concept of restoration with regard to Stravinsky seems to be dictated less by the music itself than by the vagueness of the aesthetic categories used to interpret it.)

Reference is to 'Bach', and more specifically to Bach.

'Bach': a fugue theme with built-in tonic and dominant functions, quasi-two part and with *Sekundgang* (step progression).

Bach: profile of the theme that, at least in the compressed version of bars 1, 4, and 5, shows similarities to the theme of *The Musical offering*.

HCAB: wonk eht ni esoht rof.

2. In general for Stravinsky's *improvising*. Or, more precisely: quasi-improvising. Improvising instead of *improvvisando* since *improvvisando* strongly implies 'free fantasy' (or, in the case of Beethoven, that of instrumental

recitatives), whereas improvising points in the direction of jazz, and via jazz in the direction of folk music.

Quasi: although improvisation (literally, at the piano) lies at the root of Stravinsky's compositional practice, his aesthetic is strictly anti-improvisational; it is the paradoxical aesthetic of completely controlled improvisation.

Quasi-improvising: in the case of the fugue theme in the *Symphony of Psalms*, it means continually beginning again and (Schigolch to Lulu: '. . . falsche Luft, wie ich mit meinem Asthma') the tacking together of breathless motifs according to:

the principle of additive construction. What we call the principle of additive construction on the small scale is on the large scale:

the montage principle, a term that is more appropriate to Stravinsky since it suggests the coolness of the cutting table and the cunning of the scissors. The canon concluding *Orpheus* is interrupted twice: 'cut off with a pair of scissors'. Bars 1–3 of the fugue theme are an additive structure, built up out of two:

melodic cells (C and E♭, B and D) that are rhythmically varied as pairs. This isomelodic variation technique is, strictly speaking, a serial technique. '. . . a serial relation is one which induces on a collection of objects a strict, simple ordering; that is, an order relation which is irreflexive, nonsymmetric, transitive, and connected over the collection. The term "serial" designates nothing with regard to the number of elements in the collection, to the relations among these elements, or the operations—if any—applicable to the elements or the relations among them' (Milton Babbitt). The form of serialization that operates in the fugue theme results in a melodic:

variable ostinato, in which the psychological effect is comparable to the gothic ornament shown in the illustration. The whole is understood in terms of the detail, not the other way round (additive versus divisional). The weight of the detail (in music, the individual moment) is another word for:

stasis: the whole is not more, but less than the sum of its parts. The moments (parts) derive their importance more from themselves than from the surrounding (especially future) moments. A condition for this is the disestablishment of the cadence in functional tonality as a principle of form (cf. the sonata form as a particular instance of the progression I—V—I). This

accounts for the absence of the dominant, G, at the opening of the fugue theme. Not only the absence of the G contributes to the effect of:

de-tonalization (the C is more of a *finalis* than a tonic), but also the octave placement of the B, which, except in the chromatic, descending row E♭″ to A♭′ remains immutable. Unlike most twelve-tone music, a fundamental difference exists in Stravinsky's music between the interval *n* and the interval *n*−12. If the B″ in the fugue theme is replaced with a B′, one hears a melody that resembles the original about as much as a piece of catgut resembles a violin string. In other words, the register has become crucial.

Not paradigmatic (at least not for the quality of the œuvre) is the unmistakable weakness of the close of the fugue theme. Bar 5 is a transposition of the last two semiquavers of bar 3 plus bar 4; the (by the way, not exclusively Stravinskian) rhythmic shifting that occurs in bar 5, where, what at first was thesis becomes arsis, is of too little importance to make more than a mechanically self-unrolling *Sekundgang* formula out of merely a mechanically self-unrolling *Sekundgang* formula.

But, if this is to be one of Stravinsky's strongest fugue themes (which it is), then it is because it is 'no' theme at all. 'Real' fugue themes are promises; this theme is a self enclosed thesis, due to the immobility of bars 2 and 3—there are no sequences, the continuation is not based on the harmonic movement of bar 1 (in contrast to, for example, the sighs in the theme of the fugue in B minor from the *Well Tempered Clavier*, Book I), but on rhythmically varied repetitions of bar 1. Only when the flute literally (what a memory!) repeats the oboe solo on the dominant does the oboe solo become, retroactively, a fugue theme.

Ordeals of the Memory

A thirteen-year-old is capable, while lying in bed ready for sleep, of playing the Schumann Piano Concerto (in A minor) on the record-player of his memory. During the second movement, he will probably fall asleep. If, ten years later, in another bedroom, he tries the same thing with the Stravinsky *Concerto for Piano and Wind* ('in A minor'), he will, at the very most, if he even gets that far, get stuck at the cadenza of the first movement; or worse, get trapped in a vicious circle of dove-tailing rhythms and snake-like motifs biting at their own tails. There is not much he can do: just get up and either look through the score or play the record for the umpteenth time.

The fate of the musical sleeper says something about the difference between Stravinsky and Schumann, and, more generally, about the difference between Stravinsky and all composers who write music destined for an exact memory. Stravinsky behaves as if he were one of those composers; but the listener who believes him and takes him to task will start biting his nails. The music of Stravinsky is at odds with the memory.

Draw, by heart, the emblem of the Postal Service.
Sing the beginning of *Orpheus*.
Compare the results with the originals and with each other.

Something occurs, at the latest, at figure [3] in *Orpheus* that is similar to when a word is on the tip of your tongue and thingumajig will not crystallize into speech. It is not there, but in a very special way, since except for the sound it is there. We know what it means—we can even describe it—we know its emotional impact, know how it tastes (the lip muscles are already in position), and are pretty sure whether it is a vowel- or consonant-dominated word; whether it is (in the former case) an a- or an e- word, how many syllables, why, even how many letters are in the word; and with what letter the word begins, or what kind of letter. That is, we seem to know more about the word than we ever knew. Only—drat it—what is the word?

When speaking of musical memory, one thinks first of melody. Recollection begins when a melody can easily be sung after being heard. Such melodies appear seldom in Stravinsky's music. The cavatina that Tom sings in *The*

Rake's Progress ('Love, too frequently betrayed') is an exception. More typical of Stravinsky is Parasha's aria in *Mavra:* In this aria, the gap between the apparently easy to remember and the reality of cul-de-sacs in the labyrinth of the memory is at its greatest. The listener remembers the aria—almost. Much (especially twentieth-century) music places higher demands on the memory's capabilities than Stravinsky's music does. But what is most difficult to remember is what is 'almost easy to remember'. The melodies of Stravinsky are almost easily remembered.

The first memory that a composer has to deal with is that of the performer. There is probably no composer in history who has put so much passion and fantasy into insulting performing artists as Stravinsky has—at least with regard to the performing artists who fulfil the threadbare ideals that are still cherished by today's impresarios, orchestra directors, and record producers. Stravinksy wanted to make only a tiny distinction between a train conductor and an orchestra conductor. From the performing musicians, he wanted complete subjugation to the score. His music is a translation of that point of view. Whoever—such as the famous H. who conducted a fifteen-man ensemble from the Concertgebouw Orchestra in a performance of *Dumbarton Oaks* several years ago—does not limit himself to beating out the bars and using only the most urgent co-ordinating gestures, but wants to play Maestro and goes wild like an 'Armenian rug salesman', can rest assured that the result of his efforts will resemble everything except Stravinsky. (The sparse hair of the conductor in question however was in disarray after only a minute or two.)

Whoever plays Stravinsky can hardly do without a score. In general, sight-reading a piece is easier when one has already heard it a few times. One then only partly reads the music: the memory fills in the rest. Doing this with Stravinsky will generally lead to disaster; especially when playing four hands, where co-ordination is critical. Whoever, thinking he knows *Dumbarton Oaks*, plays the two-piano version for the first time (a bit from memory, without counting) will have to pay the penalty. The ear that thought it was well-grounded in the 'rules of irregularity' was merely fooling itself. Even works which are meant to be performed 'without the music' (solo pieces, the *Violin Concerto*, *Concerto for Piano and Wind*, *Capriccio*) can, only after much resistance, be learned by heart. Performances of the *Concerto for Piano and Wind* in which the score is half-hidden in the piano are not exceptional. When Stravinsky played the première of the piece, the conductor had to sing the beginning of the second movement to him.

The seat of the performer's memory is found, to an important degree, in the fingers. One speaks of a sensory-motor memory. That is strange considering that the music of Stravinsky, and especially the *Concerto for Piano and Wind*, is characterized as being motorial. The qualities that cursory listeners (writers of programme notes and record sleeves, as well as music sociologists) attribute to Stravinsky's music are apparently not the qualities of Stravinsky's music but the qualities that the music, in one way or another, refers to.

Of course, one could give a technical musical explanation for the difficulty of memorizing Stravinsky's music. There are even several explanations, though they may not be applicable simultaneously. The limitation of the musical material to a few intervals is one such explanation. In this regard, one could speak of circular melodies: the melodies whirl around two or three intervals, are not built on harmonic tension and, therefore, have no real beginning or end, but seem to be more or less haphazardly cut from a continuum. (This is true for the larger form as well. Schoenberg said that *Babel* is a work that does not have an ending; it just stops.)

How such material is used is an extension of this first explanation: the same thing all the time, yet each time just slightly different. Anyone who listens to 'L'Oncle Armand' from *Pribaoutki* has to ask himself half-way through the piece whether or not he has heard the same thing three times already. The relationship of melody to harmony also belongs to the category of use of material. The reason that Tom's cavatina has a Mozart-like memorizability has to do with the harmonic unambiguity of the accompaniment. Conversely, the accompanying chords in Parasha's aria constantly contradict the melody or put it in quotation marks. Parasha is cautious about her serious feelings.

The dialectical relationship between Stravinsky's music and the musical conventions (styles, mannerisms, etc.) to which it refers presents another explanation. *Madrid* seems to begin like all other virtuoso orchestral works in Spanish style. The listener imagines that he is on known ground, anticipates being swept away by the prospective exotica and ends up feeling deceived. *Madrid* is more difficult to re-create mentally than Albéniz's *Iberia*, just as it is more difficult to copy the guitar that Picasso drew than to copy the guitar which Picasso used to draw his guitar. It is clear that there are just as many degrees of memorizability as there are relationships between Stravinsky's music and existing musical genres, forms, styles, and idioms. The memory has an easier time with *Le Baiser de la fée* than with *L'Histoire du soldat*.

Since the music of Stravinsky is concerned with so much other music, it can be said to be a music with a rich memory. It is strange though, that music that remembers so much hardly remembers itself. Unlike much other music that—as Stravinsky said of Handel—finishes too long after the end, Stravinsky's usually stops long before it is finished, and just after it began again for the tenth time.

This beginning again and again is somewhat childlike. (Is that what Adorno meant by 'Infantilismus'?) But not childlike in the sense that evokes endearment. It is, rather, childlike in the uncertainty of the unrhymed looking-glass world of Alice where things are never what they seem.

Of the two kinds of memory—the long-term and short-term memory—the latter is more strongly developed in children (children are good at, for example, memory games with a pack of cards) while the former is nearly all but absent. An uncle who asks his young nephew: well, what have you been up to this last six months, will only get a blank stare for an answer. What the nephew carries with him as memories are gathered into one timeless moment.

Children's behaviour is also generally without any memory of the past. This behaviour (just as Stravinsky's music) can be called additive. Building-blocks can be used as a metaphor for this type of behaviour (and music). Half an hour of hide-and-seek, ten minutes of Donald Duck, a quarter of an hour drawing, teasing the cat for a few minutes, and finally an account of the day at school: 'And then . . . and then . . . and then . . .'. Maybe that is why children, long before they have gained entry into the world of real music (real symphonies, real late string quartets), often enjoy Stravinsky. Another advantage is that most of the pieces do not last very long.

The first movement of the *Symphony in Three Movements* 'was composed sectionally, and in complete units, the first of which extended from [71] through the second measure of [80]. Another section, with a B♭-minor key signature, began at the upbeat to the measure before [59] and continued to [70]. This was followed by a draft of the first part of the third movement (!) through the canon for bassoons. The next section to be composed contained the music from [34] to [56] and from [61] to [93], where, at [81], the piano makes its appearance for the first time. The beginning of the movement was written next and the end last, which explains the non-development of the opening figure, so puzzling to commentators' (Craft, *PD*).

Stravinsky's 'and then . . . and then . . . and then . . .' is, of course, a controlled and choreographed 'and then . . . and then . . . and then . . .'. But even so, this principle of form explains why it is sometimes difficult, if we remember a fragment of his music out of context, to find it quickly in the score.

Every Beethoven-lover will immediately recognize the bars shown in

Example 1. And every Stravinsky-lover will immediately recognize the bars shown in Example 2. But, whereas the Beethoven-lover will immediately say: 'Eighth Symphony, second movement', the Stravinsky-lover will probably say: '*Danses Concertantes*' (wrong); '*Dumbarton Oaks*' (wrong); then, 'of course, *The Rake's Progress*' (wrong). The bars come from *Jeu du cartes*.

It is tempting to draw the conclusion that the individual works of Stravinsky (just as the trio sonatas of the Baroque) have weak identities—but just the opposite is true. How else could the concept *œuvre-type* have been coined (by Boris de Schlœzer) back in 1929 exclusively as a characterization of Stravinsky's works? *The Rake's Progress* is not an opera, but the opera; the *Tango* is not a tango, but the tango; and the *Requiem Canticles* is not a requiem, but the requiem. These pieces are mutually exclusive in a special way. The œuvre of Stravinsky is most similar to a network of roads: crossings, viaducts, access roads, cloverleafs, converging and merging motorways; each route has characteristics of the other routes, but no two routes could ever be exchanged. The view from the road is always the same but in a different way; always different in the same way.

Orpheus. As friends of the Greek singer offer their sympathy at his recent widowerhood, they dance an Air de danse together to the well-mannered, almost courtly elegy played by a solo violin, teetering between two adjacent notes—still tottering since the same dilemma a year earlier in the *Concerto in D* for strings. Or: the Angel of Death, the guide on the route to Hades, foreshadows the, as yet unwritten, *Agon*. Or: the Furies, who are tormenting the singer, sneer stoically—the Joker from the long-forgotten *Jeu de cartes* (a lost game, avenged?). Or: Orpheus attacked by the Bacchantes, who, basely, laugh the laugh of the devil in the age-old *Soldat*, or perhaps their laughs echo the fanfares from the *Symphonies of Wind Instruments*; finally, they tear him apart with the rage of the *Sacre*, but tempered by the *Symphony in Three Movements*.

'I am enlarging the periphery of a departure point that I consider my own, and the movement produced around it, the curve of its line, is perfectly logical, as exact as that of a wheel around its axis' (*PD*). Or, as Pascal said: '. . . an infinite sphere, the centre of which is everywhere and the circumference nowhere'.

The œuvre of Stravinsky is labyrinthine. The thread of Adriane is in every passage.

Forma Formans

Stravinsky's music sounds improvised. A musical subject is introduced, but the thought is broken off and the composer changes to another subject—like a witty speaker during a pleasant lunch, flowing with good white wine, who, after a quip pulls another anecdote out of his hat. 'Oh, yes, now I want to tell you what Misia Sert said, when she stepped into her box at the Gaieté Lyrique theatre.' (In 1921 Diaghilev decided to make his contribution to the socializing of the arts. He rented the Gaieté Lyrique, a small theatre in the workers' district of Paris and managed—through publicity in the neighbourhood—to attract the local residents into a theatre which put on mostly operettas. That succeeded nicely. After a few performances, the hall was filled with an entirely different audience from the mundane, chic people who usually attended the Ballets Russes. One evening the wealthy Misia Sert came to a performance. When she arrived at her box, she directed her binoculars into the crowded hall, saw no one well known—only unshaven faces—and said, surprised: 'There's nobody here!')

There are many stories to tell, but what they all have in common is the quick-wittedness of the speaker. That quick-wittedness—which reflects an attitude or style—forms the actual subject of the story that the words tell. And that is how it is with music, too. The composer can, if we continue with the comparison of the speaker, tell a rounded, engaging, or boring story; but can also, still by merely telling, join many varied subjects together and surprise the listener through mere inflections of the voice, gestures, twinkling eyes, and exclamations. At that moment, the form becomes content and the form of the story becomes a self-forming form.

In his inaugural lecture, 'Forma Formans', on the Fantasies of Jan Pieterszoon Sweelinck, Frits Noske (professor emeritus of musicology at the University of Amsterdam) explained the form of the Fantasies not as a previously determined structure, but as a process that develops itself during the course of the piece: the 'forma formans', the self-forming form, as opposed to, for example, the sonata form, an already formed form: 'forma formata'. In improvised music, the form originates during and through the medium of the performance, whether it is a piano solo by Cecil Taylor or the accompaniment to a dance festivity in Togo. Fortunately, the 'forma formans' has not totally disappeared in composed music in the West. We can hear it in Stravinsky—feigned improvisation. The form of Sweelinck's Fantasies is largely the result of his organ improvisations. Noske points out that the theory of the closed form was not formulated until the sixteenth century. In his treatise *Musica*, written in 1537, Nicolaus Listenius was the first to speak of the 'opus perfectum et absolutum'; in other words, music that will live on even after the death of the composer. Before then music was 'scientia bene modulandi'—the art was to *play* well, not to make up good playing rules. 'Musique en jeu'; how sad that the generation of Boulez and Pousseur used the notion, but did not understand anything about the essence of improvisation—surprising the listener, leading him down a dead end. 'Open form'. The term was applied so often in the sixties by Earle Brown, by Stockhausen (who, in *Originale*, aped the Americans), and by countless minor composers who thought to solve all compositional problems at one stroke through half-finished, indistinguishable piano filigree filled with minor ninths (preferably notated on loose sheets with circular staves that droop over the page like Dali timepieces; and preferably with a separate page of recommendations about the procedures to use in choosing a performance order); pieces to be played, if at all possible, at a piano recital in the framework of a Festival where six totally or not totally written-out piano works all sounding exactly alike were performed the previous afternoon—'too bad that Misia Sert is not here'—and not having anything to do with someone improvising, telling a story, a performer who had even one idea worthwhile enough to be interrupted.

Fortunately, Cage at least noticed that his 'indeterminate' music sounds exactly the same as his composed music. But Cage can allow himself that because he does not deal in musical problems. Cage's rhetoric is extra-musical: 'Which is more musical, a truck passing by a factory or a truck passing by a music school?'

But 'forma formans' can be feigned just as improvisation can. From the moment that music is notated, it is 'formata'. 'Formata' in the formal sense though, since even though the musical thought is fixed and every performance will sound more or less the same, the thought itself can nevertheless give the impression of being improvised—as if arising out of the playing itself. The listener pretends as well: he pretends he is listening to the piece for the first time. But he is accustomed to that, since he can do the same thing with a Mozart symphony. Jazz-lovers will admit that there is little difference, in musical experience, between improvisation at a concert, a live improvisation, that is, *real* improvising, and the thousandth listening of a recording of a

Charlie Parker solo. The literal aspect of it being an improvisation is not important: the nature of the musical content is what counts.

Jazz-lovers think that improvised music has nothing (or is not allowed to have anything) to do with composed music and that it is even opposed to it. The unique quality of a Charlie Parker improvisation, though, is not that it is improvised, but that, *à l'improviste*, a coherent musical story is told. Naturally, that 'story' (saxophone-players 'talk' on their instruments) arises out of improvisation and, while improvising, 'mistakes' can be made. The sax player can then correct such a mistake while playing, or better yet, make it part of the musical structure. This is precisely what so often happens in Stravinsky's music. Only his mistakes are premeditated. They do not get played, but 'played', acted out.

Sweelinck's 'forma formans', the written-out improvisation, has much in common with the most prevalent form in jazz—variation. Noske quotes a contemporary of Sweelinck who describes how one evening Sweelinck improvised variations on 'De lustelijcke Mey is nu in sijnen tijt' ('The Merry Month of May'), and 'could not restrain himself, being in a very sweet humour, entertaining us, his friends, and himself as well'.

Until 1960 almost every jazz improvisation was based on a repeating chord scheme of 12 or 32 bars. This kind of chain-form (or variation form) is closer to a work such as the *Sacre du printemps* than to the variation technique of the Second Viennese School. In the innumerable Variazionen für Orchester, für Klavier, für who knows what, every variation is more of an independent *metamorphosis* of a musical thought (usually a tone-row) than an interpretation of it.

Sweelinck's variations consist of consequential fragments that are notated in ever-decreasing note-values. The first variation, for example, is in semibreves, the second in minims, and so on until the last has only demisemiquaver—a rhythmic escalation. As a consequence, the variations cannot easily be interchanged. There is a more or less compelling order that is dictated by the principle of growing faster. What Noske does not explain is that the structure of acceleration per variation in the Fantasies of Sweelinck belongs to the world of 'forma formata'. No piece is less improvised than Ravel's *Bolero*. Sweelinck's organ improvisations undoubtedly had a freer form, more digressions, suddenly-appearing slow movements ('beginning again'), acceleration without a climax ('no, wait a minute, before I forget'), and unfinished thoughts. At least we can only hope so: no improvisation is so boring as acting as if you were not improvising—quasi-composing, the way organists do it nowadays, which is almost as bad as poor composing. Stravinsky does not like 'improvising' either: 'Wagner, that is improvising'. No, Stravinsky feigns the improvised gesture. He does it mostly in solo pieces, since improvisation is mostly a soloistic activity. That is why he eliminates the bar-lines in the *Three Pieces* for clarinet solo and in the *Piano-Rag-Music*—a feigned improvisation with never a clear down-beat; the same effect provoked by the clickety-clack of the train: 'no, it *is* a syncope'. Stravinsky applies it to solo parts too; the entire piano part of the strictly serial *Movements* for piano and orchestra gives the impression of being improvised—round the corner, turn left, no, better still, straight ahead, hold on—as if mice are sitting on the heels of the player. (That makes sense; Misha Mengelberg, while improvising at the piano, suddenly saw the keys as a barn full of rats. The keys he played were the nooks and crannies that he chased the rats out of. That gave rise to a musical result. One finds the best chords in search of vermin.)

But Stravinsky also 'improvises' in orchestral works. In the second movement of *Ode* from 1943, the rather childish melody at [20] never really gets off the ground (Ex. 1). The composer then decides to continue the drama (Boris Karloff is still lurking behind the tree) in the accompaniment (Ex. 2). There is the monster that eats children! The melody! Gone! (Who would ever think of such a thing? Not Bartók, he never would, he was too nice to do such a thing.) Putting the listener on tenterhooks, stumbling over your own conventions—now that is something we can learn from.

How strange is that end to *Variations*, (Aldous Huxley in memoriam), such a serious and unyielding work (Ex. 3). Dramatic final chords for the strings? Not in the least. What follows these suggestive bars is the final note (Ex. 4). Work done, no drama—so there! But this single note is the only low note that is held in the entire work. The final note becomes 'final note', a quotation, a forgotten finale, *the last chord*, the last three pages of E major by Anton Bruckner sucked up by a vacuum cleaner. Nothing is left of the Reconstructed Bicycle Wheel except one spoke.

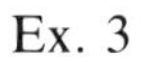
Ex. 3

Ex. 4

But that too is only suggestion. The G♯ is merely the next note in the twelve-tone row.

Zoonology

Mankind apes the animal.
Democritus

It is rather useless to speculate what somebody would have become if he had not become what he became; in Stravinsky's case, it is at least no more useless than usual. His biography is so rich in detail that more than one answer springs to mind. Such as investment manager (or blackmarketeer), bank director (or forger), lexicographer (specializing in etymology), stationer, devil's advocate, or—most likely of all—zoologist. His first autobiographical writings, the very businesslike *Chroniques de ma vie*, offer evidence to support this last conjecture when the writer remembers how he spent hours in 'the famous Aquarium' of Naples together with Picasso. The evidence piles up in other documents which have come to light, both by him and others. For instance, he had apparently already travelled from Brest-Litovsk to Smolensk with a bull in a cattle-truck in 1911. As a globe-trotter, he will visit the zoo of every city he arrives in. (In a way, he will even become part of it. In the photograph we see eight people gaping at the composer who is in undisturbed conversation with a giraffe.) As for the rest, the Stravinsky documents are inhabited by chickens, cats (Vassily Vassilyevitch Lechkin, Pancho), canaries (Iago, Lyssaya Dushka—Bald Darling), forty cockatoos and lovebirds (among them Beauty, Pretty, Whit-Whit, and Lana Turner) and Pópka the parrot, who was sometimes allowed to eat at the dinner-table. Pópka had the habit of every so often opening Bald Darling's cage, and would proceed to fly round the room in circles with the newly liberated canary. Nicolas Nabokov, a friend of the family, was warned about falling objects.

Stravinsky's behaviour towards animals was—judging by the sources—free of sentimentality; even in this respect he was fundamentally different from Wagner. This is not contradicted even by the fact that, in his work-room in Hollywood, the portrait of the deceased cat Celeste hung with those of Pope John XXIII, T. S. Eliot, and Jean Cocteau—other famous dead.

It is remarkable that not only in the descriptions of Stravinsky's surroundings did zoology play an important role, but also in the descriptions of the composer himself. The painter Pavel Tchelitchev compared Stravinsky to a 'prancing grasshopper', while Cocteau recognized in the conducting composer

'an erect ant acting its part in a La Fontaine fable'. (La Fontaine, by the way, was one of Stravinsky's favourite writers.) According to the same Nabokov, Tchelitchev and Cocteau had missed the mark, since, if Stravinsky was anything, he was a bird: 'one of those small birds with large, sturdy beaks, like cardinals or lovebirds, whose movements are quick, electric, and nervous'. We have yet to hear the last word on this.

The obvious transition is now to Stravinsky's music. *The Firebird*, *Le Rossignol*, *Cat's Cradle Songs*, *Renard*, *The Owl and the Pussy-Cat* (but not *The Dove Descending* since that is the Holy Spirit). And then there are the songs, lieder, and even a piece for choir (*Four Russian Peasant Songs*) in which ducks, swans, geese, magpies, ravens, and jackdaws take part. But this kind of list does not really say much since the firebird is not a real but a mythological bird, since the Cat's Cradle Songs may just as well have been about a tea service or Olga the maid, and since the nightingale that steals the show in *Le Rossignol* is a mechanical one, while the real nightingale sings a song which 'not even remotely resembles the song that a nightingale sings' (Schlœzer). (Yet, Stravinsky's real nightingale is his only musical bird which, with a little bit of good will, can be counted among the Messiaen family. 'For me', says Messiaen, 'the true, the only music, has always existed in Nature.' 'If we take pleasure in these [natural] sounds', says Stravinsky, 'by imagining that on being exposed to them we become musicians and even, momentarily, creative musicians, we must admit that we are fooling ourselves.')

Although Stravinsky was the last person to be interested in making stylized copies of nature, it is strange how often descriptions of his music, and especially his early music, resort to zoological terminology. One critic, in *Le Ménestrel* (6 June 1914), heard 'some croaking of frogs out of season, and the mooing of a young cow' in the *Sacre*. Ten years later the same composition was described on the other side of the ocean as a musical portrait of 'spring fever in the zoo'; in this zoo one heard 'trumpeting, braying, roaring, cackling, calling and growling' as if it were going out of fashion. In 1922 an English critic compared the brass sounds in the *Symphonies of Wind Instruments* to 'a donkey's bray'. Of course these critics hardly meant well with their animalistic qualifications and the zoological metaphor is as old as reactionary critics themselves (A. Oulibicheff heard 'odious meowing' in the Scherzo of Beethoven's Fifth symphony); but the zoological metaphors are too numerous and certainly too full of fantasy in Stravinsky's case simply to be variations on the same old theme. Sometimes the metaphor is even used explicitly in a positive sense. According to Elmo Versteeg, the character of, again, the *Symphonies of Wind Instruments* is determined by the instrumentation: 'replace the clarinet with a flute and most of the questions disappear. It is merely the clarinet in that specific register which calls up a world of folk music, grotesqueness, clowning, Romanians feasting at a wedding, one lone tree in the tundra, floods, crowing of the cock and dancing apes.' Schaeffner heard even more animals: the clucking of chickens and turkeys, the crowing of cocks (again), the quacking of ducks, and the grunting of pigs.

The animal-like aspect of such completely unonomatopoetic, un-pastoral, un-bucolic music cannot be understood from within the 'idiom' of animal sounds, but from within their structure.

Listen, a pigeon. How simply it coos:

Ex. 1

♩= 60

This is the pattern from which it varies. For instance it repeats (a) or it restricts itself to (a) with the repetition of the second half of (a), the result being (aa′). Every variation can be found to have been derived from the combinations (♪♩), (♩♪) and (♩♩). The structure of the cooing is, just like the beginning of the *Symphonies of Wind Instruments*, additive, so that the identity of each rhythmic and melodic cell is preserved. Just as important as the notes are the commas (Ex. 2). Cooing is distinguished by short first as well as last notes. What one hears (and this is true just as much for Stravinsky's music as for animal sounds) seems as if it were more or less randomly cut out of a continuum: it does not begin, it just suddenly appears; it does not conclude, it just abruptly stops. It is a *pausa del silenzio*.

Ex. 2

Symphonies of Wind Instruments, clarinet only

Characteristic of animal sounds—this is also true of bird-song—is the absence of musical development. The blackbird, the song thrush, the nightingale, the garden warbler—at any moment their song can be cut off, and, after a short pause, begin again with another random motive. From 'continually beginning anew' to controlled montage is a step from nature to culture.

The fact that songbirds are not mentioned in the quoted descriptions of the *Sacre* and the *Symphonies of Wind Instruments*—although, as far as the latter is concerned, poultry and a mammal or two are—must be explained by the distinguishing function accorded to the timbre in these compositions. Songbirds are, in the first place, distinguished by their melodic characteristics; most other animals are recognized by their timbre. You merely have to hear grunting to know that there is a pig in the vicinity; but the call of the cuckoo can vary between a minor second and a tritone (composers only hearing the falling third) and still remain the call of the cuckoo.

(In a comprehensive zoonological dissertation about the music of Stravinsky, attention would need to be paid to other than exclusively sonic correlations between the behaviour of animals and that of Stravinsky, and to the mode in which this behaviour can be interpreted. Animals, for instance, can intrigue us by natural behaviour which appears to be very unnatural. An example of this is the dynamics of the humming-bird: flying extremely fast and yet not making any forward progress. The humming-bird seems to be created in the image of the cartoon figure, whose feet—consisting of a cloud of concentric circles—suggest a high degree of velocity; furthermore, it displays strong symptoms of levitation although its horizontal displacement remains zero. Not only was the backyard of Stravinsky's home in Hollywood a *va-et-vient* of humming-birds, so too his music: from the *Scherzo Fantastique* to the pseudo-fugato at the conclusion of *Babel* [from 22$_2$], and from the semiquaver runs gone astray in the second Pas d'action in *Orpheus* to the coda of the last movement of the

Symphony in Three Movements. Although maybe this last example seems more like a dog chasing after an imaginary bone.)

And Stravinsky himself?

He reminds one of the Cheshire Cat in *Alice in Wonderland*, whose grin 'remained some time after the rest of it had gone'.

1947—Orpheus

Is a seventh chord inappropriate in modern music?
John Cage

There is scarcely any other piece of music whose beauty is as mysterious as that of *Orpheus*. And there is scarcely any other episode whose beauty is as mysterious as that of the introductory Lento sostenuto. Even the most mediocre pianist can play it on the piano. If he were to, he would notice that he actually only needs half of his instrument—even less than half. Since, except for that one augmented chord in the winds and that one C♯ in the cello, everything is white. White keys: a white ballet. Five-part, slowly sliding chords in the strings in which the 'white' notes seem to be freely combined, and the harp weaving the descending Phrygian scale through all of this.

One speaks of *pandiatonicism*. Completely white-note music could be a translation of this. The chords in the Lento sostenuto are unmistakably Stravinskian chords; that is evident, but why do they work only in this order and not in any other? Everything appears to be free but it is not. Why would changing one single note transform this snow-covered landscape into a mudhole? The answer has to be as simple as the worn-out dominant seventh chord that, with such genius, concludes the introduction. A million dominant seventh chords had been written in the last three centuries, and after all that, Stravinsky discovered the chord again. This sounds more mystical than it is. Compare it to an optical illusion: just as two parallel lines in a given background are no longer parallel lines, the dominant seventh chord in a given background is no longer a dominant seventh chord.

'What if the seventh chord was not a seventh chord?' Cage asks in *Silence*. Stravinsky had already often given the answer, and not just in *Orpheus*—in the *Symphony of Psalms*, for example, just before 'Elijah's chariot climbing the Heavens' when only one major third and one minor seventh reach to the skies in a tower of octaves.

These dominant seventh chords are pandiatonic. Pandiatonicism is not only a characteristic of Stravinsky's 'American' music though, no matter how 'American' some of the purely pandiatonic bars in his earlier works sound (Ex. 1). The bars in Example 1 do not come from *Orpheus*, but from the

Apothéose of *Apollon musagète* (1928). Pandiatonicism has something to do with neoclassicism, however not so much that it could be called a style characteristic of true neoclassical composers such as Martinů and Hindemith.

Ex. 1

Apollon musagète 98 2

For Stravinsky, pandiatonicism is strict diatonicism with notes that belong to the key but are, although institutionalized, none the less foreign to the chord. In the example from *Apollon*, all the notes belong to the key of D major (with the exception of the lowered seventh, C♮—see below, paragraph 4.2). But on no beat, except the last one, does a regular triad fall. The rhythm is tonal and regular, yet the listener is always uncertain about the structure of the phrase. The melody is diatonic and simple, yet irregular.

Stravinsky's pandiatonicism is not strictly tied to a certain period of his œuvre. Pandiatonicism appears from *Petrushka* up to and including *Requiem Canticles*. That the technique is most radically and consistently applied in the early American compositions (and consequently adopted by countless

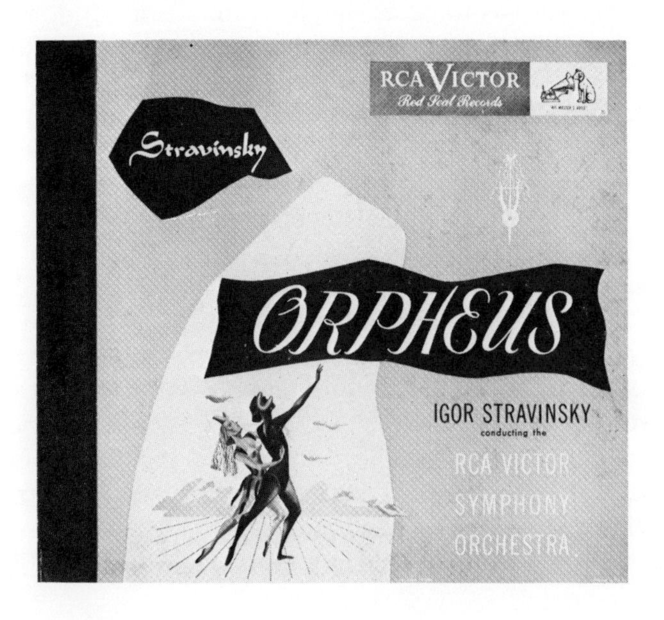

American composers) helps to explain why white-note music is automatically associated with Hollywood.

The first to attempt to formulate a more or less systematic theory of Stravinsky's pandiatonicism ('white-note collections') was the composer Arthur Berger. In his 'Problems of Pitch Organization in Stravinsky' (1963), he, as is apparent from the title of his study, strongly emphasizes questions of syntax. Another approach to Stravinsky's pandiatonicism—one which would do justice to the great significance Stravinsky placed on the chord as an object (the *Petrushka* chord, the Mighty Bear [see p. 225]) is the typological approach.

Pandiatonicism

1. Chords based on triads from the key.

In their most elementary form, pandiatonic chords are (major) triads with a bass alien to the triad. This bass often suggests another harmonic function than the triad in question (Ex. 2). Example 2 shows that the converse is equally true: the chord consists of a bass with a triad alien to that bass. The answer to the question what the fundamental is of a pandiatonic chord is not always given by the bass (Ex. 3). In example 3, from *Danses Concertantes*, the fundamental is E, not the bass G. The melody and the harmonic rhythm determine the fundamental in this case.

Ex. 2

(*a*) *Symphonies of Wind Instruments*, final chord
(*b*) *Symphony of Psalms*, 3rd movement [12]$_4$

Ex. 3

Danses Concertantes [15]

(Chords appear in Bach's music which consist almost entirely of notes from another chord [Ex. 4]. The E chord at the arrow in Example 4 consists of a B and a D♯. This D♯ is, as the continuation of the bar makes clear, not the third of B but the seventh of E; the B is the fifth of E. The tonic and the third of the chord are not present.)

Ex. 4

Invention VI, bars 51–4

2.1. Triads with a bass alien to the triad in the major (Ex. 5).

Ex. 5

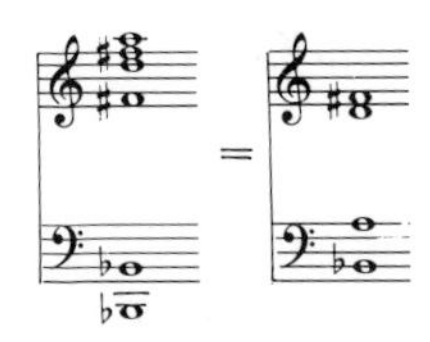

(*a*) *Symphony of Psalms*, 3rd movement [12]$_2$
(*b*) *Agon*, bars 297, 308

2.2. Triads with a bass alien to the triad in the minor (Ex. 6). Octotonic chords, especially those that regularly appear in the minor pandiatonic (*Symphony of Psalms*), are not included in this survey (see 'Octotony', p. 228).

Ex. 6

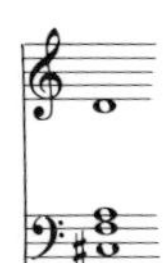

Three Pieces for string quartet, 3rd movt., bar 19

3. Triads with added notes from the key (Ex. 7).

Ex. 7

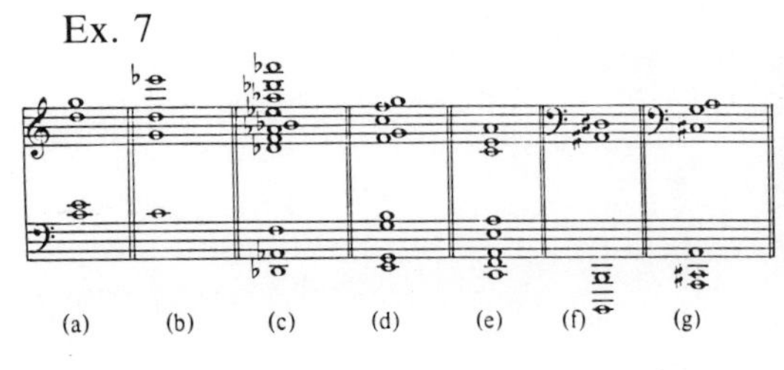

(*a*) *Sonata for Two Pianos*, final chord
(*b*) *Duo concertant*, beginning of Dithyrambe
(*c*) *Symphony in Three Movements*, final chord
(*d*) *Symphony in C* [182]
(*e*) *Apollon musagète* [58]$_2$
(*f*) *Perséphone* [59]$_4$
(*g*) *Orpheus* [3]$_5$

3.1.1. Added second in the major (Ex. 7 *a*). This chord appears quite often.
3.1.2. Added second in the minor (Ex. 7 *b*).

3.1.3. Added second plus sixth (Ex. 7 *c*). A fairly common chord (especially found in commercial music), except in Stravinsky. Apparently suitable as the final chord of a symphony in three movements.

3.2. Added fourth (Ex. 7 *d*). Occurs frequently, often in an extended open position. Furthermore, in the example here the seventh is added.

3.3.1. Added major seventh (Ex. 7 *e*). Although worn out, it still appears once in a while. This chord plays an important part in *Perséphone*, from where Example 7 *f* is taken.

3.3.2. Added minor seventh. The dominant seventh chord without the fifth in Example 7 *g* (the closing of the first scene of *Orpheus*) does not sound like a dominant seventh chord without the fifth but like a tonic chord with an added note.

Chromatic additions, that is, additions not from the key, almost always refer to octotonics.

This inventory is not an attempt at listing all types of triads with notes added from the key signature, as this would make about as much sense as a train schedule for trains that will not be leaving. Merely the combination of incomplete triads with notes added from the key signature (including the major and minor seventh) results in eighty chords. Of these eighty chords, it must certainly be the case that many appear in Stravinsky's music.

4. Chords not based on triads.

4.1. The combination of fifths with sevenths and/or ninths (Ex. 8). Four examples of this combination can be found in bars 18 and 19 in the Grand Chorale from *L'Histoire du soldat.*

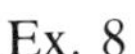

Ex. 8

(*a*) *Concerto for Piano and Wind* [8]$_{3}$
(*b*) *Symphonies of Wind Instruments*, bar 1

4.2. The combination of major and minor sevenths (Ex. 9).

Ex. 9

Threni, bar 344

This combination, prefigured in the *Sacre* (Ex. 10), superficially sounds somewhat octotonic, but it is not. Not only does the harmonic alternation of major and minor sevenths play a noticeable role in Stravinsky's pandiatonicism, so does the melodic alternation (Ex. 11).

Ex. 10

Le Sacre du printemps [104]

Ex. 11

Dumbarton Oaks [88]

(Stravinsky gratefully obtained this technique of suddenly-appearing major and minor sevenths from Bach. Especially in the Brandenburg Concertos there are many examples of freely-occurring sevenths, often as the only notes outside the key [Ex. 12]. Still today the minor seventh functions as the lubricant of the tonal functions. No tear-jerker is complete without dominant sevenths. The first application of this chord marked the breakthrough of tonality. In pandiatonicism, however, tonal functions are masked and robbed of their dynamic quality. The alternation of major and minor sevenths is one of the causes of this.)

Ex. 12

Brandenberg Concerto No 6, bar 39

5. There are many cases of pandiatonicism in which the chord can not but be explained by the melody. One example of this is the first Pas d'action from *Orpheus*. The continually varying highest voices are in strong contrast to the lower voices which move stepwise in parallel sixths. The result of this is a new chord on almost every semiquaver (Ex. 13). A computer could not have done it better.

·Ex. 13

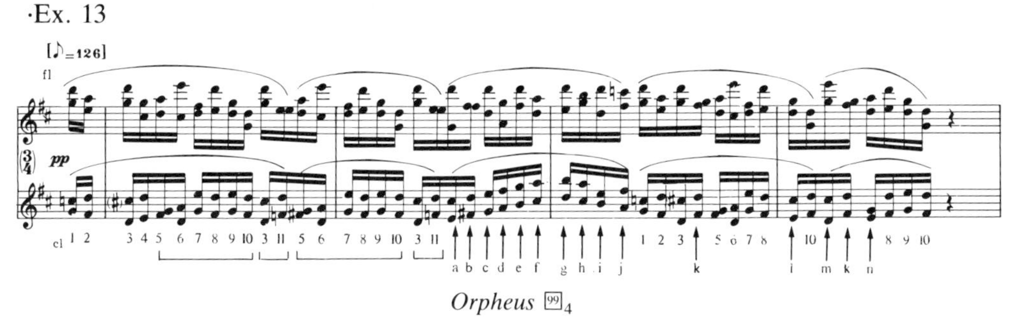

Orpheus [99]4

It is possible to make a random programme based on this limited tone material (D major with F♮ and C♮ as the only accidentals). One of the lines of this programme would read: as the number of chord repetitions increases so does the chance of a new chord appearing, reaching 100 per cent during a period of approximately ten semiquavers.

Another line would be responsible for the reduction of melodic variation during the next period (bar 2, second half).

A third line would be responsible for then adding increasingly more new chords in the following period and again increasing the melodic variation (last four crochets).

Stravinsky considered these bars to be rhythmically monotonous. But precisely because of the monotonous repetition of 'continually the same' and 'continually slightly different', these bars are a prophetic premonition of (and, at the same time, put into perspective) the music that Steve Reich and his followers would write twenty years later. Random became 'process' and pandiatonicism changed into arpeggiating modal chords.

While Orpheus is being torn apart by the Bacchantes, Apollo, his teacher, wrests the harp out of his hands and raises his song heavenwards. A plaintive, muted music is heard. The harp no longer (after the first four bars) treads the descending Phrygian scale of the introductory Lento sostenuto, but now scales the Dorian steps. The harp, just like Orpheus, is probably on its way to heaven. But it does not get very far: the web in which its notes are being caught becomes more and more perceptible, the concluding dominant seventh chord.

The only thing left to do is to wait for a new Orpheus/*Orpheus*.

II

Purcell, Pergolesi and the others

'Since I have never liked excessive uniformity in composition and taste, since I have heard such a quantity and variety of good [things], since I have always been of the opinion that one could derive some good, whatever it may be, even if it is only a matter of minute details in a piece, probably from such [considerations] and my natural, God-given ability arises the variety that has been observed in my works.'

Stravinsky was not the only Stravinsky in history. The quoted statement is borrowed from the autobiography of Carl Philipp Emanuel Bach (1714–88), the composer who vies with Pergolesi for the honour of being called the inventor of the sonata form. Carl Philipp Emanuel was more 'modern' a composer than his father. *Empfindsamkeit* and *Sturm und Drang* are terms that meant as yet nothing to the pietistic Johann Sebastian. Carl Philipp Emanuel's piano sonatas excel because of their precious capriciousness. In spite of the stylistic variety of his œuvre, his music is very personal and immediately recognizable.

Carl Philipp Emanuel, more than his father, was familiar with the new philosophical trends of his day. As musician at the court of Frederick the Great (king of Prussia and, in his free time, composer and philosopher, writer of at least a *Complete Works* consisting of thirty volumes), he came in contact with the most enlightened thinkers of his age, French as well as German. Frederick the Great's penchant towards France and French rationalism is evident not merely in the name of his summer resort (Sanssouci), but also from the fact that, for two years, Voltaire was a regular guest of the court at Potsdam. Frederick the Great carried his pro-French leanings so far that entrance to the court was denied Lessing because Voltaire had quarrelled with the German writer/philosopher. Carl Philipp Emanuel was more of a realist: Lessing became one of his best friends.

His melodic strokes of genius are plentiful, as is his harmonic daring and rhythmic cunning—his combination of construction and freedom is exemplary; and yet Carl Philipp Emanuel is still considered to be more of a forerunner than an innovator in his own right. Certainly he was a forerunner; without him the music of Haydn and Beethoven would have sounded different, while Mozart said of him: 'He is the father, we are the children.' However, the word forerunner is often used negatively. Usually what is meant is someone who precedes something, not someone who runs *ahead*. Carl Philipp Emanuel was one who ran ahead. In twentieth-century jargon, a member of the avant-garde. He was able to compose in all the musical styles that were then in vogue. He even composed sonatas which were meant to be played by *the Ladies.*

Henry Purcell, like Carl Philipp Emanuel Bach, was in the service of a monarch who divided his time and money between organizing feasts with a lot of music and fighting wars. Frederick the Great usually lost them, but William III, on the other hand, managed to set foot on Dutch soil in 1690, wearing the English crown. Among his attendants, besides advisers and soldiers, were forty-three musicians, included was Henry Purcell.

Purcell, too, could do everything: compose in every style ('faithfully endeavor'd a just imitation of the most fam'd Italian Masters', as he wrote in the preface to his trio sonatas), serve bishops, serve Catholic princes, serve Protestant princes, repair harpsichords, organs, and wind instruments. He was well paid, even though he sometimes had to wait up to a year for his fee. He wrote pavans and fantasies in the style of consort music, which had been out of fashion for at least half a century. His theatre music was universally praised, 'especially by the ladies'. Many of his opera arias are among the most beautiful ever written. And the maker's hand is always recognizable. When Purcell died in 1695, he was thirty-six, a respectable age for someone in the seventeenth century who suffered from tuberculosis. Pergolesi, who was stricken down by the same disease forty-one years later, reached the age of twenty-six.

Giovanni Battista Pergolesi could also do everything. Besides 'Mozartian' piano sonatas (Mozartian in quotes since when Pergolesi died, Mozart had yet to be born), he wrote *opere buffe*, *opere serie*, religious compositions, and chamber music. He was the founder of the *dolce stil nuovo*, the somewhat elegant Italian herald of *Empfindsamkeit.* Telemann borrowed Pergolesi's technique of cantabile allegros. 'Angelic', 'pure', 'poetic': the biographers have tried everything to describe the 'Rafael' of music. Pergolesi himself was not so angelic. During the première of *Olympiade* in Rome, he was hit on the head by an orange thrown from the audience. The performance became a scandal and Pergolesi was boycotted in Rome.

Pergolesi's fame rests mainly on his *Stabat Mater*, one of the few pieces, by the way, of which we can say with certainty that it is actually by Pergolesi. (An increasingly number of pieces by Pergolesi turn out, in the course of time, not to be by Pergolesi. The *Stabat Mater* is, exceptionally, preserved in his handwriting.) The composition—famous for its subtle interpretation of the Maria sequence of the same name—is in fact an old piece with a new text. Eleven of the thirteen movements of the *Stabat Mater* are borrowed from Pergolesi's own *Dies Irae*, which is also admittedly a sequence, but one belonging to the Office for the Dead. The same piece of music for two totally different texts. Padre Martini, in his *Fundamental Practical Science of Counterpoint on the Cantus Firmus* (1775), would later proclaim that Pergolesi composed music that 'is suitable to express happy, spirited, yes, even humorous moods, although he wants to arouse pious, devote, religious, sorrowful and mournful feelings'. One of Pergolesi's biographers hears 'the shocked Mother's heart in the face of the crucified Saviour' in the series of syncopations on the text 'Quae moerebat et dolebat', even though that same writer has just explained, several pages before, that the *Stabat Mater* was originally set to another text. So one sees the consequences of the notion that music is capable of expressing things.

The last in the list of know-it-alls, money-grabbers, and anally-fixated hypochondriacs is Wolfgang Amadeus Mozart. 'If I stay here I shall compose six in the same *gusto*, for they are very popular fare', he wrote to his father after looking at the violin sonatas of Schuster in Munich in 1777. Four years later: 'I promise you that my one object is to make as much money as possible, for after health, etc., it is the thing most worth having.'

Medical science has made large advances in the last three hundred years. Pergolesi died at twenty-six, Purcell reached thirty-six, Mozart thirty-five. But Stravinsky lived for eighty-eight years, almost as long as Pergolesi, Purcell, and Mozart put together.

Concocted Reality

In the seventies the Dutch composer Dick Raaijmakers[1] made several pieces on the theme of China. One of those was *Mao leve!* (*Mao Live!*, 1977). Next to *Mao leve!* even Andy Warhol's colour portraits of Mao pale and shrivel. The piece consists of a series of slides showing Chinese children, cut out of one of those sugar-coated illustrations which seem to have been patented by the People's Republic. The projected children observe the Long March through a Chinese teething-ring as if looking into a magic lantern. The Long March itself consists of seven sections of a map. From the loudspeakers, Chinese songs echo through the mountains. The sounds of birds and thunder create an image of an all-encompassing nature as a background to the Idea that blossomed into being during the Long March. The eighth and last slide is a portrait of Mao—the last to die. Surrounding him are artificial flowers. Out of the loudspeakers come fragments of Richard Strauss's *Tod und Verklärung*.

This description will not be any help to someone who is trying to explain why *Mao leve*! is more than just high-flown kitsch. The piece contains all the ingredients of the genre, these being consummately manipulated as well. Even the most trifling suspicions of (unacted) naïvety are immediately dissipated by the scrupulous precision with which something is made out of nothing. Although China is shamelessly reduced to the dream of the viewmaster, a great warmth and devotion, however, radiate from the maker. The affection, though, is not for China but for an image of China. 'China is more television and newspaper photos than China', said Raaijmakers in response to his pieces. 'My reality, in any case, consists sooner of *images* of reality than reality itself . . . Without batting an eyelid, I forge *my own* reality out of reality and consider it the only true one. In that way I make use of second-hand information by creating it myself.'

The China of Raaijmakers shows similarities to the lands on the globe of Stravinsky's music. The Greek descending Phrygian mode in *Orpheus* is Stravinsky's teething-ring, the cancan for girls' chorus in *Perséphone* his map of the Long March, the Spanish fioriture in the *Étude* for Pianola (*Madrid*) his Chinese sounds of nature. Not for one second is the listener asked to believe

[1] Dick Raaijmakers, Dutch composer and conceptual artist, born in 1930 in Eindhoven. One of the first in Holland to work with electronic apparatus [trans.].

in this China, this Greece, this France, or this Spain. Reality announces itself as concocted reality—no, it cannot really be like that. There is, though, one essential point in which the China of Raaijmakers radically differs from Stravinsky's foreign lands: the material of the former is 'real', that of the latter deliberately unreal—fantastic realism (with romantic roots) as opposed to pseudo-realism (with classical roots). But the extremes touch here; the borrowed material is so unadorned and coolly presented that the effect of vision ('it is so'), dream-wish ('it should be so') or fairy-tale ('if only it were so') does not stand a chance of being taken seriously. The actual effect—the image that the composer forms of his subject is what is merely imparted—exists by courtesy of second-hand information: the descending Phrygian mode is something the listener once *read* about in a book. And if the *Sacre du printemps* is indeed a vision of old Russia, it is, more than anything else, a concocted vision. Nobody understood that better than Debussy, whose musical visions and evocations suggest more a medium than a composer. Debussy called the *Sacre* 'primitive music, equipped with every modern convenience'.

Second-hand information has made the world smaller and more orderly.

But this order rests largely on appearance. There is nothing wrong with second-hand information as long as we recognize it for what it is. A map of China is not China, and the descending Phrygian mode is not Hades. The Japan of Puccini's *Madama Butterfly* (and the China of Stravinsky's *Le Rossignol*), the medieval Russia of Borodin's *Prince Igor*, the Spain of Albeniz's *Iberia*, the Flanders of Van Gilse's *Thijl*,[2] the Rome of Respighi's *Fontane di Roma*, the world of Stockhausen's *Hymnen* and the universe of his *Licht* are as close as the China of Raaijmakers, the Greece of *Orpheus*, and the Russia of *Les Noces* are faraway.

[2] *Thijl*, the name of the Flemish prankster, known in Germany as 'Till Eulenspiegel'. The legend was made into an opera by the Dutch composer Jan van Gilse (1881–1944), completed in 1940. The opera was banned in occupied Holland as being too nationalistic and received its first staging in the 1980 Holland Festival [trans.].

The Inverted Metaphor

In 1920, Yevgeny Zamyatin, a Russian of Stravinsky's generation who later fell into disfavour, wrote a short story entitled 'The Cave'. The occupant of the cave is Martin Martinych. He is accompanied by his Masha. Their scarce possessions include books, stone-age pancakes, a flat-iron, five potatoes, scrubbed lovingly to gleaming whiteness, an axe, and Scriabin, Opus 74. 'Hot as the scorched desert' is the title Scriabin gave the second prelude from this cycle; but the cold Zamyatin left his cave-dwellers in remains none the less just as bitter. Martin Martinych has to sink to stealing a few logs of wood from his neighbour.

Zamyatin chooses to use 'grotesque metaphors: outward details sometimes take on enormous exaggerations, or an epithet completely overgrows the word it is supposed to be defining. The main character in *Mamai* [another of Zamyatin's short stories], whose arms "make one think of stumpy penguin wings", himself becomes a penguin and his wife, with her Buddha-like "opulent breasts", becomes—Buddha' (C. J. Pouw). Sometimes the metaphor overgrows reality, so that comparer and the compared switch places and functions:

Glaciers, mammoths, wastes. Black nocturnal cliffs, somehow resembling houses; in the cliffs, caves. And no one knows who trumpets at night on the stony path between the cliffs, who blows up white snow-dust, sniffing out the path. Perhaps it is a gray-trunked mammoth, perhaps the wind. Or is the wind itself the icy roar of the king of mammoths? One thing is clear: it is winter. And you must clench your teeth as tightly as you can, to keep them from chattering, and you must split wood with a stone axe; and every night you must carry your fire from cave to cave, deeper and deeper. And you must wrap yourself into shaggy animal hides, more and more of them . . .

In the next paragraph, we find ourselves 'where Petersburg had stood ages ago'. (It is a much grimmer world than the Paris where Stravinsky—drunk with champagne after the première of *Pulcinella*, at a grand outdoor party given by Prince Firouz of Persia in that same year 1920—went up to the balcony of a small chateau, took the pillows, the slats, and the mattresses from the beds and threw them everywhere.) In this wilderness, the houses do not seem like rocks, but the rocks like houses. The image drives away reality. The inversion of comparer and comparable implies the inversion of reality and image. The rocks are not metaphors, the houses are; and 'the short-legged, rusty-red, squat, greedy cave god' that is the centre of this universe is not a metaphor, the 'cast-iron stove' is. Zamyatin does not push the figure of speech to the limit though; complete inversion never occurs. In the final analysis, the subject is reality, the ice-cold starving reality of Leningrad, 1920.

Stravinsky has nothing directly to do with Zamyatin, except that both, like so many Petersburg Russians, pay tribute to the spirit of Gogol. But Zamyatin clarifies something about Stravinsky: in his music, the inverted metaphor becomes a principle of style. In *Orpheus*, for example, the descending Phrygian mode is not a metaphor of Greece, Greece is a metaphor of the descending Phrygian mode.

There are two possibilities:

1. First comes reality (for example, Japan 1904), then an image of reality (for example, *Madama Butterfly*). The image shows many similarities to reality. (This can also hold for instrumental music—Bartók's *Bulgarian Dances* do not cause our thoughts to dwell on Polynesia.) If the image is strong enough, we have the tendency to consider the image as reality. Not Japan, 1904, but *Madama Butterfly* attracts our attention.

In *Oedipus Rex*, the literary subject, it is true, is Greek, but the musical subject is the dramatic form of late baroque opera, the late baroque oratorio ('Handel') and the nineteenth-century Italian aria ('Verdi').

This exemplifies the second possibility, as it appears in Stravinsky's music:

2. First comes an image of reality (*Oedipus Rex*), then reality itself ('Handel', 'Verdi'). If reality is strong enough, we have the tendency to consider reality an image. Just as Greece is a metaphor for the descending Phrygian mode, 'Handel'/'Verdi' is a metaphor for *Oedipus Rex*.

But does *Oedipus Rex* have a cast-iron stove?

Perhaps more than one, though none from such genuine cast-iron as in the beginning of the second act, when Jocaste urges calm: 'Are you not ashamed, princes, to clamour [*clamare*] and howl [*ululare*] in a stricken city, raising up your personal broils?' (Ex. 1.)

Not one, but two diminished seventh chords—only the stalest formula is stale enough. The diminished seventh chord, says Verdi, is the stumbling block for every dramatic composer since it makes things too easy for him. Of all seventh

Ex. 1

chords, this is the most symmetric; because each of the four pitches can be the root of the chord, the function of the chord is vague. Employed to modulate, it becomes a skeleton—fitting eight keys at the same time. Besides acting as a skeleton key, the chord has served to breed unrest for more than two centuries, first as unrest itself, than as a herald of unrest, and finally as the musical counterpart of '. . .' (the three dots so often used by second-rate writers, so ambiguous and therefore meaningless). To Bach, Mozart, and Schubert (immediately preceding the coda in the first movement of the string quartet *Der Tod und das Mädchen*), the chord still functioned as a dissonance; but in the hands of nineteenth-century Italian opera composers, it quickly lost its character of suspense. In bad film music—the rubbish tip of musical history—merely a remnant of the diminished seventh chord ever appears now: the tritone in the bass guitar as the hero unsuspectingly meets his destiny. Once in a while, the complete chord makes an appearance in an older Hollywood score (Ex. 2).

Ex. 2

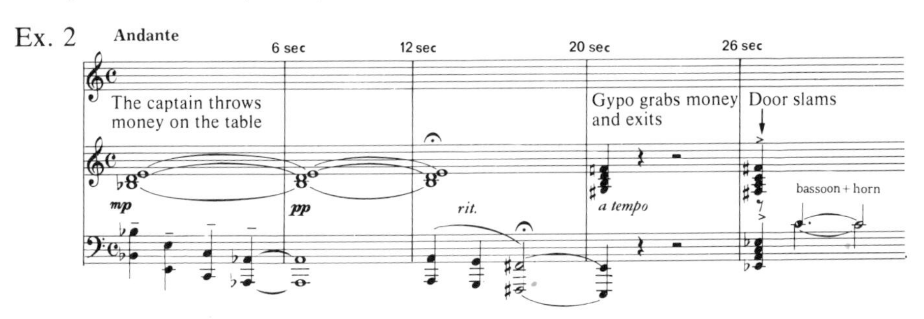

Max Steiner, film score for *The Informer*

(There follows a *cut to blind man*, and of course an entry for the cor anglais.)

The number of dim7s in Stravinsky's music (early, uncharacteristic works excepted) can be counted on the fingers of one hand. In pieces referring to nineteenth-century conventions, the dim7 denoting suspense—not the modulating dim7—appears every so often, though seldom in unadulterated form.

For instance, in the 'upper structure' of the dominant ninth chord, such as in the conclusion of the Pas de deux in *Scènes de ballet*; but *Scènes de ballet* is a work which, as much as possible, tries to conceal whether it is *about* Broadway or actually *is* Broadway).

One exception is the moment when, immediately before the da capo of Aria I from the *Concerto in D for Violin*, the orchestra and solo instrument freeze into a stack of minor thirds. Due to the harsh orchestration of the chord (with a hole in the middle register), the bell-like attacks (*sfp*) and the stiff octaves of the solo violin, the chord, perhaps for the first time this century, regains its original effect (Ex. 3).

Ex. 3

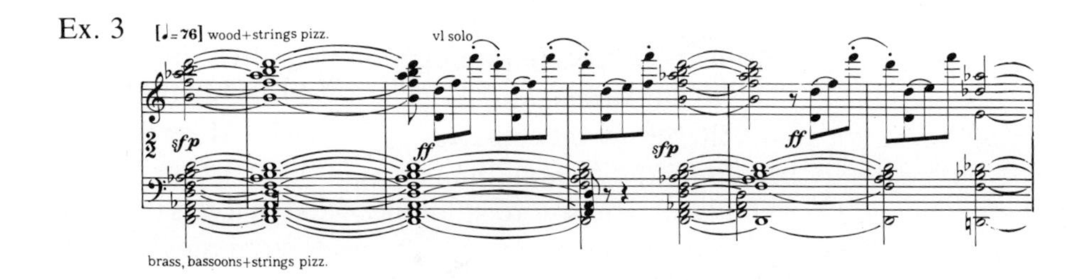

In a second exception, the previous example from *Oedipus Rex*, something else happens. Since nineteenth-century Italian opera serves as one of the models for this opera-oratorio, there are countless references to the chord. But the *clamare, ululare* is no longer a reference. It *is* nineteenth-century Italian opera. Thus nineteenth-century Italian opera, just like Martin Martinych's cast-iron stove, becomes a metaphor.

The Utopian Unison

Polyphony, harmony, unison, homophony, one-part writing, two-part writing, doublings—for centuries, these notions were sufficient to describe musical compositions. They unambiguously classified unambiguous musical structures. Twentieth-century music has forced theoreticians to redefine some of them. Polyphony now no longer means only a fabric of independent voices, but can also mean a fabric of independent chord sequences. Harmony has lost its general meaning and has become a special case of 'density' or 'field'. But when redefinition proved insufficient, because of excessive generality, entirely new notions had to be introduced.

Stravinsky's music, too, has left general music theory in disarray, not only because his music stretches traditional notions out of proportion (which is why Stravinsky is a composer of twentieth-century music), but also, and especially, because his music questions them.

Is one-part writing by definition one-part writing?

Is two-part writing by definition two-part writing?

Are doublings by definition doublings?

Orpheus. Orpheus has his Euridice back. Still blindfolded, he dances a quiet *pas de deux* with her. The music accompanying their steps can be seen as a portrayal of the situation on stage. This situation is dubious. Everything seems to be fine; but Orpheus does not know what the audience knows: it will all end in tragedy. Example 1 shows a one-part melody doubled one and sometimes two octaves lower. Every so often the doubling is derailed. Or: a one-part melody is doubled one and sometimes two octaves higher. This paradoxical musical situation calls for a paradoxical definition: parallel counterpoint. The notion of counterpoint is justifiable because if one voice is doubling the other, and the other is doubling the one, then both are independent voices and

Ex. 1

Orpheus [101]6

neither is a doubling as there is no third voice that each could be doubling. The paradox of parallel counterpoint gives listeners a choice that they really can not make. In the simplest form, the choice looks like this:

Ex. 2

Ebony Concerto [9]$_6$ (clarinet and trombone only)

This example from the *Ebony Concerto* can be described as a melody in octaves but with wrong notes. Only who is playing the wrong notes, the trombone or the clarinet?

Another dilemma involves the division of parts. The second movement of the *Symphony in C* begins with a melody in the oboe (Ex. 3). Two bars later the oboe is joined by the first violins. Along the way, as a result of octaves that go 'wrong', one-part writing tends to sound like two-part writing. The character of this two-part writing is that of a special kind of one-part writing. In the fourth bar, the listener who has now decided he is listening to two-part writing gets into trouble. If there are to be two voices, it must be possible to distinguish one voice from the other. In Example 3, which is comparatively simple due to the absence of voice-crossing and to the recognizability of the distinct timbres, the answer seems obvious: the first violins are one voice (always the upper voice) and the oboe is the other (always the lower voice). But as soon as we arrive at the arrow (↓), we start having our doubts. Is that an 'out-of-tune' unison? Who is playing the out-of-tune note then? Is the B♭ in the violins 'early'? In that case, the A in the oboe is the 'right' note, making the upper voice G, A, B♭, G; not G, B♭, B♭, G. In other words, without the voices ever crossing at the arrow, they nevertheless exchange functions—or do they? That is up to the listener—who just might change his mind each time he listens.

Ex. 3

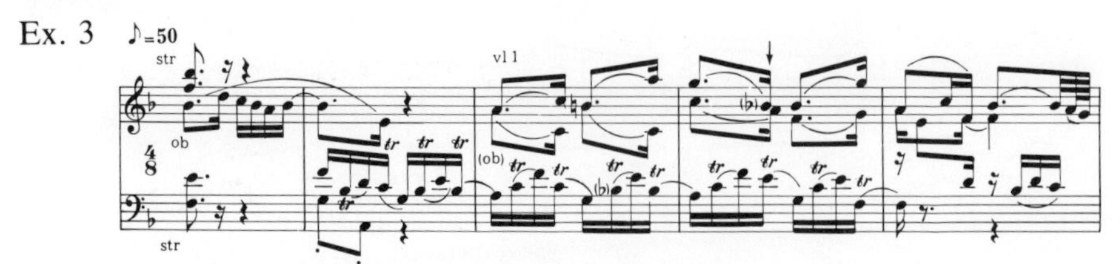

Symphony in C, 2nd movt.

Countless are the ways Stravinsky reconnoitres the border between unison and non-unison. What often occurs is that the unison gets out of hand (Ex. 4). The performers really all want the same thing, but the brass players—always considered the proletarians of the orchestra—have given up their part in the third bar already and make up their own on the spot which every once in a while gives rise to a coincidental unison or octave, but more often yields a second. The 5/8 bar (the 2/4 bar that lasts too long) is the straw that breaks the camel's back. Or was there a revolution in which it is the woodwinds who duck out? That seems perhaps more plausible. Not only is the sequence in the woodwinds rather insipid, they would never have arrived safely if the 5/8 bar had not been there.

Ex. 4

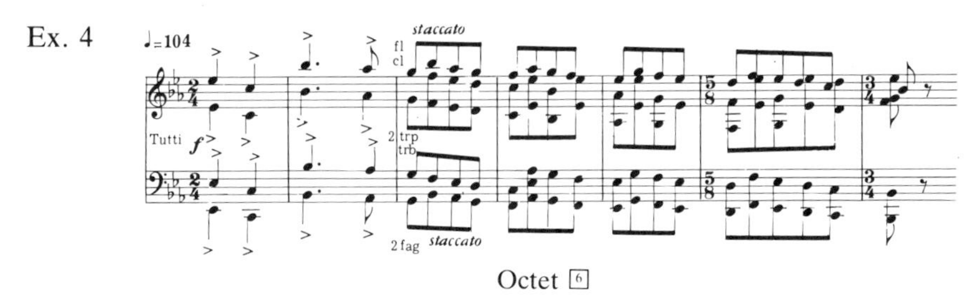

Octet [6]

(In the *Octet*, two bars at least come out all right. There are cases where things go wrong right from the start, such as at [19] in the *Symphony of Psalms* or [9] in *Babel.* Here, other parts also have the principal voice, only twice as fast. The effect is not merely traditional diminution: it is as if the copyist made a mistake in the tempo markings in some of the parts. But even in *Babel*, haste trips over its own heels.)

The voice-leading in the example from the *Octet* is divergent; voice-leading can also be convergent (Exx. 5 and 6). Example 6 calls to mind Bach, that other great illusionist of voice-leading. These bars resemble the bass in Brandenburg Concerto No. 6, with their quasi-two-part writing (heterophony) (Ex. 7), and the Allemande from the English Suite No. 3, with their motion (Ex. 8).

'Española' (from *Five Easy Pieces* for piano duet), conclusion

Symphony in Three Movements [63]3

Ex. 7

Brandenburg Concerto No. 6, Adagio, bars 27–8

Ex. 8

English Suite No. 3, Allamande, bars 10–11

But there is much more in Stravinsky's switching-yard of voice-leading that recalls Bach, ranging from the opening of the *Concerto in E flat* (*Dumbarton Oaks*), a two-part string theme that sounds like one single part (Ex. 9), to the two bassoons trampling over each other in the last movement of *Symphony in Three Movements* (Ex. 10). Play the example under tempo and two octaves higher, and the bassoons begin to resemble the sighing recorders of *Actus Tragicus* (Ex. 11). Stravinsky, like Bach, uses canon-like techniques. The slightly archaic word for canon is 'catch'. The voices almost catch each other in these canons—almost, but not quite.

The unisons and octaves in Stravinsky's music increasingly sound like a

Ex. 9

Concerto in E flat (*Dumbarton Oaks*), opening

Ex. 10

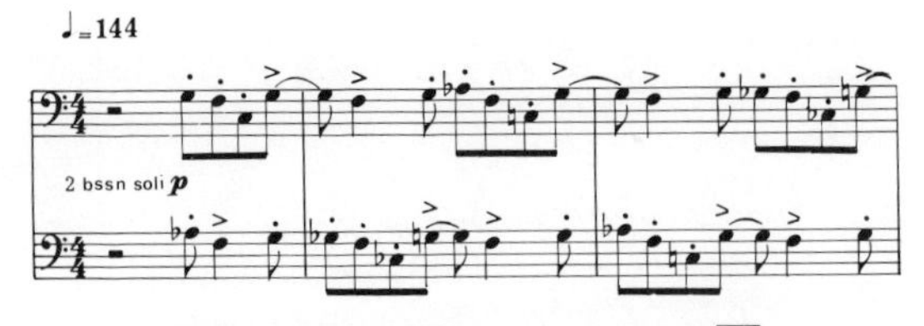

Symphony in Three Movements 148

Ex. 11

Actus Tragicus (Cantata No. 106), Sonatina, bars 7–8

musical utopia—much coveted, rarely achieved. In his old age, after a lifetime filled with shattered octaves, unisons slipping and sliding, and doublings unravelling, Stravinsky permitted himself the luxury every so often of a 'grandiose unison'. But even then he seldom gave in to a perfectly concordant passage of voices (Ex. 12). *When* the perfect consonant is actually achieved, it sounds more unison than unison—it sounds not-not-unison. This not-not-unison can be considered the culmination, in the opposite direction, of the emancipation of the 'wrong' note, where it all began—with women who sing together and not together (heterophony, Ex. 13), and with musicians who let their fancy have free reign (Ex. 14).

Ex. 12

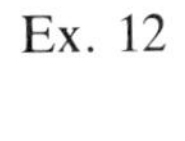

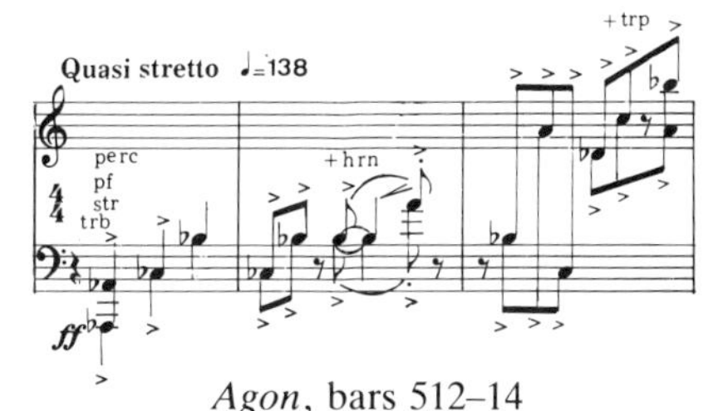

Agon, bars 512–14

Ex. 13

Les Noces [115] (without accompaniment)

Ex. 14

Marche (from *Three Easy Pieces* for piano duet), bar 26

But it is more than just the emancipation of the 'wrong' note. It is also the emancipation of hard-core playing around, when wrong notes become so prevalent that they become the norm. It went so far that Stravinsky could make the octave—the perfect consonant upon which Harry Mulisch based his book *De compositie van de wereld*[1]—sound like a *dissonance* (Ex. 15).

Ex. 15

Ex.56—*Concertino* for string quartet, bars 1–2

[1] Harry Mulisch, *De compositie van de wereld* (*The Composition of the World*). Mulisch, born in Haarlem in 1927, is primarily known as a novelist. He has written, among other novels, *De Aanslag* (*The Assault*), of which the film version recently has been awarded an Oscar. *De compositie van de wereld* (published in 1980 by the Bezige Bij, Amsterdam) is a philosophical work which attempts to relate the laws of mankind and history to the musical octave [trans.].

Poétique musicale

1. Law and Order

Two images of the 'neoclassical' Stravinsky have long competed for the honour of being the one and only true image. The first is that of the petit bourgeois, revanchist composer, recognizable in a scornfully ironical characterization by Simon Vestdijk:[1] 'Stravinsky the person, the respectable husband and the hard worker, good Christian and neo-Thomist, officially recognized celebrity, who dedicated his compositions to God'. The other is already hinted at in 1924 in the magazine *Comoedia*: '. . . I was able to ask the young Russian maestro several questions without giving him the feeling of being submitted to an interview. He answered with the marvellous indifference of a banker explaining his minor business affairs to an agent of the sûreté.' What emerges here is a considerably more realistic image—that of the grand bourgeois Stravinsky and his potentially polemic attitude of businesslike artistry. We recognize the aristocratic pose in the portraits taken in those years: the enlightened despot in Amsterdam, with monocle and bowler, 'The Artist as Duke of Omnium', or 'Ramses XXXXVI with cane' in a Paris studio.

But it is true—even though we must for the first time draw an emphatic distinction between life and work: what began as an infectious form of showing off ended up in earnest. Façade became genuine behaviour: the icy behaviour of the composer who, since his return to Paris from Switzerland (1920), alienated his audience; who suffered from the popularity of compositions that he himself considered in the past perfect tense; and who, in as much as his compositions were not appreciated for the wrong reasons (as witnessed in the works of his epigones), fell just as much in disfavour with the avant-garde as with the average listener. 'And to say that this Paris which lifted me in triumph seventeen years ago can offer me nothing better now than a public appearance in a chamber-music concert of this kind. One would think that one was in Zagreb' (*PD*), the composer complained bitterly in 1927, having just finished *Oedipus Rex*. *Oedipus* did not bring him much luck either: after three performances the opera-oratorio disappeared from the repertoire.

[1] Simon Vestdijk (1898–1971), Dutch author and essayist. His essays on music have recently been collected (in 12 vols.) and published in Holland [trans.].

Probably not for the 'right' reasons, as formulated by, of all people, Schoenberg ('. . . it is all negative: unusual theatre, unusual setting, unusual resolution of the action, unusual vocal writing, unusual acting, unusual melody, unusual harmony, unusual counterpoint, unusual instrumentation'), but for the 'wrong' reasons, as accurately expressed—as often occurred in Holland where Stravinsky was concerned—by Willem Pijper:[2] 'If the writer of this actionless opera had previously only written choral music for song competitions or if he had busied himself with arranging potpourris for wind bands, even then one would have had to call this opera-oratorio a scandalous pasticcio . . . the work of an incompetent craftsman . . . composed in a muddled artistic conscience.'

Stravinsky's behaviour during the fifteen years before the Second World War is characterized by the cynicism of the dethroned god who would rather be misunderstood than vilified. As fate would have it, the French citizen (since 1929) had most success in America while the American citizen Stravinsky in the fifties and sixties was most praised in Europe.

Stravinsky's situation was typified by his desire to take complete control. He began an active performing career as conductor and pianist of his own works in 1924. The fact that conducting remained up to the end of his life his largest source of income says something about the social position of composers and sheds some light on Stravinsky's deep-rooted hatred of conductors, easily illustrated by countless amusing anecdotes. A side-effect of this performing career was a decreased production in the thirties ('merely' eleven works, including 'merely' four major pieces: *Symphony of Psalms*, *Perséphone*, the *Concerto for Two Solo Pianos* and *Symphony in C*).

Also typical of his situation was the desire to preface every new composition—starting with the one-act *Mavra* and the *Octet* (from 1922 and 1923, respectively)—with a lecture, an interview, a statement, a radio-talk, or a newspaper article.

Moreover, his situation was typified by his writing an autobiography, *Chroniques de ma vie* (vol. 1, 1935; vol. 2, 1936), prompted by the desire to resolve misunderstandings about himself and his works. The autobiography may well be reliable,[3] but the tone 'consistently contradicts what Stravinsky thought, felt, and said at early periods of his life' (Craft, *PD*).

The book, which might be considered modern for its day because of what is

[2] Willem Pijper (1894–1947), Dutch composer and critic [trans.].

[3] That is—*un*reliable. In an appendix devoted to 'Walter Nouvel and *Chroniques de ma vie*' in *Selected Correspondence*, vol. 2 (New York, 1984), Craft points out 'numerous errors of both commission and omission'. The few dates that Stravinsky does give are for the most part incorrect, including that of the première of *Le Sacre du printemps* [trans.].

not said, has become infamous for one tiny sentence, the much-quoted 'music is powerless to express anything at all'. Many an offended melomaniac has contested these heretical words with barbed tracts, words which, as Craft rightly points out (*PD*), are nothing more than a polemical summary of the Kantian hypothesis that, to be truly beautiful, a thing should signify nothing but itself. An expression of belief in the autonomy of music has become the stick used interminably to beat the composer who only wanted to give music back to music.

A composer like that must have the passion of a sewing machine, the sensibility of an adding machine. Does not this man have any feelings to express?

Stravinsky to a journalist: 'Suppose you went out and narrowly escaped being run over by a trolley car. Would you have an emotion?'

Journalist: 'I should hope so, Mr Stravinsky.'

Stravinsky: 'So should I. But if I went out and narrowly escaped being run over by a trolley car, I would not immediately rush out for some music paper and try to make something out of the emotion I had just felt' (*PD*).

The roots of Stravinsky's later aesthetic 'theory' are found in these kinds of anecdotal, mainly apodictic statements. Merely to formulate this 'theory' typifies his undermined position. In 1942 six lectures that the composer had given three years earlier at Harvard University were published under the title *Poétique musicale*: it is the somewhat cramped staging of what began as a colourful and unordered procession of aphorisms, *bons-mots*, insights, and paradoxes. The artist as bank director: now that would have been a lively form of demythologization; to leave the unmentionable unmentioned and only talk about the concrete: that would have been a cheerful reaction to the usual philosophy of artists; but, in *Poétique musicale*, recalcitrance suddenly appears as '*dogma*', pretence as 'objectivity' and 'crap' is elevated into an '*academic* course'. This, together with the need to give no less than 'an explanation of music' and the methodical placing of oneself 'under the stern auspices of order and discipline' is just like stirring up clear waters. Of all the cloaks, both borrowed and stolen, ever worn by Stravinsky, the academic robe fitted worst.

In *Poétique musicale*, formalistic pseudo-objectivity is characteristic of the argumentation with which the author attempted to justify his deep-rooted aversion to 'revolution'; art is 'constructive', 'the contrary of chaos', 'revolution is . . . temporary chaos', 'a state of turmoil and violence'. Obviously one must look for the origins of such sophisms in the rancour of the former Russian landowner. With much verbal ado, the cantankerous speaker in Boston denied the revolutionary contents of his music. Though he would be the first 'to recognize that daring is the motive force of the finest and greatest acts', he none the less considered himself 'no more academic than . . . modern, no more modern than . . . conservative'. Even the *Sacre* was not revolutionary, no, the author 'was made a revolutionary in spite of [him]self', 'for revolution is one thing, innovation another'.

The Stravinsky of *Poétique* is like a wasp who tries to remove its own sting, who says it will not harm a fly, or better, thinks it *is* a fly, a responsible, hard-working, cultivated, reasonable fly that believes in a Supreme Fly, but a fly that, oh dear, is continually being hit by the fly-swatter, first from the right, now from the left. As far as that goes, there is not much difference between *Poétique* and *Chroniques de ma vie.* Both writings seem prompted by the desire to hit back. *Poétique* is, of course, about 'music as a form of speculation in terms of sound and time', about 'the dialectics of the creative process', 'the composing of music', 'the formal elements of the craft of music', 'musical typology', 'the problem of style'—but these subjects seem more like a front. Order and discipline make a good alibi when launching a philippic against the (although never mentioned by name) 'vanguard *pompiers*', with their 'taste for absurd cacophony' and their habit of speaking about music 'as they do about Freudianism or Marxism'; against the public that is unjustly entrusted with the task of returning a verdict on the value of a work of art; against the stupid critics who 'are not at all shocked by the ridiculous device of the *Leitmotiv*' but who automatically call modern anything 'discordant and confused'. (What it was that Stravinsky thought sounded so awful is not explicitly mentioned. He did not mean Schoenberg in any case, who was 'fully aware of what he was doing'. Not that Stravinsky was informed about what Schoenberg did. He knew *Pierrot Lunaire* and he had at least heard the Chamber Symphony, Op. 9, the Suite, Op. 29 and probably the Serenade, Op. 24. Of all the nonsense that Adorno asserted about Stravinsky, the theory that Schoenberg's influence on Stravinsky is already apparent in *Petrushka* and the *Sacre* is the easiest to disprove.)

Fortunately, *Poétique musicale* is also a high-spirited book; rancour was not the only source of inspiration. The polemical élan with which the composer created confusion in the hallowed halls of music history was a result of musical and not personal motives. The firmament of Stravinsky's music history had not changed much since the appearance of *Chroniques*, although this must have escaped the American audience of 1939. Once again much was made of the wonders of Gounod, Chabrier, Weber (no 'n'), and Tchaikovsky. Later, European readers would be surprised by other things: Bellini, who gloriously outshone Beethoven as a melodist; Berlioz, whose originality could not disguise his 'poverty of invention'; and Verdi: 'there is more substance and true invention in the aria *La donna è mobile* than in the rhetoric and vociferations in the *Ring*'. (No less inventive is Stravinsky's consistently wrong spelling of Wagner's *Gesamtkunstwerk*—now *Gesammt Kunst-Werk*, now *Gesammt Künst Werk*.)

No matter how heatedly worn-out conventions and barrel-organ melodies were defended, *Poétique* was first and foremost a plea for 'order', 'discipline', 'method', and 'laws'. These words control the sentences, paragraphs, and chapters like traffic police. Apollo has disguised himself for the occasion as chief inspector and carefully keeps track of his earthly representative, making sure he misses no chance to show himself off: as the epitomization of an aesthetic law-and-order ideal; as head of the Department of Public Works, for whom composing is the same as 'putting into order a certain number of . . . sounds according to certain interval-relationships'. One has recognized in this potentially polemical attitude a unique attribute of modern, twentieth-century artistry, thus confusing a side issue (which appears like the main issue) with the main issue (which appears like a side issue). This side issue in the guise of the main issue is no more than a bevy of slogans taken from the reservoir of rallying-cries of French aesthetics as formulated in the period between the two World Wars.

Order, method, laws, balance, taste, health, construction: this is but a selection from the arsenal of catchwords around which thoughts about art in France were arranged, thoughts about very different kinds of arts works, made under very different circumstances, with very different aims, in very different styles, and using very different media. The fact that the meaning of these concepts could also differ from composer to composer indicates that they did not so much define what the new music was, but what it was *not*. It was not romantic, in the broadest and most popular sense of the word. Although one sees the term rarely used, anti-romantic was the key concept of French art just before and especially after the First World War. That Jacques Rivière considered dadaism as the furthest consequence of romanticism just goes to show how broadly the term romanticism could be interpreted. This view on the unregimented, anti-intellectual programme of this programme-less movement perhaps explains why dadaism never took hold in Paris, even though it superficially fitted into the post-war mood of 'mockery, scandals, proclamations, feasts lasting seven days, tamtam, alcohol, tears, sadness, novelty and dreams' (Cocteau).

Positively formulated, the anti-romantic spirit was called classical or classicistic. Classicism was not restorative in the first instance. But it turned out that the concept classicism, when taken over by the most diverse social and artistic groups, became just as flexible as the term 'order' which they bandied about. To the supporters of the Action Française, classical was equal to the art of the *ancien régime*; the classical work of art was a 'triumph of order and measure over self-centred romanticism' to Gide (whose communism was a personal version of the classicistic ideal); to Cocteau, classicism was identical to '. . . s'évader d'Allemagne! Vive le Coq! A bas l'Arlequin!'

Yet all of these versions of the new classicism had one thing in common: fulfilment of the need for 'discipline'. The ideology that satisfied this requirement more systematically than any other was that of neo-Thomism. This ideology, a version of the medieval scholasticism of Thomas Aquinas adapted to the needs of the time, fo-med the philosophical foundation of the neo-Catholicism which flourished after the First World War. Although France had experienced other *renouveaux catholiques* (for instance, after the Dreyfus affair), this neo-Catholicism had one new attribute: it satisfied less than ever a religious need. It was, first and foremost, the property of the intellectual and artistic élite, its adherants being armchair Catholics—'Catholics without belief' (Bäcker).

Neo-Thomism replaced Bergson's philosophy of becoming with a doctrine of being. Bergsonism, which considered the individual as continually fluctuating from one state to another and never forming a definitive synthesis of the 'ego', rather than as one personality always remaining equal to itself, contrasted with neo-Thomism, which posed universal principles, the eternal truth, order, dogma, and the state of unchangeability. It reconciled reason and belief, was intellectualistic, provided answers to every question just like any totalitarian ideology, and formulated statutes for classicism especially for the spiritually homeless artists. These statutes were called *Art et Scolastique.*

2. *Art et Scolastique*

Perceive thy religion, O, Catholics, perceive thy grandeur.
Raïssa Maritain

Art et Scolastique stemmed from two articles in the magazine *Les Lettres* in 1919 and was published in book form in 1920. The study apparently commanded much respect and not only within France, since a mere four years later the book, as *Kunst en Scholastiek*, received the Dutch *nihil obstat* from Father B. Kuhlmann and Father R. R. Welschen.[4] The author of 'this little work' (this at least is how Father C. A. Terburg OP the Dutch translator of this substantial neo-Thomist art catechism, described it in the preface) was

[4] J. Maritain *Art and Scholasticism*, trans. J. F. Scanlan (London, 1947), is the edition used by the translator. The authors used the Dutch translation by C. A. Terburg OP (Amsterdam, 1924), which was even more Maritain than Maritain. Contrary to the original French and English versions which appeared to

Jacques Maritain (1882–1972). By now, Maritain's name has been forgotten, along with his hundreds of writings, partly because of increasing secularization. Only in Nijmegen[5] does the memory of this illustrious emancipator of Catholicism live on, a memory of a man who spent his entire life attempting to give Catholicism a new, combative, modern and serious image with the fanaticism of the convert he was, a theologian claimed by Pope Paul VI as his teacher. 'Neither rightist nor leftist, neither traditionalist (obscurantist, anti-modern) nor faddishly modern; neither pessimistic nor optimistic—though more the latter than the former'; that is how Brooke W. Smith, Maritain's biographer, described this theologian's philosophy of history, and thereby, implicitly, the theologian himself. This description says it all: Maritain's philosophy can be explained any way one wants. Therein lies at least part of the explanation why his neo-Thomist aesthetics could be so influential between the wars. Another part of the explanation lies in the virtuosity with which Maritain was able to bend 'our modern view of life' at will. In practice, this not only meant that he endorsed the contemporary artistic *parti pris*, but also provided it with a theoretical (i.e. doctrinal) foundation. For a start, Maritain greatly emphasized the fact that art is a result of active labour and that the work of art is an artifact. The 'artisan' of the Middle Ages is held up as an example for the artist; he is expected to be 'a good workman', whose so-called *habitus* is concerned solely with 'the work to be done'. In what Stravinsky wrote about himself (in *Poétique*) and in what others wrote about him, these terms also regularly appear. 'Stravinsky, like medieval man, is an artisan . . . The work to be done always posed him a problem of craft [*métier*], never one of beauty' wrote Ansermet in 1921, and in 1929, Honegger published an essay entitled 'Strawinsky, homme de métier'.

Within the, apparently, modern notion of the work of art as an artifact, neo-Thomist aesthetic found a place for 'the rules of art', 'order' (Augustine's *splendor ordinis*), 'form' ('that is to say the principle determining the peculiar

be serious books, the Dutch version has the character of a catechism, due to the provision of summaries of every paragraph in the margin in bold print, as well as the addition of twenty-four prints of Maritain's favourite medieval art including the over-representation of Maritain's strong favourite, Fra Angelico. It should be mentioned that one modern print was included in the preface of the translation: a portrait of the philosopher himself by Otto van Rees in the same style which modern Roman Catholics—and later ecumenical—painters use to portray their Saviour. Also curious is the mention of the *nihil obstat*, omitted in the English translation (as well as the lack of a translator's preface). For those who do not know the work by Maritain, it is perhaps interesting to mention that a large part of the book consists of footnotes, the most important of which are even included in the Table of Contents. One could say that the authors here are not only writing about Maritain and Stravinsky in this chapter, but also about Catholicism in general and its manifestation in the Netherlands. The English translation used in this chapter is more sober than the lofty style of the pre-war Dutch [original footnote elaborated by trans.].

[5] Nijmegen is a university town in the south-east of the Netherlands, which was until recently a bastion of Catholicism. It is worth mentioning that one of the two copies of the English translations of *Art and Scholasticism* which could be located in Holland was in the library at the University of Nijmegen [trans.].

perfection of everything which is, constituting and completing things in their essence and their qualities, the ontological secret, so to speak, of their innermost being, their spiritual essence, their operative mystery, is above all the peculiar principle of intelligibility'), and, most importantly, the intellect. Continually being bandied about in *Art et Scholastique* is the idea that art is 'a *virtue of the practical intellect*' and that 'every virtue inclines solely to the good (that is to say, in the case of a virtue of the intellect, to what is *true*)'; which leads to the conclusion 'that Art as such (Art . . . and not the artist, whose actions often run contrary to his art) never makes a mistake and involves an *infallible correctness*'.

Even in his theory on the 'purpose' of art, in which autonomy and the 'gratuitousness' of the work of art are strongly emphasized, Maritain follows the dominant tendency of the era. He refuses to submit to 'the domination of an art which deliberately contrives means of suggestion to seduce [the] subconsciousness'; 'its [art's] *effect* is to produce emotion, but if it *aims* at emotion, at affecting or rousing the passions, it becomes adulterate'. With these imperatives, Maritain joins in with 'all *the best people*' who, after all, 'nowadays, want the classical'. The neo-Thomist can, for the moment, think of 'nothing . . . more sincerely *classical*' than Satie, and borrows Cocteau's voice by quoting from *Le Coq et l'Arlequin* in singing the praises of this 'master craftsman'.[6]

It must be said that Maritain was adept at making the new art—in so far as this art pleased him—dance to his own tune. That tune was seven centuries old: what in the neo-Thomist aesthetic appeared to be a vital, modern, anti-romantic attitude was in reality merely the expression of a fanatical, romantic nostalgia for the Middle Ages, for 'relatively the most *spiritual* epoch in history'. Deep down, Maritain considered the entire post-medieval era as an age of decadence caused by anthropocentric humanism, the foundations for which were laid in the Renaissance. This is the background against which the aesthetic and philosophic Manicheism of *Art et Scolastique* must be seen, including the furious polemical attacks on artists and thinkers who had already

[6] Although two years after the appearance of *Art et Scolastique* Maritain was to publish a book entitled *Antimoderne*, he did grant the *nihil obstat* to a number of phenomena of contemporary art in the former book. A futurist was allowed to portray a woman with 'only one eye, or a quarter of an eye'; he was allowed to say that ' "a galloping horse has not four hoofs but twenty" ', so long as it did not give way to 'artificial "deformation" ', to '*deformation* in the sense of violence or deceit', as is done by 'certain Cubists'. It pleased Maritain to see that some artists made 'a most praiseworthy effort to attain the logical coherence, simplicitly and purity of means, which properly constitute the veracity of art'. If it were up to Maritain, an artist would once again be 'humble and magnanimous, prudent, upright, strong, temperate, simple, pure, ingenuous', and his ideals would include those from the age when 'more beautiful things were . . . created', when 'there was less self-worship' and when 'the blessed humility in which the artist was situated exalted his strength and his freedom'.

been dead for many centuries. Neo-Thomistic aesthetics are not a reaction *to*, but a crusade *against*: against the Renaissance and 'the spiritual acephaly of the age of enlightenment' in general, against Descartes, Rousseau, and Luther in particular; against 'idealist fancy fair' in general, against Kant and Leibniz in particular; against Tolstoy (even though his spirit 'has no followers among us' Catholics), against Chateaubriand, against Zola, in short, against everything to which the holy Thomas would never have given his blessing.

To put a political interpretation on Maritain's neo-Catholicism: Christianity is neither rightist nor leftist, it is simply true, and therefore 'compatible with all forms of legitimate government'. During the years when *Art et Scolastique* was being written, the ideologist of neo-Thomism was himself a pronounced right-wing Catholic of the type then well known in the Netherlands and later in (Fascist) Italy, who combined anti-capitalistic inclinations with anti-democratic convictions. (This type is known in the Netherlands through *De Gemeenschap* [*The Faithful Community*], a strongly French-orientated periodical, begun in 1925 as 'the monthly for Catholic reconstruction' under the influence of Maritain's intimate friend, Pieter van der Meer de Walcheren.[7]) This rightist mentality can be seen in the numerous articles that Maritain published in *La Revue universelle*, the mouthpiece of the Action Française. Because of these articles, Maritain became generally recognized as *the* philosopher of this monarchistic, anti-democratic movement. (The Action Française wanted to rescue France from the secular, anti-clerical Third Republic in which, according to its mentor Maurras—unconditionally revered by Maritain—all power rested in the hands of the Jews, the Freemasons, and the Protestants. Only when Pius XI officially condemned the movement in 1926 did Maritain sever all contact with them.[8]) In one of his articles for *La Revue universelle*, Maritain spoke out more forthrightly than in *Art et Scolastique* about the primacy of Catholic art: 'Truth to tell, I believe it to be impossible outside Catholicism to reconcile in man, without diminishing or forcing them, the rights of morality and the claims of intellectuality, art or science.'[9]

This was the balm used by many an artist—seduced by the call of order, form, rules, and intellect—to soothe the wounds of their souls.

[7] Pieter van der Meer de Walcheren (1880–1970), Roman Catholic man of letters, promoter of Catholic talent in the Netherlands and close friend of Maritain. He was baptized in 1911 in Paris, witnessed by the (also converted) Maritain and Bloy couples. He passed the last seventeen years of his life as a monk [trans.].

[8] Two months before Pope Pius XI issued his condemnation against Action Française, Maritain had attempted to mediate between the Pope and Maurras. A year after the condemnation, Maritain published a book (*Pourquoi Rome a parlé*) in which he justified the behaviour of the Holy Father. In later editions of *Art et Scolastique*, the only quotation from Maurras (a prediction of the future, of a 'truly democratic barbarism of the mind') has disappeared.

[9] The article in question, 'An Essay on Art' [included in the trans. of *Art et Scholastique*], deals in specifying Maritain's position on the 'gratuitousness [of art]'. This position apparently left the impression that 'gratuitousness' could exist without neo-Thomist interests. This was—how could it be otherwise?—a

'Look!' cried Raïssa Oumansoff—tied to Maritain through a *mariage blanc* —in her diary on 12 March 1925. 'Here is another group of young Catholics falling into his [Maritain's] arms; they beg for intellectual direction, discussions, meetings.'

Maritain had already accomplished his most spectacular conquest: that of Jean Cocteau. Cocteau's recovery through God had progressed so miraculously that he published a seventy-page letter to Maritain in 1926, which Maritain then answered with a seventy-one page open letter.

'You, who are so transparent, a soul disguised as a body, an imprint of a countenance, a sudarium, your feebleness is a terrible force, the force of a labourer', wrote Cocteau.

'Your excuse is friendship', replied Maritain.

'Art for art's sake, art for the masses, it's all equally absurd. I propose art for God', wrote Cocteau.

Whether it was now God, country, the republic, or, as far as Cocteau was concerned, Pétain, did not really matter. Max Jacob summed up the essence of French neo-Catholicism when he wrote in a letter to Cocteau: 'One should swallow the Host like an aspirin'.

3. *A Summa Theologica of Music*

> The order after the crisis, that is the order I claim.
>
> Jean Cocteau

In 1936 a Spanish journalist quoted Stravinsky as having said: 'My art is the product of Christian dialectics, and this is a reason why I cannot accept

misunderstanding. Maritain distinguished two types of divagations: 'art *on nothing*' (meaning that art 'ought to tolerate no human interest or any superior law in the artist, absolutely nothing outside the sole concern of artistic manufacture') and 'art *for nothing*'. The latter divagation concerns the 'idealistic heresy' of omitting 'to distinguish the *art* . . . from the *artist*, who, as working man, can have as many ends as he pleases', in other words, the heresy of 'the elimination of every *human end* pursued'. One was allowed to create gratuitous art as long as one was not a *Parnassian*, a Symbolist, certainly not a Mallarmé, not a Gide, nor a composer who 'gladly restricts oneself to irony and pure entertainment'. Truly gratuitous were Verlaine (Catholic), Claudel (Catholic), Ghéon (Catholic) and Bloy (Catholic). It is not surprising then that the freedom of the artist did not have as bright a future as suggested in the main text of *Art et Scholastique.* What was said there (that 'the pure artist considered in the abstract as such, is something completely unmoral' [above morality, trans.]) was taken back in the footnotes and appendices. There it appeared that 'in the normal order of things, that is, one which posits *a public*, a social life, a State, and in that state a Church whose authority is fully recognized . . . the rules which are externally placed upon the artist, should arise by themselves, resulting solely from the effect of social bonds', but these days, 'we lack . . . these things' and 'we allow the faithful to be poisoned by so many works of art and so-called works of art, which cannot but be unbearable for the Christian' and 'against which a strong reaction is necessary'. The conclusion, in another context, is that: 'Catholicism . . . must in certain cases deny to art, in the name of the essential interests of the human being, liberties which art would jealously assert.'

surrealism or communism'. Here speaks a man plagued by feelings of guilt about his double life (it was twenty years before the death of his extremely bigoted wife made marriage to his mistress possible); who sought refuge in the fold of the church; whose correspondence was populated by a multitude of saints; who had a dyptich of Saint Suaire on his piano; who threatened to break with his mistress when she neglected to have her new apartment consecrated by a priest; and who illustrated many a musical sketch and letter with a cross.

That cross was no ordinary cross, but a Russian cross such as found in the church to which the composer returned in the twenties—the Russian Orthodox church into which he was baptized. In 1926 he wrote to Diaghilev that, for the first time in twenty years, he felt 'an extreme spiritual need' to take communion and he asked Diaghilev 'to forgive me the transgressions of all these years'. (Apparently, the impresario never honoured the request to destroy the letter.) In the same year Stravinsky, for the first time ever, set a religious text to music, a *Pater Noster* for four-part chorus.

Stravinsky's 'conversion' was different from Cocteau's in that French neo-Catholicism was not a deciding factor. Nor was Maritain—if we are to believe Stravinsky—although the neo-Thomist 'may have exercised an influence on me at this time, though not directly, and, certainly, he had no role in my "conversion"; until just before the latter event I knew him only through his books'.

Little is known about the personal relationship between Maritain and Stravinsky, partly due to Stravinsky's silence on the matter. In a letter from Maritain to Stravinsky, it appeared that the composer and the neo-Thomist met each other initially in June 1926. In Stravinsky's version of his relationship with Maritain, they became 'personal friends' in 1929, though it was a friendship with reservations: in a letter of 1936 Stravinsky admits that Maritain's 'entourage produces a light nausea in me'; he calls Maritain 'one of those people of superior intelligence who are lacking in humanity', although, in the same breadth, he recognizes 'the great value of his work in Christian and Thomist thought'. Only towards the end of the Second World War, when Stravinsky faced another spiritual crisis and sought refuge with the heroes of French neo-Catholicism (Bloy, Bernanos, Bossuet, and Thomas Aquinas as author of the *Summa theologica*), did he again regularly meet the philosopher, who, like himself, had immigrated to America.

Their *incompatibilité d'humeur* had never stood in the way of their mutual admiration. 'To be with him was to learn', Stravinsky later confided about Maritain to Robert Craft. Maritain reciprocated the admiration. A choice quotation from Stravinsky was never misplaced in an article in *Reflections on*

Sacred Art; the composer received a book by Bloy in gratitude for the pleasure a new work of his had given Maritain; and although Maritain was so careless as to write that Wagner and Stravinsky belonged in the same line of development, diametrically opposed to Gregorian chant and Bach, he was not above placing a footnote in a later edition of the same book in which he apologized for such stupidity, since, on the whole, Stravinsky's 'remarkable, disciplined œuvre with its profusion of truth' was still 'the best lesson in creative greatness and strength', an œuvre 'that really did meet the rigours of strict classicism'.

But apologizing does not undo the mistake. Besides, the remark made about Stravinsky in 1919 is not the only reason to suspect that Maritain had not the faintest idea about music. What can we think of an art legislator who writes about a close friend's music: 'in contrast to emotional "phenomenism" and pure "constructivism", the music of Arthur Lourié is ontological music'; who, philosophizing on the music of his favourite proselyte, continually makes a fuss about: 'the universe of the non-me', 'art and beauty', 'secret substance of the person', 'sensitive materials', 'essential postulate of music', Nietzsche, Plotinus, Proust, and Bergson; but who, when turning to a specific musical subject, relies on cliché after cliché. 'The artist's friends therefore, who know what the artist wanted to do—as the Angels know the Ideals of the Creator—derive far greater enjoyment from his works than the public . . .' This comment in *Art et Scolastique* only goes to show why Maritain wrote only one essay on a composer, of which Lourié is the subject. Art and scholasticism, therefore, must merely mean theologically standing up for someone who, according to your wife, is 'an extremely great musician'; who set her texts to music (an improvement on Raïssa's 'Si j'étais sûre de plaire | A Jésus mon doux Sauveur', sung to a melody by César Franck), and whose *Sonate liturgique* contained the Good News for, in any case, Guy de Chaunac, who, as a result of the piece, became Père Robert.

After reading the half-hysterical diary of the feminine half of the famous *compagnie thomiste* and hearing Lourié say in 1929 that 'our melodic capacity is directly proportional to our capacity for goodness and love', one may very well ask how Stravinsky could possibly have placed his trust in this composer to such an extent that he recommended Lourié as an authority on his own music, accepted the publication of a neo-Thomist interpretation of *Apollon musagète* based on a short score which was far from completed, allowed him to make a piano reduction of the *Symphonies of Wind Instruments* and, up to *Perséphone* (1929), played through every new work to him, in other words, made him his right-hand man and *valet de chambre*.

The question who this Lourié really was has remained unanswered by every Stravinsky biographer up to now, including Lourié's compatriot, the Russian musicologist Mikhail Druskin. But, as far as Druskin is concerned, this is not very surprising considering that Lourié does not even appear in the *Lexicon of Soviet Composers*, or the Russian *Encyclopaedic Musical Lexicon*. After all, Lourié belongs to the generation of composers, including Roslavetz and Golyshev, who have been carefully erased from the annals of Russian musical history. As far as that goes, the West also has ignored the emigrants of this generation—Lourié, Golyshev, Vyshnegradsky, Obukhov. When Lourié died in 1966 in Princeton at the age of seventy-two, at best one could say he enjoyed some local fame. In one of the few obituaries, he was remembered as an 'old-fashioned Russian intellectual, with all that this implies: a universal curiosity, a philosophical sense of art and a mystical-cultural orientation'. This old-fashioned Russian intellectual was the same man who, forty years earlier, on a business trip to Berlin in his capacity as assistant and right-hand man to Lunacharsky, the People's Commissar of Public Education, threw away his return ticket, thereby turning his back to his native land—albeit without rancour—where he was one of the undisputed leaders of the musical avant-garde. He had been part of the group of futurists which included Mayakovsky, Tatlin, Kulbin, and Khlebnikov, and had been the first to set poems of Anna Akhmatova to music. In 1910, even before Rimsky-Korsakov's grandson founded his Society for Quarter-Tone music in Leningrad, Lourié had experimented with micro-tones in that same St Petersburg. In the following years he wrote compositions which rivalled Scriabin in their harmonic experimentation and made an attempt to systematize atonality before Schoenberg and Webern.

This biographical commentary does not fulfil its purpose since it does not really explain anything. On the contrary, up till now, readers of biographies of Stravinsky have been faced with a *fait accompli* by the presence of Lourié, like a new character that enters out of nowhere half-way through a play. Now that Lourié has received a past—thanks to recent research into the eclipsed Russian musical avant-garde of 1910–30—the sudden entrance and the sudden shining role of Lourié in Stravinsky's life becomes, strangely enough, even more of a mystery. One thing is certain: regardless of the reason why Stravinsky had so much trust in Lourié, it was *not* because of Lourié's past as a composer. In the mid-twenties—more than ten years after the completion of the post-Scriabinesque cantata *Le Roi des étoiles*—nothing was further removed from Stravinsky's musical thinking than the harmonic experiments of Lourié's *Poèmes and Synthèses.*[10]

It remains a fact that Lourié—as a mouthpiece for Maritain—was largely responsible for formulating Stravinsky's *homo faber* philosophy as reflected in Stravinsky's own writings and in publications written under his supervision or with his permission.

How did the Procrustian bed of neo-Thomism as made up by Lourié look? An example: In 1925, Stravinsky was asked for the umpteenth time his opinion on modern music. His answer: 'Gentleman, you are undoubtedly on the wrong floor.' That same year marked the period in which French composition and musicography was dominated by the slogan 'back to Bach'. 'You know the formula: it is the order of the day', wrote Charles Kœchlin. And in that same year of 1925, Prokofiev characterized Stravinsky's *Sonata for Piano* in a letter to Miaskovsky as 'Bach but with pockmarks'.

This lively language atrophied into the formulations that we read in Lourié's 'Leçons de Bach'. What does Stravinsky do, according to Lourié? 'Stravinsky, after playing the role of the bellicose king of the underbrush, of the steppes and the jungle of the non-conformist . . . restores [the canon] of Johann Sebastian and utilizes it as a polemic against modernism.' And what did Bach represent to Lourié? An 'artisan', a 'creature with no other aspiration than to praise the Lord', manufacturer of an art that 'represents the affirmation of the *personal* and the victory over the *individual*', that is, 'in the sense that Jacques Maritain gave these words'.

This sense Stravinsky knew only too well. He let 'the philosopher Jacques Maritain' speak for himself in the *Poétique*. In that mighty structure of medieval civilization, the artist merely held the rank of artisan, he quoted approvingly. 'And his individualism was forbidden any sort of anarchic development, because a natural social discipline imposed certain limitative conditions upon him from without.' Not only, as noted before, did all the themes of French neoclassical aesthetics pass in review in *Poètique*, but they were elaborated with a neo-Thomist bias. Nowhere does Maritain reverberate so strongly as in Stravinsky's criticism of the 'musical culture [of] our contemporary epoch': his criticism of 'the individual caprice and intellectual anarchy'; of the tendency 'to reduce everything to uniformity in the realm of matter' and 'to shatter all universality in the realm of the spirit in deference to an anarchic individualism'; of the 'cosmopolitanism' that 'provides for neither action nor doctrine'; of the—'what an abortive neologism'—'modernism', that

[10] Years later, Stravinsky would deny ever hearing or seeing even a single note composed by Lourié. This denial, at least concerning a few works from the time Lourié was in Paris, is contradicted by Stravinsky's correspondence. See *PD* 291.

'in its most clearly defined meaning . . . designates a form of theological liberalism which is a fallacy condemned by the Church of Rome'. If that were the case, we might as well go back to the Middle Ages.

A photo exists of Stravinsky sitting at an outside table with Roland-Manuel. Roland-Manuel, who took Stravinsky's sulky statements and made them into the flowing *Poétique musicale*, is busy writing. Stravinsky, surly and impatient, is looking the other way. A book lies on the table. It could be Valéry's *Cours de poétique* (the poet was not the only one to notice striking similarities between Stravinsky's poetics and his own), but closer inspection reveals that the book is too thick to be Valéry's. Then it must be *Art et Scolastique*: it might be a coincidence that both Stravinsky and Maritain first use exactly the same quotation from Baudelaire's *L'Art romantique* (but what could Stravinsky possibly be doing with something like *L'Art romantique* otherwise?), then the same remark by the seventeenth-century painter Poussin. But the cat is out of the bag when both writers quote on the same page first from the same verse of Bellay's *Les deux Marguerites* and then precisely the same line from Montaigne's *Essais*.[11]

[11] Compare *Art and Scholasticism* pp. 134, 44, *Art et Scolastique* (1935, third imp.) p. 205, and *Poétique musicale* (1945, ninth imp.) pp. 101, 115, 80 [in *Poetics of Music* (1970, third imp.) pp. 65, 73, 52]. In passing, it might be mentioned that the quotation of Poussin is rather carelessly copied. Maritain quotes: 'le but de la peinture, disait Poussin, est la délectation', while Stravinsky writes 'Poussin a très bien dit que "la fin de l'art est la délectation" '

Did Stravinsky in this case belong to the *pompiers d'avant-garde*, that group that he himself so despised, who 'even go so far today as to familiarize themselves, albeit reluctantly—but *snobisme oblige*—with the great Saint Thomas Aquinas . . .'?

On Influence

If ever a Stravinsky school existed, it was in Boston around 1950. It was there that a group of composers was formed, discussed in 1951 by Aaron Copland in an article for Minna Lederman's book *Stravinsky in the Theatre*.

Copland and Walter Piston were the first American composers to whom Nadia Boulanger revealed the secrets of European music in Château Fontainebleau. This luxurious château, surrounded by woods, was the setting of the American Conservatory, founded in 1921, where the then thirty-four-year-old Nadia Boulanger was lord and mistress. She had abandoned her own career in composition in 1918, the year her sister, the composer Lili Boulanger, died.

Nadia Boulanger knew precisely what was beautiful and what was not. In her lessons (that approximately *all* American composers born between 1900 and 1940 attended), she rarely spoke about Schoenberg, Hindemith, and Bartók, but often about Stravinsky, Bach, and Mozart. Nadia Boulanger had a brilliant mind and an overbearing character. In contrast to most French composers, she spoke fluent English. She admired *clarté* and *discipline*, as exemplified in the works of Albert Roussel, the much underrated master of French neoclassicism, the symphonist who said of the present orientation of the arts in 1924, but in fact referring to his own music, that it had 'clearer lines, more emphatic accents, more precise rhythm, a style more horizontal than vertical, a certain brutality sometimes in the means of expression, contrasting with the subtle elegance and the misty atmosphere of the preceding period, an attentive and sympathetic glance towards the robust frankness of Bach and Handel'. Replace Bach and Handel with Stravinsky, 'frank' with 'unabashed' and one gets a fairly good description of American music in the first decade after the Second World War. Harold Shapero, Irving Fine, John Lessard, Lukas Foss, Gail Kubik, Andrew Imbrie: the neo-neoclassicists, composers of countless sinfoniettas, serenades, and concertinos, either with or without solo winds, of high-spirited, often somewhat short-winded, white-note music. But this Stravinsky school did not appear out of nowhere. Around 1925, while still in France (at the same time as Ezra Pound, George Antheil, and Hemingway), Walter Piston played his music to Paul Dukas and Dukas exclaimed: 'C'est Stravinskique!' Copland, a contemporary of Piston, was called the Brooklyn Stravinsky once he was back in the States. Although Copland's music may seem like Stravinsky's, it is more 'American' than even the most 'American' piece by Stravinsky. Copland's pandiatonicism is cruder and harsher, but more than anything else, cheerful and longer of breath. Copland takes his time. Furthermore his music is Music Minus One: instead of panoramic vistas, constant changes—the Grand Canyon of the C major scale. Jazz and folk music are unequivocally part of the musical style. Jazz in Copland becomes real jazz. And folk music becomes real folk music.

The second generation goes further: this time there are no vistas. The music becomes more classical: many piano sonatas, serenades rather than symphonic poems; and the more the chords sound like Stravinsky the better. Listening to Fine's Partita for woodwind quintet is a kind of illicit joy for a Stravinsky-lover: the right notes, flashy harmony, clever time-signature changes. But still, it is different. It does not start with Stravinsky, but, just like Copland, with another Stravinskian: Francis Poulenc, the Babar of the French china shop. It is Stravinsky squashed and then blown up with air. The air comes from France: fresh 'Luft', not 'von anderem planeten', but direct from Fontainbleau, from Boulanger, the Groupe des Six with Poulenc in the foreground in torn Punchinello trousers, and let us not forget Ibert, le bœuf sur le toit, Parade, street noise, real car horns, in a word: An American in Paris. Milhaud had been in California, by the way, every alternate year since 1940.

The best was Shapero. At least that is what Stravinsky thought. In 1947 at the age of twenty-seven, Shapero wrote his *Symphony for Classical Orchestra.* The title says it all. This is how Beethoven would have composed had he known Stravinsky (one hears Shapero thinking). Completely stripped of the superficialities of American music (Gershwin, Bernstein), the piece is a formalization of neo-classicism: strict form, long breath, much pandiatonicism and, according to the best European recipes, octotonicism in the transitions. Of course, behind the brilliant technique you can see the pokerface of the art director, but that hardly contradicts the mien of the true classicist.

Arthur Berger, older by eight years, also belonged to the 'school'. He was initially a Schoenbergian but was converted around 1940 to neo-classicism—independently of Shapero and Fine, with whom he later became friends. The greatest consequence of his conversion was that a critic could write about one of his new pieces: 'one might easily guess it to be one of [Stravinsky's] smaller ballet scores'. It is odd that this kind of judgement is not usually considered complimentary. If someone had written: 'One might easily have guessed it to be one of Schoenberg's smaller chamber music works', then one would have had more trust in the score. With some justification, Berger complained that 'twelve-tone composers enjoy a certain immunity from the accusation of being servile followers'.

No, one may steal from Schoenberg, from Bartók, from Prokofiev, from Poulenc; but to steal from Stravinksy is forbidden.

If a composer at the beginning of the fifties had played for his friends his new Piano Sonata in which this bar appeared:

Ex. 1

no one would have cried: 'That's just like Webern!'

And if this bar had appeared:

Ex. 2

nobody would have remarked: 'A bit too much like Bartók.'

And if this bar had turned up (which would have been highly unlikely in America):

Ex. 3

no one would have said: 'It sounds like Boulez. Or Stockhausen.' At most: 'Very interesting'.

And supposing this bar was played (which would have been very likely in America):

Ex. 4

nobody would have thought: 'Sounds like Hindemith'. At most: 'A little boring, that bar'.

But if the following bar were to turn up:

Ex. 5

everyone would have jumped up all at once and shouted: 'You can't do that! That's too much like Stravinsky!'

(How can this be? A lengthy account of general characteristics and personal techniques will not help. Perhaps the answer is very simple. The last of the five musical examples is the most interesting. In no other example is tonality dealt with so 'dialectically'. The other examples are either chromatic or diatonic—in any case, unambiguous. But the last example suggests different musical inclinations. It is tonal, but at the same time non-tonal. The music can take off in any direction, which is not the case with the other examples.)

Fortunately, Fine and Shapero and all the others did not worry too much about accusations of epigonism. Everyone, after all, has been influenced by Stravinsky: Milhaud, Gershwin, Prokofiev, Poulenc, De Falla, Lutoslawski, Henze, Blacher, Britten, Walton, Khachaturian, Antheil, Stan Kenton, Frank Zappa, Piazzolla, Dallapiccola, Varèse, Shostakovich, Ravel, Dutilleux, Casella, Luigi Russolo, Petrassi, Nabokov, Orff, Messiaen, Conrad Beck, Willy Burkhard, Tcherepnin, Egk, Fortner, Willem Pijper, Thelonius Monk, Bernd Alois Zimmerman. And what about all those little *Sacres* composed between 1920 and 1940 in the Soviet Union, Poland, Hungary, up to and including the Netherlands: umpa, umpa-pa, um, strings thumping away, never enough time-signature changes.

No, to say that a piece of music sounds like Stravinsky every once in a while does not really say much. Put more strongly: a genuine Stravinsky school cannot, by definition, exist, since Stravinsky's music has not yielded a musical system that other composers can use.

Stravinsky's influence can be seen rather in a specific *attitude* towards already existing musical material. This attitude can best be described as the (historical) realization that music is about other music and is not primarily suited to express personal emotions; that new music implies the existence of other music; that music is only *music*—Orpheus may well be able to coax stones into dancing, but he will never be able to get his woman back.

On the horizon of this description looms the concept of *classicism*. Not as a historical style, but as the rationalization of an artistic attitude.

Classical in this instance means music in which the composer creates only the form 'but leaves the finding of some content in this form to "the listener's power of imagination" '. '. . . the listener, too, must autonomously collaborate at fulfilment.' Romanticism imputes to music 'concrete content, condemning the listener to passivity'. 'Where music makes use of such intensified means that it despotically sweeps the listener under its spell and robs him of his own power of imagination, it ceases to be "music"—that is, it oversteps the boundary of what in the classical sense is allowable.' (Friedrich Blume in *Die Musik in Geschichte und Gegenwart.*)

Such a description comes closer to forming a theoretical basis of music similiar to Stravinsky's than does an analysis of the pandiatonicism in the Sonata for Piano Four Hands by Shapero.

In this regard, classicism is radical. It manifests itself in art as avant-garde and defines the attitude of the artist who holds back, distances his work from the audience, withholds information. This attitude is diametrically opposed to that of a quiz show compère, a chat-show host, leaders of advertising campaigns, and the people who make recommendations in TV adverts. Classicism is not searching for balance and harmony, eclecticism, the golden mean, the beauty of a dinner-jacket and white shirt, 'just act naturally and that's crazy enough'. Precisely what a TV personality does: be conspicuous by not being conspicuous. Just like composers such as Henkemans,[1] Lutoslawski, and Henze at their worst: music in dinner-jacket, music that orchestra directors love.

Stravinsky's classicism is always slightly irritating, the music is unfinished. 'The music calls for action, not consideration,' says Wim Markus. Once again, this sounds like the encyclopedic words of Friedrich Blume. But it cannot be emphasized enough: renewal is concealed in the old. It hides itself. Only a sharp sleuth will discover it and thereby change history.

The true influence of Stravinsky keeps beginning all over again.

[1] Hans Henkemans, (b. 1913), Dutch composer and pianist.

1952—*Cantata*

The *Cantata on Anonymous XVth–XVIth Century Lyrics* was composed in 1951–2. It calls for soprano, tenor, female chorous, and a small instrumental ensemble consisting of two flutes, oboe, cor anglais (doubling the second oboe), and cello. Duration: about half an hour. The piece is rarely performed. Perhaps that has something to do with the closed character and modest lyricism of these Lyrics. The *Cantata* is the antithesis of a spectacular composition. Its beauty is difficult to discover. After one hearing the music seems simple and languid: simple because of the diatonic melodies, and languid because of the regular rhythms in a solemn tempo. It is restrained music that demands a special concentration and attention from the listener. To him who is at rest and can hear the piece under the best conditions, it will reveal its beauty in good time, like the king's daughter in the fairy-tale, jealously guarded in the tower.

The piece was completed in 1952. Careful study of the works composed between 1948 and 1951 reveals that the *Cantata* assumes a key position in Stravinsky's development from American 'optimism' to European-orientated serialism. It is part of a transitional period which began with the *Mass* for chorus and winds in 1948. The *Mass* is downright anti-romantic, anti-subjective. It sounds 'medieval', but does not as yet use ancient, strict canon techniques, as does the *Cantata*.

Between the *Mass* and the *Cantata*, *The Rake's Progress* was written. It was the first and last time that Stravinsky worked uninterruptedly for three years on the same piece. The opera is somewhat an outsider, since it does not really fit into the line of development begun by *Orpheus*. Stravinsky interrupted that development in order to put on the shoes of an opera composer and make a portrait of an 'opera': 'starting with a hero, a heroine, and a villain, and deciding that these people should be a tenor, a soprano, an a bass' (*Mem*). He had once called the opera an archaic form and he did not feel much inclined to contribute towards the renewal of the genre. Three years of mimicry, one must assume.

In 1951, on the occasion of the première of *The Rake's Progress* in Venice, Stravinsky came to Europe for the first time in twelve years. A second trip followed in 1952. He began to develop in the direction of conceiving his music serially, undoubtedly a result of his revived confrontation with the Old World.

His music was initially orientated towards Renaissance canon techniques (such as reflected in the use of five-, six- and eleven note tone-rows) and only later towards twelve-tone technique; Renaissance and early baroque on the one hand, and the most classicistic of the Viennese School, Anton Webern, on the other, were applicable as stylistic examples.

The interest of the newest generation of European composers at that time was directed exclusively towards the Viennese School. Atonality was rediscovered and contrasted with the prevailing fashion of optimistic sinfoniettas and concertinos, preferably for trumpet or piano and thumping strings. (Rediscovered is the right word, since Fascism and the Second World War had caused everyone to turn away from the *entartete Kunst* [degenerate art] of the Viennese.) Leibowitz, Eimert, and, in Holland Kees van Baaren,[1] were the pedagogues who determined the state of music for the next fifteen years.

America was a different story. Stravinsky—Milhaud in his wake in California and Nadia Boulanger minding the shop in Château Fontainebleau—with his cheerful, white-note music, was still the main attraction of musical thought. Except for a handful of dissenters such as Milton Babbitt and Carl Ruggles, American composers wrote 'American' music: *New York Profiles* and neo-classical divertissements, preferably spiced with jazz-rhythms. The Viennese School was a Central European oddity.

The completely different historical orientation of the post-war generation of European composers certainly did not escape Stravinsky's notice during his travels to Europe. Robert Craft took him to performances of *Wozzeck* and *Erwartung*, operas that Stravinsky was hearing for the first time. (It was no coincidence that Stravinsky did not know this German music. He went out of his way to remain ignorant, just as he went out of his way to hear a Verdi opera, gladly even changing the date of a concert he was to conduct.) Craft, whose role as advocate for the Viennese School can hardly be overestimated, conducted Schoenberg's Serenade, Op. 24 and Suite, Op. 29 in 1952 and began two years later on his project of recording Webern's complete œuvre.

During his work on 'To-morrow shall be my dancing day', the second ricercar of the *Cantata*, Stravinsky attended rehearsals of the Serenade and the Suite, asking about the techniques used in the pieces. Even so, the *Cantata* has about as much to do with the Viennese School as a Raphael with a Kokoschka. As far as pitch material and harmony are concerned, the *Cantata* belongs to the pieces composed just prior to it: *Orpheus*, the *Mass* and, for that matter, *The Rake's Progress*. ('Westron Wind', the only movement of the Cantata in a fast tempo, seems almost like an aria left over from the *Rake* with

[1] Kees van Baaren (1906–70), Dutch composer and pedagogue, teacher of, among others, Louis Andriessen, Jan van Vlijmen, Peter Schat, and Misha Mengelberg [trans.].

its continuous rhythmic figure in the accompaniment and its tonal character, as if it were a duet from a 'classical' opera.)

What is different about the *Cantata* is the *method* of composition. Thinking serially: starting with a tone-row means, in the first place, thinking contrapuntally. To Stravinsky, serial counterpoint implied specifically an ancient composition technique, not a new one. Counterpoint belongs with modes, not with tonal or chromatic music. Counterpoint is modal, pre-tonal, Palestrina, Obrecht. The modes form the material of the melody, or in this case, the cantus firmus, and the cantus firmus forms the basis of contrapuntal thinking. This is why similarities in Stravinsky's serial and non-serial music and in his polyphonic and homophonic music can be found in the construction of the melody. Melodic thinking is what guaranteed continuity during the musical upheavals at the beginning of the seventeenth century—the transition from modality to tonality, from counterpoint to monody, from vocal to instrumental music. It is precisely in this period that the cantata, along with the opera, developed as a new musical form. The early cantatas are compositions for solo voices (with or without chorus) and instruments and consist of different movements which alternate between polyphony and monody: monody—the medium of expression *par excellence* in baroque music—is reserved for the movements with solo voices.

From the outset, the cantata developed along two lines: the secular and the religious. The secular cantatas had their roots in the madrigal. Monteverdi, not one to have scruples when it came to money or fashion, quickly added a basso continuo part to the second printing of his a cappella madrigals. Now that was modern music. Similarly, the religious cantatas were no more than a series of motets with an added basso continuo. Does not composing really mean 'putting together'? But it was not long before real cantatas were being written. The first results of this new discovery show similarities to Stravinsky's *Cantata*. The texts are, in contrast to the texts of motets for example, strophic, usually ballad-like poems, either religious or secular (or, typical of the Renaissance, both at the same time). They are regularly interrupted by refrains, whose contents are outside the domain of the main texts; these refrains are called ritornelli. Many of the strophes have the same bass. Homophony and polyphony are alternated each movement.

As far as form goes, Stravinsky's *Cantata* refers to the discovery of the cantata form, but musically refers to a (somewhat) earlier world about 1,400 miles north-west of Italy: the England of Elizabeth I, Shakespeare, and John Dowland. Dowland was himself in Italy with the idea of studying with the madrigalist Marenzio (a plan defeated by a chance meeting with some compatriots who were conspiring against the queen). After being dismissed from his post at the Danish court for licentious behaviour, he finally returned home. Dowland was a brilliant composer and lutenist, a know-it-all, just like William Byrd, twenty years his senior. Affluence under the regime of Elizabeth I (woollen mills, the ending of religious conflict, the beginning of colonization, the organization of the welfare system) gave rise to many good composers: since where affluence is, art follows. These composers wrote, besides consort music, madrigals and music for virginal, airs and catches. Catches were canzonas for more than one part, frequently for solo voice and canonically accompanying instruments.

Affluence gives rise not only to art, but to luxury and refinement as well, and thereby refinement in art. Dowland's airs are endowed with harmonic and melodic jewels not dared for the next 300 years of history—extremely sophisticated settings of dissonances (a minor third in the melody, a major third in the accompanying chord, just like, well, 250 years later, Chopin used), contrapuntal diamonds not sweatingly extracted in the mines, as in the German motets; no, merely found lying in an overflowing treasure-chest.

This is the world to which the two ricercare in Stravinsky's *Cantata* refer.

> Come kiss me, sweet, and kill me.
> So shall your heart be easéd,
> And I shall rest content and die well pleaséd.

Words Gesualdo could also have written—between being flogged.

The text of the *Cantata* consists of four beautiful poems in which religious and erotic emotions melt into a sublimated unity. This sounds high-flown, though the poems are not in the least. 'To-morrow shall be my dancing day' is not about a fifteen-year-old girl trying to get to sleep the night before her first ball; no, this is God's Only Son Himself speaking, with a delicate smile on his lips. Death, too, is no longer the ultimate sacrifice for humanity, but merely a gesture towards the beloved:

> Then on the cross hang'd I was,
> Where a spear to my heart did glance,
> There issu'd forth both water and blood,
> To call, to call my true love to my dance.

'The Lyke-wake Dirges'

A 'Lyke-wake Dirge' precedes and follows each of the two ricercare and the duet of the *Cantata*, so that one gets the impression that the dirges have the main role. The dirges are less 'Elizabethan' than the ricercare. More timeless, a barely moving musical continuum, they seem like an evocation of the '"Totenklagen" [dirges] so characteristic of the Burgundian-Netherlands culture at the end of the Middle Ages' (Lindlar). The women are guarding the corpse. What are the men doing then? Digging the grave? Composing?

When good music is about death, and especially about overcoming death by way of—what else—love (*The Rake's Progress*), women sing (or preferably children, such as in Fauré's Requiem or Bach's Passions), and they sing in the third church mode, the Phrygian. The *Cantata*, as in the medieval Totenklagen, begins with the descending tetrachord characteristic of this mode (Ex. 1). More characteristic of the Phrygian mode is the ascending minor second with which the scale begins—unique among the modes.

Ex. 1

The association of this scale with sadness, death, and the fear of death must have its origin in a distant past. The Phrygian lament also appears in Spanish flamenco, probably borrowed from Arabian music which can be traced back to Jewish synogogue music—in all probability the formula has an Old Testament origin.

The instrumental entry preceding the descending melody (Ex. 2, which in turn is the 'intonazione' for the melody with which the women's chorus begins) sums up the two characteristics of the Phrygian mode.

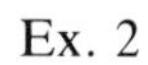

1. The upper voice, a descending and then ascending major second, is, apart from the Phrygian pentachord to which it belongs, a melodic key in Stravinsky's music, in early and late works, in the beginning, middle, or end of pieces, usually as a 'chorale', as a Song of Songs, from the *Sacre* up to and including the *Requiem Canticles*.

2. The Phrygian formula E—F—E is hidden, though it sounds more emphatic than is suggested in the example, being the lowest and loudest notes of the most penetrating instrument in the ensemble, the cor anglais (Ex. 3).

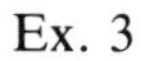

The Phrygian second is also a melodic key in Stravinsky's music, from the mother's lament at having to relinquish her daughter in *Les Noces* to the opening of *Threni*, from the variation theme of the *Octet* to the descending Phrygian scales at the end of the first movement of the *Concerto for Two Solo Pianos*, and at the beginning of *Orpheus*. But the genuine Hades appears in *Symphony in C*. (Ex. 4).

Ex. 4

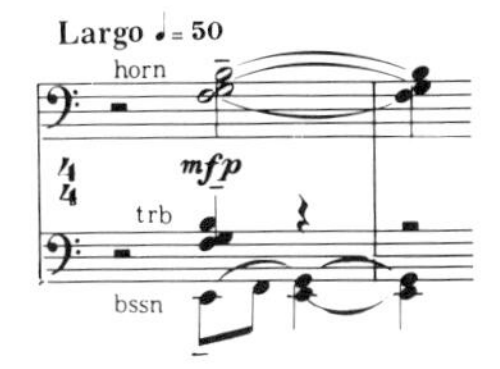

Symphony in C [135]5

The third and most important aspect of the opening bars of the *Cantata* is the pitch collection. The complete pitch collection forms a hexachord on E (Ex. 5). To analyse the pitch material by means of six-note groups can help to clarify the riddle that is posed to the listener by the inexplicable beauty of the piece. This is as true for a melodic as it is for a harmonic analysis.

Ex. 5

As far as the melody is concerned, a hexachordal structure relates the eleven-tone row (*almost* twelve-tone) of the tenor aria (Ricercar II, Ex. 6) to the simple melody in C major in the beginning of the soprano aria 'The maidens came' (Ricercar II, Ex. 7).

Ex. 6

Ex. 7

The hexachord of the soprano aria becomes compressed in the opening bars of the tenor aria, from ½ 1 1 1 ½ to ½ 1 ½ ½ ½ (Ex. 8).

Ex. 8

Instead of being explained as triads (simple stacking of simple thirds) with added tones, the harmony can be better explained as being part of a hexachordal system. So, too, can the chords of Example 9, taken from the second line of the opening chorus, the first 'Lyke-wake Dirge'.

Ex. 9

It would be obvious to treat the first chord as a G major triad with a Hollywood major seventh and the second as a G major triad with a New Orlean's blue note F, but one could also consider the harmony to be the alternation between the (as yet incomplete) hexachord (Ex. 10*a*) and the (complete) hexachord (Ex. 10*b*).

Ex. 10a

Ex. 10b

Making the F♯ the lowest note of a hexachord instead of G as a fundamental of a major triad has a few musical advantages. The listener must place the music in a Phrygian context, thereby hearing more clearly the relationship between the musical material of the various movements and relieving the music of conventional, tonal references. This latter is especially advantageous, since the *Cantata* alludes to the world of pre-tonal music in which harmony is primarily a result of the congruence of melodies.

The significance of chords related by thirds is an essential difference between tonal and pre-tonal music. In tonal music, every triad has either a tonic, subdominant, or dominant function. Pre-tonal music differentiates the various steps of the scale to a much greater extent. The Italian madrigalists in particular (Gesualdo) suggested tensions between steps—such as the mediant relationship (for example C to E or C to A minor)—that are much more refined than any possible between the three tonal functions. In the *Cantata* as well, relationships by thirds are more prevalent than tonal relationships. Thus, a modal cadence is emphasized in the 'Lyke-wake Dirges' by way of a melodic third serving as leading note—an elegant musical formula which was thought to have been abandoned around the year 1500 (Ex. 11).

Ex. 11

Ricercar 1: 'The maidens came'

Ricercar 1, the second movement of the *Cantata*, is an air for soprano solo accompanied by the entire ensemble. The soprano enters with a melody based on the same hexachord as the preceding 'Lyke-wake dirge' (Ex. 7). A strict canon in inversion between the first flute and the cor anglais forms the accompaniment. (This one you have to look up yourself—Stravinsky neglected here to write in those convenient brackets.)

Two other idiosyncrasies of modal music are used in 'The maidens came'. The first is the iambic rhythm (Ex. 12), which refers more to medieval music than to Renaissance music. (Just as in films when to give the feeling of the thirties, one uses cars from the twenties.)

Ex. 12

The second idiosyncrasy concerns a technique not unique to the *Cantata*, but one which is characteristic of Stravinsky's vocal music generally—the incongruity of the rhythm of the text with the rhythm of the music (Ex. 13). Only in the last bar do word and musical accent come together. (That is the way it should be; not only did Russian nyanyas and the troubadours make skilful use of recalcitrant accents between words and music, but, of course, John Dowland did too. Only Brahms and popular hits stay on course. Gide was actually the only one in Stravinsky's circle to be bothered by it, and apparently Maeterlinck had complained about Debussy's *Pelléas*.)

Ex. 13

Exactly half-way through 'The maidens came', a moving cadence suddenly occurs out of nowhere during 'How should I love, how should I love and I so young?' We will quote the fragment in its entirety (Ex. 14) and not hesitate to add another three beats ourselves: not only to show what Stravinsky suggests musically, but primarily to show how Stravinsky, by avoiding the obvious, composes transitions upon which the listener is compelled to dwell. (The three added bars could have been composed by Stravinsky since they keep to the harmonic, melodic, and rhythmic conventions of the style being used.)

Ex. 14

This cadence is characterized by the descending bass, played not by the cello, but by the cor anglais; it is the one time that the cello is silent, so that the only conventional bass line is played by a non-bass instrument. This descending bass causes the fragment to function tonally—one long cadence in D minor (marked by the Roman numerals in Ex. 14). No matter how handsome this cadence is—including suspensions that Bach could not have done better—and no matter how logical the three bars are to the musical progress, it is precisely these three bars that would have reduced the music to that of an epigone.

So what does Stravinsky do? (Ex. 15.)

Ex. 15

The cadence is interrupted, leaving one note in mid-air—the F, seventh of the G minor chord—which proceeds to become the fundamental of the following melody. A dissonance becomes a consonance by merely standing still, not stirring, while the surrounding notes that made it dissonant simply disappear. Alienation? Montage? One does not hear the scissors, just the interruption of the rhythm so that the tonal cadence is no longer tonal, but, for that matter, not-not-tonal.

The canons are strictly worked out.

Ricercar II: 'To-morrow shall be . . .'

The second ricercar, the tenor aria, is the heart of the *Cantata*. It is also the longest movement, taking up two-fifths of the total length of the piece. It was apparently important enough to the composer to compose an 'ending for separate performance'. But then again, not *so* important: the 'ending' is just one chord. And a trivial chord at that, rather arbitrary, like a poet finishing up a poorly-paid poetry-reading session with a 'well, that's it folks'.

Ricercar II is built around five canons. A ritornello concludes each canon, and every new canon is preceded by the first canon plus ritornello. The first canon plus ritornello also concludes the movement. A 'Cantus cancrizans', and two slightly varied repetitions precede all of this. These cantus are also separated by ritornelli. (A small detail for those taking notes: the ritornello, when functioning as refrain for the 'cantus cancrizans', is four bars long and cadences in C minor, and, as interlude for the canons, is three bars long and cadences in B minor.) The form in its totality is shown in Figure 1. The total number of bars of the nine canons (the five different ones plus the four repetitions of the first canon) has a symmetrical structure: 12—12—12—9—12—9—12—12—12.

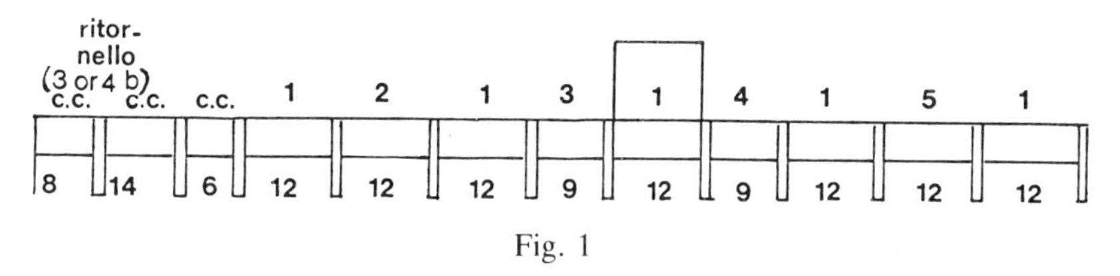

Fig. 1

In contrast to the canons, the 'cantus cancrizans' and the ritornello are monodic. The 'cantus cancrizans' is the 'Invitation to the Dance' made by the Main Character: God's Son telling the story of his life in the canons, but also the young lover singing to his sweetheart. The ritornello is the beginning of an elegant pavan in B minor—'To call, to call my true love to my dance'. It is distinguished instrumentally by the flutes: silent during the canons, they lead the 'dance'.

The second ricercar, except for the ritornello, is based on an eleven-tone row, or more properly, an eleven-tone melody. This row is different from the dodecaphonic row, not because it is *not twelve* tones (the eleven-tone row as twelve-tone row with something gone wrong), but because it consists of merely six *different* tones—tones 4, 7, 8, 9, and 10 are repetitions of tones 1, 3, 1, 2, and 3 (see Ex. 6).

Although use is made of the real (not the tonal) inversion as called for by Schoenberg's twelve-tone technique, the inversions generally maintain the harmonic characteristics of the row which is being inverted, as with Ockeghem or Isaac. Besides the inversion (I), the retrograde (R) and the inversion of the retrograde (IR) are used. All of these forms in most of their transpositions appear in the piece, except for the inversion of the retrograde (actually the retrograde of the inversion) which appears only as IR6 (= RI8). In real terms this retrograde inversion is a transposition, but not in tonal terms. Outside of the 'cantus cancrizans', the retrograde inversion appears just once—as a mistake, a contradiction—when the tenor sings at that point: '[The Jews on me they made great suit] and with me made great variance.'

The impression left by the second ricercar is that of music straying further and further from its starting-point. This impression corresponds with the compositional strategy of the movement in which each successive canon makes use of one or more transpositions which lie further from the basic row—not as far as the first note is concerned, but as far as the harmonic characteristics are concerned. However, the number of common tones between two transpositions is not a measure of their harmonic relationship. The ninth inversion (I9)—being a minor third below the basic row—has four notes of the possible six in common with the basic row but is only minimally related to it harmonically. This inversion appears in the last new canon, canon 5, at the words: 'And rose, and rose again on the third day'. The tenor is apparently listening to the text, since he reaches his highest pitch in the ricercare here, F♯′ (Ex. 16).

Ex. 16

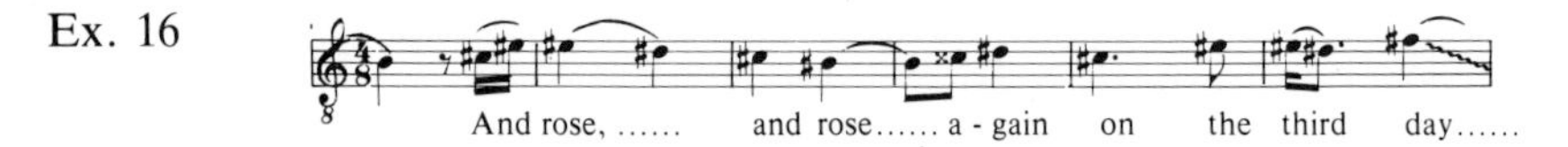

This is not the only example of word-painting. A sad modulation to D♭ major occurs, quite pitifully, at the words 'So very poor, this was [my chance]', while the voice-leading in the oboes becomes poverty-stricken (Ex. 17).

Ex. 17

The word 'Betwixt [an ox and a silly poor ass]' in this same canon gives cause to add an extra note between the first and third notes of the row. Suddenly, starting at this note, the oboe plays the melody of 'The maidens came'. Soft porn for those reading between the lines?

And of course the melody climbs during the singing of 'My Father's voice heard from above', although the 'voice' itself is now at its lowest point in the canons. (Stravinsky's God, generally, has a forked tongue—two-part male chorus in *Babel*, two solo basses in *The Flood.*) God seems to have a low voice.

Besides being childish, all of this is also a reference to the *Augenmusik* of the mannerists at the beginning of the seventeenth century, although the mannerists went even further—two semiquavers at the same pitch when singing about the beautiful eyes of a beloved damsel (Ex. 18).

Ex. 18

This is literally music for the eyes. Generally speaking, the term refers to music in which the visual appearance of the score in some way relates to the text. A good example in Stravinsky's *Cantata* is the word-painting of Barabbas in the second ricercar. This criminal breaks the laws of the ricercar—he does not keep to his row and manages to free himself of all his accidentals. And when Jesus begins to lament 'They scourg'd, they scourg'd me and set me at nought', the cello, too, breaks loose, thrashing away at the cross.[2]

What Stravinsky neglects is to allow the musical crucifixion of his main figure. But Bach had done that already so often, and usually on his own name (Ex. 19).

Ex. 19

'Westron Wind'

The penultimate movement of the *Cantata*, 'Westron Wind', is a duet for soprano and tenor, which refers, more than any other movement, to music that Stravinsky wrote prior to the *Cantata*, especially *The Rake's Progress.* 'Westron Wind' could have been a duet between Tom Rakewell and one of his girlfriends. It is the only movement with a fast tempo. The voices sing a melody with relatively long note-values above a rushing, continuous accom-

[2] A play on the word 'kruis' in Dutch (or 'Kreuz' in German), meaning both 'sharp' and 'cross' [trans.].

paniment. (This old French aria technique—slow melodies accompanied by fast, instrumental movement—is dying a slow death these days in television commercials.)

As so often in Stravinsky's music, there is more the suggestion of musical development than actual development. What in fact happens is that the movement keeps starting afresh. Something that begins to look like development occurs between numbers [2] and [4], but that, too, is mere appearance. The modulation to E minor is no more than the shifting of the wind, returning to its original compass point five bars later.

Once more, the 'Lyke-wake Dirge' is heard after 'Westron Wind'; but it is different this time from the previous three times in two significant ways: the leading note of a third in the closing melody has changed into a fifth, and the Dirge modulates, cadencing for the first time to an A major chord. This chord is an apotheosis in the most literal sense of the word, a big word, though, for two bars of music, but the fact remains that an A major triad has only been heard twice so far, rather obliquely, even though the entire *Cantata* pivots on the pitches A and C (and their mediants F and E). The effect is that one realizes that pure, major triads have almost never been used in the *Cantata*. That single chord makes obvious what up until that moment has been concealed.

Taken together, the movements of the *Cantata* reveal a symmetrical form (Fig. 2).

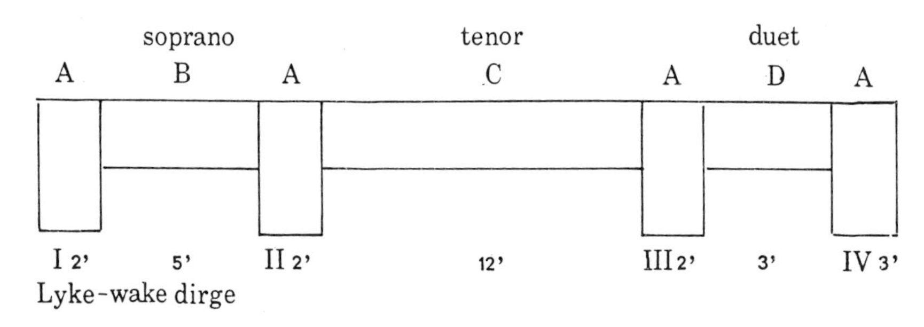

Fig. 2

The durations have been rounded upwards.

Philosophie der neuen Musik

. . . but Schoenberg was shorter than I am.

Stravinsky entertained a lively interest in death. He loved death-masks. He called Beethoven's 'more human' than the portraits of the living Beethoven. His own father 'impressed [him] in his death more than he had ever done in his life'. Stravinsky practised the musical *In Memoriam* with more than just average devotion. The deaths of Debussy, Natalie Kussevitzky, Dylan Thomas, and Aldous Huxley each yielded a musical masterpiece. Perhaps the *Chant funèbre*, composed in 1908 in remembrance of Rimsky-Korsakov, is also a masterpiece. Half a century later, Stravinsky would remember the work as his best and most advanced prior to *The Firebird.* Rumour has it that the allegedly lost manuscript lies mouldering in the catacombs of a church in Leningrad.

Just as Stravinsky had a preference to affect musically dead forms and conventions, so too did he prefer dead composers as a model for his art. It may not be a complete coincidence that serial technique only became a usable 'thing' after Schoenberg passed into history in 1951.

Three years earlier, in 1948, Stravinsky had listened to a composition by the son of an acquaintance. It is not known what occurred during the listening session, but the son did reveal to his mother afterwards 'that Stravinsky had absolutely no idea of how the music was constructed' (*PD*).

Not only did Stravinsky have no idea, he hardly knew Schoenberg's music. He had forgotten that he had been at a performance of *Verklärte Nacht* ages ago in St Petersburg (twenty-five years later, the memoirs of the conductor Siloti would help to jog his memory); and it was mainly coincidence that he was at a performance of the Chamber Symphony, Op. 9 in 1928 and of the Suite, Op. 29 in 1937 (a work which had had its première in, of all places, Paris ten years earlier). Stravinsky's only recorded memory of Schoenberg was as the composer of *Pierrot Lunaire.* At least Schoenberg is mentioned only in that capacity in *Chroniques de ma vie* and in *Poétique musicale.*

On 8 December 1912 Stravinsky attended the fourth performance of *Pierrot Lunaire* in Berlin. He kept his ticket for the rest of his life. Besides the performance, he also attended a few rehearsals. He followed the score that Schoenberg had given him, just as, we can assume, Schoenberg had done while in Stravinsky's company a few days earlier during a performance of *Petrushka.* During this stay in Berlin, Stravinsky was for the first and last time a guest in the Schoenberg house. He is said to have met Berg and Webern as well, although, alas, he had no recollection of this later.

Stravinsky made no secret of his admiration for *Pierrot Lunaire.* 'Schoenberg is a remarkable artist. I feel it,' he wrote to Florent Schmitt shortly after his expedition to Berlin. *Pierrot Lunaire* was reason enough for him to continually support Schoenberg publicly. He called the Viennese who had 'chased Schoenberg to Berlin' 'barbarians' in an interview with the *Daily Mail* in 1913. Even in 1936 he admitted that he 'admire[d] Schoenberg and his followers' and in *Poétique musicale* he defended Schoenberg by saying that 'one cannot dismiss music that he dislikes by labeling it cacophony'.

One should not, though, conclude that Stravinsky was really interested in Schoenberg. Even his admiration for *Pierrot Lunaire* had its reservations; the 'Beardsley'-like aesthetic of the piece was not to his taste. His comments leave one with the impression that he was not necessarily pro-Schoenberg, but rather, against the reactionary criticism of him. Against, for example, Vincent d'Indy, who publicly called Schoenberg 'a madman' in 1928, and against self-satisfied French chauvinism in general. Until the mid-thirties, Paris was distinctly anti-Schoenberg. If something of Schoenberg's happened to be played there (incidental performances of *Das Buch der hängenden Gärten* in 1920, 1922, and 1924, the Second String Quartet in 1922 and 1924, the Five Pieces for Orchestra, Op. 16 in 1922), the criticism was for the most part dismissive and, not uncommonly, anti-Semitic in tone. *Pierrot Lunaire*, once again, was the only piece that gained general recognition after its Paris première in 1921.

Stravinsky's and Schoenberg's musical lives crossed only that once, during the Berlin performance of *Pierrot Lunaire.* A discussion of *Pierrot Lunaire* in which Stravinsky is not presented as an admirer has yet to be written. For that matter, so is a discussion of Stravinsky's *Trois poésies de la lyrique japonaise* in which Schoenberg is left unmentioned. Schlœzer, in his monograph on Stravinsky (1929), notices 'some influence of Schoenberg'. Vlad (1958) is reminded of not only *Pierrot Lunaire* but of the *Six Little Pieces* for piano as well. According to Kirchmeyer, 'in no other work of Stravinsky is . . . the influence of Schoenberg so strongly present, or at least so clearly traceable'. Routh (1975) considers the confrontation with *Pierrot Lunaire* responsible for the 'Schoenbergian chromaticism' of the songs. Siohan (1959), with more nuance, discovers Schoenberg in the third song, 'Tsaraiuki'. Tierney (1977) comes to the surprising conclusion that the Japanese songs have certain qualities 'that *probably* derive from Schoenberg's *Pierrot Lunaire*, which influenced Stravinsky *greatly* when he composed these pieces' (italics added).

To start with, the first song, Akahito, in which the dance of the 'Rondes printanières' from the *Sacre* is continued to a certain extent, must be left out of consideration. Before leaving for Berlin, Stravinsky had already written the final double bar of this movement. Even the conclusion that Stravinsky's ensemble is borrowed from *Pierrot* is unfounded. Although the ensembles are similar, Stravinsky's ensemble is also almost identical to the orchestration he had used in a sketch of Akahito in October 1912.

What is left are the notes (not the orchestration) of the second and third songs. Not only would it be impossible to deny Schoenberg's influence by way of chronology, it would be useless since the songs simply do not sound like Schoenberg, despite the extended free-atonal chromaticism and despite the major sevenths of the opening of the third song, 'Tsaraiuki', which is not Schoenbergian but more Webernesque. The Webernesque theme makes the song seem contemporary with the Passacaglia from the *Septet*, composed forty years later. Even though this chromatic experiment can be traced back to Stravinsky himself—to the octotony of *Le Roi des étoiles* or the already fairly Japanese-sounding bars from *Deux poésies de Balmont* (1911 in Ex. 1)—it

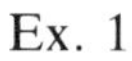

Ex. 1

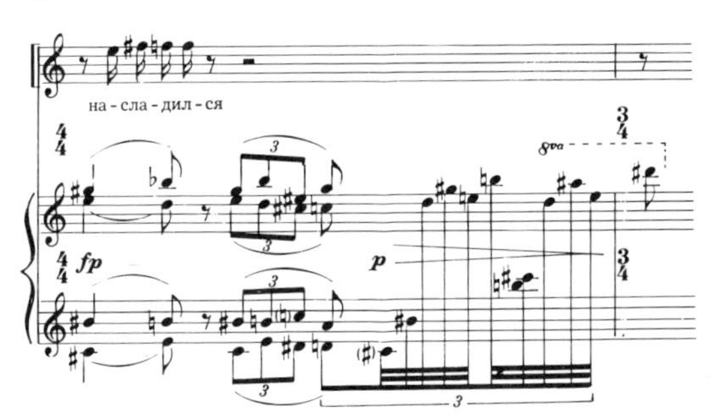

'Golub' [The Dove], bar 13

may very well have been inspired by *Pierrot Lunaire.* But inspiration is different from influence. (Schoenberg's Serenade could have been inspired by *L'Histoire du soldat.*) Stravinsky had cause to be annoyed with Boulez more than once, but not the time that Boulez called Schoenberg's influence on the Japanese songs 'd'une façon impressioniste'. The stubbornness with which Schoenberg's significance to these songs is continually imputed so vehemently can have but one explanation—the tradition of copying others when writing about music. That Schoenberg was emphasized half a century ago is defensible. When in 1915 Debussy admitted his concern that 'Stravinsky is leaning dangerously in the direction of Schoenberg', by Schoenberg he simply meant atonality, which was approximately the same thing in those days. Schoenberg was not yet even Schoenberg then, but merely a *pars pro toto*. Knowledge of the *pars*, let alone of the *totum* was as good as *nihil*. Ravel and Debussy were only being logical when they heard Schoenberg's influence in *Le Rossignol*, since what was being developed musically during the Chinese court scene in the second act of this opera was what was tried out first in the Balmont and Japanese songs.

Thirty-three years were to pass before Schoenberg and Stravinsky—in the mean time both living in the same city—would breathe the same air. The air was that of the mortuary where Franz Werfel lay. Stravinsky saw 'the angry, tortured, burning face of Arnold Schoenberg' and later at home Schoenberg spoke indignantly about his fellow composer: 'Can you imagine someone going around shaking hands at a funeral?' Four years later, Stravinsky was in the audience during the speech Schoenberg gave thanking the city of Vienna for making him an honorary citizen. Two years later Schoenberg's death put an end to the question of who was the best living composer in Los Angeles.

Only then could Stravinsky compose *his* septet and *his* variations for orchestra. In articles and interviews after 1951, he posed as an authority on and advocate of the Viennese School, dipped his pen in holy water while reviewing Schoenberg's letters and had, secretly at first, scores and recordings of Schoenberg's music brought to him, in so far as these were not sent to him by Schoenberg's widow. Of course, the European avant-garde's orientation towards the Viennese School also whetted Stravinsky's curiosity, and Robert

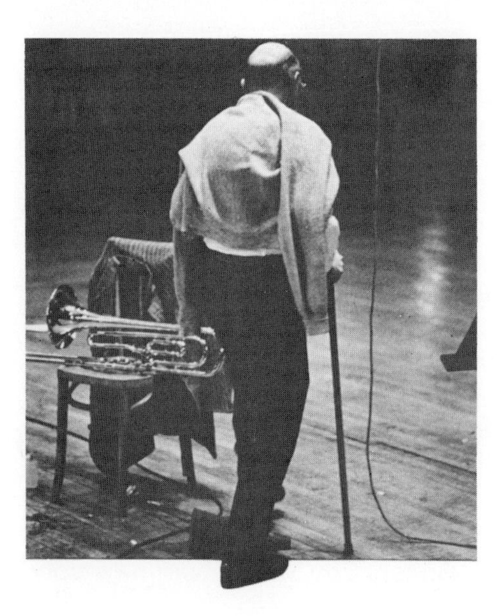

Craft kept him informed of his own activities as a conductor of Schoenberg and Webern. But it is debatable whether Stravinsky would have notated his first row in 1952 if Schoenberg had not already been laid to rest. The fact that this first tone row was not a twelve-tone row and that the structure and use of later twelve-tone rows were modelled more on the constructivist Webern rather than the expressionist Schoenberg is not the point. The Viennese School was history, that was the crux. And the Viennese School were always the others, the representatives of 'Mitteleuropa', separated from him by a 'gigantic abyss', the kind of abyss that cannot be bridged. 'The principle of developing variation that led to the twelve-tone technique and at the same time legitimized it, is known just as little in the serial scores of Stravinsky as in his earlier scores', wrote Adorno, who detested Stravinsky but who sometimes had a clear insight into his music.

The Webern of *Movements* studied with Strauss Jr., the Webern of *Agon* with Rameau, the Webern of *Canticum Sacrum* with Gabrieli and all of these Weberns together studied with Stravinsky.

1955—*Greeting Prelude*

Extremely small composition for extremely large orchestra.
'Singing telegram.'
45 sec.
Happy Birthday to You: forwards, backwards, upside down, distorted, mixed up and all at once. Elaborate gaiety.
Especially suitable for 'critics and children'.
For critics: from melody to abstract interval pattern, from tune to series.
A lesson.
For children: 'A Young Person's Guide to Serialism'.
A game.

Ex. 1

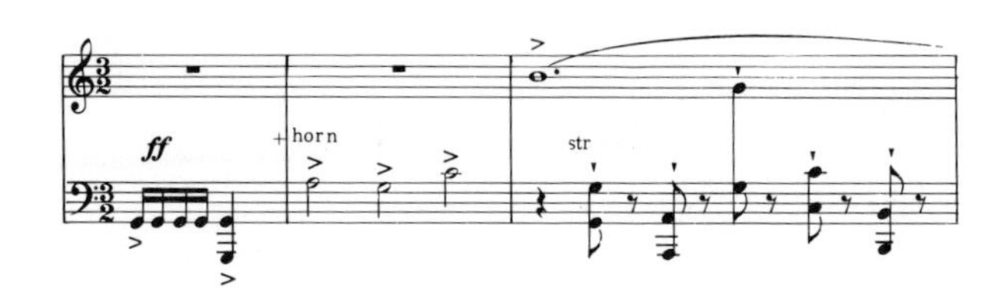

Melody still recognizable as melody, though G is octave too low, B octave too high—first step towards abstraction. B no longer B of melody but B of Webern. See: Pseudo-chromaticism.

High B skips in the groove. Meanwhile same notes in low strings, twice as fast, higgledy-piggledy, up- becomes down-beat (Ex.2).

Ex. 2

From bar 9 *Durchführung.* German discovery: hard work. But bass just goes on singing tune. Other voices do not really work so hard either: rather, they lead bass through hall of mirrors.

Thus from melody to series. Musical *Alice in Wonderland.* 'Happy Birthday to You' = 'Here lie, son, the severities of a hamburger (random: it's the sesame).' The Lewis Carroll of music conducts cellos: 'He relies on these verities of a Hamburg: err, and omits these same.'

What's going on?

How are these similar:

Ex. 3

Boccherini, Sonata in B flat for cello and piano (2nd movt., opening of theme)

Ex. 4

Donizetti, *Lucrezia Borgia* (prologue)

Ex. 5

Michael Haydn, Symphony in G (2nd movt., opening of first theme)

Ex. 6

Rachmaninov, *The Island*, Op. 14 No. 2.

and

Ex. 7

Clayton F. Summy, *Happy Birthday to You*

Answer: series (Ex. 8).

Ex. 8

See (long ago): variations (*Octet*) or variations (*Concerto for Two Solo Pianos*) or variations (*Sonata for Two Pianos*) (Ex. 9).

Ex. 9

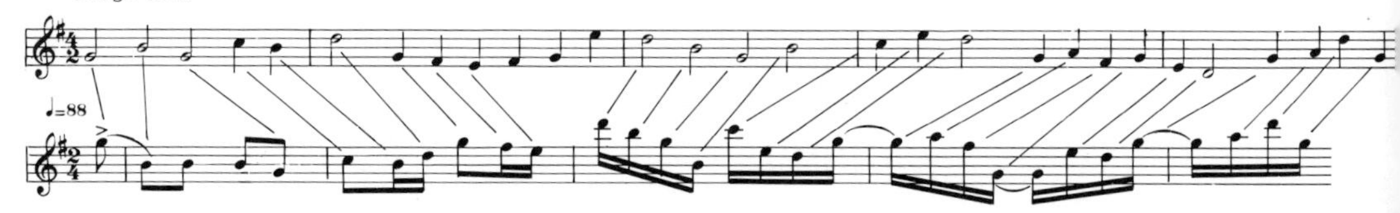

Sonata for Two Pianos (2nd movt., theme and variation 3)

By now, Stravinsky's greetings even more complicated. Violas with upside down hamburgers. Later on, violas playing hamburgers backwards. Advantage: music always nonsense.
Too late: 45 sec. up.
Well, who'd have thought it, children eat serial for breakfast.

New York: Robert Craft and Vera Stravinsky

Shake the hand that shook the hand.
Saul Bellow

New York, 15 July 1979

Central Park. A terrific view of a six-foot-four Nubian beauty, slender, in shimmering, red shorts, roller-skating past, walkman on her right hip.

'He loved the view of Central Park, no matter how short it may have lasted for him.'

Vera S. bought the luxurious mansion on the corner of 73rd and Fifth Avenue in December 1970. The composer lived there for seven days. The elderly couple moved into the house on 30 March 1971—Vera S. leaving behind a hotel suite, I.S. (even Robert Craft never used the familiar Igor) a hospital room. In accordance with Russian superstition, they brought salt and bread with them. I.S. kept asking to be pushed through the rooms of the house in his wheelchair. 'It's ours, it's ours', was his commentary, from which one could tell that he was his old self again. But the owner—whose manuscripts and personal papers had been valued at three and a half million dollars a few months earlier (a bargain according to the Washington *Star*)—was extremely worried about whether he could afford it or not. He could; six days later he was dead, and Vera S. and Robert Craft continued to live there.

An almost rustic quiet. Iago the canary who could trill like Galli-Curci was no more, neither was the purring Celeste, the 'puss*partout* cat'. I compared the room with the description that I remembered of the house in Hollywood: here a Sunday in spring brought inside, there the stuffed fortress of a collector. 'The furniture is recent, American, ordinary'. It had apparently been replaced and, although not striking, it was anything but ordinary—ah, but the 'French dynastic chairs offering you their *sentiments les plus distingués*' were here. 'Every room in the house is a library, for we have more than ten thousand books.' And, yes, here too the bookcases were filled to the brim, behind me one with lavish expensive prints of twentieth-century art, a little further one in which I suspected that Asafiev's *Kniga o Stravinskom* [*Book about Stravinsky*], irritably annotated by the composer, lay in wait—but just a little too far out of reach to be able to steal a look. No idea where all of the works by Picasso, Giacometti, Klee, Miró, Moore, Dufy, Bakst, Larionov, Goncharova, Tchelichev, Chagall, and Léger had gone. Though there were paintings by Vera S. above the mantelpiece, photographs of the composer and the narcissistic portrait of Nijinsky admiring his own reflection. The 'innumerable objects on tables and shelves' had been reduced to an orderly amount of knick-knacks, a mobile that had apparently replaced the 'Calder-like plaything' bought at Bonnier's, artificial flowers in glass and the like. The extra large waste-paper basket in which fanmail of the sort 'Dear Sir, I already have signed photos from Socrates, Stockhausen, and Schweitzer. Would you mind . . .' was deposited had also disappeared. But I did recognize those wooden sculptures in front of the mantelpiece as 'a pair of eighteenth-century wooden ducks from Long Island'.

I did not get much further in my inspection of the room. My attention kept being drawn towards the huge pile of envelopes, packages, and porfolios on the large coffee table a few feet to the right. Inscriptions in black and red pencil, in the unmistakable handwriting of the composer. Finally, here was my chance to illicitly appropriate a tiny piece of what was for me—and not only at that very moment—the most desirable object in the United States. Thank God the timely entrance of Craft brought an end to this painful situation.

I should have known: the Craft I saw was different from what I had expected. Even if he was twenty-four when he wrote the first page of his *Chronicle of a Friendship* on 31 March 1948 and even if thirty-one years had gone by, still, I expected to meet a somewhat nervous, lanky American, who spoke carefully, and yet hurriedly; not a greying, somewhat puffy, brooding, quasi-Anglo Saxon, who moved stiffly, worried about his health and whose careful manner of speaking (yes, indeed) was, in accordance with his elegant New England accent, closer to the *tempo giusto* of his affected thoughtfulness, à la Sherlock Holmes's 'Ah, Watson', than to the *ritmo di tre battute* of his distinct humour, irony, and intellectual (and apparently infectious) mannerisms.

After the briefest of introductions he sat down, took a skilfully-bound booklet from the table between us which turned out to be the sketches of the sixty-five-year-old *Three Pieces* for string quartet, removed his glasses and, with his nose in almost physical contact with the yellowed paper, proceeded to discuss the genesis of the piece and to analyse the various versions, thereby, considering how detailed his commentary was, assuming that I knew the score down to the last harmonic, which certainly gave my ego a boost. It was but a small step from the *Three Pieces* to the *Sacre*, *Petrushka*, *Renard*, the *Étude* for pianola and the *Three Easy Pieces.* Here was a new case of musical kleptomania, there was a sketch that was more radical than the final score, somewhere else an unpublished revision—my head started to spin. Apparently the bibliography of Stravinsky's œuvre was even more complicated and bewildering than I had ever imagined.

That was Craft the Researcher. Stravinsky's former Secretary made his appearance when the discussion turned to more trivial items which varied from Xenia Yurievna Stravinsky's uninteresting memoirs to Rozhdestvensky's bizarre plan to perform *The Rake's Progress* in Russian. The decided tone which Craft the Diary Writer tended to use while candidly putting Stravinsky in perspective was difficult to detect. His witticisms, down-to-earth asides and ironic parentheses were announced in advance by a meaningful tightening of the corners of the mouth or by one or two false starts which resulted in gasps. It was obvious (and this confirmed the impression left by the critical asides in *Stravinsky in Pictures and Documents*) that he was not speaking on behalf of his former employer. The combination of involvement and detachment which characterized his statements, unusual for someone in his position, could only strengthen one's faith in his quality as a biographer. A genuine Eckermann would never have made such remarks as '*Le Rossignol* is not a viable opera' in the presence of a perfect stranger.

(M. in Los Angeles was another case. M. seemed to be a living metaphor of the history of California: beginning as a cinema musician and ending up, for the time being, as the 'official' biographer of Stravinsky. A fragile, old man—the epitomy of amiability—snorting between two puffs of his sixth Gauloise smoked in half an hour, he expressed his fear that he would not live long enough to finish his lifework. And to be perfectly honest, the only thing he really still wanted to do was to *listen* to Stravinsky's music. M. had become a friend of Stravinsky during the latter's California years and as organizer had done a lot of work for his music. M. left the impression, infinitely more than Craft, of having been cloned from Stravinsky. In my memory, his small apartment on the edge of Hollywood consists entirely of paintings by Vera and photos of the composer—among others, a splendid silhouette-like study by Arnold Newman in which M. not only stands across from Stravinsky, but actually *is* Stravinsky; the photo seems to document the meeting up of the young and old Stravinsky. When M. showed me his Stravinsky library/bedroom, it became apparent why it had occurred to me in our previous conversation that he might not be the *ideal* biographer of Stravinsky—above the bed hung a sign in calligraphic writing: 'Stravinsky slept here on 3.20.1969 from 8:30 to 9:30 pm'.)

I do not remember any more whether Craft was talking about the proofs of *Les Noces* from Delage's collection or about the mistakes in Buckle's new biography of Diaghilev when I heard a door close and the approach of shuffling footsteps. Turning round, I saw Vera S. enter. She looked hesitatingly at Craft, like someone who was not sure if she had rung the right doorbell. Craft immediately rose to introduce us. If I would excuse her, she had been painting the entire afternoon—her hands and smock were the best witnesses to the truth of this statement. She lit a cigarette and exchanged a few words of a domestic nature with the quasi-foster son who was clearly acting as master of the house. Initially it was difficult to understand her: she had a soft voice, spoke Franglais ringing of Russian and sometimes appeared to have trouble finding the right phrase. Only Craft, clearly becoming impatient, could help her out. A few times, later in the conversation, he would switch over to a grammatically correct though somewhat vacillating French, which noticeably relieved her. My Americanese, as effortless as it was blundering, seemed reckless to me in her presence.

Ever since Vera S.'s entrance, a continued feeling of surprise and disenchantment had come over me. The effect would have been exactly the same if, instead of Vera S., Madame Bovary or John Shade had entered the room (Dr Kinbote was already present). Just as normal, just as strange. No distinction between fiction and biography could ever exist for me any more. For the first time I could properly value Craft's literary craftsmanship. The image of the composer that he had created over the years was so minutely detailed, so exactly documented and so vivid that Stravinsky had become unthinkable, causing a paradoxical metamorphosis to occur. Stravinsky had become 'Stravinsky'. Stravinsky entering the room in his wheelchair had become an impossibility, he *had* to be dead (if he had ever actually existed). And Vera was part of 'Stravinsky': 'Vera'. Suddenly though, 'Vera' had become Vera and it took me some time to work out approximately how these two women (one of whom, to make things even more complicated, was older than the other) were related.

'Actually, you should interview Madame. She is writing her memoirs. A Slavist is translating them from the Russian.'

Craft's well-intended suggestion embarrassed me—I had *nothing* to ask Mrs Stravinsky. I already knew everything and what I did not know were things ('In what way does the incomplete and unfinished fragment of *Kozma Prutkov* differ from other music written just after the *Sacre*?') about which I could only bother Craft. Anyway, I had not come here for stories and I was not a biographer. To interview Vera S. as the widow of the composer under the present circumstances could only be taken, and rightly so, as a sign of disregard; besides, the questions which I could ask within the bounds of decency during this first meeting were not only questions to which I already knew the answers, but also questions to which Vera S. assuredly knew that I already knew the answers. To ask her about her life as a film actress, costume designer, and painter (about which I could already write five full pages and that would seem to be enough) was not in the least possible. It would be hypocritical. Of course, I would ask about her current pictorial occupations, if only because a stack of copies of the recently-published *Vera Stravinsky—Paintings* was lying on top of a bureau a few feet away. I had already glanced through the book and some of the prints—pale gouaches in aquarium colours—were actually quite good. But no interview, if you please. Tea with Madame, that is what I wanted.

Craft had picked up the threads of his story again—his suggestion was mainly out of politeness. He was busy with a publication of the correspondence, so he told me, between Stravinsky and Cocteau ('the idea of staging *Oedipus Rex* was indisputably Stravinsky's'), between Stravinsky and Ansermet, Stravinsky and Suvchinsky, Stravinsky and Boulez ('Stravinsky's letters, from the period in which he was still on good terms with Boulez, are sometimes brutal, perhaps the most critical mail the French emperor ever received') and the letters from Nadia Boulanger to the composer. Boulanger's letters were the most gushy of them all, consisting mainly of 'kisses and worship'. According to Craft, the recently-deceased breeder of composers was just as destructive as she was influential: she preached the gospel according to Stravinsky and the rest was rubbish. Stravinsky more than slightly detested this lackey.

'Remember how, every year when it was Boulanger's birthday, dinner was ruined by trying to get him to send a greetings telegram?'

Yes, she remembered only too well, and I recognized in the manner in which she commented on the annual inconvenience her habit 'of emphasizing certain words in order to, together with lowered shoulders and a tone of ironic peevishness, show her disapproval'.

She was so charming. So charming in fact that I was slightly embarrassed by the way Craft impatiently waited for her to finish one of her few interruptions. Am I exaggerating, or did he act like a real son who could do it much better, quicker, and more rationally than his elderly mother? Fortunately, Madame did not let him get the better of her when the conversation turned to the possible publication of the correspondence between I. S. and his first wife, Catherine Nossenko. By the following dispute, not lacking in tension and irritation, it appeared that widow and orphan whole-heartedly disagreed.

'Stravinsky always saved everything.' (Later that afternoon, Craft showed me a bound collection of reviews from the Russian period, filled with handwritten comments in the margin.) 'But in the sixties he began to burn everything. Only, strangely enough, he wrote 'To be destroyed after my death' on some packages. Why, I keep asking myself, didn't he burn them immediately?'

Vera S., in a cheerful, jesting voice: 'We didn't have a fireplace in Hollywood!' Of her more serious counter-arguments, I remember only the emphasis she laid on the 'typically Russian, very far-reaching intimacy' of the letters ('Mayakovsky, for instance, was such a sullen person, but his letters are striking because of their tenderness', I read later in my notes made during and immediately after the conversation).

Craft, too, had his scruples. He had written an article, heavily laden with quotations, about the controversial correspondence, 'Igor, Catherine and God' ('the first time I call them by their first names'), offered it a couple of times to magazines—even had the proofs—but kept retracting it at the last minute. He would, if I cared to listen, read it to me and told a story full of Mother-hatred, Father-fear, a triangle, bigotry, guilt, and reproof. (A short while afterwards the article appeared in *The New York Review of Books* under the title, 'Catherine and Igor Stravinsky'. The passages that were the real reason for his wanting to read it to me had been left out.)

Vera S.: 'Mama had to know everything'. This was in reaction to a quote from a letter read by Craft in which the composer, who had the great fortune of having a wife and a mistress who 'were very fond of each other', revealed that he had lived for sixteen years with the fear that his mother would find out about his liaison with Vera.

Vera S. suddenly became very communicative. She began to talk about those days—the haggling with her step-children over the inheritance, the jealousy which had plagued her life. Yes, in the past she could be used for anything. 'They were *scared* of their own father. If they needed money for a new car or to fix a leak in the kitchen, they wrote to me to see if I couldn't persuade Igor to send them money. We had to support *them* instead of them supporting us.'

And she told much, much more, but it is no use writing it all down, besides—that is just the way it is—it was exactly what I wanted from her: to say things which I knew would be senseless to write down. She spoke to me in such a way that I had the feeling of visiting an old aunt whom I had not seen since entering primary school and who started calling up memories of my (may his soul rest in peace) uncle whom, really, son, if you had known him, you would really have loved. When I left, she radiantly showed me a photo: he had the smile of someone who had just won the million-dollar lottery with a fifty-cent ticket, and she—lipstick filled laugh, chin on his shoulder, arm stuck through in front of his—like the girl on whom he is going to throw it all away. 'You can tell that we were living in America in this picture. He looks so happy. He never looked like that in France.'

I promised myself that I would send her a birthday greeting next Christmas.

I returned five days later. Since I was still in New York anyway and since the estimated eight cubic feet of sketches and manuscripts would not immediately disappear back into the vault, I should, according to Craft, take advantage of the opportunity. Chance of a lifetime! But what could I accomplish in two hours? Thumb through everything, mouth wide open? That would not leave all too serious an impression. Limit myself to trying to catch in the act the mystical moment of creation, or, rather, more Stravinsky-like, the moment of production, of just one envelope-sized sketch? That would not show my gratitude. Or check if the D in the first horn in bar 21 in the Epitaph of the *Ode* should not really be a D♭? But of course it should be a D. Could not I just stay there for a week, no, my entire vacation, oh, a year or so? Would not it be fascinating to prepare a critical edition or a detailed reconstruction of the genesis of *Les Noces* on the very spot? Fascinating because, by definition, it could not be accomplished: the riddle would only increase. (The riddle of any work of art that is worth the trouble is, no matter how large, always smaller than the riddle of its genesis, especially if the genesis reveals the development of an idea. Almost all 'insights' or 'first ideas' that form the basis of a work of art are banal, except to the creator himself. And why they were not banal to the creator is disclosed only at the end of the long or short road paved with erasures and pencil shavings. The reconstruction of the genesis of a work is more educational than studying in a conservatoire, more exciting than the best thriller, and more unpredictable than the price of oil; in the final analysis, it is the reconstruction of a vicious circle.)

It was therefore somewhat difficult to hide my disappointment (although diluted with a drop of relief) when, after arriving, I noticed that, for reasons left unclear, the coveted manuscripts were once more under lock and key. Had something gone missing? A figuration much too obviously cut out, a hastily torn-off ostinato? If this were so, then one could not tell by the behaviour of Stravinsky's deputy that he might suspect *me*. I could only blame myself for creating the single cloud that troubled the sky of our discussion for connoisseurs only (which made up for the promised goods being absent). Craft made suggestions and promises of his own accord, which I gratefully accepted; but when I finally pulled a carefully-prepared list of questions out of my pocket (questions of the most general nature: in which library is *The Book of the Homeless*, that kind of thing), I noticed surprised irritation in his reaction to this unexpected personal offensive. To *my own* irritation, I might add. The last thing I wanted to do was to ask for favours—there were only two people in this house who were in a position to give favours and one of them had died some time ago. But maybe I was being too touchy. The man opposite me, after all, had had to sit in *my* place for more than twenty years.

I can just imagine how Craft would have described this afternoon in his *Chronicle* if the friend of the family, R., had sat in *his* chair and he in *mine*.

'Afternoon with R. Two hours of conversation actually a veiled monologue.

I do little but listen fascinated, not because he wants me to, but because I don't have much choice. He speaks in a slow, lecturing voice; his monologue navigating between musing and oration, between Schoenberg's sense of humour (*sic*, he knew Schoenberg personally), Moldenhauer's indigestible biography of Webern and, prompted by Allen Forte's recent book on *Le Sacre du printemps*, the disastrous practice of thinking in systems typical of leading Amerian theoreticians; touches port at President Carter's recent television address and the threatening unemployment, throws a few reputations overboard after manœuvring the straits of the *petite histoire* and through the eye of the hurricane of cultural gossip, to dock at the supplement of a weekly magazine from a country of which he does not speak the language. Besides an article about *Stravinsky in Pictures and Documents*, an essay about the long-deceased humoristic magazine *Mandril* is included in the colour supplement. He asks me to describe the magazine, and after I say that I did not think it was that funny, just as corny as its model, *The New Yorker*, an expatiation follows, substantiated abundantly by quotations from Joyce and Shakespeare, on the geographic and historical limitations and, consequently, the necessarily transitory nature of humour based on word-play.'

I also took notes during this conversation. Those from the last twenty minutes are illegible. *Polish falseness*—that must have been Stravinsky's hypocrisy which Madame discussed last time. *Henze*. 'Wears a Mao tunic now, but with lots of money in the pockets', I remember Auden's remark. But the note refers to another anecdote: how Stravinsky, shortly after the beginning of an opera by Henze dedicated to him and, visible to those who were supposed to see, left the hall. *Le moineau est assis—Prose* (?). A little higher on the same page, crooked and crammed together, and only with great difficulty recognizable as grammatical French. 'The sparrow is sitting.' The sparrow in the *Chants russes*, I suppose, who sits 'on some else's hedge'. But what is the sparrow doing? Has it suddenly discovered its talent to write prose? Insoluble riddle. A cursory graphological check reveals that this note was made precisely at the moment in which I broke out in sweat. The double whisky that I had just downed so quickly (that is, in imitation of my host) obviously landed on an empty stomach. 'How do you feel now, Mr Stravinsky?' 'Quite drunk, thank you, Mr President.'

Salvation was just round the corner though. In the adjacent room, barely visible through the half-open sliding doors, dinner was being served by the maid, or the successor to Evgenia Petrovna.

'The cooking is regularly French but periodically Russian: caviar, blini, piroshki, kulibyaka, borsht, stroganov, kasha, kissel.' Or shchi for a change?

The room had, in the mean time, inconspicuously filled up with prattling company. In a desperate attempt not to divulge the shameful state I was in, I greeted—Dutch hypocritic, exaggeratedly polite, well, almost subservient—a certain Dr so-and-so whose name I could not catch and a girl with a laconic New York accent whose shockingly down-to-earth remarks, spoken as if she were typing a letter, concerned the fate of a certain Jim (Mike?) and, if I was not mistaken, the stifling heat outside. She then asked if my visit 'had something to do with Stravinsky'. For a moment, I completely forgot that the composer had been lying in Venice under Manzù's marble memorial for almost eight years.

Brought back to reality, I courageously bid Madame farewell, hopelessly slipping over the sibilants. 'I'm so sorry that I didn't get a chance to chat with you today,' she says. I flatter myself with the thought that she will be ninety-one on 25 December and need not unnecessarily compliment complete strangers. Cautiously, she embarks towards the dining-room, her dinner companions making room for her.

> The thread of gold cordial flowed from the bottle
> With such languor that the hostess found time to say
> Here in mournful Tauris where our fates have cast us
> We are never bored—with a glance over her shoulder . . .

That is how Osip Mandelstam poeticized the then Vera Sudeikina née de Bosset, the widow of the illustrious absentee of 2 East 73rd.

It was an hour before everything was back in order as I walked through Manhattan. Continually humming the first thing that inexplicably came into my head. 'Pussy said to the Owl, "You elegant fowl! How charmingly sweet you sing!"' Almost half a century ago, Vera S. had been taught this Edward Lear fable by Serge Nabokov, brother of the novelist. For her, it was her first acquaintance with the English language, for Stravinsky, the text of his last composition.

> They sailed away for a year and a day
> To the land where the Bongtree grows

A dodecaphonic mousetrap.

'In the Swiss years he drank white Neuchâtel while composing, and in the French years red Bordeaux. In America it has been Scotch, Jack Daniels, Jim Beam, or even a bumper of beer.'

I do not have to make up the notes of the song, just carry the tune and I cannot manage merely that any more. Even as a drinker he was my better.

1943—*Ode*

Ode is a piece that balances on the threshold of musical audibility. It is, despite the rather powerful middle movement, more the shadow of music than music. It seduces one into senseless contemplation about the music that lies behind the notes (even though what undoubtedly lies behind the notes is at most other notes; encouraged to make connections by the sound of the notes, we can only draw on our remembrance of other notes). The opening of the Eulogy, the first movement of this 'Elegiacal Chant', is just like the opening bars of Schubert's Fantasy in F minor for piano duet: their impact is out of proportion to the meagreness of the score. Musical analyses rarely make a point of such discrepancies. Those more exacting who define a musical composition as functional cohesion or as a network of internal relationships may suggest that such bars receive their meaning from the bars that follow them and the way in which they relate. The bars *in themselves*, so they say, mean nothing. But the bars *do* mean something in themselves. And if the explanation cannot exclusively be found in the musical substance (this chord and not that chord combined not with this phrasing but with that phrasing etc., etc.), then the explanation must be sought in a network of external relationships. For his Harvard Lectures Leonard Bernstein rewrote the beginning of Mozart's Symphony No. 40 in G minor. He made it into a banal piece by making the structural irregularities (such as the asymmetrical construction of periods) regular. But the result was no mere banal piece, it was a banal piece with a wonderful theme.

Ode is very simple music. Few of its notes are what could be called 'interesting'. The history of the piece consists of one single anecdote and one footnote. Even the composer had nothing to say about it. The piece exists merely in lists of works. In books about its creator, it is generally mentioned just in enumerations. Only Tansman seemed to like the music: 'Rarely has so much been said with so little.' At least Tansman dared to write that himself. There was no one to quote in 1948.

If it makes any sense at all to describe music, then preferably describe music that is known, or at least that has a chance of being heard. A description of *Ode* is a description of an imaginary piece.

The third movement, the Epitaph, is the strangest. There can be no doubt that this is music by the American Stravinsky, even though the first half of this movement is dominated by reminiscences of *Symphonies of Wind Instruments.* Only those reminiscences do not have the allure of real reminiscences since they call no past to mind. They are echoes which do not sound like echoes, but rather as unreflected sound. Even the composition which is called *Symphonies of Wind Instruments* consists of such non-echoes. The origin of *Symphonies of Wind Instruments* is long before the *Symphonies of Wind Instruments.* Only 'Wind Symphonies-like' exists.

A year before Stravinsky composed his *Ode* on one side of Hollywood, Schoenberg composed his ode on the other. It is the *Ode to Napoleon.* The title is ironic. Schoenberg's piece is Middle European expressionism hook, line, and sinker. When Schoenberg moved across the ocean, his music did not come with him—as Stravinsky's music had. Stravinsky's jump over the ocean was made within the bounds of one piece: suddenly, in the fourth (American) movement of the *Symphony in C*, Broadway-like string tremelos are heard. Not only is Schoenberg's ode European (the return to octaves and E flat major has nothing to do with America), it is *directed* at the war-torn continent. 'Napoleon' meant Hitler. Stravinsky's ode is predominantly concerned with death and money. The death of a lady in whose memory the piece was composed and the money of her husband—Stravinsky's former publisher—who commissioned the work. Who now actually died did not concern Stravinsky too much. The *Élégie* for viola was composed in memory of someone he barely knew. Death had always been the best guarantee for beautiful music, and so it would remain.

Schoenberg's ode is first and foremost a vehement and impassioned piece, Stravinsky's ode is first and foremost affected silence. Saying this lends a poetic aura to Stravinsky's ode, although that is not the intention. Stravinsky never composed so-called poetic music. Sometimes, like in the first and third movements of the *Ode*, he wrote soft, distant, introverted music, but never 'like the flutter of angels' wings'.

It's not difficult to point out the weaknesses of the *Ode*.

The trio for the three solo strings is rather obvious.

The combination of major and minor thirds, at least by the end of the piece, starts to seem like a self-regulating mechanism.

Broken triads, parallel thirds.

And the formal construction is naïve, too.

But it's just like your sweetheart's pudgy fingers. Without those pudgy fingers, she would not be your sweetheart.

There is a word for it—beauty.

III

Monsieur, le pauvre Satie

Seventy years after its creation, *Le Sacre du printemps* is still so potent that it can give someone who is hearing it for the first time the feeling that his life is being changed, or at least that his ideas about music are being turned topsy-turvy.

It is highly unlikely that a young musician who, as an experiment, listens to Britten's *War Requiem* after a long night spent with a lot of Talking Heads, David Bowie, the Police, and perhaps too much beer, will have the feeling that 'this is it'. If, instead of Britten, he puts on *Viderunt omnes* by Perotin, preferably on compact disc with the volume as loud as possible, the chance of having this feeling increases.

The relationship between the historical age of a piece and its musical novelty is complicated. Being novel appertains not only to being unknown, but to being able to change one's views, opinions, and reference points. One can imagine a time when the symphonies of Beethoven will not be played any more and musical taste will be determined completely by Satie, Steve Reich, Praetorius, *pelogs*, *gagaku*, 'nature sound explorations' (rock groups specializing in the harmonic series), and Pythagoras Therapy (sessions of twenty to thirty hours in which ten clients, in a circle, each play their own monochord). And one can imagine someone in this imaginary time inventing a new kind of music: loud and short, rhythms hammering away in rows based on the Fibonacci-series, performed on newly designed instruments; and that someone declaring that everything else is now obsolete except for a completely forgotten nineteenth-century *Einzelgänger* [loner] who *wrote* music in which he confronted *two* musical ideas with each other—a Belgian who lived in Germany or Austria who was called Beethoven.

This is less imaginary than it sounds.

Vivaldi: famous, forgotten, rediscovered.

Bach: locally famous, forgotten, rediscovered.

Gesualdo: forgotten, rediscovered.

Joachim Raff: famous, forgotten.

Ives: unknown, discovered.

And now to the point—Erik Satie: twice forgotten in his own lifetime, discovered, and once again forgotten; rediscovered for the umpteenth time in the sixties; and now once again, for the time being, finally immortal—that is, dead as a doornail and ripe to be forgotten for the hundredth time.

It should be kept in mind that the list of Satie's innovations is very impressive. And that is precisely the guarantee that Satie can never, in the final analysis, be canonized. It probably would have surprised him greatly to learn that his piano pieces could become part of the background to chic parties in the seventies, sound-tracks to films about nature or famine in South America and be recorded on convenient cassettes included in sleep-therapy packages. What was once new can now be yawned at.

The list begins in 1887, a century ago. In his Sarabandes, Satie writes parallel ninth chords which served as an example for Debussy's piano music (Chabrier being left out of the picture for the moment).

In 1891—he has met Debussy in the mean time and will have an unrelenting, lifelong admiration for him—he works on an opera based on a text by Maeterlinck, even before Debussy starts thinking about his *Pelléas*.

In 1893 he composes the *Danses gothiques*, the first modern example of music without any structural development. The material of each independent movement is mutually interchangeable, meaning that, sixty years before Earle Brown and Cage, one can speak of 'open form'.

In 1913 Satie writes *Le Piège de Méduse* (words and music) for an ensemble almost identical to that used in *L'Histoire du soldat*. It is an absurdist piece of music theatre. Twice Stravinsky publicly denied knowing the piece, though by 1918 he had been a friend of Satie for some time and had even dedicated the 'Waltz' from the *Three Easy Pieces* for piano duet to him in 1917. (Yet it must be admitted that *Le Piège de Méduse* was not performed until 1921.)

1914: *Sports et divertissements*, a series of piano pieces and at the same time an *objet d'art*. The music, printed in facsimile, is encircled with texts and drawings.

1917: Satie writes the first neoclassical piano piece and gives it a name which announces the coming of the craze of -isms: *Sonatine bureaucratique*.

In the same year comes *Parade*, the ballet filled with revolvers, typewriters, sirens, rattles, the Wheel of Fortune and Morse-code transmitters. With this, Satie becomes the leader of a new musical movement: against impressionism, against refinement, especially against art; and in favour of cubism, cabaret, music-hall and jazz (then still being called negro music).

Two years later: *Socrate*. 'Étrange, n'est-ce pas?' was Satie's commentary. All 'white', minimal, and repetitive music is potentially in *Socrate*. Little occurs in the music, and absolutely nothing occurs in the piano piece *Vexations* (*c.*1895). But this nothingness can go on for twenty-one hours. Compared to this, Philip Glass is a composer of *Humoresken* and *Albumblätter*.

But the list is not complete. Yet to be mentioned is the *musique d'ameublement*—the first disposable music; contrary to the piano pieces from the middle period, this music has *not* permeated the repertoire of the seventies and eighties. And, last but not least—this is especially for those interested in the sociology of music—Satie's temporary membership of the Radical Socialist Party in the district of Arcueil. Even here Satie was ahead of his time.

Satie, either directly or indirectly, influenced all his contemporaries—at least those west of the Rhine. He did not want to establish a school, but was constantly being declared spokesman or master of this or that movement. That is why he continually had to be innovative. He kept making history by composing without history.

John Cage is one of the more recent rediscoverers of Satie. In 1948, in order to convince the public at the Black Mountain College Festival—consisting mostly of German refugees—of the necessity of listening to *twenty-five* concerts of Satie's music, Cage gave a lecture in which he greeted Satie, along with Webern, as the father of 'the only new idea [in the field of structure] since Beethoven'. Ten years later, in an 'imaginary conversation', Cage presented Satie as a historical example of his own musical philosophy which, just as Satie's, was, paradoxically, without precedent. Like our imaginary discoverer of Beethoven, Cage belongs to the composers who ignore the fact that they work within a tradition, even though they search for historical prototypes.

Few of Stravinsky's pieces now, in the eighties, have the confusing propensity that the *Sacre* still has: of proclaiming itself novel.

'*Apollon musagète* is lovely, but Satie's *Socrate* is lovelier.'

'*L'Histoire du soldat.* Typical of the early twenties.'

But what is new becomes old. And sometimes what is old becomes new again. Countless contemporaries who called Stravinsky a composer who followed fashion, have been, for the moment, shown by history to be wrong.

'The only way to escape Hollywood is to live in it.'

Ragtime

Actually, ragtime was a boomerang. French and Spanish colonists brought polkas, quadrilles, cancans, galops, pasodobles, and habaneras to *Nouvelle Orléans* and black pianists flung back ragtime. They gave the whites a taste of their own medicine. They merely played galops, quadrilles, and cancans, imitating an entire orchestra of winds, banjos, and basses on the piano, but added rhythms in the right hand which were new to Western ears, even shocking, and which had their origin in African musical culture. The whites thought the rhythms were syncopations (as if it were Brahms!), but the new rhythms were anything but syncopations and to the pianists, anything but new.

(African music, especially on the west coast, is polyrhythmic: a tri-rhythm within a two-part bar is not an irregular division of a bi-rhythm, not a so-called anti-metrical figure, but an autonomous rhythm. Every eight-year-old Ghanaian boy has a 3–2–3 rhythm in a four-part bar in his bag of musical tricks.)

The cakewalk came before ragtime. This was music played by whites dressed like 'negroes'. In Europe John Philip Sousa's white band, playing syncopated marches alongside square marches, spread this music around. A few years after Sousa's visit to Paris, Debussy composed *Le petit nègre*.

The ragtime rage began around the turn of the century. The flood of ragtimes in music shops began with Scott Joplin's *Maple Leaf Rag*. European immigrants were ripe for a new kind of piano music that went beyond the worn-out salon music tradition of flower-waltzes, butterfly-dances, imitations of musical boxes, and Chopin preludes. The ragtime had considerable significance for the development of black culture in the United States. It was the first *written* music from the blacks and also their first instrumental music whose form was not dictated by the text. The formalization of the (additive) African rhythms—as had first occurred in the ragtimes—would leave indelible tracks in Western art music. The ragtime was modern also because of its form. Ragtime was played in one constant tempo, had no contrasting middle section as did the minuet, had no development, but was a 'montage' of independent sections. Ragtime had a chain form: AABBACCD. Joplin even removed the A after the BB in *Cascades* so that a real chain was made: AABBCCD. Rather like the *Sacre*, one could say.

It did not take long before the white orchestras confiscated ragtimes, just as the word jazz was confiscated in 1917 by the white Original Dixieland Jass (*sic*) Band. In no time at all, the genre had become commercialized.

The answer to this was a new piano genre which developed from an entirely different background—the blues. It is difficult to say who played the first blues basses, but it is certain that by the end of the twenties a new piano style had begun to evolve which was much different from ragtime. Boogie-woogie was, just like the blues, counted in four, with the ternary rhythm of the blues guitar in the left hand. Boogie-woogie disposed of ragtime's chromaticism, the secondary dominants, the passing tones, the slick riffs. Whoever listens to Clarence 'Pinetop' Smith or Jimmy Yancey gets the feeling that playing the piano is being invented all over again. What is so noticeable about their style (Monk's too, some time later) is how much is left out—especially the ogling at white music publishers that became so evident in ragtime. After all, blacks in the age of ragtime were treated as second-class citizens.

Ragtime was cheerful music, but early boogie-woogie was no longer cheerful, just as little as was (sung) blues. It was not until the thirties, in the hands of virtuosi such as Pete Johnson and Albert Ammons, that boogie-woogie also became entertainment. The boogie-woogie that Europe came to hear after the Second World War ('boogie-woogie, jitterbug and jive!') was just a pale shadow of the rap notes that resounded in the twenties.

Early orchestral jazz did not fare any better. Not until the end of the First World War did the first jazz orchestras appear in Europe. The drummer Louis A. Mitchell, who was spotted in the Parisian *l'Empire* in 1917, was introduced in the press as 'l'ambassadeur du bruit'. His orchestra of fifty black musicians pushed its way on stage at the Casino de Paris in 1919 and had such a 'succès hot' that New York papers wrote: 'French now want colored musicians.'

It is possible that Stravinsky heard Mitchell's orchestra. Ansermet, who had already been to America and had written an enthusiastic article about Sidney Bechet in 1919, informed Stravinsky about the ragtime rage. He had even brought back the instrumental parts of a couple of ragtimes, which Stravinsky pieced together into scores.

Stravinsky's own *Ragtime* for eleven instruments was not *per se* a contribution to the rage, but more an answer to it. There are continual gaps in the melody, the harmonic rhythm is constantly disrupted, and the cimbalom in the orchestra suggests rather that a Hungarian invented the portrayed genre than a black American. Stravinsky would never compose true jazz, let alone third-stream music. He was interested in the confrontation of styles and genres and not in mixing them. Even the *Ebony Concerto* is not jazz. When he pointed to traces of blues and boogie-woogie in his own music, even in his most serious works, such as *Orpheus*, he was often mistaken. The examples from *Agon* which he named ('Bransle simple', 'Bransle double') could be anything really, except blues and boogie-woogie. The only notes in *Agon* that actually seem like a boogie-woogie lick, in the Gaillarde, played by two flutes, he neglected to mention (Ex. 1). These notes are just as slick as those from a genuine piano entertainer.

Ex. 1

1921—*Les cinq doigts*

Kur-dáa, tang ka da dááa! Táng ka táng ka . . . etcetera.

This and no other way is how the *Symphony in Three Movements* begins. Orchestral violence results in such song. All music which is sounded is the outcome of a certain amount of physical energy. Even the better kind of electronic music allows the listener to hear that the cones of the speakers are hard at work, and the best electronic music, like Dick Raaijmakers' *Canons, Ballade voor luidsprekers* [*Canons, Ballade for Loudspeakers*], makes a subject out of the cones.

Stravinsky always sang his instrumental melodies monosyllabically. His singing of the beginning of the *Symphony in Three Movements* would probably have sounded like this: 'Ta-táa, ta ta ta táá! Tá ta tá ta . . .', etcetera. Not only does the sounding of music demand a certain amount of physical energy, so does the composing of it. It can almost be taken for granted that composers sing the vocal parts of songs or choral works while composing; but there can also be times during the composition of a piece for, let us say, string orchestra when the composer—while playing through what has been written so far—sings certain parts, an important inner voice, for instance, since he does not have that vital eleventh finger to play all the notes. In the simplest case, the right hand plays the accompaniment (old barrel organs have a stop called *accompagnement* which is used for the second and third beat of the waltz and for all the beats except the first of a polka or galop) while the left hand plays the bass.

Whether the composer now actually sings or hears the melody in his mind is neither here nor there. Some bars sound as if they have been sung and others do not. And whether the composer composes at the piano or not is also rather immaterial. Stravinsky always composed at the piano—sometimes one hears this and sometimes one does not. Seldom, however, does one come across bars in piano reductions of his orchestral works that are easy to play. In most cases, you wish you had a pianola for the continually added inner voices, the elaborations in the upper voices, the labyrinthine voice-leading, the widely-spaced chords. Stravinsky may have composed at the piano, but orchestral music that could easily be reduced for the piano left him with a healthy suspicion.

What begins as playable on the piano (Ex. 1) ends up as unplayable (Ex. 2).

But also the unplayable was played, since even the added notes were tested during composition.

Ex. 1

Ex.92—*Symphony in C* [64]4

Ex. 2

Few bars of the orchestral works can be completely reproduced on the piano, but all the notes have been tried out on the keyboard, sung, heard, and checked. Even the hermetic work *Threni* was sung and played down to the last note (Ex. 3). Here we have Stravinsky's own basso profondo.

Ex. 3

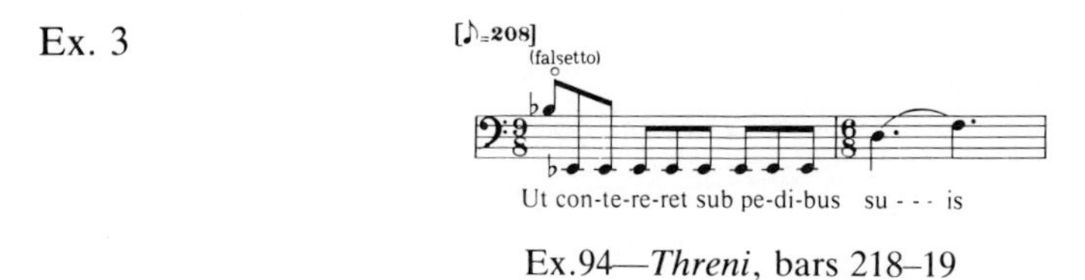

Ex.94—*Threni*, bars 218–19

The five hammer-blows that introduce the speaking chorus are Stravinsky's right and left hands (Ex. 4).

Ex. 4

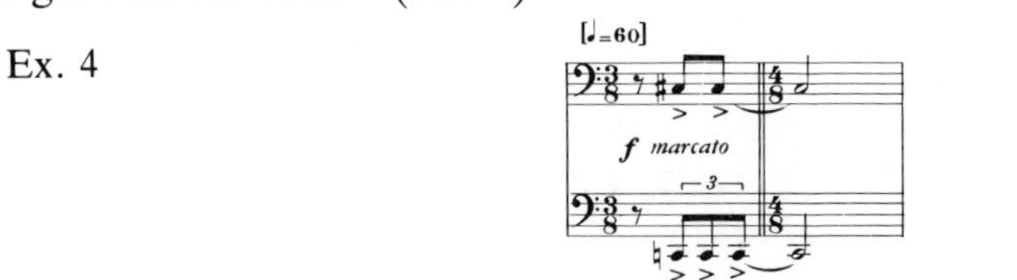

Threni, bars 26–7

The spread-out fifths that frequently occur in *Threni* 'chime in' nicely on the piano (Ex. 5 and 6). Example 6 is not only an example of composing at the piano, but of composing the piano: a strong attack, sudden diminuendo, and finally the slow decay of the tone.

Ex. 5

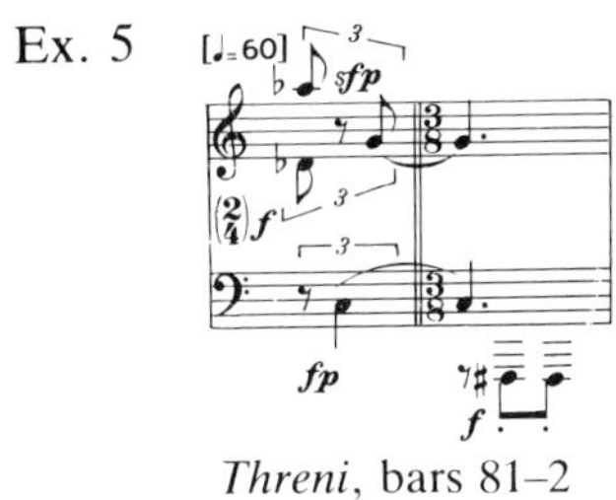

Threni, bars 81–2

Ex. 6

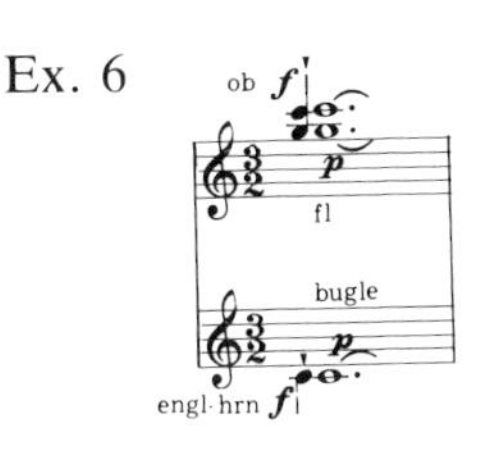

Threni, bar 246

Examples of this kind of orchestration can be found everywhere, throughout his entire œuvre: the combination of string pizzicato with held chords in the winds, of two flutes or two clarinets where one plays staccato and the other legato, and especially strings playing and plucking at the same time—a combination which, in its strictest mode, formed the basis of the first, unfinished version of *Les Noces*. The term *pizzarco* might be used for this technique. *Pizzarco* basses are frequently alternated with and/or doubled by timpani. We will ignore the doubling of the piano in the orchestra for the moment since the orchestral piano is a totally different instrument from the piano in the living-room. *Pizzarco* basses are the instrumental translation of piano basses which, once returned to the piano, hardly sound like piano basses.

Not only orchestrations, but sometimes even musical gestures betray their pianistic past (Ex. 7). First the bass in the left hand, then both hands on the second beat with the chord, and then some fast notes in the middle voices. Any pianist who see these notes will be filled with a sense of satisfaction.

Ex. 7

Symphony in Three Movements [29]

Every once in a while, a few bars from a piano reduction will sound better than the original orchestral version. One such example is the shuffling of the cards from *Jeu de cartes* (Ex. 8). Here too, in principle, the strings double only the first beat of every bar.

Ex. 8

Jeu de cartes, opening

(Vera Stravinsky thought that the harpsichord arpeggios in *The Rake's Progress* sounded like the way Stravinsky shuffled cards [Ex. 9]. This shuffling occurred, as we hear, by allowing the two packs of cards to slide into each other, helped out by both thumbs. And the cards *have* to be shuffled because this arpeggio announces the devil, Nick Shadow, with whom Tom Rakewell—just like the soldier in *L'Histoire du soldat*—must play a round of cards in order to win back his soul. These are devilish arpeggios.

Ex. 9

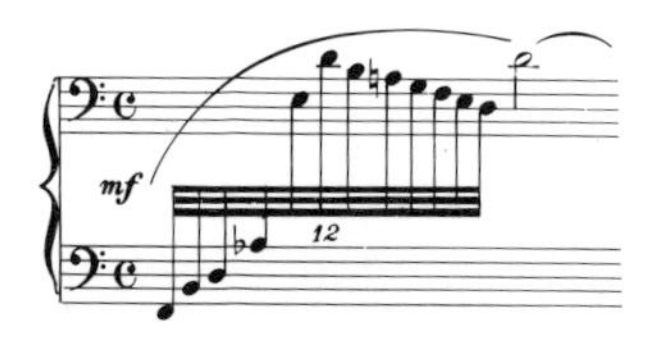

The Rake's Progress, Act I [47]

Or did Vera mean perhaps the arpeggios shown in Example 10. Only magicians can shuffle so quickly. And, of course, devils.)

Ex. 10

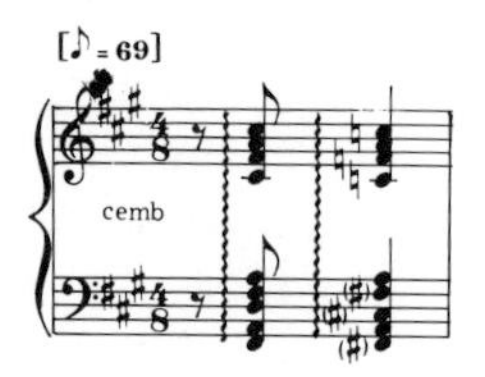

The Rake's Progress, Act III [186] 10

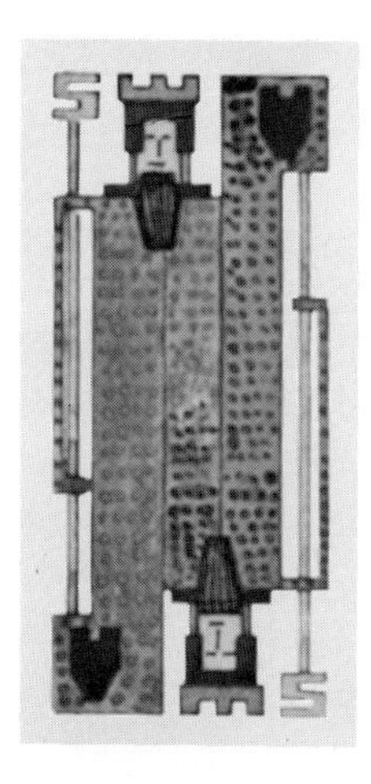
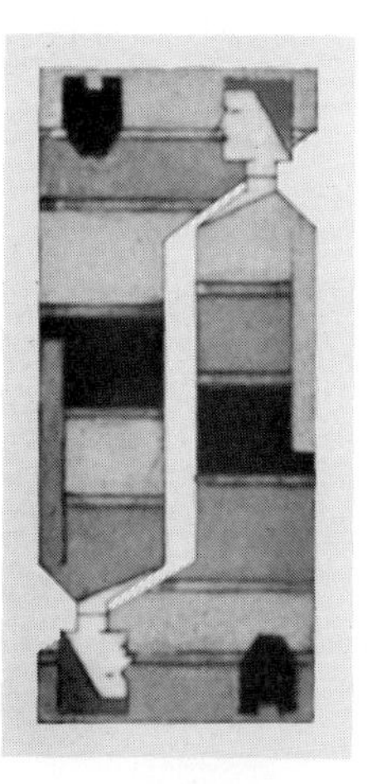
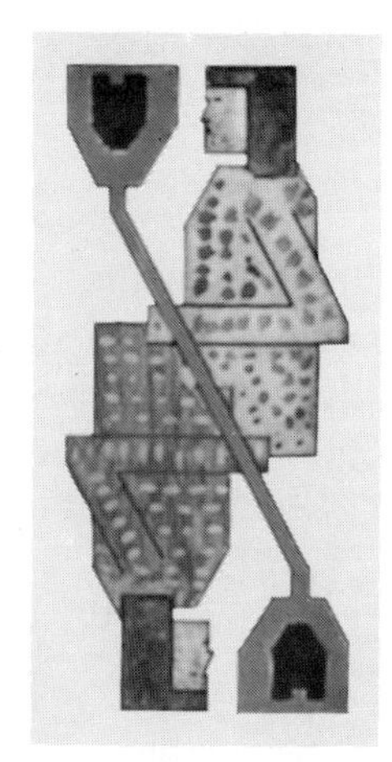

Playing cards designed by Schoenberg

Just as an orchestra and a harpsichord can sound like the shuffling of cards, so can the piano sound like an orchestra. In the *Five Easy Pieces* for piano duet one can hear balalaikas, Spanish guitars, mandolins, percussion instruments, clarions dented tubas, and all kinds of other instruments heard in a village square or café. Stravinsky quietened down the rumbustious holiday spirits of these pieces in the orchestral version he later made. The two *Suites* have become pieces for salon orchestra, suitable for young people's concerts filled with well-behaved children.

But the *Five Easy Pieces* are an exception, as are the other eleven piano pieces in which all kinds of instruments are suggested: the *Three Easy Pieces* and, up to a point, *Les cinq doigts*. (The orchestral version of *Les cinq doigts*, precisely like the other pieces for four hands, are easy to programme in promenade concerts.) The rest of Stravinsky's piano music *sounds* like piano music. The *Sonata for Piano*, the *Serenade in A*, the piano part of *Duo concertant*, none can be orchestrated. They are not written for the 'muted upright' on which Stravinsky composed, but for the same concert grand on which *Movements* and the *Concerto for Piano and Wind* are performed.

This grand piano is the musical instrument modelled least after the human voice. Its tone is no 'tone', just as its black is not a colour. Its tone has no real duration. Romantic and impressionistic composers considered this a limitation and geared their music towards overcoming this limitation. They loved to sit behind their autumnal-imbued grand piano, letting the instrument 'sing' and suggest a world of colours, greater and more varied than the world of the symphony orchestra.

Stravinsky's piano is the black grand, the instrument for which Gottlieb Schröter—inspired by Pantaleon Hebenstreit's playing of the dulcimer—was one of the first to design a mechanism. The keyboard is a portrait of Stravinsky's musical brain.

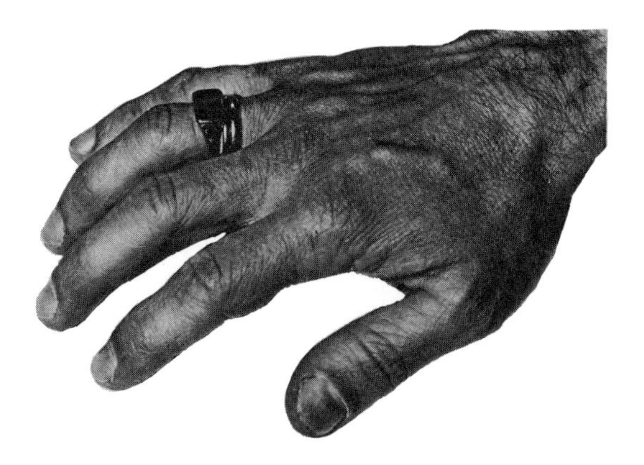

1917—*Les Noces* (*Svadebka*)

In 1926 the Viennese avant-garde magazine *Musikblätter des Anbruch* dedicated a special number to the subject of 'Musik und Maschine'. 'Maschine' in this case meant, in particular, the player piano, or pianola, an automatic or semi-automatic piano that replaced the ten fingers of the pianist with eighty-eight artificial fingers, programmed on rolls of perforated paper. According to H. H. Stuckenschmidt, one of Germany's most prominent advocates of new music, the 'last two years have been crucial. The first compositions for mechanical instruments have already been composed, the first performances have already taken place.' The writer had the Donaueschinger Musiktage in mind, where compositions specially written for the Welte piano—by, among others, Hindemith (*Toccata*) and Ernst Toch (*Der Jongleur*)—had been played. The opportunity offered by the so-called Welte system of reproduction in which live piano-playing could be directly recorded with a high degree of accuracy in the dynamics was not used by these composers. The pieces were not 'played in', but directly punched on to the music roll.

In the same issue of *Anbruch*, Ernest Toch called the heart of this mechanical music 'Kühle'. This 'Kühle' was not 'lack of warmth', but the 'presence of non-warmth'. Toch was interested primarily in music that 'could no longer be performed at all by human beings, but exclusively by mechanical instruments', music that 'is composed in or proceeds from the spirit of the instrument'.

Toch was not the only one interested in exploiting the specific possibilities of the pianola. Stravinsky declared, upon his arrival in New York, that he was not going to compose during this tour, but make new versions of his compositions for pianola. This was in 1925, when the pianola had reached the pinnacle of its popularity, with an estimated one in three American households owning one. 'Not a "photograph of my playing", as Paderewski has made of his, through recordings . . . but rather a "lithograph", a full and permanent record of tone combinations that are beyond my ten poor fingers to perform.' Apparently, Satie's words of admiration from 1922 in *Les Feuilles libres*, responding to the first Paris concert where mechanical music was presented, were still ringing in his ears. Satie had, in that article, compared photography with lithography.

The history of the pianola stretches over the first three decades of this century, pre-and post-history excluded. More than two million pianolas were built in the United States alone in this period. Production during the peak of popularity in the twenties reached a quarter of a million a year. The most famous companies included Hupfeld in Germany, Pleyel in France, and, the biggest of them all, the Aeolian Company, originally an American factory. The Aeolian Company sprouted so many subsidiaries at the beginning of this century that it grew into a gigantic industrial empire greatly resembling a modern multinational. One of its subsidiaries, the Orchestrelle Company, contributed towards the war effort during the First World War by building, in its English piano factory, fighter planes which, once in the air, encountered Germany planes made in the Steck pianola factory, owned by this same Orchestrelle Company.

Just as impressive as the production figures of the pianola and piano roll industry are the quantity and diversity of types of pianolas and piano rolls. The jungle of the so-called automatic musical instruments industry can only be compared to the current jungle of the gramophone and hi-fi industry. The comparison is not arbitrary, since the pianola was primarily a sound-reproduction system. The juke-box is the electric successor of the coinola (a pianola that played only after inserting a coin) and the gramophone record is the successor of the reproduction rolls of Welte, Duo-Art (a product of Aeolian), Ampico, and DEA, on which one could hear original, and 'original' piano compositions or arrangements played by Rubinstein, Cortot, Prokofiev, as well as Teddy Wilson (as imitated by J. Lawrence Cook), Art Tatum (as imitated by J. Lawrence Cook), or Fats Waller (as imitated by J. Lawrence Cook). The majority of the repertoire on Duo-Art was, just as that of today's record industry, light classics and entertainment music—foxtrots, waltzes, marches, opera potpourris. The piano roll was also similar to the phonograph record since it allowed the performer to sound more perfect than he ever could in reality. The reproduction rolls actually outdid the gramophone on this point: a wrong note (a wrong hole in the roll) could simply be covered over and replaced with the right note (the right perforation made by hand). Intervention of this type by the human hand made even the impossible, such as chromatic glissandos, possible.

The development of the gramophone record, and to a certain extent of the radio, brought about the downfall of the pianola. Not only did the gramophone record make the instrument superfluous, it absorbed it as well. The gramophone record on which old piano rolls are recorded is an example of music reproduction reproduction.

The history of the pianola is 99 per cent the history of a medium of reproduction. In this form, the instrument has value only as a curiosity and belongs in the museum between the musical box and the barrel organ. The history of the pianola as a means of production is the history of a missed opportunity.

The first to exploit the possibilities of the instrument in order to enrich musical language was the American composer Conlon Nancarrow. The pianola in his compositions does not merely sound like a piano played by a superhuman virtuoso, but like a mechanical synthesizer producing sounds that one would think possible only with the assistance of electronics. The most peculiar fact is that Nancarrow was converted once and for all to the pianola in 1949, only after the instrument had been put away forever in the attic of musical history.

It is odd that the pianola hardly played a role in the new music of the twenties considering that the aesthetic of the mechanical was a decisive factor in musical thought during that period. Composers wrote pieces in the image of 'a watch', 'a well-oiled engine', 'a sewing machine', or 'a tractor'. When, at long last, *Anbruch* in 1926 began a new column on 'Musikautomaten', just prior to the special number on 'Musik und Maschine', the pianola had already had its longest day. It was a little late to observe that 'the importance of the *boîte à musique* lies in its nature of enriching the language and not (or only slightly) in the possibility of a fixed interpretation'. The list of composers who wrote specially for the pianola is limited, just as limited as the interest in their experimentations was. Much has been written about the pianola as juke-box.

Little has been written about the already very meagre history of the pianola as a 'language-enriching' instrument.

It is generally assumed that Stravinsky was the first to write an original composition for the pianola—*Étude* (1917). According to the composer, his interest in the instrument was awoken in 1914 when he attended a demonstration by the Aeolian Company in London. Since the Ballets Russes had for two years been making use of pianola arrangements for rehearsals, it is quite possible that before his visit to London Stravinsky was already familiar with the instrument.

The score of the *Étude* is notated on six staves. The Aeolian Company, who commissioned the work, produced the official roll. Stravinsky perforated a roll for himself with his own hands.

The *Étude* was not intended for the fully-automatic pianola, but for the more current semi-automatic pianola. The player of this instrument, the so-called pianolist, is not unlike Nabokov's Martin Edelweiss, who 'in childhood, seated on the floor with his feet resting on the piano pedals . . . would hold the stool with its round, revolving seat between his legs and handle it like a steering wheel, taking splendid curves at full speed, pushing the pedal again and again (which made the piano hum), and slitting his eyes against the imaginary wind'. The pianolist *steers* his instrument: the pumping pedals are regulated by the feet, and he uses his hands to regulate control knobs for dynamics and tempo as notated on the roll. The *Étude* is a musical portrait of Madrid city life and a genuine performance of the piece is just as tiring and just as exciting as riding along the Gran Via in a pedal-wagon.

It is said that Stravinsky's only original composition for pianola (*Madrid*, the last of the *Quatre études*, is an orchestral arrangement of it) leaves the superhuman possibilities of the instrument unused. And indeed, most of the notes of the original can be found in the arrangement that Stravinsky's son Soulima made for two pianos. Not all the notes. A few typical virtuosities of the pianola have fallen victim to the limitations of the human machine, such as repeated semiquaver triplets becoming semiquavers. Another instance, of shattered octaves becoming unisons, is shown in Examples 1 and 2. But even if such passages could be performed live, the result would still be different since there is a difference in dynamic nuance and articulation, as well as a difference

Ex. 1

Étude for pianola, bar 22

Ex. 2

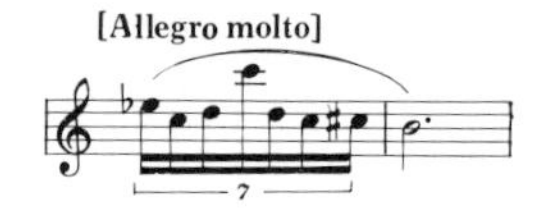

Madrid (for two pianos), bar 23

in acoustical space, between a performance on two pianos (doing it on one piano is physically impossible) and one on pianola. Besides, the pianola just does not resonate like a normal piano. According to Stravinsky the pianola 'compares with the glossy, emulsified "tone" of a Chopin recitalist's Steinway somewhat as a Model-T Ford compares with a six-door Cadillac'.

The pianola in the *Étude* has a polemic relationship with the piano as embedded in the nineteenth-century tradition in which 'the work is for the interpreter the tragic and stirring *mise en scène* of his own emotions' (Liszt). The automatization of the interpretation was the paradoxical consequence of striving towards de-automatization of musical thought. Interpretation became reproduction.

This de-automatization by mechanical means became complete in *Les Noces*. Nicolas Nabokov called *Les Noces* a ritual 'and the mechanism of the ritual is by no means "motoric". It is like clockwork. The ritual unwinds like the springs of one of those quaint *Euphoniums* of the XIX century, with their holed-up metal discs. It slows down mechanically without any loss of pitch, contrary to the early gramophone.' This characteristic is most clearly present in the unfinished version of *Les Noces* from 1919. The instrumentation of that version calls for two cimbaloms, harmonium (double manual), pianola, and percussion. A later planned version for an ensemble of *four* pianolas (two of which replaced the cimbaloms) was never executed. The mechanical cimbalom that Pleyel was supposed to construct for Stravinsky has yet to come.

The most authentic of the three more-or-less completed versions of *Les Noces* is the one from 1919. It comes closest to the ideal of a 'cérémonie scénique'. It is more conductor-proof than any other of Stravinsky's compositions: the conductor is conducted by the pianola, and the roll has been perforated directly, not with a pianist as intermediary. The sound of the orchestra is somewhat rickety: the pianola sounds like a second-hand piano,[1] the harmonium like a bad imitation of an organ and the cimbalom something

[1] At least, if the pianola part is not played—as is usually the case with the sporadic performances of this version—on three pianos. Stravinsky never completed the 1919 version of *Les Noces* because he was afraid that the problems of synchronizing the mechanical and non-mechanical music were insoluble. The English pianolist Rex Lawson proved that these problems can be solved, when he assisted in an authentic peformance of this version in 1981 conducted by Boulez.

like a do-it-yourself harpsichord. If the final version of *Les Noces* for four pianos and percussion (not including the vocal parts) is an electric locomotive, then the 1919 version is a steam engine; not any less powerful, but noisier (Ex. 3 and 4), no less solidy constructed, but with more frills (Ex. 5 and 6). Stravinsky was able to hear the first performance of the 1919 version a few years before his death.

Ex. 3

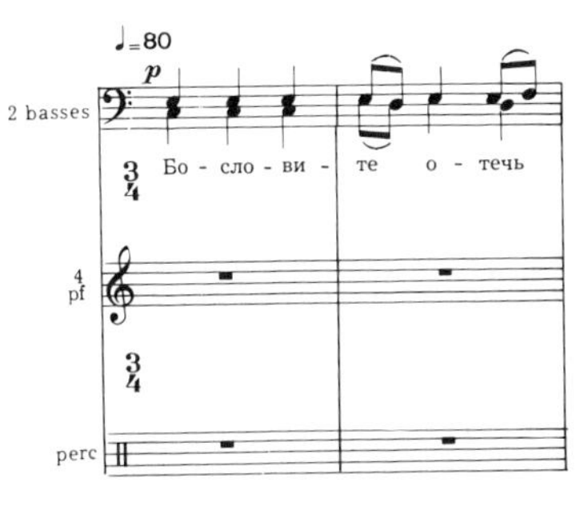

Les Noces (1923 version) [50]

Ex. 4

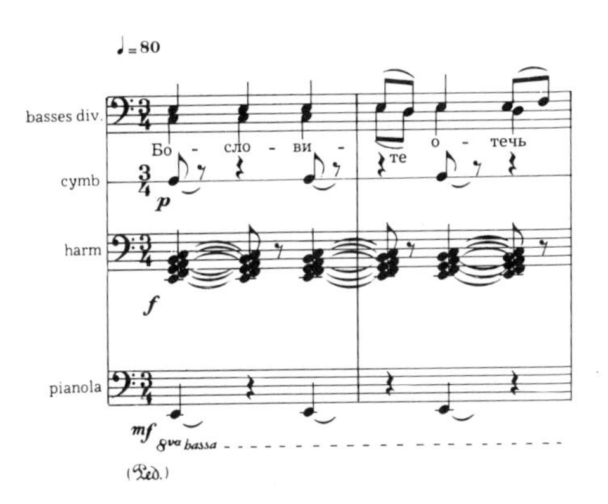

Les Noces (1919 version) [50]

Money matters. Money was the reason Stravinsky arranged one old composition after an another in the twenties, first for Pleyel, then for Aeolian. In 1924, when he signed a seven-year contract with Duo-Art Reproducing Piano for between $2,000 and $4,000 a year requiring him to make in total twenty-eight records, it was no longer for the good of mechanical music or to directly make perforated rolls of scores, but for the mass production of authorized 'recordings'. It is not surprising that this contract was dissolved before fulfilment. The pianola had had its heyday by 1930. Two years

Ex. 5

Les Noces (1923 version) 58 7

Ex. 6

Les Noces (1919 version) [58]5

S.
A.
T.
B.
G.Cl

previously, the first gramophone record on which Stravinsky conducted his own works had appeared. All of those poor people who had broken open their piggy-banks in order to invest in a pianola and collect the complete works of Stravinsky on rolls were rudely awoken from their dream by the master:

...j'estime que le phonographe est actuellement le meilleur instrument de transmission de la pensée des maitres de la musique moderne

(IGOR STRAWINSKY)

On Montage Technique

The *Symphonies of Wind Instruments* is an aloof composition. That may explain the vicissitudes of the piece. It began with the first performance. The piece must have sounded like a brass band tuning up, coming as it did after a big orchestral work. In 1921, within sophisticated concert life, winds were still associated with military and brass bands, with banality, with fat men wearing caps, playing in the town square. And the sight seen during the première of the *Symphonies* did not do much to contradict this. After the performance of the Marches from Rimsky-Korsakov's *Le Coq d'Or*, almost the entire orchestra marched off the stage. The remaining twenty-three musicians were separated from the conductor by a gulf of many yards and a forest of empty music stands, looking a little like naughty schoolchildren who had to stay after class.

In the fifties, a piece for winds evoked, at best, a feeling of endearment: all right you lot, you can have a chance now. Thank goodness it did not happen too often. In the Netherlands, only Willem van Otterloo[1] ventured once in a while to perform his own *Sinfonietta* for winds, an exciting musician's piece that would be great as a sound-track for a children's Western.

Stravinsky's *Symphonies* is not an exciting musician's piece, and one will not hear any heroic blaring, like in the Fanfare of Dukas's *La Péri.* Short, bitten-off motifs, alternating with unspectacular, held chords, rounded off after ten minutes with a meagre, cold 'chorale'. One is forced to the conclusion, wrote an English critic in 1922, 'that disordered polyphony of this kind would be quite as well accomplished if left to the orchestral players themselves'.

Up until the fifties, the piece was rarely performed. The few conductors who nevertheless wanted to include it in a programme received a letter from Stravinsky full of instructions and corrections. It was not until 1947 that Stravinsky decided to revise the score completely, and five years later a new score appeared, even more direct, scanty, and stricter than the original. This score, too, was not played so often. Boulez was one of the few who regularly performed it—that is, before he became a Wagner specialist. He probably considered the piece a historical example of *penser la musique aujourd'hui:* montage form, serialization, de-tonalization, structural orchestration.

[1] Willem van Otterloo (1907–78), Dutch composer and conductor [trans.].

The genesis of the piece is just as bizarre as its history. Fragments can be found in three different sketchbooks. Most of them are for harmonium. If Stravinsky had ever visited Schoenberg's Verein für musikalische Privataufführungen—where a harmonium was rarely missing—musicologists certainly would have written essays about influence. But Stravinsky never visited the Verein, not even when a couple of his songs were performed there. Webern, who was there, thought these songs to be, by the way, 'ausserordentlich gelungen'; 'Strawinsky war herrlich',[2] he wrote to Alban Berg. (To Craft, these sketches for harmonium go to prove that Stravinsky unjustifiably claimed that his musical ideas were always inseparable from a specific timbre. Other examples are more convincing—like the three orchestrations of *Les Noces*—for is a harmonium, as it were, anything other than a wind ensemble attached to a keyboard?) In the sketchbooks mentioned above are also fragments for violin or cello solo accompanied by winds. Some of these reached their final destination in the *Concertino* for string quartet (that was later arranged as—or rather, returned to—the *Concertino for Twelve Instruments:* obbligato violin, obbligato cello and ten winds), some in the *Symphonies of Wind Instruments.*

Before the completion of the *Symphonies*, part of it—the final chorale—had been published in a version for piano in a supplement to *La Revue musicale.* This supplement was entitled *Tombeau de Claude Debussy*, appearing in December 1920—a delayed reaction considering the master had already been in his grave for two and a half years.

The *Symphonies of Wind Instruments* displays its birthmark in a good way: montage is not only a principle of construction, but also a structural principle. This is—musically announced already in *Le Sacre du printemps*—an entirely new way of dealing with form.

The concept of montage, gradually becoming a magic word in modern art, was originally part of theatre vocabulary. Plays in Belgium are still 'montaged', not staged. The word means: to build, to make stacks (like the index cards, for example, on which Joris Ivens[3] registered the shots for *The Bridge*), to give form by means of assembling parts. Meyerhold's productions were called a 'montage of attractions' by Eisenstein; they were 'suites' of contrasting, consequential, dramatic episodes.

Eisenstein, himself a theatre director, came to formulate a theory of montage helped along by developments in literature (Russian Formalism) and

[2] 'exceptionally successful', 'Stravinsky was superb' [trans].

[3] Joris Ivens (1898–), Dutch political film-maker, known for such films as *Spanish Earth* (1937), *Indonesia Calling*, and *Regen* (*Rain*, 1929), a film with music by Hanns Eisler depicting an outburst of rain in Amsterdam [trans.].

politics. Both the First World War and the Russian Revolution greatly changed the way man viewed the world. His image of reality, and therefore reality in his imagination, was literally blown to smithereens.

The continuity of the story, of the drama, was ruptured. The Formalists had already introduced the concept of 'decomposition'.

Around 1925, the time of *Strike* and *Battleship Potemkin*, Eisenstein formulated his political theory on 'dialectical' or contrasting montage technique: adjacent shots should relate in such a way that together A and B will produce C, which is not actually recorded on film.

That does not sound very epoch-making any more, but it created a way of filming that was diametrically opposed to that of Eisenstein's contemporaries. Even his friend Pudovkin considered montage no more than a method 'which controls the "psychological guidance" of the spectator'. Montage was, according to Pudovkin, 'the complex, pumping heart . . . that was to support narrative'.

Eisenstein's montage of 'shocks', however, introduced a way to make films in which the montage became *evident*, thereby vesting it with intrinsic meaning. Logical or compelling sequences were avoided: the images themselves became 'verifiable' and referred exclusively to their own meaning. In this way montage became a part of the contents.

In 1920, the year that the *Symphonies of Wind Instruments* was composed, setting out for the movies meant going to the fair and seeing the Keystone Cops, Chaplin, Mack Sennett.

Pure artistic experiments in film montage thrived towards the end of the First World War. Stravinsky, who met Marinetti though not Eisenstein, almost certainly saw works by dadaists such as Richter, Eggeling—*La Symphonie diagonale* (1924)—and René Clair; perhaps even Robert Wiene's *The Cabinet of Dr Caligari* (1919), in which case, the insipid dénouement—where we see that the Doctor is mad and then that everything was but a dream—must have seemed to him a much too easy pretext for making a film about a madhouse.

Stravinsky, who later regularly went to the cinema and became a television addict (preferring cowboy and animal films), used compositional techniques in the *Symphonies of Wind Instruments* analogous to the film experiments of the same period: short, continually-returning fragments each with their own identity, abruptly alternated with contrasting structures, every one of which can be defined by a limited number of characteristics. One of the characteristics of these characteristics is that they are not developed. Fernand Léger's *Ballet Mécanique*, for example, complies fairly well with this definition, but was made six years after the *Symphonies*. One could say that the *Symphonies of Wind Instruments* was the vanguard.

The fact that this composition can better be compared with the film experiments from the twenties than with the montage of the Western is not only based on historical consequence. It is also based on the contents of the montaged fragments and the way in which they are montaged.

In cowboy films, the sequence of independent images is (and always was) subordinate to the telling of the story: the whole is more than the sum of the parts. In the historical experimental films—and the same is true for Stravinsky—the whole is less than the sum of the parts since each part retains its own self-contained identity. The montage itself, being one of these parts, also retains its identity, in the sense of that which cuts.

Merely six different musical ideas are used in the *Symphonies of Wind Instruments*. These ideas all return several times, barely transfigured, and sometimes so cursory that the listener starts to think that any segment lasting a bit longer is merely a delay in the montage. It is the deferral of the interruption of the continuation. The music becomes a double negation.

A more cheerful contemporary of montage is the collage. This nimble kindred spirit, dressed in train tickets, spectacles, and toilet paper, also handled music. One can hear it in the *Groupe des Six*. In 1917 Satie conquered the world in Paris with his *Parade* of typewriters; many a ballet replete with sailors, whores, polkas, and tangos were to follow. But none was linked to the aloof world of the *Symphonies of Wind Instruments*. Stravinsky never used *objets trouvés*. The objets he uncovered, such as Tchaikovsky's *Le Baiser de la fée*, he *dis*covered himself.

There is a considerable difference between collage and montage. In collage, the relationship between the various elements is imposed exclusively from outside. In montage, the parts are related in a material aspect (for example, harmonically). The collage externalizes the structure of the montage into a colourful flea market. In collage, the separate elements are less important than the contrast which they form among themselves. In montage, the contrast between the structurally related elements causes one to seek the identity of the separate elements. The connection between the separate elements in the *Symphonies of Wind Instruments* can best be illustrated in terms of tempo. All the elements have their own tempo, but the various tempi are arithmetically proportional (2 : 3, 3 : 4) to the basic tempo of the piece, the heartbeat of the final chorale (♩ = 72). It is, however, puzzling that in a rhythmically perfect performance, the secret of this proportion is not revealed. The relationship between the tempi only becomes evident in a performance just barely deviating from the exact 2 : 3 and 3 : 4, in which each part, in accordance with its musical identity, receives 'its own tempo'.

Stravinsky knew that. Nothing would have been easier than to notate the piece in one tempo, using triplets or semiquavers in the faster sections. This kind of notation would have guaranteed precise execution of the tempi.

Stravinsky's choice of varying the note values is a choice for the paradox of the correct wrong tempo, for the 'verification' of the material and its 'dialectical' montage. Only because of montage C does fragment A become A and B become B.

And only during this last sentence, Stravinsky would, leaning over slightly, have placed his hand behind his ear and ask: 'что вы скажите?'

A Kind of Brecht

Enemies should be killed by shooting at their images.
Bertolt Brecht

Brecht was a confirmed communist. Reactionary critics who, when writing on Brecht, speak of 'the pitfall of dogmatism into which many an artist stumbles when finding himself in a creative crisis', are knocking at the wrong door. If ever Brecht was dogmatic (as in, perhaps, the radical *Lehrstücke*), it was for political and not for artistic reasons. The form Brecht gave to his works was, in the first place, a result of a political attitude. It was a question of life or death for an anarchistic anti-bourgeois like Brecht to fight the onset of Fascism in the Germany of the twenties (political exploitation of unemployment, racism and rancour) with words and action. Fascism: the grand evocation of the myth of 'race', the massive culture of ruins, the pomp and circumstance of the immutable, the empty gesture of empty grandeur.

Brecht was concerned with completely the opposite. His plays give shape to the changeable; they are about the constant changeability of human thought and human behaviour, about the continual struggle between passion and intellect, between good and bad, between surprising and being surprised. Galileo disavows the absolute truth of science because he prefers to eat well. Galileo is not a monumental hero, or, if you will, an anti-hero, he is merely a model, an example of ambiguous behaviour, just as Stravinsky's *Tango* is an ambiguous image of a tango.

Anyone who sees in Brecht's Galileo a man tormented by inner contradictions does not understand Brecht's way of writing. 'People who suffer bore me', Brecht attributes to Galileo. The emotion is no spontaneous outburst, it is ritual, as in Chinese theatre. The actor takes his hands from his face and turns as pale as death: he had white powder on his hands. Brecht called this *gestus*, which evokes alienation and results in insight, not in empathizing with the play. The audience, or the listener in the case of Stravinsky, is witness to an act, the effect of which is the opposite of the 'feeling of naturalness' that so-called great art gives us (beauty as a dream). 'Das ist die ewige Kunst!' ['That is eternal art'] shouts Jack in *Mahagonny* when he hears someone playing the piano in E flat major.

Alienation for Brecht is, besides being the outcome of a specific way of writing proceeding from a political attitude, a way of acting: the actor has at his disposal the means to transform 'being compelled'—which may well move the audience, but renders it helpless—into 'facing the situation'. This 'facing the situation' does not merely direct one's attention more to the nature and cause of behaviour, but especially raises the audience from will-less accomplice to what Brecht calls: co-producer. The attitude of the first audience, the actor, 'should be one of a man who is astounded and contradicts'. He will quote. He will not play someone deceived, but play the role of someone who says: 'While he furiously threw up his arms, he spoke: "I've been deceived" '. This kind of momentary historicizing—a look through the inverted inverted telescope—emphasizes detachment, just as placing history in the present does (looking through the inverted telescope). This detachment is advantageous in two ways: it promotes rational insight and is also surprising and amusing. 'From the first it has been the theatre's business to entertain people, as it also has of all the other arts', says Brecht. That is exactly what the clown does, who, after protracted investigation finally realizes what the violin in his hands is, plays a few bars of *Paganiniana* perfectly, and then breaks the instrument into tiny pieces and starts nibbling them. The clown commentating on Paganini is a copy which is better than the original. That is why *Le Baiser de le fée* is better than most of Tchaikovsky's piano pieces and *Perséphone* better than Massenet. 'We must realize that copying is not so despicable as people think', according to Brecht. 'Copying is primarily: carrying out procedures, reproducing expressions, taking on attitudes.' It is no longer surprising that the Latin word *componere* also means 'to adopt an attitude'.

The way in which history is placed in the present is a technique shared by Brecht and Stravinsky and used not merely to adapt historial works of art (Bach, Shakespeare), but especially to disclose the author's or composer's own reality in terms of a historical metaphor. The Chinese fairy-tale which was the model for *Der gute Mensch von Sezuan* can be compared to the dragging Protestant part-song which was the model for the chorale in *L'Histoire du soldat.* Even the montage form, the alternation of songs, dialogues, quotations, and acted-out scenes that we know from Brecht can already be found in the score of *L'Histoire du soldat*: the first performance of Stravinsky's music theatre piece was in 1918, nine years before the première of *Mahagonny* (*Songspiel*). In 1927, while *Oedipus Rex* is being opened, Brecht cries out: 'One must simply copy that'.

For the history of twentieth-century art, the similarities of techniques which Stravinsky and Brecht used are more important than differences between

Stravinsky and Brecht. *Aufstieg und Fall der Stadt Mahagonny* is an opera which Brecht believed to have 'launched [a change] which goes far beyond formal matters and begins for the first time to affect the theatre's social function'. Stravinsky—if Brecht's words had ever reached his ears—in all probability would not even have understood what Brecht was talking about. The differences between Brecht and Stravinsky, therefore, concern especially content. While Brecht, in *Der Jasager und der Neinsager*, uses a Japanese Noh play to analyse historically and materialistically the master-servant relationship in order to make the possibility of changes in that relationship evident, Stravinsky dwells on mystifying orientalism in *Le Rossignol*—an opera from 1914 based on a fairy-tale by a Danish romanticist about a Chinese emperor. (Look! That Japanese jewelry box on Ravel's piano; the East, mysterious, enchanting, truly breathtaking, how surprising, those strange customs in faraway lands; but not quite so far away: the trips to Spain made by Diaghilev and his friends, followed by the rest of the Parisian *beau-* and *demi-monde*, skirting revolutions in their Daimlers and Hispano-Suizas, making a large detour around the corpses, and photographing flamencos all the while. Der Flamenco lässt sich photographieren. And beyond Spain, buying waterpipes in Fez—a pinch of cocaine as a souvenir for Jean—and on the way back, crying in front of the Caravaggios in Venice and chatting about the *géométrie secrète* of the Renaissance painters. Henri Sauguet, later to become a composer of popular film music, noticed that the caviar was being served in soup bowls at one of Misia Sert's parties.)

The personages in Stravinsky's operas are mythicalized. Whereas Brecht uses the devil as a metaphor for a crafty merchant, Stravinsky, in *The Rake's Progress*, uses a crafty merchant as a metaphor for the devil. As far as Stravinsky's instrumental music is concerned, a metaphor is made out of (musical) reality. 'Greek' in *Orpheus* is the metaphor of the Phrygian mode.

The apotheosis in *Apollon musagète*—with its compelling, steady tempo and its languid harmonic rhythm—is nothing other than a moulding of the catharsis in Greek drama, which is the consummation of so many of Stravinsky's instrumental works (*Symphonies of Wind Instruments*, *Three Pieces* for string quartet, *Symphony in C*). 'Dynamic calm' enters (although it had been there from the start). Yet the calm is that of a summer day with a chance of snow. That sounds somewhat un-Brechtian, and we realize that Brecht condemned suggesting purification, overcoming conflict and suffering, in traditional theatre. But it remains to be seen if the dissimilarities between the writer and the composer are as large as suggested by this formulation. Wim Markus called Stravinsky's apotheoses 'the actual launching of the work of art'. The apotheosis is 'more real' than the preceding montages, comparable to the announcements of the occurrences to come in Brecht's epic dramas projected onto the curtain before each scene begins. They identify the play as anti-naturalistic and give final form to that which is in the state of formation.

History, too, has taken care that the similarities in form between Brecht and Stravinsky have become more influential than the differences; in progressive middle-class theatre, alienation is used precisely in order to allow the viewer to identify with the emotions of the characters. Underacting has become the watchword for interpretations of realistic social dramas.

1918—*L'Histoire du soldat*

When, in the seventies, *Rolling Stone* editor Jonathan Cott was in Amsterdam for a few days, he visited the harpsichordist and Bach specialist, Gustav Leonhardt. He had a chorale setting by Bach with him and wanted Leonhardt's views on the peculiar harmonies and passing notes. Leonhardt looked at the chorale and asked: 'Do you have the text of the chorale with you?' No, he did not, even though Leonhardt's question was rather obvious: the text could shed some light on why some of those extravagant notes were there.

Still, Cott's quest for truth beyond the text made sense. Even if he had known the text by heart, the secret of the setting's beauty would have remained largely unresolved.

Not only do the spectacular voice-leading, the dissonances, the suddenly appearing chromaticism in the chorale setting belong to the treasures safely stored away in the corners of the basement where the *aleph*—the combination of fast tempo and slow melody that mocks all the laws of time—can be found, no, behind all that, behind the spectacular the ordinary that is anything but ordinary can be found (Ex. 1). The first five beats of Example 1 sound fairly ordinary. That is, there are no shocking harmonies or chromatic passing notes. These do not appear until the next bar, and even there they sound more ordinary than they really are. Since, in reality, something extraordinary is going on in those first five beats.

Ex. 1

J. S. Bach, 'Christus, der uns selig macht', bars 14–18 (from *Organ Works*, vol. v)

The chorale melody in the upper voice—no more complicated than the melody to 'Baa, Baa, Black Sheep'—is in G major. But the first G in the melody is the third of an E minor chord. The second chord, the last beat of the anacrusis, is certainly the dominant of G; but how does the C resolve? It resolves in the wrong direction, only to end up in something which is without doubt a G major chord, including everything—an F♯, for example—except a G. When the G, after some delay, finally is heard, a C appears in the melody on the second beat of the bar (a Stravinsky chord): a C which again, against all the rules, resolves upwards. The chromaticism that follows is of the spectacular kind; we will skip that, just as we will skip over the fact that the entire fragment is a canon in the double octave as well, and that, like a wandering soul from the Middle Ages, a Machaut-like cadence occurs in the fourth bar (see ↓ in Ex. 1).

The more the labyrinth of Stravinsky's music branches out, becoming ever more entangling, the stronger the desire becomes to find something like the Truth: a point in the music—just a couple of bars—in which it is all there, the Aleph, or the mirror in which everything is reflected. And then, suddenly, perhaps only after the thousandth hearing, one knows for certain: these bars from *Orpheus*, they are the précis, the focal point, in which all the riddles are resolved. One is overcome by insight for a euphoric moment. A split second. Something like that cannot last long—euphoria is something which is rather remembered. And then the same thing happens a few weeks later, only this time with the Sarabande from *Agon*. 'Of course, it has to be *Agon*. *Agon* is the undisputed epicentre. Every side road in the history of music, every dance step, all the evenings on the town and dinners in smart restaurants, not to mention all the techniques of orchestration, all the gibberish and irony: it is all brought together in *Agon*. This has got to be explained.' And so the listener is whirled about, from experience to experience, to the most grotesque extremes: 'Those simple piano pieces, *Les cinq doigts*, in which almost everything is left out. Is that not *really* the music which provides the true insight?'

Some music digs deep without being profound. It bores down into the deepest depths, only to reveal that there is nothing there to discover. What is truly profound is usually hidden just below the surface, perhaps in very simple children's pieces with just a few notes, three, four, five, for three, four, five fingers. But then the right notes, or the right wrong notes. 'I played the wrong wrong notes', Thelonius Monk lamented, unhappy about a concert he had just given.

The Great Choral from *L'Histoire du soldat*: a row of four-voiced chords of defying meagreness, almost nothing, but still, the *inquisición* of four hundred years of Protestant church music.

Creaking and groaning, the chords push their way forward through a bleak landscape. It is an inverted crusade, the pillaging only becoming worse and worse. At figure [4], the all-time low of the First World War is reached. It is 1918, Switzerland, and although Luther, Zwingli, and Calvin are protecting you, nevertheless, the heaviest fighting ever to have occurred in Europe is taking place close by.

Here is the focal point, here is where Stravinsky summarizes himself in fifteen chords:

Ex. 2

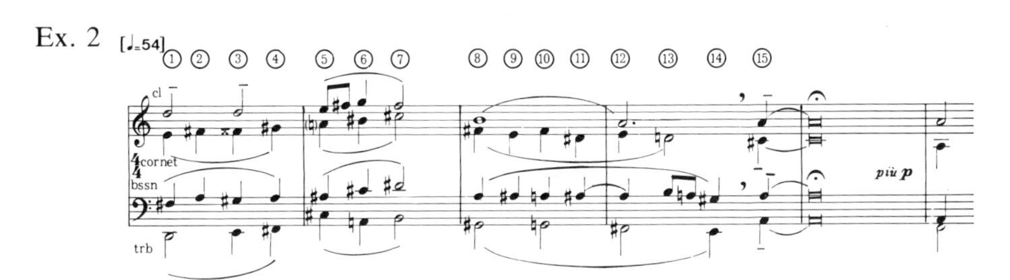

Chord 1 is from *Le Roi des étoiles*, but remains sounding up to the *Septet*. It is the pandiatonicism of the *Mass*.

Chord 2 is from Bach. D major. Here it is neoclassical.

Chord 3 is octotonic, it has already made an appearance in *Le Roi des étoiles* and will return in the *Variations*. Boulez called it the tic of major-minor.

Chord 4 is created by avoiding:

Ex. 3

that is, avoiding octotony in the alto and avoiding parallel chords. The rule of forbidden parallels holds for the entire chorale. Even what is literally parallel does not sound like it (Ex. 4). Chord 5 is a variant of chord 3. There is a C♯ instead of an F♯ in the bass to avoid repeating chord 3 a tone higher.

Ex. 4

Chord 6 = chord 3 and
Chord 7 = chord 1.

Together, the seven chords also form a modulation—referring to Bach—from D major to B minor, as strung together by amateur organists (not only Swiss) every Sunday on romantic little organs, or preferably harmoniums in small churches (Ex. 5). This is an example of notes that are wrongly right (wrong).

Ex. 5

But back to the Great Choral.

From the first chord onwards becoming more obvious after chord 8, the chords develop according to their own, new rules. According to the main rule, all the harmonies (chords 3, 4, 5, 6, 8, 9, 10, 11, 12, and 14) are, in principle, built up of both a fourth or a fifth and a seventh or a ninth. The combination of chromaticism and diatonicism—which can take on all sorts of shapes: chromatically-sounding diatonicism, diatonically-sounding chromaticism—is a consistent characteristic of style for Stravinsky.

Chord 8 is a textbook case. It is polysemic. With an added B♯, it is a dominant seven-nine chord in root position. At the same time, it is a reference to a Tchaikovskian four-three chord with a suspension (Ex. 6). It is also chromatic, and it is also bare.

Ex. 6

Chord 9 is a motto of Stravinsky (Ex. 7). Because of its ingredients, it can be used in early as well as late works. Even Bach uses it, though with him the A♯ is a suspension.

Ex. 7

Chord 10 is pandiatonic. The added major seventh is probably an early influence of light music. Milhaud will use the major seventh five years later as a showy *septime ajoutée* in the final chord of *La Création du monde.* The ninth in the bass becomes something of a fetish for Stravinsky around that time: in the piano music (*Piano-Rag-Music*, the piano part to *Duo Concertant*) as well as in the orchestra, for example *Renard* and *Pulcinella* (and gratefully pilfered by Poulenc in *Les Biches*). The *Histoire* chorale was apparently composed at the piano.

Passing-chord 11 leads to the most vulgar chord ever produced by octotony, chord 12, much loved by big-band arrangers and striptease accompanists.

Chord 14 is a combination of dominant and tonic, denying and confirming the tonal functions at one and the same time; the resolution of this chord, chord 15, sounds like an embarrassing revelation—like the comedian who polishes the moon. But something is going on even with this chord: since it has no fifth, it sounds almost like a deceptive cadence (*Trugschluss*) with a doubled third. (Bach used this chord fairly often as well. Example 8 is from 'Es ist das Heil uns kommen her', a chorale in the fifth volume of the *Orgelwerke*, the volume including the chorale variations on 'Vom Himmel hoch'.)

Ex. 8

The deceptive cadencing of chord 15 is an alleged deceptive cadencing (double deception). The genuine deceptive cadence does not occur until the next bar. But that chord is part of the continuation of the chorale and not a cadence, so that it too is guilty of double deception. This F major chord, third in the bass, without a fifth, sounds Russian, more Russian than the entire *Firebird*.

But neither is the Great Choral from *L'Histoire du soldat* the Aleph. Not because its beauty cannot be described, but because what is being described is transient. Even the 'I' of Borges notices happily after a few sleepless nights that oblivion visits him once more. Sometimes it is *Orpheus*, then *Les Noces*, then again *Canticum Sacrum*, suddenly there can be no doubt—the end of the third movement, Aria II, from the *Concerto in D for Violin*, those two flutes and the solo violin, they go beyond all description. 'In that single gigantic instant I saw millions of acts both delightful and awful; not one of them amazed me more than the fact that all of them occupied the same point of time, without overlapping or transparency.'

'. . . infinite wonder, infinite pity' (Borges).

On Authenticating and on Making Current

> My ideal has always been to play music not from our own time . . . in such a way that an imaginary listener from then would recognize the piece.
>
> Gustav Leonhardt

Today, Bach is played better than he was eighty years ago. Bach has been authenticated. Performance practice today on historical instruments as developed by Nikolaus Harnoncourt and Gustav Leonhardt is not better because it is authentic, but is authentic because these musicians have a better insight into Bach's music. Their playing style not only differs from the romantic orchestral style, but also from the anti-romantic 'sewing-machine' interpretations that, though contrasting with the romantic style, none the less hardly elucidated Bach.

Old instruments offer many advantages: the gut of baroque string instruments sounds more transparent and richer in high harmonics; the string orchestra is lighter, more elastic and lively, especially with one player per part. Even the technical disadvantages of the old instruments are advantageous: there is a special reason why the aria 'Zerfliesse, mein Herze' from the St John Passion is in F minor. Bach *knew* that when the transverse flute plays in this key, it sounds as if a shadow has fallen over the instrument. Almost all the notes have to be played with fork fingerings. Bach needed this veiled timbre: 'dein Jesu' is, after all, in this aria just recently 'tot'. Only when the great flute sonata in B minor is played in an old Werckmeister tuning can one hear just how modern the chromaticism of the harpsichord part is.

The use of boys in the choir also has its advantages. We are finally relieved of the Wagner Ladies: with their heaving bosoms and flowered dresses; with a vibrato a mile wide, always much too loud and—in the wrong way—not in tempo; and with bellowing crescendos, as if an infernal gale is blowing up from the Teutonic forests. Good riddance. And now if we could only do something about the male soloists, who sing Bach as if it were a consecrated Viennese *bonbon*, tasted on the lips and tip of the tongue, weighed and licked clean, oh, so dignified and religious, and who continually strive to be polite and nice for the ladies, with no attack whatsoever, but rather with warm crescendos and swells of caramel and fudge: in a word, the Liberaces of baroque music. But one cannot change everything at once. The boys' choirs are at least an enormous step forward; finally one can hear the expressiveness of Bach's notes instead of that of ladies from comic books.[1]

Authenticity is not only a result of better insight into the sound of baroque music, but also of better insight into its dynamics. These dynamics come from the beat and not, as in romantic music, from the bar. The orchestral crescendo, a discovery of Italian opera composers and unjustly credited to the later Mannheim School, was undoubtedly revolutionary, but Bach, assuming he had even heard it, did not avail himself of it. Bach's dynamics never carry across the bar, his music is conceived proceeding from the first beat. This is an essential trait of baroque music: unlike music since Beethoven in which one plays towards a point, baroque music is played proceeding from a point.

Timing in authentic performance practice is also more free than in romantic interpretations, more free, too, than in the 'new objectivity' from the thirties to the fifties. It seems to be so free because it is not free at all: rubato on 'borrowed time' (in general, not equal semiquavers, but a slightly longer first semiquaver compensated by the other three being shorter) leaves the beat intact, differing from romantic rubato on 'stolen time', in which the metre fluctuates, literally being played out of tempo. No matter how precisely Webern notated the rhythm of his music, the continual ritardandi and accelerandi are a consequence of late Romantic thinking.

Rubato in the Baroque—that of 'borrowed time'—gives freedom *within* the tempo: lengthening of values is compensated within the rest of the beat. In France it became a rule, the rule of *inégalité*: play long on the down-beats, and short and light on the up-beats. Rubato on 'stolen time', what nowadays is generally regarded as rubato, had to wait until the Romantic period to flourish, as did ritardandi and accelerandi.

One needs a searchlight to find ritardandi in Stravinsky's music, although written-out ritardandi (comparable to the baroque hemiola) often occur, as in the last four bars of *Apollon Musagète*.

The development of authentic baroque interpretation in the sixties was not only a reaction to romantic performance practice, but also an answer to the anti-romantic clean-up begun in the thirties. Hindemith, Glenn Gould, Landowska, I Musici: they were all a necessary step.

Stravinsky was in the front line of this company. Bach's music, 'pure

[1] The authors mean here specifically Bianca Castafiore, a character from *De Avonturen van Kuifje* (*The Adventures of Tintin*), a classic series of Belgian comic books about a young reporter and his tribulations [trans.].

architecture . . . is played in symphony concerts by Wagnerian orchestras . . . This is what I call a deformation, an attack on music, a great ignorance, a misunderstanding, a stupidity' (*PD*). This statement is more than half a century old. It dates from 1923. In *Poétique musicale* (1942), Stravinsky pleaded for an authentic performance of the St Matthew Passion. That was in the lingering days of the great Mengelberg,[2] when the harpsichord was played only by matrons in home-weave clothes, with their hair tied up in a bun, and when recorder players wore sandals and were vegetarians. 'Its first performance in Bach's lifetime was perfectly realized by a total force of thirty-four musicians . . . nevertheless in our day one does not hesitate to present the work, in complete disregard of the composer's wishes, with hundreds of performers, sometimes almost a thousand. This lack of understanding of the interpreter's obligations, this arrogant pride in numbers, this concupiscence of the many, betray a complete lack of musical education' (*PM*). Does one detect here a slight distaste for symphony orchestras? Twelve years lie between *Le Rossignol* (1914) and *Oedipus Rex* (1926) in which Stravinsky wrote *nothing* for symphony orchestra (*Pulcinella* is by Pergolesi, *Mavra* is for just winds and solo strings), but rather made an important contribution to new instrumental combinations: *L'Histoire du soldat*, for example; *Renard* for seven winds, cimbalom, three percussionists, and five solo strings; *Symphonies of Wind Instruments*.

'If oboes d'amore and da caccia were common I would compose for them. What incomparable instrumental writing is Bach's. You can smell the resin in his violin parts, taste the reeds in the oboes' (*Conv*). Stravinsky said that in 1958, before Harnoncourt's Concentus Musicus recordings in which Stravinsky's conception of Bach became reality for the first time.

Choosing idiosycratic instrumental combinations (the most famous of which is *Les Noces*, and look how much trouble it cost Stravinsky to realize the very timbre for the piece) is also a form of authentication. *L'Histoire du soldat*, *Les Noces*, *Symphonies of Wind Instruments*, *Renard*, none of these can be arranged. Timbre has become a parameter of the musical language, just as with Bach.

Another consequence of this authentication of instrumental timbre is that symphony orchestras must now limit themselves more and more to music specifically written for them. They cannot really play Bach any more, Mozart is getting more difficult, but Stockhausen is fine.

[2] Willem Mengelberg (1871–1951), conductor of the Concertgebouw Orchestra from 1895 to 1941. The tradition of performing the St Matthew Passion of Bach at Easter is of great importance in Holland; it is performed in almost every town, usually with hundreds of performers [trans.].

Authentication is not merely the result of instrumentation. Which instruments and how they sound is only a prerequisite. There is more: the right notes, the right rhythm. Although it might seem otherwise, Stravinsky's *Concerto for Piano and Wind* has more to do with Harnoncourt's Bach than with Hindemith's Bach. The sewing-machine neoclassicists composed à la Bach, Stravinsky composes Stravinsky's Bach. He invents his own style, he makes his Bach contemporary. (Leonhardt and Harnoncourt also do this; their interpretations are typically contemporary, as contemporary as modern European city planning: repairing the old façades, forbidding cars in the city centres, renovating the worker's neighbourhoods; creating new sections of cities with high-rise apartment buildings has become old-fashioned.) Stravinsky's rhythms are the authenticated interpretation of the baroque rubato on 'borrowed time'. Everything is conceived proceeding from the down-beat, but the beat itself has become *inégal*: down becomes up and an up (sometimes a few beats later) turns out to be a down-beat. Even the *Concerto for piano and wind* is first and foremost anti-mechanical. It is the only sewing-machine ever made from catgut.

Ostinato Basses

In the salon of a Swiss villa—the starting-point for a search for Stravinsky's residences circumscribing Lake Geneva—was a Steinway grand. It was blacker than most other Steinways, and also shinier. It was as if the thick carpet of snow outside had continued on indoors.

'I tried out some basses, mostly repeated motifs. If you try to make Stravinsky-like basses, you've got to continually shift the down-beat.'

'Not necessarily. You can just limit your choice of notes. Start with an ostinato bass of a minor third and you'll see that Stravinsky often merely adds the upper octave of the lower note: the bass is in three, but in a four-four bar, like in the *Symphony in Three Movements* (Ex. 1). By the way, did you notice

Ex. 1

how much this sounds like the horn fragment near the end of the "Danse sacrale" written thirty-odd years before?'

'Really simple ostinato basses of a minor third without shifts of the beat—like in French opera, or for that matter, in Russian opera when the czar enters—don't occur very often in Stravinsky.'

'I know of only one example. Somewhere in the third movement of the *Concerto for Piano and Wind*. But in that case, the lowest third is the third *below* the tonic.'

'There are other examples. Like in *Oedipus Rex*. Or in *Symphony in C*, where any musical movement of the main theme is held back as much as possible by the bass, an ostinato of a minor third. Here, though, the notes are the mediant and dominant. Sometimes the irregularities happen simply because of what is left out, because of the rests. Montage technique also means leaving holes.'

'There is a good example of a bar rest in an ostinato in *Jeu de cartes*. After that rest, at [185], the ostinato continues for six bars, utilizing a structure fairly exceptional for Stravinksy: bar 4 is a mirror. Only, it does not mirror the music, but the bars: bar 5 = 3, bar 6 = 2, and bar 7 = 1. A very special mirror unknown to serial composers.'

'In *Dumbarton Oaks*, there is an ostinato of a third, too, although after the first three bars, hardly any note comes on the beat. And still, the fragment does not sound so restive. It sort of seems like the French technique of leaving out the bass on the first beat in order to give the melody more room. But here, the melody has been left out.'

'Chopin often does that, leaving out the bass. The most elegant example is the first page of the Ballade in G minor: the melody is always on the beat, the bass *never*. A completely different story from the Viennese waltz—boom, chick, chick, boom, chick, chick. Chopin is also exacting in his choice of the octave in the bass. In the accompaniment of the Ballade in F minor, the bass is continually in a different octave. That must certainly appeal to a composer like Boulez.'

'Why didn't Stravinsky like Chopin? After all, Chopin is the true classicist among the romantics.'

'Perhaps the classicist Chopin was obscured in the first half of this century by sentimental women who tastelessly played the waltzes and nocturnes, out of tempo and with everything arpeggiated, and then fainted.

'I meant, by the way, these bars from *Dumbarton Oaks*. This fragment from Stravinsky's Brandenburg Concerto has little to do with Bach, and even less with Chopin.' (Ex. 2.)

'The consequence of placing a minor third in the bass, clearly, is that the

Ex. 2

key becomes ambivalent. Is this in B flat major or G minor? This ambiguity is typical of this kind of situation. That is one of the functions of such an ostinato. Though it is true: effective ostinati of a minor third generally are irregular. The final dance in the *Sacre*, to mention a case in point. Not only continual changes of bars, but within those irregular bars, an irregular rhythm in the bass. Stravinsky never writes long passages in which the bass seems to go on automatically. Only B-composers do that. Or C-composers like Orff, when it's time to be *volkstümlich.*'

'What about this, then?' (Ex. 3.)

Ex. 3

Polka (from *Three Easy Pieces* for piano duet)

'Do you really think this is a contradiction? That Polka is a children's piece. The subject is musical simplicity. The upper voice shows that it is not a childish piece, but one that is *about* simplicity. Remember, bad writers write boring books about boring office clerks. The bass just has to make a leap of a fourth here. That is not stupid, that is music about stupid music. At the beginning and end of *Oedipus Rex*, *Symphony in C*, *Concerto for Two Solo Pianos*, you can find steady basses of minor thirds, but the regularity has a special reason: a literary reference or a musical subject of the piece. In *Oedipus Rex*, it is about musical petrification, the choir as sculpture, and about radical de-chromaticization of the musical material. Don't do the obvious, unless you can use it to your advantage. Sweet-talking Mussolini, for example. Don't use an ostinato third to compose a kind of sabre dance, but for exactly the opposite, for something that suddenly appears out of nowhere yet suggests a moving quietude. Wide positions, long note-values. "And the sun descended over the hills." *Perséphone* does that, in the beginning of the third movement: *Perséphone renaissante.* First come triplets in the woodwinds, accompanied by mumbling in the bassoons and then: like sliding into a warm bath.' (Ex. 4.)

'Stravinsky on Ravel's divan, and then falling off.'

'The references to French oratorios are numerous indeed, but the melodrama had already had its day when *Perséphone* was written. He should never have taken that gig from Ida Rubinstein. People talking while the music's going—even if they are gorgeous dancers—is always hopeless. But it is a fabulous piece.'

A Visit to Lake Geneva

Geneva, 29 December 1979

What our eyes first fell upon when entering Geneva were the large, cream-coloured signs on both sides of the Boulevard. On the posters, in large letters—STRAVINSKY. Only not Igor but Theodore. Theodore was the oldest of four children; a quick calculation showed that he was at present just as old as his father was when he composed *Canticum Sacrum* (ad honorem Sancti Marci nominis). Evangelium secundum Marcum XVI.15: 'And he said unto them, "Go ye into all the world, and preach the gospel to every creature" '. Just before the Second World War Theodore wrote *Le Message d'Igor Strawinsky*—a worthy, pious, but none the less rather dull book that, except for the name of the author, does not betray itself as being written by a son. The signs that tell us of an exhibition of his work are great in size and large in number. They suggest a local fame. Sometimes it is not much fun being the son of your father.

We drive along the Quai du Mont-Blanc in the direction of Morges. The direction of *L'Histoire du soldat*, *Ragtime*, *Piano-Rag-Music* and the *Three Pieces* for clarinet solo. The direction of *Cat's Cradle Songs.* And, last but not least, of *Pulcinella.* And the direction of the remainder of 1915–20.

It is not a genuine pilgrimage: that would have begun in Amsterdam. No, a friend of a friend, a Princess Edmond de Polignac, reincarnated exclusively for us, has lent us a country villa on the estate M., near Geneva. And since we are here, why not reconnoitre Stravinsky's Switzerland? And since that Switzerland is more or less congruent with the contour of Lake Geneva, and that contour is not even 150 miles long, it will not have to take more than a day to do it.

The evening before, we made a list of place-names and addresses. That was more trouble than expected. One begins these things with a certain amount of indifference, as if it were not really serious. But the indifference is caused by embarrassment, more feigned than real, and therefore not easily sustained. Such a list gets progressively more and more detailed; if one is going to bother to do something, why not do it properly right from the start? But that is where the trouble begins, since where do you stop? For example, if you want where and when, why not—just as important—what? The prospect of standing tomorrow in front of Les Tilleuls and not knowing if he completed the 'Danse sacrale' with 'a raging toothache' here, or in the Hôtel du Châtelard is oppressive. Before you know it, you are busy making a biographical reconstruction à la Deutsch's *Mozart: Die Dokumente seines Lebens*, and before you know it (see if you can keep 'the warm Slavic hospitality' out of the story and the young father 'as the perfect aspirant-painter—checkered shirt, luxurious cravat, long-haired wig, Rembrandt-cap, easel over the shoulder and palette in hand' and 'Uncle Serge' and Larionov and Massine and the Russian colony in Ouchy and the do-it-yourself wallpaper hanger and the measles of Maria Milena and the drunken peasants in the train—everyone of them a pointer along the way, enter, hup, march!) between parentheses you have once again proven the unreconstructability of 'historical reality'. Just like the incomparable Deutsch.

Deutsch's book is a textbook case of musico-historical philology. Everything included is historical 'reality', because the documents are factual. Documents convey lies every once in a while, but lies are also facts. Books such as Deutsch's *Dokumente* are called objective but that is not their most prominent merit. Their greatest charm lies in the paradoxical effect they have on the reader: they make fiction out of 'historical reality'. The more we know about a historic figure, the more elusive he becomes. Nothing casts more doubt on Stravinsky's authorship of *Les Noces* than the fact that just after the première of the work, the composer ordered a black cashmere smoking jacket from the Parisian *couturier* James Pile (*Dokument seines Lebens*, 20 July 1923). So, a biography is, in the first place, invention. Invention, of course, should not conflict with the documents of historical reality, but on the other hand does not necessarily have to coincide exactly with the description of historical reality. Good biographies, like Hildesheimer's Mozart, present themselves as invention. 'If we could describe what a person actually went through in one hour—what a book that would make'; that is the desperation of anyone who calls himself a biographer.

It was obvious that with this list we would not get anywhere. The final result of our combined effort was a mysterious collection of chalets ('bois de Malèze'—a chalet near Salvan, Les Fourgères near Diablerets), pensions (Les Sapins and Rogie Vue in Morges), hotels (Châtelard in Clarens, Victoria in Château d'Oex), place-names (Lausanne, Leysin), and question marks. Especially question marks, as sources continually contradict one another. Did he move to Rogie Vue in 1915 or January 1916? And La Pervanche, the end of August or September 1914? For that matter, do you spell Rogie with or without an 'e'? And so on. There are times when one is convinced that the solution to the Mystery of the Universe lies hidden in the answers to such questions (or perhaps, more precisely, in the serene and lucid state that might result from answering these questions). It is all or nothing. There is a book about Hawthorne that gives not only the *name* of the ship on which his *grandparents* emigrated to America, but the *complete* inventory on board, including the exact number of cows from which the passengers received their daily milk ration. In principle, such books deserve our sympathy—so long as they are not the fruit of a passion in which the safety of the archive, the comfort of the duster, and the reward of diligence are as much cause as purpose. Positivism, much scorned, may be a disguise for desperations: Or the anything but positivistic search for secret signs, much closer really to mysticism, may take on positivism's outward appearance.

'. . . and thus the least things in the universe must be secret mirrors to the greatest', wrote De Quincey in his autobiography.

After completing the list, we made a historical map. We drew, in chronological order, lines between Stravinsky's temporary residences in Switzerland. 'Connect the dots and see a familiar fairy-tale figure.' But it was not a fairy-tale figure that appeared, nor a circle, nor an aleph, but a hieroglyph whose meaning remained deeply hidden.

Morges. Les Sapins and Rogie Vue cannot be found. We do not have enough information. Schaeffner places Rogivue (*sic*) in the *banlieue* of Morges, near the *route de Lausanne.* But the *banlieue* has been devoured by the city in the mean time, so it is hopeless searching for what the French biographer, almost fifty years earlier, described as a house 'with strange, irregular architecture', and Ramuz, at the same time, described as a 'villa très 1880', a house 'with a turret and a slate roof'. Unsuccessful, we continue on our way. Before the actual village, we turn left. We ride along a quay overlooking Lake Geneva, which, according to the map of Morges, is called Lac Léman. Quai de la Baie, a bend to the left, a bend to the right, Quai Lochman. At least that is what the map says, but apparently it has changed its name because by a landing we see a sign attached to a streetlamp with the inscription: *Quai Igor Strawinsky*. It is freezing, it is blowing, there are four inches of snow on the ground, but we are getting warmer. We park the car because just behind here must be Place St. Louis.

No. 2, Maison Bornand. There we stand, a bit numb, not really knowing what to do because, after all, we are modern people and know all about the autonomous work of art and biographical fallacy and the abolition of genius,

and where Boulez, let us see, about a quarter of a century ago, composed *Le Marteau sans maître*—that does not disturb us one bit even though it is a splendid work. What a dump Morges is and goodness how ugly they have made the square with all the iron fences and traffic islands and the diagonally-striped traffic-cones. Where are the women who, whatever the weather, are supposed to be there in the shade on the pavement, knitting, listening to the din coming out of the window, a noise worse than 'the band-saw of the carpenter', and who indulgently mutter: 'That's the Russian gentleman'?

But where that Russian gentleman is supposed to be sitting, behind the writing-table which—how did Ramuz put it?—oh, yes, which resembles the instrument-table of a surgeon, where bottles of every sort of colour stand (in their hierarchical arrangement, they clearly are an affirmation of a higher order), and also pieces of erasers of various types and sizes, and rulers, razors, drawing-pens, and even an original invention—an instrument with small wheels to draw staves—all this subjected to an order radiating clarity so that it is actually no less than the reflection of an inner clarity that shines through all these pages and pages, large as they are—more complex, more convincing, more irrevocable—where the effect is amplified by the various colours: blue, green, red, black—no, even two sorts of black, normal and India—each with its own destination, meaning, and use: one for the notes (collected in bunches or spread over the page like fruit in a pergola), one for the text (one of the texts), a third for the second text, others for the titles and still others for all the dynamic markings—in place of that gentleman sits a clerk with leathered elbows puffing over inventories, dossiers, tables and balance-sheets from the Greffe de tribunal—registre du commerce—tribunal du district.

Inside there is nothing to see, but it is enough just to look at, alternately, the second floor (Ramuz) and the third floor (Ansermet) of this splendid seventeenth-century (White), or eighteenth-century (Schaeffner), or late eighteenth, early nineteenth-century (Ramuz) house. What is striking is that the house is much more monumental than it appears in photos. And the strangest thing about the house is that there is nothing strange about it. Why does the house not carry a trace, if only the octotonic creaking of the shutters, of the intimate privileges that it has enjoyed? If anything, the opposite seems to be true. Across the street from Maison Bornand is a church which between its one hundred and forty-fifth and one hundred and forty-eighth years commanded the view of the temporary resident of 2 Place St Louis. The church remained untouched, the resident did not. Years after he left Morges, he quoted, by way of dedication in the score of the *Symphony of Psalms* and *Symphony in C*, the text engraved over the door of the church: A LA GLOIRE DE DIEU.

Before we continue on our journey, we walk round the outside of the house. In the garden that borders on the eastern façade is a statue, a black, tarnished man, covered by a long, wide greatcoat, peering belligerently into the unseeable horizon. On his head lies a tuft of snow. The text on the plinth reads: MANRU, OPERA DE PADEREWSKI. This must be, therefore, either Manru or Paderewski. Who is Paderewski? Good question. Paderewski composed the Minuet in G major but was also President of Poland. On the other side of the house there also used to be a garden, but it gave its life to progress. The enclosing walls and entrance gate with its decorative wrought iron are gone as well. Not only is there no garden, there is no statue. A miserable plaque next to the entrance betrays the work of the local gravestone maker. On the left side of the marble monstrosity is a much too large coin, in *haut relief*, with the composer's profile, and next to it, his name and the message that he (i) lived here 'with his family' from 1917 until 1920, and (ii) composed *L'Histoire du soldat* during that period.

On the way to Clarens, thirty miles further and a few years back. From the car radio sounds a Strauss-like *lied* about a 'Bursche' with a 'Loch' in his pocket—or maybe it was his soul. He was right, whoever it was who said: a German is someone who, if he has got something in his eye, acts as if he must wipe away a tear. Less true was the second part of this ethnological aphorism which stated how this differed from a Swiss, who, when moved to tears, acts as if he has got something in his eye. The difference between Wagner and Debussy, Strauss and Ravel, and Schoenberg and Stravinsky was never expressed more clearly, although there was little room left for the Swiss in the comparison. Not capable of being moved is different from reserve and self-control. Wandering through Geneva was more like a visit to a wax museum; compared to the clerk who, in a bank protected by heavily-armed police, cashed your traveller's cheques, the statue of Calvin in the Place du Cirque was spontaneity itself. The people here 'tend to analyse each other so much, to judge, to compare themselves with each other, that they, in the final analysis, do not act anymore, let alone react'. For a stranger passing through, it would hardly be in good taste to write something like this, but then, there was no need to, since this comment had been written by Ramuz himself, and Ramuz was Swiss born and bred. He, who once had been considered the hope of Vaudian literature, had written a hefty stack of books, although by now, thirty-three years after his death, he enjoyed fame exclusively as the librettist of *L'Histoire du soldat* and the translator of *Renard*, *Les Noces*, and some songs by Stravinsky. Except perhaps in Switzerland; though not a single title of his was to be found in the Librairie Naville in Geneva, there was still a

Ramuz *Society* and six or seven of his books yellowing in the bookcase at our temporary abode. We felt obliged to read them, albeit not one of the books could hold our attention for more than ten or eleven pages. Such was obviously the plight of previous readers as well since only the first few pages of some of the books had been cut.

Naturally, interest in the work of Ramuz was a diversion, based more upon his friendship with Stravinsky (*Une amitié célèbre* is the title of the book that Pierre Meylan wrote in 1961 about the collaboration between poet and composer) than the literary quality of *L'Histoire.* Even Ramuz's *Souvenirs sur Igor Strawinsky* did not whet that interest, as it was a rather cosy and capricious book, full of *la vie quotidienne*, life's little pleasures, and oh, the days of honour and glory. There were a few infectious descriptions of Stravinsky, and a few perfect characterizations of his 'pose', and it was only proper that the most quoted passage from Ramuz's entire œuvre was his detailed description of Stravinsky's worktable. But because virtually every sentence, every word, seemed to endorse village virtues and idealism, even the truest truism ('One must be, at one and the same time, a savage and a civilized being') smacked of muesli and Walden Pond. The tone of melodramatic simplicity, sentimental unaffectedness, and tormented humility was unbearable. Ramuz had made himself so small that he easily fitted into the bottle that he (as he announced at the end of the book) put his *Souvenirs* into and let float down the Rhône.

One begins to wonder how Ramuz could become one of the most important influences in the life of Stravinsky—and according to Craft, that influence was real. What was the basis of the friendship between writer and composer? 'Bread when it was proper, wine when it was proper'? Or was this friendship, at least as far as Stravinsky was concerned, based mainly on Ramuz's usefulness? That could at least explain why, when Stravinsky returned to France in 1920, Ramuz as good as disappeared from the composer's life and why 'mon grand ami' from the diplomatically written *Chroniques de ma vie*, is remembered in later writings as someone primarily with whom he always got drunk. It would also explain the extravagant 'And now, Stravinsky, where are you?' with which Ramuz began the third chapter of his *Souvenirs.* Here was a man completely left in the lurch, not only by his personal friend, but by the saviour of the fatherland—'this land was a land without prestige, *you have bestowed that on it*'. Ramuz did not skimp on the encomia: where William Tell, Scriabin, and Lenin fell short, Stravinsky succeeded.

'You are distant to me in space as you already are distant to me in time. I have barely seen you three or four times these last few years; in your room at Pleyel, rue Rochechouart (the old Pleyel) and then only too briefly. Perhaps you have changed, are no longer the Stravinsky I have known. Perhaps these "souvenirs", if they ever reach you, will displease you; perhaps you will be angry that I have written them.' The tone of that account is not merely aggrieved, but self-pitying, almost jealous. Ramuz addresses himself very consciously to a VIP, to one whom 'the papers call "world-famous" ', 'whom people interview', someone 'surrounded by prominent women who keep track of your whereabouts by telephone'. But just look at me a moment; while 'they prepare your *Musagète* in America with lots of interviews and dollars', I sit here 'in a small land where you are absent', but 'to which you are still indebted'.

Poor Ramuz, you must have known very well that you were letting yourself be used and still you did not have the heart to let your readers doubt for even one moment that your years with Stravinsky—the dinners, the walks, the train trips, Muller's morning gymnastics, the Spanish flu, the war rationing, the March revolution—were perhaps the most important years of your life.

> Entre Denges et Denezy
> Un soldat qui rentre chez lui.

Still greater luck that you wrote in a major language and not in Dutch. Otherwise your fame might well have been overshadowed by Martinus Nijhoff, because Nijhoff over-trumped the original with his translation of *L'Histoire.* Right from the start, Nijhoff succeeded in making clear (as you had not) that what happens to the soldier will amount to nothing—whatever he tries, he cannot get even one step further, for the patch he follows seems to be the way between two different cities, but is really one between synonyms.

> Op den straatweg van Sas naar Sluis
> een soldaat op weg naar zijn huis.[1]

The road from Clarens to Montreux also seems imaginary. The village apparently has been abandoned, since this is now the second time we have gone as far as Montreux. Twice we drove too far and twice we have turned back. The third time, though, we are rewarded with success. The village lies on a hill. Yes. We go slowly to the top, searching for 'a giant rented house, somewhat banal, lying a little bit above the station' (Schaeffner). There is the station, and before we know it, the car is on the platform. But there is nobody to chase us away. There is not a single person in sight. The station buffet

[1] 'Somewhere twixt Rockhill and Lode | A soldier on his homeward road.' The English translation by Rosa Newmarch carries the same implications as Nijhoff's, 'lode' being defined as a vein or fissure in a rock where metallic ore is found—a 'rockhill' one might say. In the Dutch version stand the words *Sas* and *Sluis*; a *sluis* being a lock or sluice, and *sas* an archaic Dutch form for lock [trans.].

appears to have been shut since 1915. All right, let us go up the hill then. Even the streets are dead. The one creature we notice seems to have been conceived around the same time as the *Sacre*. We ask him where the Hôtel du Châtelard is. He explains that the hotel burnt down a few years ago, but answers as if he really does not know what we are talking about, saying something just to have something to say.

'You want to bet that we never find the house?'

We try to comb the village as systematically as possible and a quarter of an hour later, ready to go back down to the lake admitting defeat, I suddenly recognize the photo from Schaeffner's book.

'You can't tell from this distance. All the houses look alike.'

'Yes, but this *is* the house—Les Tilleuls.'

Les Tilleuls—you can barely read it, but it is there, on the façade next to the bay window, at the height of the second storey. We saunter around the house but the only sensation that takes possession of us is of a climatological nature: there is a piercing wind and, oh no, it is starting to rain as well. Les Tilleuls is even more silent than Maison Bornand. We have all the sympathy in the world for the old woman peering out at us from behind the curtains on the ground floor. Our concern for this house must certainly be puzzling to her. Maybe she thinks we are house inspectors and that we will soon force her to sign an unpayable renovation plan. We therefore walk on a bit further.

Behind Les Tilleuls is a stretch of land, a garden in disarray, with another house on it. It is smaller—instead of five floors, it has two. This must be La Pervanche. Ansermet lived here, next door to Stravinsky, whom he did not yet know. Their meeting did not take place until 1911 (according to one) or 1912 (according to the other). A few years later, Stravinsky rented La Pervanche from Ansermet. At that time Ansermet had a large black beard making him resemble the Charlatan from *Petrushka*. That, at least, is how Stravinsky remembered him in 1966, but the memory was most certainly distorted by bile, as the composer and his former neighbour lived for almost a quarter of a century as enemies. It is true that, facing death, they settled their differences, but Stravinsky was someone who would forgive but not forget. If Ansermet said that Stravinsky introduced himself to him 'leaving the hall after one of my concerts', then Stravinsky would contend that Ansermet introduced himself to him 'in a street in Clarens'. For years, Ansermet had been one of Stravinsky's most fiery advocates; he had conducted more premières than anyone else—the *Song of the Volga Boatmen*, *Le Chant du rossignol*, *Renard*, *Les Noces*, *L'Histoire du soldat*, *Pulcinella*, *Capriccio*, the *Symphony of Psalms*—had written articles about the composer, intervened in arguments, and with the acumen of the former mathematician that he was, corrected scores; until he enraged the composer at the end of the thirties by arbitrarily cutting *Jeu de cartes* to two-thirds of its original length. That would have been forgivable, if only he had not then tried to justify his interference.

Ansermet knew that for Stravinsky the world consisted of two sorts of people—those who were for him and those who were against him—and it should not have surprised him (that is, if he were ever told of it) that Stravinsky imputed to him a 'strange megalomania' and wrote in the margin of Ansermet's apologia regarding the cuts in *Jeu de cartes* such peevish comments as: 'My God, what philosophical jabbering', 'what boasting' (gretchnevaia kasha'); that Stravinsky put question marks by statements about 'symphonic dialectic' and 'form' versus 'substance' and—still in the margin of the same apologia—that he suspected that this 'Protestant minister' wanted to become a second Stokowski. And yet, Ansermet's 'philosophical jabbering' anno 1937 did not fundamentally differ from his 'philosophical jabbering' anno 1921 (*L'œuvre d'Igor Strawinsky* of which Stravinsky, via Henri Prunières, editor of *La Revue Musicale*, personally approved). And the 'philosophical jabbering' anno 1921 did not fundamentally differ, except in value judgements, from the '*a priori* arguments and up-to-date phrases' that the conductor put forward in 1961. Compared to Adorno's psychopathological analysis of Stravinsky in the *Philosophie der Neuen Musik* (which the composer never paid the slightest attention to in any of his writings and of which he certainly never made head or tail), Ansermet's elucidation of Stravinsky in *Les Fondements de la musique dans la conscience humaine* was the picture of clarity and goodwill. But it was unfortunately still the work of an incorrigible schoolteacher and a formalist in both body and soul. How else could one set oneself the task of, for example, *demonstrating* that dodecaphony was *ipso facto* nonsense and could only lead to nonsense? In his blind faith in the phenomenology of Husserl, he left no room for the notion that, precisely in art, wrong premises can lead to 'valid' consequences. *Réflexion pure* and *réflexion seconde* had become for him shibbolethim—speaking these were enough to make the world divulge its secrets. And nothing less than that, as *Les Fondements*, almost a thousand pages long, discussed *everything*; supplying an ultimate unravelling of the mystery of music, of music history (*La Création historique de la musique dans l'empirisme*), of man (*Les quatre principales modalités européennes*), of human thought (*Notes sur les structures de la réflexion*), of God (*La Phénoménologie de Dieu*), of the history of conscience (*Évolution de la conscience*).

Rather than discussing the 'phenomena', Ansermet oddly enough placed them in an eternal and immutable hierarchy of values, a periodic table of existence. The final message of the book was therefore less of a phenomenological than of a moral-theological nature, so that it did not matter much whether it was about art or God. As far as music was concerned, the message was simple—Beethoven is a more universal, humane, richer, etc. composer than Stravinsky; the rest of the book consisted of a rationalization by a metaphysicist who pursued the illusion of the scientifically provable truth (and therefore—superiority) of personal taste. In such a book, so many brilliant things can be said (and they are), but in the final analysis there is little more to conclude than: amen. One remembers such a book especially for its rancour, its convulsiveness, its ideological fanaticism and its anti-Semitism wrapped in phenomenological terminology.[2] And as far as Stravinsky is concerned, more revealing than pedantic remarks about wrongly barred castanets was the fact that Ansermet, when he really began to criticize, criticized only works after *Jeu de cartes.*

'And about revisions of old works. *Petrushka*, for instance.'

'But not about *The Firebird.*'

'No, of course not. Who was the first to perform the 1919 version of *The Firebird*?'

'Is that the version Bozzetto used?'

In Geneva a few days before, we had seen Bozzetto's *Allegro non troppo*, an Italian cartoon film, a kind of parody on Disney's *Fantasia.* A cartoonist is forced to draw appropriate illustrations to the musical carrying-on of an orchestra of old ladies and a fat, stupid conductor; Sibelius's *Valse triste* as the beautiful dream and sad reality of an alley cat, Debussy's *Faune* as the adventures of an old goat and a spring chicken, Ravel's *Bolero* as the story of creation, *The Firebird* as, well, as what? There was a snake that decided to eat the forbidden fruit himself, there was an all-devouring monster, washing machines flew about; it would thus appear to have something to do with lost innocence and the consumer society. Here the cartoonist seemed to be less inspired by the quadrophonic super-technicolour performance by ghost-

[2] Ansermet's anti-Semitism is of the more sophisticated (and perhaps more treacherous) variety: calling a Jew a Jew only when something queer is going on. That is what Ansermet does with Webern, first rebuking Webern's call for a *Zukunftsmusik*, then recognizing it as 'a Jewish idea'. In his exposition on 'Jewish modality', the writer concludes with his unfathomable existentialist axiom that 'the Jew is a *me* who speaks as though he were an *I*', that the Jew 'suffers from thoughts doubly misformed' and does so without any 'sense of transcendency', making him 'suitable for the handling of money'. And also according to Ansermet, the 'historic creation of Western music' could have got along just as well 'without the Jews'. And to make it appear that he is writing a philosophy without value judgement, he allows Ernst Bloch to call Schoenberg a 'stupid Jew' in order to wash his own hands of guilt, since 'it should be noticed that a Jew made this remark to me'. (*Les Fondements de la musique dans la conscience humaine*, vol. 1 [Neuchâtel 1961], pp. 235, 423 ff., 534.)

conductor von Karajan than by the bouncing, bubbling, burping pandemonium into which the Japanese synthesizer virtuoso Isao Tomita had transformed *The Firebird.* Not that it made much difference; the future cultural historian will mention the Italian as well as the Japanese contribution to late twentieth-century commercial culture in the chapter 'Walt Disney and the Decay of Civilization'. Stravinsky, for that matter, contributed his two cents' worth as well. That is, six-thousand-dollars' worth in exchange for the use of the *Sacre* as background music for the prehistoric (what else!) scene from *Fantasia.* Afterwards he said that he was *forced* to accept the money, that the *Sacre* was not protected by copyright in the United States, and that Disney had warned him that he would use the music even without his permission; but a year later, in 1940, it was the same Scrooge McDuck in him that sold Disney an option for *Fireworks*, *The Firebird*, and *Renard.* Perhaps he would not have done so had he known how *Fantasia* was made; how the *Sacre* was played on a victrola and at the same time was commented on by Disney and his colleagues.

H: The music here is a little too long.
WALT: . . . I would like to see a sensational blow-up there . . .
A: A terrific explosion . . .
WALT (*comparing continuity with what he hears*): This fits to a tee, doesn't it? I'm afraid Stravinsky wouldn't recognize himself. (*Loud crash in music*) Oooh, gee—hurray! That's swell! We can bring this out as strong as we like.'

Here, in Les Tilleuls, the music for *Fantasia* was composed, on a muted piano in a room eight feet by eight feet. Only, which room?

Inside is a corridor ending with a door. We ring the bell.

A man opens the door, a schoolteacher type in his mid-twenties.

Yes, he knows that Stravinsky had lived here, but on which floor he could not say. To judge by the expression on his face and the questions he asks, he is interested. He offers to call the director of the festival in Montreux, someone like that is bound to know. A little later he returns; the only thing that Mr K. could account to us was that the *Sacre* was composed here. That we already knew.

Does he know anyone else who could help us? After considering a bit, he gives us the name of Mr B. Mr B.'s hobby is the history of Clarens.

We go to Mr B., but Mr B. is not at home.

We ring the bell again at Les Tilleuls. Mission failed, maybe he has another idea? He tells us that La Pervanche has been used for a long time as a rectory so that perhaps the local minister could help us. We take down the address of the church and the minister.

The church turns out to be open, only there is not a soul to be found. Even our repeated shouts receive no reply. Nobody answers the door at the minister's quarters across the way. According to a passer-by, the minister left early this morning.

22 Les Tilleuls, Clarens, 1931

23 Les Tilleuls, Clarens, 1979

Back again. Maybe the helpful man at Les Tilleuls has yet another suggestion. And he does: there is a man who lives on Rue de la Poste who is in his eighties and he has a unique photo collection.

After some searching we find Rue de la Poste. We ring the bell, wait a bit, and as we turn to go, an elderly woman opens the door. As we finish our story, she tells us that her father is old and crippled and that he honestly could not help. In the mean time, we hear shuffling in the hallway. An ancient man appears. He more or less stands aided by two crutches. He asks his daughter something. She screams back her reply: 'These are two gentleman who . . .' Grandfather almost topples over. His daughter wants to get rid of us. We politely say good day, walk back to Les Tilleuls and get into the car. But first we take a picture. The same picture that Schaeffner took for his book about Stravinsky fifty years earlier.

We return home, this time taking the route through France, the southern shore of the lake. The bend of the short side of the lake begins immediately outside Montreux. People say that there have been more butterflies here recently than in previous years. It is difficult to tell in the winter though. Left and a little ahead of us must be Château d'Oex, Leysin, Salvan, and Les Diablerets, tucked away in the bend of the lake. But we do not know what to look for, and even if we did, we would not know where to look. Half-way along the southern shore we stop at the last point—Evian-les-Bains. According to I.S., who stayed here nine years ago, the people taking a cure here in the summer can choose 'between a fast death in the Casino and a slow one by mineral water'. In the winter, there is no such choice. One is supposed to be able to see Morges from the boulevard when it is clear, just as with a clear head one can see *Requiem Canticles* from *Les Noces*; the number of miles separating the two places does not differ much from the number of years separating the two works.

We drive around for a while and suddenly come across a sign—Hôtel Royal. Above the name, there are a lot of stars. From here the path ascends through a bare hay-field, with a tree here and there. We approach a colossal building. The man who built this purgatory 'for octogenarians' must have really had it in for old people. The site of the hotel is just as desolate as a bunker in the dunes. Ten years ago, the entrance was crowded with people looking for Stravinsky, by then like 'a stone, still warm for a while after sundown' (*ThC*); now we are the only ones here. 'Prochaine ouverture—fin avril 1980' reads the placard posted on one of the four whitewashed doors. The steps are grey with ground rubble and traces of cement. A gas oven rests upon a rubbish container. On the steel bin itself is a sticker—*récupérateur.* A 'récupérateur' is a regenerator and a regenerator is a device used to recycle obsolete waste products.

We do not even get the chance to taste the *couronnes*, *rondures*, *royales*, *caprices du roi* and all the other kingly *pâtisseries* that are served by the house for tea.

Back in Geneva, we decide not to end our day looking for Maxim's Bar. The bar probably will not exist any more. And even if it does, the waiters who once enjoyed the virtuosic cimbalom playing of Aladar Rácz and who were astonished by the visitor wearing a monocle, a red tie, and a green waistcoat, trying to write down a Serbian *kolo* on music staves hastily drawn on his cuff, those waiters must be long dead and gone.

We spend the evening just as Stravinsky and Ansermet did sixty-five years earlier. *Nous jouions à quatre mains.* And just like Ansermet and Stravinsky, we play the Brandenburg Concertos. But all that is mere coincidence. In the first place, you cannot very well start playing canasta so early in the evening; secondly, it is fun to play piano duets; and thirdly, the Reger transcription of Bach is lying on the piano at Madame B.'s so defiantly—a rare copy of an edition that today would be called the result of bad taste.

We play and we play well—light bass, good phrasing—but not quite totally relaxed. It is too difficult for that. Cutting the lawn with nail clippers. The upper part especially demands skill and endurance; it is apparently intended for pianists with four right hands. What you hear seems like a musical vivisection. The Anatomy Lesson by Reger—sinewy music, the bones stick through the pages and what was curved has become flattened.

When we reach this point:

Ex. 1

Brandenburg Concerto No. 2in F, 1st movt., bar 26

we can no longer keep our mouths shut, and as if by previous agreement, indicate to each other that we would like to stop, realizing we want to say the same thing: 'Of course, *Dumbarton Oaks* is about Reger's piano duet version of Bach that he always played with Ansermet!' Only in *Dumbarton Oaks*, the inside of Bach becomes the outside. We hear not so much the overcoat of Bach, as the lining, the stitching, the shoulder padding, the hem, and the tacking, still dangling loose (Ex. 2).

Ex. 2

Dumbarton Oaks [22]

A key to a riddle had almost been lost together with the bad taste of yesteryear.

Id est: Hermetic Music

Threni = 5 phonemes.

'Id est Lamentationes Jeremiae Prophetae' = 5 words.

Threni contains, just like the Lamentations of Prophet Jeremiah, 5 movements.

An introduction, consisting of an orchestral fragment of 5 bars and an *explicatio tituli* of alternately 3/4 and 2/4 bars, precedes the 5 sections.

The piece begins with a 3-note motif, repeated 5 times.

From the Lamentations of Prophet Jeremiah, 3 parts are employed.

The middle movement, 'De Elegia Tertia', consists of 3 sections. The 15 Hebrew letters (15 = 3 × 5) sung in that movement each occur 3 times.

In 'De Elegia Prima', 5 Hebrew letters occur. 'De Elegia Prima' has 5 sections. The 3 odd sections consist of 5 episodes each: an orchestral introduction concluding with a rhythm of 3 against 2, a speaking chorus, an orchestral interlude concluding with a 3/8 bar of 2 quavers on the 2nd and 3rd beat, a second speaking chorus and a melodic canon for tenor and contralto bugle accompanied by woman's chorus and high strings.

Sections 2 and 4, the even sections, are called '*Di*phonas': *two*-part retrograde melodic canons for 2 tenor soloists (5 [sections] = 3 + 2).

A Hebrew letter precedes 'De Elegia Prima' and the further Hebrew letters divide its 5 sections.

'De Elegia Tertia' consists of 15 episodes, divided over 3 sections. In each episode, one Hebrew letter is sung 3 times, each letter resulting in a 5-voiced chord (except the second letter of the alphabet, *beth*—actually meaning 2—which results in a chord spread over 3 voices in the chorus and 3 in the instruments, that is, 2 groups x 3). Each episode is divided by a letter into 3 parts.

The last movement, 'De Elegia Quinta', consists of 5 sections. The last section consists of 5 chords in the horns. The fifth chord is a *third* doubled in the octave (8 = 3 + 5).

In the twelve-tone row on which the work is based, the most frequent interval is the *fifth*. Harmonies of fifths, often very widely spaced, occur invariably in the piece.

Evidently, the numbers 3 and 5 are essential to the structure of *Threni*. These numbers are the 3rd and 4th terms in the Fibonacci series. Their ratio therefore approaches the golden ratio (Fig. 1).

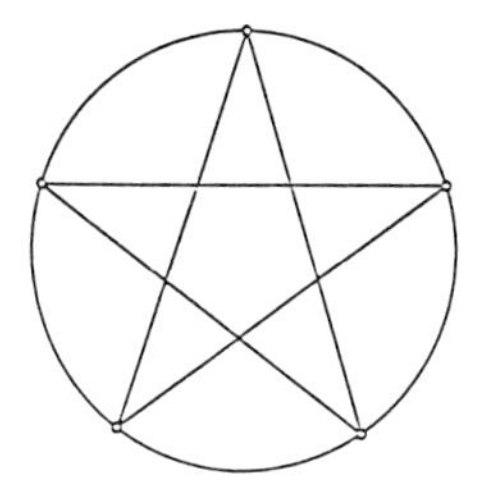

Fig. 1

The lines connecting the points which divide the circle into 5 equal parts form a pentagon, a five-pointed star (the star that directed the Three Wise Men from the East), the diagonals of which divide each other in the golden ratio.

Geometrically, the golden ratio can be calculated by means of a right-angled triangle, in which side AB is half the length of the base AC (Fig. 2).

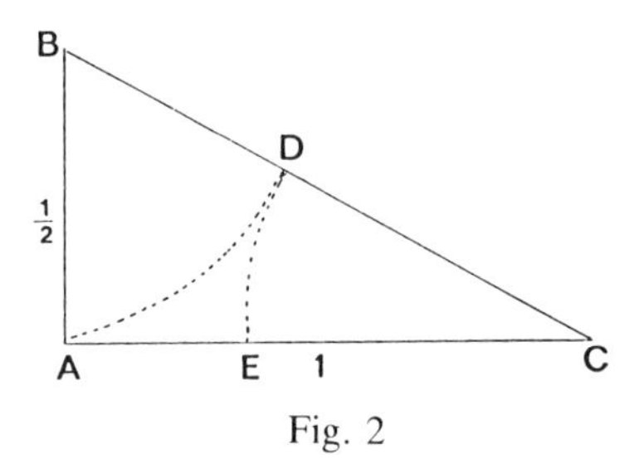

Fig. 2

Draw a circle with a centre B and a radius BA. This circle intersects the line segment BC at point D.

Draw a circle with a centre C and a radius CD. This circle intersects the line segment AC at point E.

The base AC is divided into two fragments which are related by the golden ratio, that is: AE:EC = EC:AC.

Mathematically, the golden ratio is expressed by a formula which employs $\sqrt{5}$. If AC = 1 (see fig. 2), then EC = $\frac{1}{2}(-1 + \sqrt{5})$; this number is symbolized by Φ (phi), and, rounded to three places, equals 0.618, the golden ratio equalling 1.618.

The Five-Pointed Star (the pentaculum Salomonis, or the Seal of Salomon) was first used as a symbol to describe the golden ratio by Luca Pacioli (*c.*

1450–1515). He accorded the golden section (*sectio divina*) five divine characteristics:

Just as God, the proportion is unique.

Just as the Holy Trinity is a union of one Godhead, the proportion is one ratio consisting of three terms.

Just as God cannot be described in words, the proportion cannot be expressed in a conceivable number nor be expressed rationally.

Just as God, the proportion resembles itself.

And finally, the divine proportion, 'dal ciel mandata', is the expression of the *quintessence*, according to Plato the fifth element that consists of 5 regular figures joined together stereometrically and enveloping one another: a stereometric duodecigon, consisting of 12 pentagons.

Jeremiah's 'Lamentationes' consist of 5 stanzas.

The first stanza consists of 22 lines.

Each line begins with the consecutive Hebrew letter, forming an acrostic on the Hebrew alphabet, which has 22 letters.

The second stanza also consists of 22 lines, each beginning with the consecutive Hebrew letter.

The third, and central, stanza consists of 66 lines and is therefore 3 times longer. Here, too, a different Hebrew letter precedes each line. Each letter appears 3 times.

Again, both the fourth and fifth stanza consist of 22 lines.

As in the Vulgate, the Hebrew letters are excluded from the fifth and last stanza.

Stravinsky followed this structure: 5 movements, of which the longest is the third. He did not use the text of all five stanzas, but limited himself to *Lamentatio* 1, 3, and 5. The lines from the third lamentation are spread over 3 sections. Applying the text numbering to the musical movements results in: 13335.

IV

Stravinsky

. . . I think my music deserves to be considered as a whole.

(1971)

'Stravinsky' is an adjectival, not a nominative form in Russian, hence I am not Stravinsk but Stravinsky-y(an). Are any consequences of this fact discernible in my music? Certainly it has been characterized as adjectival frequently enough, in the sense of a descriptive mode, Stravinsky the adjective modifying such nouns as Gesualdo, Pergolesi, Tchaikovsky, Wolf, Bach . . . A study of 'Stravinskyan' would also have to include a differential comparative analysis with English and French of the processes of my Russian thought-language—which lacks the pluperfect tense, the definite article and the copula (for we say 'I happy', not 'I am happy') . . .

(1971)

Everybody who makes something new does harm to something old.

(1966)

'Mortify the past.' The past as a wish that creates the probability pattern of the future? Did John of the Cross mean that, and the fear of changing the past which is fear of the present? I mortify *my* past every time I sit at the piano to compose, in any case, though I have no wish to go back or to relive a day of my life.

(1968)

One evolves, and I have the luck to have very little memory, which is what enables me to begin each new step of my life forgetting the past.

(1935)

Play a scale in C major metronomically and ask someone else to do the same. The difference in the playing is the proof of the presence of personality . . .

(1930)

Creation is its own image and thought is its own mirror. As I think about this metaphor language—it gives me claustrophobia—the word mirror frightens me. Seventy-five years ago as a child alone in my room, I once saw my father instead of myself in the looking glass, and my already strong case of father-fears became mirror-fears as well. I expect Purgatory to be lined with many-dimensional mirrors.

(1968)

. . . I have not been able to change. I do not understand the composer who says we must analyse and determine the evolutionary tendency of the whole musical situation and proceed from there. I have never consciously analysed any musical situation, and I can follow only where my musical appetites lead me.

(1968)

One has a nose. The nose scents and it chooses. An artist is simply a kind of pig snouting truffles.

(1962)

My instinct is to recompose, and not only students' works, but old masters' as well. When composers show me their music for criticism all I can say is that I would have written it quite differently. Whatever interests me, whatever I love, I wish to make my own (I am probably describing a rare form of kleptomania).

(1960)

[Technique] is the whole man. We learn how to use it but we cannot acquire it in the first place; or, perhaps I should say that we are born with the ability to acquire it. At present it has come to mean the opposite of 'heart', though, of course, 'heart' is technique too . . . A technique or a style for saying something original does not exist *a priori*, it is created by the original saying itself . . . 'Thought' is not one thing and 'technique' another, namely, the ability to transfer, 'express' or develop thoughts. We cannot say 'the technique of Bach' (I never say it), yet in every sense he had more of it than anyone. [. . . Technique is . . .] creation, and being creation, it is new every time . . . Technical mastery has to be *of* something, it has to *be* something . . . At present all of the arts, but especially music, are engaged in 'examinations of technique'. In my sense such an examination must be into the nature of art itself—an examination that is both perpetual and new every time—or it is nothing.

(1959)

I prefer thinking to understanding, for thinking is active and continuous, like composing, while to understand is to bring to an end.

(1965)

My agenbite of inwit is that I do not know while composing, am not aware of, the value question. I love whatever I am now doing, and with each new work I feel that I have at last found the way, have just begun to compose. I love all of my children, of course, and, like any father, I am inclined to favour the backward and imperfectly formed ones. But I am actually excited only by the newest (Don Juanism?) and the youngest (nymphetism?). I hope, too, that my best work is still to be written (I want to write a string quartet and a symphony), but 'best' means nothing to me while I am composing, and comparisons of the sort that other people make about my music are to me invidious or simply absurd.

(1968)

STRAVINSKY:	SCHOENBERG:
1. Reaction against 'German music' or 'German romanticism.' No '*Sehnsucht*,' no '*ausdrucksvoll*.'	'Today I have discovered something which will assure the supremacy of German music for the next hundred years.' (Schoenberg, July 1921.)
2. Fox (eclectic and abundant variety). (Aron)	Hedgehog. (Moses)
3. 'Music is powerless to express anything at all.'	'Music expresses all that dwells in us . . .'
4. Chief production is of ballets.	'Ballet is not a musical form.'
5. Learns from others, a lifelong need for outside nourishment and a constant confluence with new influences. Never a teacher. No writing about musical theory.	An autodidact. After the early works, no influence from other composers. Also a teacher. Large amount of writing on musical theory. His philosophy of teaching is 'Genius learns only from itself; talent chiefly from others. Genius learns from nature, from its own nature; talent learns from art.'
6. Composes only at the piano.	Never composed at the piano.
7. Composes every day, regularly, like a man with banking hours. Hardly a scrap unfinished or unused.	Composed fitfully, at lightning speed, and in the heat of inspiration. Therefore, many unfinished works.
8. Remote-in-time subjects: *The Rake's Progress*.	Contemporary subjects (protest music): *Survivor from Warsaw*.
9. Metronomic strictness, no *rubato*. Ideal is of mechanical regularity (*Octuor*, Piano Concerto, etc.)	Much use of *rubato*.
10. Diatonicism.	Chromaticism.
11. *Secco*. Scores contain minimum of expression marks.	*Espressivo*. Scores full of expression marks.
12. Prefers spare, two-part counterpoint.	Preferred dense eight-part counterpoint (the choruses, op. 35; the *Genesis Prelude* canon).
13. 'What the Chinese philosopher says cannot be separated from the fact that he says it in Chinese.' (Preoccupation with manner and style.)	'A Chinese philosopher speaks Chinese, but what does he say?' ('What is *style*?')
(. . .)	(. . .)

(1968)

Would you 'draw' your recent music? For example:

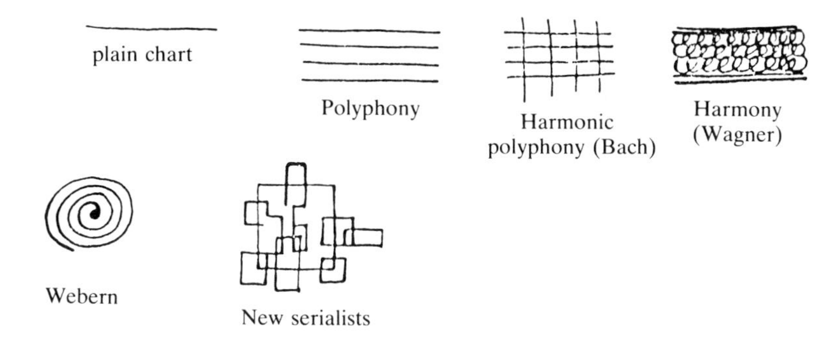

This is *my* music:

(1959)

So the danger lies not in the borrowing of clichés. The danger lies in fabricating them . . .

(1939)

. . . I was, and still am, a pious Aristotelian: imitation is the beginning of art.

(1971)

Composition begins with an appetite, or taste, for discovery, and the emotion is born after the discovery, following rather than preceding the creative process . . .

(1945)

In music as in love, pleasure is the waste product of creation.

(1971)

[A young composer] should go directly underground and do nothing but compose; that is, not strive for Foundation awards, academic prizes, college presidencies, foreign fellowships; not attend culture congresses, not give interviews, not prattle on the radio about music appreciation, not review new scores (except his own, pseudonymously); and not push, promote, manoeuver, advertise, finagle, operate.

(1971)

In fact my processes are *determined* by esthetic accidents, except that they are not really accidents . . .

(1971)

To be deprived of art and left alone with philosophy is to be close to Hell.

(1971)

We have a duty towards music, namely, to invent it.

(1939)

Although I have been concerned with questions of musical manners all my life, I am unable to say precisely what these manners are. That, I think, is because they are not precompositional, but of the essence of the musical act: the manner of saying and the thing said are, for me, the same. But am I not unusually conscious of the manner question, nevertheless? All I can say is that my manners are my personal relations with my material. *Je me rends compte* in them. Through them I discover my laws. . . . I have been told that such things merely indicate the culture-consciousness found in all *emigrés*, but I know that the explanation is deeper than that, as I worked and thought exactly the same way in Russia. My manners are the birthmark of my art.

(1968)

I have often considered that the fact of my birth and upbringing in a Neo-Italian—rather than in a purely Slavic, or Oriental—city must be partly, and profoundly, responsible for the cultural direction of my later life.

(1962)

Was I merely trying to refit old ships while the other side—Schoenberg—sought new forms of travel? I believe that this distinction, much traded on a generation ago, has disappeared. (An era is shaped only by hindsight, of course, and hindsight reduces to convenient unities, but all artists know that they are part of the same thing.) Of course I seemed to have exploited an apparent discontinuity, to have made art out of the *disjecta membra*, the quotations of other composers, the references to earlier styles ('hints of earlier and other creation'), the detritus that betokened a wreck. But I used it, and anything that came to hand, to rebuild, and I did not pretend to have invented new conveyors or new means of travel. But the true business of the artist *is* to refit old ships. He can say again, in his way, only what has already been said.

(1968)

How does a man grow old?
I don't know, or why *I* am old, if I must be (I don't want to be), or if 'I' am 'he'. All my life I have thought of myself as 'the youngest one', and now, suddenly, I read and hear about myself as 'the oldest one'. And then I wonder at these distant images of myself. I wonder if memory is true, and I know that it cannot be, but that one lives by memory nevertheless and not by truth. But through the crack of light in my bedroom door, time dissolves and I see again the images of my lost world. Mamma has gone to her room, my brother is asleep in the other bed, and all is still in the house. The lamp from the street reflects in the room, and by it I recognize the simulacrum as myself.

(1962)

. . . music expresses itself.

(1962)

1957—*Agon*

. . . a present fixed with the help of the past, and not vice versa.
Jean Genet

Agon goes a step further.

Prior to *Agon*, Stravinsky wrote ballet music and music resembling ballet. What for the most part was missing from early Russian ballets became one of the most important subjects of 'neoclassical' ballets (*Apollon musagète*, *Jeu de cartes*)—references to classical music and, especially, references to the rhythmic conventions of classical ballet. Prancing, curtsies, gambolling, stepping in place, springs, or, more properly: arabesques, battements, jetés, assemblés, pirouettes, and pliés. The violin is a particularly good means of playing melodies dressed in tutus, both in ballet and on the concert platform.

Classical ballet (which should actually be called romantic ballet) draws from a reservoir of steps and figures built up in the nineteenth century, steps and figures which are still taught today in ballet class. To accompany these classes, a voluminous piano repertoire is available—from Chopin to Moszkowski—though primarily comprised of completely forgotten composers of salon music, every one of whom made much use of rhythms that Stravinsky would restore to honour, beginning in 1928. Stravinsky's manipulations of these rhythms could not always hide the true nature of the original salon music: light, sometimes as featherweight, rarely as heavyweight. Even in *Orpheus*, the land of roses and moonlight where Tchaikovsky was king looms in the distance.

Stravinsky loved classical ballet.

Did he bow in the third position after the première of *Orpheus*?

'Mr Stravinsky, who has been writing ballets since 1909 . . . knows very well the logical anatomical basis of the Five Absolute Positions. In the Third Position (the heel of one foot locked against the instep of the other, weight equally distributed, with completed turnout), Mr Stravinsky would have found it awkward to execute the traditional stage bow derived from the Imperial Russian Theatre. He took it in Fourth Position—with weight equally divided, the forefoot twelve inches in advance of the back' (Lincoln Kirstein).

The composer celebrated his eightieth birthday with the performance of three ballets choreographed by Balanchine: *Apollo*, *Orpheus*, and *Agon*.

Agon was a summary of the history of ballet; not only the romantic (so-called classical) ballet, but the actual classical ballet as well—dances from seventeenth-century France and related forms from earlier and later periods. *Agon* was also Stravinsky's last ballet (not including the bit of children's pantomime in *The Flood*), the conclusion of fifty years of composing for dancers and seventy years of watching dancers. And, last but not least, *Agon* was a summary of a history of music. There were plenty of holes in this history of music, but through those holes peered a couple of great composers: Machaut, Dufay, Rameau, Webern, Stravinsky.

In order to write a history, one is obliged to study manuals. Preferably manuals which include everything. One such is Marin Mersenne's *Harmonie universelle*, which appeared in Paris in 1636 and 'includes the theory and practice of music. In which is discussed the Nature of Sound, of Movement, the Consonances, the Genres, the Modes, Composition, the Voice, Songs and all types of harmonic Instruments'. This book of more than 1,300 pages is, at least concerning the section on acoustics, of historical importance: the Laws of Mersenne have yet to be disputed.

Mersenne devotes fourteen of the 1,300 pages to Dance Forms; enough for Stravinsky as will become evident, though not very much for a verbose Capuchin—then again, quite a lot for a Capuchin of the opinion that the most expensive and magnificent ballets are nothing compared to the efforts of a fly.

Second Pas-de-Trois

The Second Pas-de-trois in *Agon* consists of three dances: Bransle Simple, Bransle Gay, and Bransle de Poitou. These are the first three Bransles that Mersenne depicts. He names five in total; that is, twenty less than Thoinot Arbeau in his *Orchésographie*, but Stravinsky did not know of that book as yet.

The opening rhythm of the bransle simple is easy to look up in Mersenne. He uses the old Greek arsis/thesis signs to describe the basic rhythms.

The bransle simple according to Mersenne:

– ◡ ◡ – –

The Bransle Simple according to Stravinsky:

Ex. 1

The two trumpets that play this in *Agon* come from yet another seventeenth-century French book on dance.

The rhythm of the castanets in the Bransle Gay—a regular, persistent rhythm that sounds as if it keeps falling on the wrong beats—is also derived from Mersenne (Ex. 2).

Ex. 2

The bransle gay is quicker than the bransle simple; it has a triple rhythm, to the beat of the 'Swiss tambour': ◡◡–. Is it a coincidence that the first two notes of Mersenne's musical example (Ex. 3) are the inversion of Stravinsky's melody (Ex. 4)?

Ex. 3

Mersenne

Ex. 4

Agon

'The third is called bransle à mener, or de Poitou; its metre is the sesquialtera, that is, hemiola.' Stravinsky notates a 3/2 metre. He certainly would have used the basis rhythm, if only Mersenne had mentioned it. But he did not. No need to be disappointed though, since two bransles later (in the Bransle de Moutirandé), Mersenne gives ◡◡–. Stravinsky can just as well use this rhythm to begin his Bransle de Poitou (Ex. 5).

Ex. 5

trb

f

Stravinsky stylizes the hemiola that Mersenne mentions (two times three beats divided into three times two beats) by having the trumpet and trombone continually play after the beat—or before the beat, or in four, or in leaving out the beat, in short, anything to trip up the 3/2 metre.

First Pas-de-Trois

The first Pas-de-Trois in *Agon* also consists of three dances: Saraband-Step, Gaillarde and Coda.

In the Saraband-Step, the solo violin is together with two trombones while a xylophone plays a kind of music that would chase Beelzebub himself from the dance floor.

What kind of Saraband is this? It has nothing to do with Bach. Did Stravinsky dig up yet another reference book? One about Piranesi, or Athanasius Kirchner, or Paracelsus? *The Times* described *Agon* as an 'imitation of Boulez and Arbeau', and according to Craft, Stravinsky was so curious about this Arbeau that he scarcely noticed the reviewer's malice.

Arbeau as a source for the seventeenth-century dances in *Agon*: a source Stravinsky did not know of while composing, but for someone who is making up his own history, that is more of an advantage than a disadvantage.

Though Arbeau was no alchemist, he was a dance teacher. In his *Orchésographie* (1589), he advises his pupils to spit and blow their noses sparingly and to be suitably and neatly dressed: 'your hose well secured and your shoes clean . . . not only when you are dancing the gaillarde'. A kind of Arthur Murray one might say, who was of the opinion that 'nowadays the gaillarde is danced regardless of rules' in the big city. He also adds an interesting remark concerning the bransle de Poitou: that the young women of Poitou stamp with their wooden shoes on the second and third beats of triple time.

Arbeau gives a lengthy description of the gaillarde, the second dance of the First Pas-de-Trois from *Agon*. 'The gaillarde should consist of six steps as it contains six minims played in two bars of triple time, thus:

Ex. 6

However, it consists of five steps only because the fifth and penultimate note is lost in the melody, as you see below where it is deleted and replaced by a rest of equivalent value. So there remain only five notes and, allowing one step for each note, you must count five steps and no more' (Ex. 7).

Ex. 7

Agon starts to become visible (Ex. 8).

Ex. 8

Agon, bar 178

Arbeau continues with a description of the various steps: *révérence*, *pieds joints*, *pieds largis*, *pied croisé* and many others. From the illustrations, it would appear that the gentleman removes his hat solely while performing the *révérence*.

RÉVÉRENCE

RU DE VACHE GAUCHE

PIED EN L'AIR GAUCHE

There are even some dancers so nimble as to be able to 'move their feet in the air' while executing the *saut majeur*. Such a leap is called the capriole. Leaps were, even long after the period of the basse-dance, exceptional.

CAPRIOLE

The bransles, too, were subject to lengthy discussion in Arbeau. Once more 'some ignoramuses have corrupted the movements of the bransle de Poitou'. The bransles were accompanied by the violin, but we knew that already from Stravinsky.

The third dance of the First Pas-de-Trois is called Coda. That is the name normally corresponding to the last dance of a *pas de deux*, *trois*, or *quatre* following the conventions of classical ballet. To Stravinsky, this coda is not an end but a beginning: for the first time in his music, a complete twelve-tone row appears. But this beginning also sounds like an end: like a mocking farewell to composing 'mit zwölf Tönen'. These tones are played like a German march: *eins*, *zwei*, *drei*, *vier*, on and on up to *zwölf*. It has already become unbearable by the fourth note and the violin (again) starts playing an Italian gigue, the real coda. When the violinist obeys the laws of 'twelve-tone music', the music starts sounding like a satire: exactly in tempo, a trill here, a glissando there, in a word, the kind of music that is nowadays again being called ping-pong music. The violinist imitates a violinist playing Webern.

Pas-de-deux

Stravinsky abides by the form of the *Grand pas de deux* of romantic ballet in his Pas-de-Deux: Adagio, solo for the male dancer, solo for the female dancer, coda. Even if the music resembles Webern, the choice of having a string orchestra play it none the less stems from the tradition in Stravinsky's own ballets (*Orpheus*), which in turn stems from the tradition of romantic ballets. There is no *pas de deux* in romantic ballet where the music does not irrevocably fade into an 'Adagio for Strings', preferably supported by frequent chords in the harp and followed by manly horns for the gentleman's solo and plenty of feminine flutes for the lady's solo.

So, too, in *Agon*. Only the string orchestra has been stripped, torn to shreds. Often the only thing remaining is the inevitable solo violin. It grabs on to one note, plays a remnant of Webern or suddenly remembers *L'Histoire du soldat*, *Apollon musagète*, or Little Tich, the clown from the *Three Pieces* for string quartet. The mandolin in the Coda is Tchaikovsky's harp, just back from the Viennese dry-cleaner.

In *Agon*, the dance is a grimace, a game more forbidding than the dance parties in the house of the Quintessence. *Agon*, which means 'competition', could be the music to the ballet described by Rabelais in *Gargantua and Pantagruel*: 'a ball in the form of a tournament—which was not only worth seeing but eternally memorable'. The hall where this takes place is, according to Rabelais, covered with a pile tapestry, in the form of a chessboard. Thirty-two dancers enter. Each party has its own musicians, 'with various fantastic instruments, all differently yet perfectly tuned to one another and marvellously tuneful. These changed the tone, mood, and time of their music as the progress of the ball required; and this surprised me, when I considered the number and variety of the steps, back-steps, hops, leaps, returns, flights, ambuscades, retreats, and surprises.'

The ballet that Rabelais goes on to describe consists of three movements, each movement in a faster tempo, danced by hopping and leaping 'chess pieces'. Every move appears: capturing pieces, jumping knights, castling, and the pawn that becomes a queen; and everything danced 'with such agility that they made four moves to one beat of the music'. There is so much laughter, by both parties alike, that even Heraclitus himself, 'such an enemy to laughter—which is peculiar to man—would have relaxed his frown at the sight' and nothing but hand–clapping can be heard. Pieces revolve about like 'children's spinning tops', vaulting, capering, and wheeling, too. It is anything but a dignified ceremony, even the courtly Lady has long since disappeared. *Agon* is a *game*, with the devil as challenger and the history of ballet as opponent. 'I will say more. If this superhuman spectacle confused our thoughts, amazed our spirits, and transported us out of ourselves, we were moved even more by the fears and emotions raised in our hearts by the sound of the music', Rabelais writes, as if nothing has changed for the last four hundred years. Perhaps little has changed. The last bars of *Agon* sound like the end of a Florentine ballet from 1380. Only with the last chord does it become apparent that no candles are being blown out, but that the switch is being turned off. With one flick of the wrist, out go the lights.

The World, a Comedy

Since every work of art is a kind of feigning, there are two types of artists: those who are aware of their feigning and those who are not (or who do not want to be). The first type of artist has a choice: he can, by a sleight of hand, conceal his feigning, or, he can make a subject out of it. The one who makes a subject out of feigning is, in the most general sense of the word, an ironist; of course this does not stop him from being able to do anything he wants: sing praise to God, write bloodthirsty historical plays, mythologize a day in Dublin, compose 104 symphonies. His art has the characteristic of 'the fully-conscious artist whose art is the ironical presentation of the ironic position of the fully-conscious artist' (D. C. Muecke). This artist will 'stand apart from his work and at the same time incorporate this awareness of his ironic position into the work itself and so create something which will, if a novel, not simply be a story but rather the telling of a story complete with the author and the narrating, the reader and the reading, the style and the choosing of the style, the fiction and its distance from fact . . .'

Many of Stravinsky's compositions begin with an intrada-like clamour: 'watch out, I'm going to play a piece for you now'. (The story and the telling of the story.)

The Rake's Progress begins like 'just another' festive opera, *Oedipus Rex* like another opera-oratorio, the *Concerto for Piano and Wind* like another orchestral suite à la Bach, but, from the first bar on, the musical subject is 'played upon' and the expectations of the listener get confused. (The style and the choosing of the style.)

Le Baiser de la fée, based on original compositions by Tchaikovsky; *Pulcinella*, based on original compositions by Pergolesi; Stravinsky, based on original compositions from musical history. (The fiction and the facts.)

But how are we supposed to imagine music 'complete with the author'?

Not like this:

Ex. 1

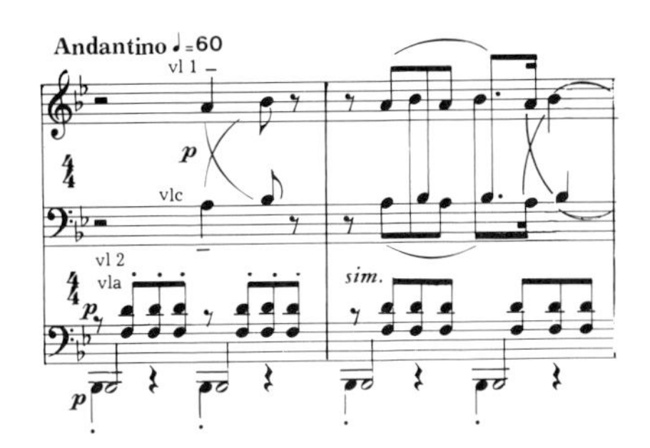

Concerto in D for string orchestra, beginning of 2nd movt.

This is a (wonderful) example of, for the most part, 'real' music, music that, above all else, wants to suggest a naturalness and leaves the impression of having written itself. But music does not write itself. Music is not a sunny backyard where, on Sunday morning, we sleepily dream away; that is why we have sunny backyards. And just to show that it is not so, the 'author' in the third bar lets us hear (Ex. 2):

Ex. 2

Abruptly awoken, but awoken with a shiver of pleasure.

At this point the listener asks himself: what am I actually *hearing*? Stravinsky's music continually questions its own working. Not that every listener can be expected to answer that question; it is enough that he hears the question being posed. If he does not even hear the question, he will stop listening and complain that this music 'has no feeling'. This music is not meant for him.

Thomas Mann called God's 'attitude one of all-embracing irony' and His gaze 'the gaze of absolute art, which is at once absolute love and absolute nihilism and indifference'. This God greatly resembles the author whose profile the

Schlegel brothers, founders of the German Romantic school, sketched and who represents the fully-conscious artist. Although one speaks of romantic irony in this connection (what in itself would seem ironic to listeners of Wagner, though not to readers of Jean Paul, Heine, Flaubert, or Gogol), it is an irony that defines more a type of artist than a historic period. As an ironist, Stravinsky is a contemporary of Gogol. (No wonder we recognize him in the main character of *The Portrait:* 'Next he bought all sorts of scents and pomades; then he rented the first magnificent flat on Nevsky Avenue he came across, without haggling over the price [Gogol was wrong on this account]. He further acquired (quite by the way) an expensive *lorgnette* and (also quite by the way) a huge quantity of cravats, many more than he would ever be likely to use. He then visited a hairdresser's and had his hair curled; drove twice in a carriage through the main thoroughfares of the city without rhyme or reason; went into a pastrycook's and gorged himself on sweets; and, finally, treated himself to a dinner at one of the most select French restaurants in town about which the rumours that had reached him were as vague as the rumours about the Chinese Empire.' The scene must have occurred around 1912. And if we, following Gogol's example, drop the thread of the story and imagine the morning in which a benefactor was woken by the telephone at seven o'clock and told by an intermediary that Igor did not sleep a wink all night because he, after serious deliberation, stipulated a thousand dollars less than was proper for *Threni*, then we are reminded of the tailor who 'charged too little because he was drunk; but all you had to do was add ten kopeks and it was a deal'.)

Stravinsky's affinity to Pushkin was even greater. Stravinsky shares with Pushkin, whose 'creative way of thinking', according to the literary historian V. V. Vinogradov, was 'thinking in literary styles', a place of honour in the Order of Proteus. In 1940 Stravinsky wrote a short, admiring essay on Pushkin. Of course this does not say much, since there probably is not a Russian who has not written at least a short, admiring essay about Pushkin, if only in his journal, just as there probably is not a Russian composer who hasn't begun his career, just as Stravinsky did ('Storm Cloud', 'Faun and Shepherdess'), by setting the verses of Pushkin. But Stravinsky's panegyric sets itself apart from so many other panegyrics in that the author, with a supreme tone, distances himself from 'the majority of my compatriots' who see in Pushkin 'our national glory', 'our first classicist and romanticist', 'the creator of that-or-the-other type' and, for Stravinsky the most contemptible, 'the forefather of the Russian revolution'. Stravinsky's Pushkin seems strikingly similar to Nabokov's Pushkin; he is the poet who says: 'The aim of poetry is poetry'; who says: 'Poetry, may God forgive me, must be slightly stupid; who, as Stravinsky concludes, 'craved poetry reduced to pure art, to art alone, amply deep and amply mystical in itself.' Stravinsky's Pushkin also resembles Stravinsky himself, especially the author of the *Poétique musicale.*

The writer of *Eugene Onegin* does not wear his heart on his sleeve, is not a romantic catalyst of all-consuming emotions, no tyrant demanding absolute subjugation, and does not want to replace reality with his art. He has an ironic spirit and writes with the belief that things are always more complicated and contradictory than would appear at first glance. Whereas we recognize only a part of this Pushkin in Tchaikovsky's opera about Tatyana and Onegin (even though, for example, the canon that Lenski and Onegin sing just before their senseless duel is a hundred times more ironic than many a scene in Wagner), he is perfectly recognizable in Stravinsky's *Mavra*. Parasha has not seen her hussar for seven days and, oh dear, she really misses him. But her voice and the instrumental voices that accompany her talk at, not with, each other. There is method in that madness of talking at each other though, since each voice has its own periodicity, but the method is too complicated for one to be able to predict when the three, or at least two of the three, periods will come together. It seems more like luck than wisdom that every once in a while the voices—suddenly—harmoniously unite. The notes that Parasha sings (we can not understand her—she is singing in Russian and we arrived at the theatre too late to read the programme), these notes make us aware that her feelings are mixed, complex, and, in any case, are not unambiguous. Musically formulated: saying tonic (in the bass) but acting as dominant (in the other voices). This used to be called 'cubistic', but this cubism is timeless (Ex. 3).

Ex. 3

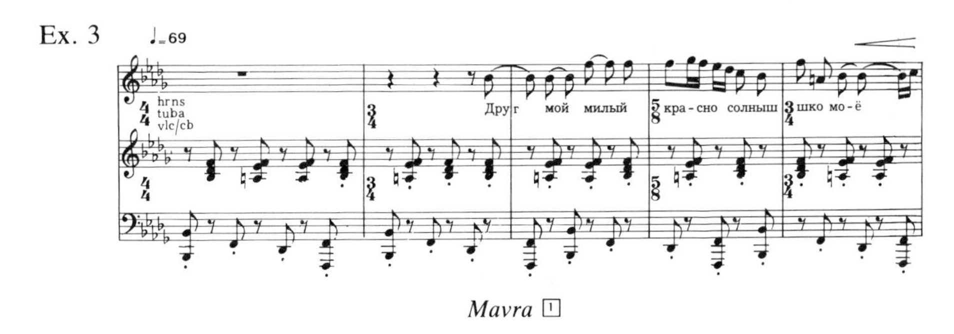

Mavra [1]

'There is', writes D. C. Muecke, 'yet another feature of irony which appears regularly in discussions of irony. We can choose from among a number of terms: detachment, distance, disengagement, freedom, serenity, objectivity, dispassion, "lightness", "play", urbanity.' It cannot be coincidence that precisely these terms (or their pejorative counterparts: lack of feeling, coldness, superficiality, etc.) rate highly in the descriptions of Stravinsky's music.

Stravinsky is first and foremost an ironic *buffo*-composer, no matter how serious the music may get. But his good humour is not carefree. The clown who acts as if he is stumbling, but would crash fifty feet were he really to fall, is not merely funny. And anyway, look how often the performances of the Stravinsky circus continue long after the lights have gone out. The only thing left is an empty arena, no human being can be seen, and it is 'cold, cold' (Stravinsky about Racine and himself). And if we look carefully, we see that the arena is not an arena but a mausoleum. Without embarrassment, and with a countenance which betrays not the slightest emotion, the ironist can allow himself the use of big words. *Memento mori*, for example or just 'death'. But nothing is tragic about this death, it is merely the confirmation of the insoluble absurdity of a world in which things are always contradicting each other.

The eighteenth-century writer Horace Walpole called the world 'a comedy to those that think, a tragedy to those that feel'.

'. . . песню пою'
('. . . I sing my song')

Making folk music into works of art was very fashionable in the second half of the nineteenth century. And not only in Russia, even though the example of the Mighty Handful (Borodin, Cui, Mussorgsky, Balakirev, Rimsky-Korsakov) is rather obvious. In Austria, even Mahler was moved by folk tunes. Hungary, Spain, Norway, almost every country had its composers who strove for a 'national' music in which simple melodies gave expression to the ideals of the unspoiled countryside, the stalwart farmer and his healthy way of life. At least, that is the only thing the twentieth-century town dweller still hears in the music of these nineteenth-century urban composers. The tone-poets themselves often upheld high-minded cultural and political ideals (Rimsky-Korsakov) and spoke in lofty words on democracy and cultural identity.

The charm of folk music was the charm of uncorrupted simplicity. The attitude towards folk music was one of endearment, and consequently one of superiority and even arrogance. It was pre-eminently a romantic attitude. (Once again, the ideals of the simple farmer and his country virtues are passionately avowed. Just look at the ubiquitous folk groups, with an Irish harp in one hand, a hank of sheep's wool in the other, waiting for the home-made bread to rise, politely singing 'Greensleeves' on television.)

Stravinsky begins his autobiography with a description of his earliest musical memory. The description is not romantically idealized, but is factual. His first memory is of an enormous, red-haired peasant, clothed only in a short red shirt, two bare legs covered with reddish hair sticking out underneath; all the children were afraid of him; though dumb, he could click his tongue very noisily, and sang a song which alternated rapidly between two meaningless syllables, accompanying himself with rhythmic puffs from the most primitive bagpipe ever (right hand under left armpit pumping away). His second memory is that of the unison song of village women returning homewards from their work in the fields. To the approval of his parents, the son, after his arrival at home, gave a pretty true imitation of the women's choir. (These are not the adventures of a Russian peasant's son, but of a two-year-old boy from St Petersburg who, as the son of a celebrated opera singer, enjoyed the privilege of spending the summer in a country dacha.)

In these reminiscences, what is important is not the quality of the folk music as a source of inspiration, but the quality of Igor Fyodorovich's reproduction of it. That will become clear in his later, notated compositions. 'The Russian feeling' always prevailed in the *émigré*'s comings and goings, except in the procedure of composition itself. For his composing, merely the technique of folk music was important, not its geographical origin. Stravinsky never wrote 'Russian folk music', since folk music is music that is 'created instinctively by the genius of the people' and it is a 'naïve but dangerous tendency' to want to imitate it. And in an interview from 1930: '[Folk] music has nothing to gain by being taken out of its frame. It is not suitable as a pretext for demonstrations of orchestral effects and complications. It loses its charm by being *déracinée*.'

After *The Firebird* and *Petrushka*, which make use of almost literal quotes from folk music, the *Sacre du printemps* replaces stylized quotations (and thereby the romantic anecdotal) with the spirit of Russian folk music. This spirit should not be thought of as an incorporeal medium or a soul hidden in matter, rather as primarily a collection of melodic and rhythmic structural principles. When Stravinsky, in the *Sacre*, decided to use concrete examples as models, these examples are interesting less because of their similarities with their final shape than because of the distance separating the original from the final. It is the distance between the concrete and the abstract, between anecdote and essence.

Bartók—who, unlike Stravinsky, as an ethnomusicologist conducted actual research—understood this, perhaps because of this research. According to Bartók, the origins of Stravinsky's 'rough-grained, brittle, and jerky musical structure, backed by ostinatos, which is so completely different from any structural proceedings of the past, may be sought in the short-breathed Russian peasant motives', consisting 'of four, two, or even one bar'.

After getting their fingernails dirty, researchers have been able to dig up several original folk melodies in Stravinsky's early works: three in *The Firebird*, eight in *Petrushka*, four in the *Sacre*, (merely four years ago, that was but one), two in *Les Noces*, and not a single one in *Renard*. But even if in the distant future, ten in each composition are found, or twenty, or maybe thirty-two, that will not afford a better insight into Stravinsky's *music*. Stravinsky's silence about folk music is telling. He avoided discussions on it, according to Craft. At least, Stravinsky provided insufficient information. This reticence was undoubtedly coupled to an aversion (shared by too few of his collegues) to 'poshlost' (banality).

Stravinsky transformed musical thinking by dealing with characteristics of folk music on a syntactical level; usually, though, musicologists mention only the characteristics of the construction of melody and (additive) rhythm in this context. But folk music also has other characteristics—even if they do not belong to the list of musical parameters as compiled by modern researchers—such as performance and its distinctive sound. Folk music is imperfect. In folk music, one is allowed to play out of tune.

Stravinsky makes this audible. Heterophony for him, just like in folk music, is frequently a 'failed' unison. The opening march from *Renard* is a circus-like melody, played by a trumpet, two horns, and a bassoon, accompanied by the cymbal and the bass drum of the marching band. That the horns and the trumpet continually leave out notes of the melody while the bassoon plays the melody in its entirety is not only a result of 'a refined orchestration in which hocket technique is combined with instrumental heterophony in the unisons', but also a reference to street musicians, who, while marching, leave holes in the melody while they empty the spit from their instrument, or because they have just tripped over a stone, or because they have such a hangover from the night before.

Playing out of tune is a parameter of folk music. The two clarinets in the *Sacre* that have parallel major sevenths ([94]), not only execute a 'type of parallel intervals that breaks the rules of counterpoint', but also play like two peasants who are actually in octaves but awfully out of tune.

Just as sevenths can be more than just sevenths, elaborations can also be more than just elaborations. In the middle voice of the Galop from the *Five Easy Pieces*, one is reminded less of the subtle embellishments of a preciously manicured eighteenth-century harpsichordist than of a circus musician who, wanting desperately to show off, adds a couple of notes *à l'improviste* to the melody (Ex. 1).

Ex. 1

The directness and crispness that folk music can have, for example, that of Georgia, but also of Sardinia—music without acoustical space—finds an outlet in Stravinsky's music. Even in *Agon*, the instruments sound as if they are being played by a group of vagrants who have only just narrowly escaped the plague.

Not endeared, but fascinated by folk music.

Stravinsky did not want to raise folk music to the level of art, but wanted to raise his art by means of folk music.

Anyway, where in the world did he hear all that folk music, asks his Russian biographer Druskin. During holidays in the country? According to Stravinsky's writings, there was not much more folk music in St Petersburg than the tritone street cry of the knife-grinder. But once again, Stravinsky is silent about 'influences' that really matter. Anyone who has heard a Georgian male-voice choir will understand better why Stravinsky's music is Stravinsky's music. We say that the *Mass* sounds like Machaut; a Soviet musicologist says that the influence of Georgian melodies can be shown. This Soviet musicologist (L. Blazhkov) is right, just as we are, since the harmonies in Georgian choral music sound like those of Machaut. Besides, Stravinsky himself denied knowing Machaut's music before he composed the *Mass*. But that does not necessarily mean anything, just as it does not necessarily mean anything that he copied out sixteen polyphonic Georgian songs in 1904. It would only have deepened the insight into Stravinsky himself if the composer (true or untrue, it does not matter) had admitted prior knowledge of Machaut and of Georgian choral music. It would merely have made more evident what interested Stravinsky in this music, namely not 'the medieval', nor 'the Russian', but chords, voice-leading, a way of singing.

Stravinsky's relationship with the Russian language is comparable to his relationship with Russian folk music. The desire to evoke a Russian Taj Mahal was not why the *émigré* Stravinsky composed on Russian texts; rather, it was the fascination with the sound of the language, its prosody, the way word and musical accents remain asynchronous.

'Perhaps the strongest factor in my decision to re-enter the Russian Church rather than convert to the Roman was linguistic.'

The Metamorphosis of Misha

1. Mighty bear. Dreaded companion to man in vast Russia. According to legend, himself once a man. But love and friendship were denied him; he turned his back on man, put on a new, fear-provoking face and returned to the protection of the forest.

Mighty, and invincible. And so he is portrayed on the coats of arms of prominent Russian families. A symbol of strength, but also gentle and cuddly—the animal that loves honey.

Sometimes he was captured and taken along by showmen and peddlars. He became Misha—as this is the bear's proper nickname—and he danced to the music of the organ-grinder. He is still a bear when he appears in *Petrushka*, accompanied by his owner's clarinet (Ex. 1).

Ex. 1

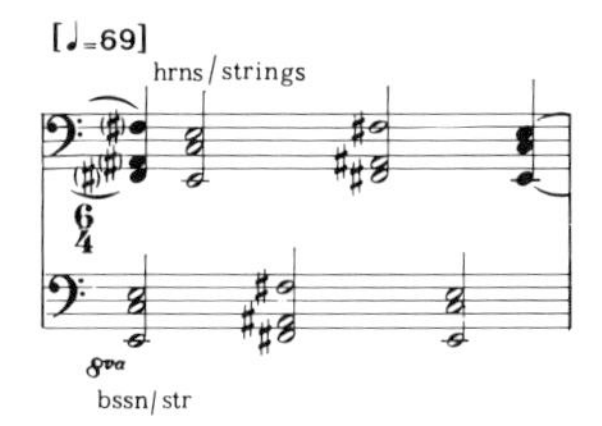

Misha! Your clumsy feet trample over so much Russian orchestral music. How ponderous and sluggish you sound—always thick, low chords, always octaves with thirds. Your appearance carries with it the melacholy of fate. And though not without grace, your dancing, your desire, will be lost in the flow of time. In *Petrushka* you are still decked out in exotic harmonies, but merely two years later, in the *Sacre*, you are stuck fast in the 'Ritual Dance of the Ancestors' (Ex. 2).

Ex. 2

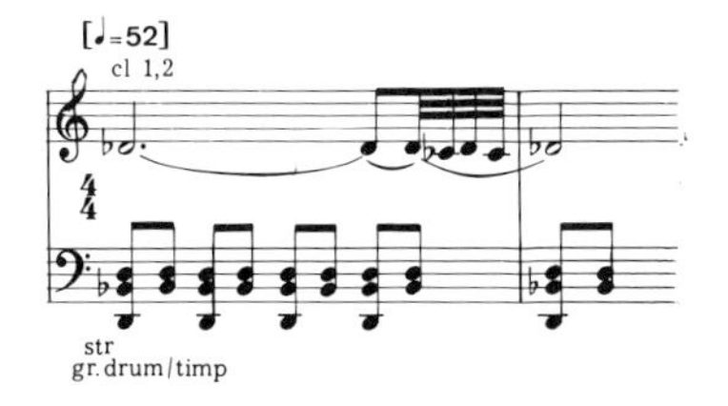

As an atavistic memory, though none the less threatening, you fleetingly appear in the *Symphonies of Wind Instruments* (Ex. 3).

Ex. 3

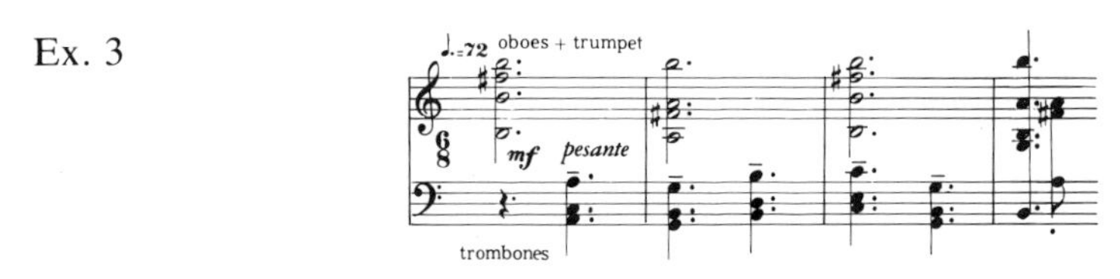

Yet look, Misha! You should have stayed in the sanctity of the deep, Russian wood. You could have lingered calmly by the Great Gate of Kiev—sluggish, naïve, but still proud and invincible. Now, Misha, you will be chilled to death by the mundane, decadent West.

There you are, once again. Though now not flesh and blood, merely as a symbol, the symbol for what you always were—Mother Russia. One month after the Russian February Revolution in 1917, as Father Igor arranges the *Song of the Volga Boatmen* (the replacement of 'God Save the Tsar' and instead of Degeyter's 'Internationale') for a benefit concert for the Red Cross in Rome, you appear in all your majesty. Omnipresent. From the first note to the last. Both high and low. As if you are standing on your hind legs and for the last time raising your voice in full glory (Ex. 4).

Ex. 4

But time waits for no one. Slowly you were transformed from bear into 'bear', and from 'bear' into an abstract musical idea—a clamp on the hand of the pianist (Ex. 5).

Ex. 5

Concerto for Piano and Wind, beginning of 2nd movt.

Ultimately you will be petrified into one single chord, cornerstone of the music for an eastern cathedral; a soldier in full armour, opening and closing the gates of the first chorus in *Canticum Sacrum*; sentinel of Venice and its patron, the Holy Saint Mark, to whom the sacred chant is dedicated (Ex. 6).

Ex. 6

2. He treads no longer. The mighty bear has become a musical formula. But a formula with a long history in liturgical music. Close spacing in the bass, octaves and thirds in parallel motion as happens when men raise their voices in harmony and the women listen. In Slavic lands and in the West, examples of early polyphony exist in which equal voices move in parallel motion: faux bourdon. Stravinsky's version of it has a specific musical function: the third next to the fundamental in the bass works to de-tonalize. It is used preferably in strongly tonal works, as reflected even in their titles: *Concerto in D for Violin*, *Symphony in C*. In both of these works, root position major chords are seldom encountered. Even, no, especially in the closing chord of the first movement of the *Symphony in C*, the bass, the mediant of the key, is so strongly emphasized that the tonic function of the C major chord is affected, the tone B almost being heard as the dominant of E instead of the seventh of C) (Ex. 7).

Ex. 7

In the *Symphony in Three Movements*, thirds and sixths (forming octaves) shape the first movement to a certain extent also melodically (Ex. 8).

Ex. 8

The bear is engulfed—forged into steel as in the monument by Tatlin.

'. . . a war film, this time a documentary of scorched-earth tactics in China'.

Octotony

Two, or at most three, musical examples might be adequate to characterize the worrying state of Dutch composition in the years just after the Second World War. And half an hour of leafing through an overwhelming amount of piano sonatinas and symphoniettas is enough to get a good idea of the Dutch spirit after the war: national unity, progress, positive mentality, anti-communism, keeping up with the Joneses, in short, reconstruction. Optimistic rhythms applied to lively melodies with here and there a dissonance: what was once called *en vogue* was now called 'cool'. There was a future.

And the future was in one's hand, except for the students of Pijper and their uncrowned king-in-exile, the irresistible Henk Badings[1] who stood on the brink of Dutch art even *during* the war by way of his opera on Rembrandt, commissioned by the Nederlands-Duitse Kultuurgemeenschap [the Dutch-German Cultural Community].

More than thirty-five years later we can take advantage of that situation. In spite of the fact that none of the works referred to above are worth their weight in gold, composers such as Henkemans, Van Delden,[2] and Van Lier[3] enriched music theory with a scientifically useful term—octonony.

The octotonic scale consists of a regular alternation of major and minor seconds. Just as the whole-tone scale (or enhemitonic hexatonic, henceforth enhemitonic) has only two forms with different pitch content, the octotonic scale has three forms with different pitch content. The limited number of possible transpositions of the scale is a direct consequence of its symmetrical structure. Messiaen, who applies the scale regularly in his music as do his kindred spirits of La jeune France, regards the scale as one of the so-called *modes à transpositions limitées.* The Italian composer Vito Frazzi speaks of *scale alternate* in his treatise of the same name (Florence, 1930) (Ex. 1).

Ex. 1

[1] Henk Badings (1907–1987), Dutch composer who, well known outside the Netherlands, had a rather difficult time in Holland due to his opportunistic behaviour during the German occupation in the Second World War [trans.].

[2] Lex van Delden (1919–88), Dutch composer and former critic [trans.].

[3] Bertus van Lier (1906–72), Dutch composer [trans.].

Dogmatic and automatic use of this scale leads to malingering music, reeling around in circles, biting its own tail, scurrying hither and thither. Main themes cannot be differentiated from transitions, secondary themes sound like codas. The principle is as simple as it is effective: one places the upper tone of a major second (each octotonic scale has four of them) in the bass, while with the right hand one shifts around back and forth through the scale (preferably sequences with vivacious rhythms) and, lo and behold, a new sonatina for piano is born. The notes of this kind of music are not gained through the sweat of the brow, but grow on trees. Yet it does not have to be like that.

Stravinsky's music stipulates insight into octotony.

The octotonic scale has a synthetic construction. Historically and structurally it is a derived from a harmonic sequence, specifically the succession of four major triads related by minor thirds (Ex. 2).

Ex. 2

(In a somewhat different arrangement:

Ex. 3

Le Sacre du printemps [42]4

they awaken the suspicion of recognition.)

Using the same pitch collection, these four major triads can be expanded to dominant ninth chords (minor ninth) with an added minor third (Ex. 4). Within the octotonic context, these chords should be seen as a combination of two dominant seventh chords separated by a minor third (Ex. 5).

Ex. 4

Ex. 5

(More than just a suspicion:

Ex. 6

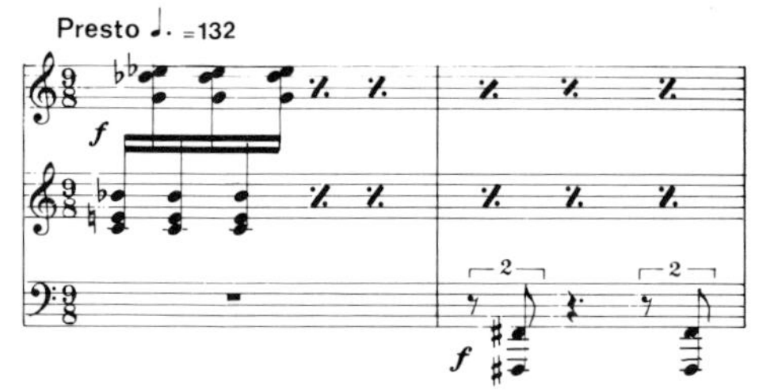

Le Sacre du printemps [37]

this is starting to resemble Stravinsky.)

Besides being the combination of two dominant seventh chords, this chord also has the characteristic of being a major triad with an added minor third. It is a motto of Stravinsky's entire œuvre:

Ex. 7

(*a*) *Le Roi des étoiles* (1912), motto

(*b*) *Symphony of Psalms* (1930) [24]$_2$

(*c*) *Symphony in C* (1940) [179]$_3$

(*d*) *Orpheus* (1947) [46]

(*e*) *Threni* (1958), bar 170

(*f*) *Requiem Canticles* (1966), bar 265

or one could say, a 'distinguishing mark':

(*g*) *Le Sacre du printemps* (1913), bar 2

(*h*) *Les cinq doigts* (1921), III. Lento, opening

(*i*) *Dumbarton Oaks* (1938) [33]

(*j*) *Danses Concertantes* (1942) [54]

(*k*) *Scènes de ballet* [1]

(*l*) *Symphony in Three Movements* (1945) [112]$_2$

In each of the dominant ninth chords in Example 4, two successive major triads (from Example 2) can be differentiated. The combination of two non-successive major triads gives rise to another chord—the dominant ninth chord (minor ninth) with added tritone (Ex. 8).

Ex. 8

This chord, probably only in the United States still called bitonal, has become known as the *Petrushka* chord (Ex. 9).

Ex. 9

'The dissonant combination of C and F♯': paradoxically, the customary description of the *Petrushka* chord emphasizes its most traditional aspect. What is new about it is not necessarily the structure of the chord, but the fact that the combination of two major triads separated by a tritone has been removed from the context of late romantic chromaticism and roving harmonies (Scriabin). The chord's anti-tonal notation (for example, an A♯ instead of a B♭) gives visual expression to the becoming autonomous of what used to be an augmented six-four-three chord. The *Petrushka* chord is not a harmonic function but an *objet sonore avant la lettre*.

The harmonic structure of the *Petrushka* chord emanates from a development that goes back to the beginning of the nineteenth century. But the *Petrushka* chord is also a chord taken from *The Firebird*. The difference between the two chords is a difference of function, also reflected in the notation: what in *Petrushka* is the combination of two independent triads is in *The Firebird* still a 'tonally' notated seventh chord with appoggiaturas (Ex. 10). Only after many pages and just as many adventures does the '*Firebird* chord' betray its roots: the *succession* of the two chords of which it is composed (Ex. 11).

Ex. 10

The Firebird, bar 11

Ex. 11

The Firebird [48]

This succession of two triads separated by a tritone (the second one in this case is a passing chord) is a harmonic piquancy belonging to the groomed fairy-tale world of late nineteenth-century Russian, especially St Petersburg, dramatic music. There are a plethora of examples in Rimsky-Korsakov (Ex. 12).

Ex. 12

Rimsky-Korsakov, *Mlada* (1892), Act III [8]$_6$

Rimsky is the first consciously to apply the octotonic scale as melodic material, the first to describe its structure explicitly. In his memoirs, he delves into the history of *Sadko* (1867) and answers the question, 'what musical tendencies guided [his] fancy' while composing this 'symphonic picture'.

'The beginning of the Allegro 3/4, depicting Sadko's fall into the sea and his being dragged to the depths by the Sea King, is, in method, reminiscent of the moment when Lyudmila is spirited away by Chernomo in Act I of *Ruslan and Lyudmila.* However, Glinka's scale, descending by whole notes' (Rimsky could hardly have spoken of a Debussy scale while discussing an opera that was sixty-two years old) 'has been replaced by another descending scale of semitone, whole tone, semitone, whole tone—a scale which subsequently played an important part in many of my compositions.' (Ex. 13.)

Ex. 13 Rimsky-Korsakov, *Sadko* (Symphonic Poem, 1867 version), bars 135–44

In Example 13, the octotony is still related to the diminished seventh chord.

Ex. 14

The Firebird, bar 7

Example 14 from *The Firebird* is historically more important in an analysis of octotonic harmony. After removing the two minor third appoggiaturas, a rudimentary form of octotonic harmony remains: the French six-four-three chord, a chord which also belongs to the harmonic arsenal of the enhemitonic scale. The French six-four-three is the harmonic key to *The Firebird.* It forms the link between octotonic and enhemitonic harmony. An example of the latter is the beginning of 'Lever du jour', [89].

It was neither Rimsky (octotony), nor Debussy (enhemitony): the genuine ghost which scares the firebird into becoming a high flier is the anything but fairy-like Alexander Nicolaevitch Scriabin. When *The Firebird* is formally octotonic but does not sound as if it is (Ex. 15), we hear Scriabinesque, impelling chromatic sequences in the upper voice and leading notes in the bass (Ex. 16 and 17).

Ex. 15

The Firebird [57]$_{6}$

Ex. 16

Scriabin, Prelude, Op. 11 No. 2, bar 57

Ex. 17

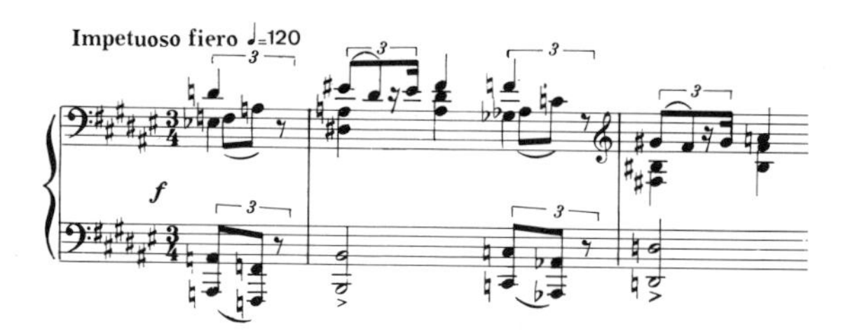

Scriabin, Prelude, Op. 48 No. 1, opening

Example 16 (Scriabin, 1895) shows how three of the four octotonic seventh chords can become closely related within a rather conventional tonal idiom. In Example 17 (1905), typical of later Scriabin, the tonal functions have disintegrated and the leading notes in the bass do not resolve. The first chords of this prelude in F♯ (which begins with a seventh chord on F!) combine to form an octotonic scale and really sound octotonic, especially because of the successive bass notes F, B, A♭, D.

(Of course, the history of octotony goes back further. When Chopin left Warsaw in 1830 for Vienna, besides taking 'a silver goblet filled with Polish soil' in the coach with him, he took the octotonic scale. An early example of this scale is found in the *Polonaise-Fantaisie*, Op. 61 (Ex. 18).

Ex. 18

Chopin, *Polonaise-Fantaisie*, Op. 61, bar 240

This octotony, however, is not the result of a combination of triads, but of a broken diminished seventh chord with passing notes. Although such rudimentary forms of octotony are historically important, they need not be included in an analysis of Stravinsky's harmony since one of the most essential aspects of octotony is absent—the combination of major and minor thirds. Incidentally, Chopin took this combination with him from Poland too: minor third in the melody, major third in the harmony. But the alternation of minor and major seconds lasting four bars in the *Polonaise-Fantaisie* is less characteristic of octotony than this languid gesture:

Ex. 19

—a sigh from Scriabin [Prelude, Op. 15 No. 2], forty-five years after the death of Chopin. The seductiveness of this double dissonance must have been great.)

The Firebird as Magpie

[Composing] is certainly more difficult now, and it always was.

Ravel's music is easily admired. At the beginning of this century, the *Rapsodie espagnole* left a deep impression, not only in Paris but in St Petersburg as well. 'The *dernier cri* . . . incredible as this seems now' is what Stravinsky wrote in 1962. But 'now' was nearly half a century after he almost literally borrowed the ending of the *Rapsodie espagnole* for the last twenty bars of the 'Infernal Dance' in *The Firebird.*

That was not quoting, nor was it paraphrasing, nor commentating nor parodying; it was imitating. Imitating is something that young composers do. It is a legitimate way of gaining compositional proficiency. 'One learns through imitation', according to Brecht (and Chekhov and Horace and so many others). But a composer needs to free himself from the masters who truly influence him.

'Ravel? When I think of him, for example in relation to Satie, he appears quite ordinary.' That is what Stravinsky said four years earlier, in 1958, nearly half a century after he wrote a 'Berceuse' in *The Firebird* that sounds suspiciously like the *Pavane de la Belle au bois dormant* from Ravel's *Ma mère l'oye*, composed two years earlier. Even the romantic eruption half-way through the 'Berceuse' (185) reminds one of Ravel, of the first movement of the *Rapsodie espagnole* (4): the same musical motion, the same chord. Very beautiful. Something like what you just have to have composed once in your life.

'Ravel? But Ravel is ten years older than I am. As for Ravel's talent, it is Rimsky-Korsakov's fifty years younger.' Stravinsky said this in 1924. But this same Ravel was the discoverer of the string-harmonic glissando (in *L'Heure espagnole* as well as in the last movement of the *Rapsodie espagnole*, Feria 1), a novelty that Stravinsky would later claim as his own, referring to *The Firebird.* Stravinsky is sometimes even ungracious about Ravel. 'Ravel turned his back on me after *Mavra*'. But who actually turned whose back on whom?

Even in *Petrushka*, Ravel's dazzling octotonic arpeggios from the *Rapsodie espagnole* (and from the dizzying piano works *Miroirs*, *Gaspard de la nuit*) shine like stars in Stravinsky's eyes (Exx. 1 and 2). And they continued to do so for some years; examples abound.

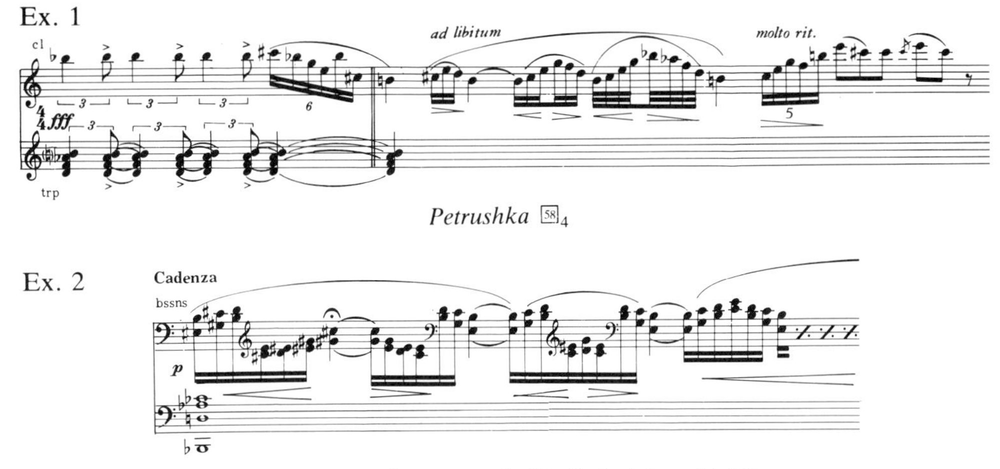

Petrushka [58]4

Ravel, *Rapsodie espagnole* ('Prélude à la nuit' [8])

Initially, Stravinsky and Ravel were very good colleagues, friends even, though Ravel was seven years older—not ten as Stravinsky maintained. Ravel was 'my uncle'.

This uncle, besides being present at the première of the *Sacre du printemps*, was also at the dress rehearsal. And Stravinsky sat with the composer and his mother in the box during the première of *Daphnis et Chloë* (June 1912). He thought it was superb. He asked Ravel to come to Switzerland to work with him on an orchestration of Mussorgsky's *Khovanshchina* (and they slept together in the same bed when they had gone to Varèse in search of paper and the hotels turned out to be full). Nothing but good words. In Switzerland they worked on songs for similar ensembles, Ravel on the *Trois poèmes de Stéphane Mallarmé* and Stravinsky on the *Trois poésies de la lyrique japonaise*, inspired by Schoenberg's *Pierrot Lunaire*. Both were VIPs. Once, when Stravinsky was ill, Ravel cried at his sickbed.

Even in 1914 Stravinsky writes in a letter to Alexander Benois (set designer for, among other things, *Petrushka*): 'I love Ravel very much, not sentimentally but actually.' Two years later, in a letter to Diaghilev, he wrote: 'I greatly admire Ravel's *Rapsodie*.'

But on the evening that Ravel and Marcelle Meyer played *La Valse* for two pianos for the first time for Diaghilev and friends (where else than at the home of Misia Sert, to whom the work was dedicated), Stravinsky succeeded in saying not a single word about the piece the entire evening. That was in 1920. Since then, the admiration was past tense.

That Stravinsky and Ravel chose different musical directions is insufficient explanation for their estrangement. Their directions had always been different.

Ravel was a composer who, unlike Stravinsky, hardly reacted to fashions in music. He went his own way and created a new music that would reverberate throughout the twentieth century. There is hardly a television film today in which one or another Ravel derivation does not serve as background music. But that is the negative side of influence, influence on the surface of music. Truly exemplary is the lining of Ravel's music, the tight structure, the refined harmonic connections, the meticulous orchestrations.

The similarities between Stravinsky and Ravel are more important than the differences though. Just like Stravinsky, Ravel was interested in writing compositions about musical genres—about a dance form, for example—or about a specific style (eighteenth-century French harpsichord music). In this way, the subject of *La Valse* is the Viennese waltz. But, at the same time, *La Valse* is the apotheosis of the waltz. Since then, not a single composer has succeeded in composing a piece in three-four that has stood the test of time. Ravel's apotheosis was a final apotheosis. Did Stravinsky ever get so far? And who has managed to compose a bolero after 1928? In 1935, while travelling around Morocco with friends, no longer in a fit state to compose, Ravel said: 'If I were to write something Arabic, it would be more Arabic than all of this here.'

The *Rapsodie espagnole* was also a genre composition. Although it may have been a model for parts of *The Firebird*, the piece itself had yet other music as model: the 'folkloristic' orchestral pieces about exotic Spain, with flamenco-like cadences, festive Andalusian dances, slow movements depicting nocturnal scenes, and string orchestras imitating guitars, preferably with the violin under the arm—Rimsky's *Capriccio espagnol* for example, or the piece that was model for that piece, Glinka's *La Jota Aragonaise*. Stravinsky, in the same breath, called *La Jota Aragonaise* and Glinka's *Une Nuit à Madrid* 'incomparable'.

Stravinsky's *Tango* was less final than Ravel's *Bolero*. Astor Piazzolla would raise the genre to great heights once more in the seventies.

Stravinsky was influenced by Ravel up to his thirtieth birthday. And being influenced is different from 'making use' of Weber in the *Capriccio*, of Verdi in *Oedipus Rex*, or of Purcell in *Three Songs from William Shakespeare*. Stravinsky estranged himself from Ravel because he had been too close to him. He could hardly bring himself to value Ravel's music any more since he loved it too much. They were too similar. And, 'ceux qui se touchent, s'extrèment'.

There was another composer who shared the same fate—Scriabin.

'Our local genius' Stravinsky called him in 1962.

In St Petersburg, *Le Poème divin*, *Prometheus*, and *Poème de l'extase* 'were thought to be as up to date as the Paris Métro'.

This is the tone used by Stravinsky in later years to talk about the composer without whose music many a page of his own earlier works would be unimaginable, albeit unimaginable in a different way than without Ravel's music. The relationship of Stravinsky to Scriabin is more complex; it had to be, if only because Scriabin's aesthetics and philosophy of art were completely alien to Stravinsky. Scriabin's ideal of a musical Universe—orchestras and choirs wandering through a paradisial India, hugging one another, and the audience too, playing and singing against a background of sunrises and sunsets, since merely the introduction to *Mysterium*, the Prefatory Action, was supposed to last seven days—belonged to a world of Blavatskian utopianism that Stravinsky, even then, considered much out of date.

'To answer your question, perhaps I have been influenced by Scriabin in one very insignificant respect, in the piano writing of my Études, Op. 7.' 'Perhaps', 'insignificant', 'Études'—Stravinsky allowed himself to go that far when he was almost in his eighties and Scriabin had already been in his grave for more than half a century. When Stravinsky wrote his piano pieces he was just twenty-six and Scriabin was the celebrated composer of exuberant piano music filled with literally unheard-of harmonies. The *Études* could have been by Scriabin, certainly. But *The Firebird*, composed not quite two years later, is that suddenly no longer Scriabinesque? Stravinsky thought so. When in 1962 he elaborated on the styles which are recognizable in *The Firebird*, both Rimsky-Korsakov and Tchaikovsky are expanded upon, though not even the name Scriabin is mentioned.

But what is the Dance of the Firebird if nothing more than a copy of the Allegro volando from Scriabin's *Poème de l'extase*? An ability to read music is not even needed to see it with one's own eyes: the flittering in the violins, the plucking in the basses, it is all one and the same. And it sounds the same too: virtuosic gyrations in mid-flight, flashy chromaticism in the melody, octotonic harmony in the middle voices, and everything propelled by a light bass of diminished fifths.

Scriabin 'had no insight at all', Stravinsky wrote in 1960. He apparently had forgotten what he had written to Florent Schmitt half a century earlier, on 21 July 1911 to be precise: that he was 'playing only Debussy and Scriabin'. In 1913, while Stravinsky and Scriabin are both living in Switzerland, the former actually invites the latter to visit him.

30 September 1913: 'Yesterday I played your Seventh Sonata again and my opinion has not changed. I await you eagerly so I can show you and tell you what I like so especially in it.' The letter in question has been dug up by Scriabin's biographer Faubion Bowers. Since Scriabin never turned up, Stravinsky simply had to go to him. A week later he wrote to V. V.

Derzhanovsky, editor of *Muzyka:* 'He played me his latest sonatas and they pleased me incomparably.' One can certainly hear that, and not only in the lush harmonies of *The Firebird.* Even in the *Sacre*, the inventor of 'mystic chords' has left tracks: parallel dissonant chords, repeated on different steps of the scale, often octotonic. Playing these chords provides a certain physical pleasure. And Stravinsky *played* Scriabin. He played Scriabin on the same piano that he played the *Sacre* on before he wrote down the notes (Exx. 3, 4, and 5). Incidentally, the last chord of Example 5 is identical to the chord which begins bar 238 of the Sixth Sonata (Ex. 6).

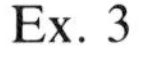
Ex. 3

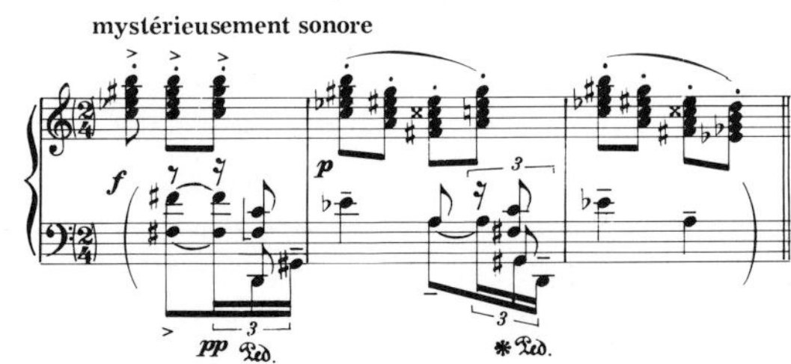

Scriabin, Sonata 7, Op. 64 (1911), bars 36–8

Ex. 4

Le Sacre du printemps [45]

Ex. 5

Le Sacre du printemps [53]10

Ex. 6

Scriabin, Sonata 6, Op. 62, bar 238

It is particularly because the late sonatas of Scriabin and the *Sacre* sound so different that it is interesting to look at their similarities. The ear easily passes over them. They are structural similarities. The glowing lava of Scriabin has solidified into the pumice of Stravinsky. Harmony, the clearest manifestation of the kinship, has coagulated. Example 7 shows how this has been put into practice. The bars from Scriabin's Étude, Op. 65 No. 3 form the same chord that dominates the last page of the *Sacre* (Ex. 8).

Ex. 7

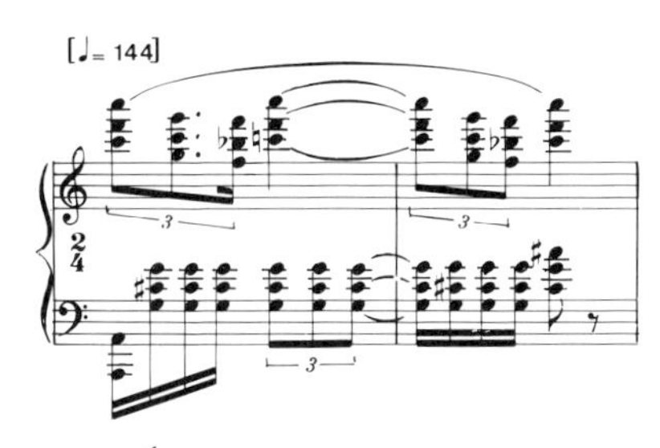

Scriabin, Étude, Op. 65 No. 3, bars 45–6

Ex. 8

Le Sacre du printemps 199

This chord can be reduced to a chord of six notes (Ex. 9).

Ex. 9

This six-note chord is a variant of Scriabin's '*Prometheus* chord' (Ex. 10).

Ex. 10

If Examples 7 and 8 are compared to the *Prometheus* chord, it appears that a B♭ has been added in both cases, that the E♭ is missing in Scriabin (but of course it immediately follows a bar later in the bass) and that Stravinsky adds an E. The addition of the E causes the melody at the end of the 'Danse sacrale' to become *diatonic* (Ex. 11).

Ex. 11

The combination of diatonic melody (the 'folk melodies' of the Mighty Handful) and chromatic harmony in the *Sacre* forms the most significant difference from Scriabin's music. Besides, in the example from the *Sacre*, the harmony is octotonic: the middle voices run through a standard version of octotony, a succession of the four dominant seventh chords of C, F♯, A, and E♭. The enharmonic notation of this harmonic sequence—that has slowly but surely become cliché—betrays the influence of a late romantic musical propensity. It is true that Scriabin's music sounds romantic and the *Sacre* does not; but behind Scriabin's romantic gestures hides the herald of a new, typically twentieth-century musical way of thinking. *Prometheus* and the Seventh and Tenth Sonatas are not only proto-psychedelic sound-visions, but early examples of a predilection towards non-development as well, of which Stravinsky took advantage. After the gigantic C major into which *Poème de l'extase* resolves, not a work of Scriabin's can be found in which musical material is *durchgeführt*. The diabolical *Vers la flamme* is merely the pianistic escalation of transpositions of continually the same chords.

Tracing influences can be dangerous. The critic who, for example, after the first performance of Stockhausen's *Gruppen* can think of no more to say than that Berlioz already placed orchestras in various parts of the hall, takes the sting out of the new. This is how new music is, in the wrong way, written about in history books: it is categorized.

True renewal is only possible by the grace of tradition. But tradition is something different from convention.

'[Conventions] differ from traditions in that they are modified rather than developed.'

In music, it is a good tradition to break conventions.

1912–*Le Roi des étoiles* (*Zvezdoliki*)

There is no more dangerous a spirit than the Zeitgeist. The Zeitgeist is a lazy, conceited, disporting despot. He sees nothing, he explains nothing, he simply is. He has free power of attorney and slouches lazily on his tattered chaise-longue conducting a chorus of fools, from early morning to late at night. He robs the people of their voice, but is democratically elected. The Zeitgeist reduces fertile ideas into paralysing formulas: civil disobedience is reduced to 'the sixties', an energetic avant-garde withers into 'you know'. It is no coincidence that the Zeitgeist is often a pseudonym for decadence. Amateurs of 'general ideas'—one of the most cunning disguises of this calendar ghost—can feast on Russia at the turn of the century, when every self-respecting artist placed his talent in the service of Promethean thought, sensualism, or (specifically Russian) apolcalyptic emotions; and thereby, especially in the latter case, often taking refuge in the gospel of the antichrist, cultivating hypochondria and, for those with Artsybashevian sympathies, experimenting in sexual and suicidal rites. Mother Russia as an out-of-control Baba Yaga. Of course, we must thank the Zeitgeist for Kandinsky, Bely, Malevich, Blok, and Balmont (*in spite of* this Zeitgeist); but the victims were more numerous. They might only be remembered as witnesses for the prosecution. Those who escaped from the Zeitgeist could do so only through inventing their own Zeitgeist (so that it ceased to be one), through taking advantage of the Zeitgeist, or by negating it (by first recognizing it).

Diaghilev rightly called himself an 'incorrigible sensualist', but in Paris, he made the Ballets Russes—and the Zeitgeist—dance to his piping.

Scriabin's *Promethean Fantasies* has been preserved because it was written by Scriabin; but the camouflaged piano concerto that carries the name of the hero who stole fire from the gods is not only a finale to a totally burnt-out aesthetic, but also the prelude to a musical dawn.

Stravinsky composed music to Balmont's apocalyptic *Le Roi des étoiles* (*Zvezdoliki*) (one of the most quoted early symbolic poems) in 1911–12, shuttling between his telluristic consecration of spring—actually just as much inspired by the Zeitgeist—and his vision of a Saturnalian universe; but he announced his musical future in the motto inscribed above the Balmont cantata (Ex. 1): undisguised major/minor in the initial chord, pandiatonicism in the third chord and in the melody a foreshadowing of the Laudate from the *Symphony of Psalms*.

Ex. 1

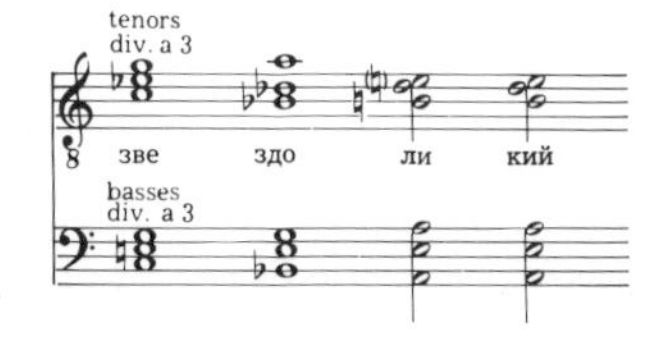

In the cantata, the new is embraced by the old: neither the first part (bars 1–23), nor the coda (bars 42–8) pay much regard to the motto. The coda, with its languid thirds in the oboes and its whole-tone chords (bars 40, 41) is a copy of Debussy's style. Actually, we are reminded of the new only by the closing chord (bar 48, a pandiatonic variant of the octotonic chord which closes the first choral phrase in bar 7) (Ex. 2). The coda is, furthermore, the conclusion of the period (early Stravinsky) in which style quotation is not necessarily 'style quotation'.

Ex. 2

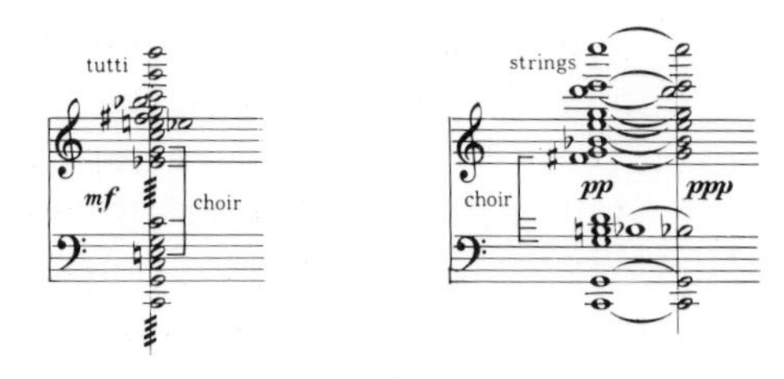

Le Roi des étoiles, bars 7, 48

The first part is more idiosyncratic and experimental; it is simultaneously the furthest consequence and the scrapping of the harmonic language of *The Firebird*. (The supposition propounded by Schaeffner and since then, 1931, repeated by others that, with *Le Roi des étoiles*, Stravinsky turned down a road that 'could have brought him in the neighbourhood of Schoenberg', is none the less the consequence of a misunderstanding. Not only is the elimination of harmonic gravity suggested by the text—this statement could possibly be inverted—but this music acts only as preparation—the unsuspected execution of Scriabin's Prefatory Action—for the following chorus, for the 'new'.)

When a bare major triad with an added minor third appears in bars 1–23, it is an exception to the rule of parallel chords and strongly octotonic-tinted chromaticism. Octotonic chords function as musical punctuations (bars 7–8,

11, and 23), sometimes also as points of departure for more advanced harmonic experiments (Ex. 3).

Ex. 3

Le Roi des étoiles, bars 15–17

What is heard in bars 15–17 is, at the same time, both the consequential application of the octotonic principle and its own undermining: hardly any chords *sound* octotonic, though *all* the chords are comprised of notes from one of the three octotonic scales:[1]

	1–8		11–12			: scale 2
chord number		9			13	: scale 1
			10		14:	scale 3

The 'wrong' bass notes B♭ and G, the 'wrong' soprano E in the orchestra, and the 'wrong', C♯ twice in the choir indicate that Stravinsky—unlike his Dutch colleagues almost half a century later[2]—did not think horizontally in synthetically structured modes, but intuitively experimented with late romantic harmonies.

Upon reaching the chorale, the octotony is done away with. The octotonic chords that remain (and that never really disappear during the succeeding forty years) are uprooted, functioning only as passing chords. The only genuine octotonic-tinted harmonic sequence (the four dominant seventh chords a minor third apart in bar 29) occurs not in the chorale itself, but in the solemn hymn for male voices. The rest is prophecy: octotony as apposition; bare major triads with added major seconds (bars 25^2, 28^3, 30^1), with added minor seconds (bar 30^2), or with added minor thirds (24^1, $27^{1,3}$, 28^1, 30^3, 31^3,

[1] See 'Octotony', p. 228 [trans.].

[2] See also 'Octotony', p. 228, especially footnotes 2, 3, and 4 [trans].

32[2]), and pandiatonicism (33[2], the final chord of the chorale) are what stand out (Ex. 4).

Ex. 4

Le Roi des étoiles, bars 24–33

Between the Scriabinesque twilight and the Debussian afternoon, Time forgets the hour. For, when the King of the Stars finally speaks 'Do you keep the word?' and 'we' shout 'We do', the granite chords appear, unambiguously, for the first time, that will continually appear, time and time again, for the next sixty years, in order to enchant Time, like an indefatigable Averroës in the form of a clock with one hundred and twenty hands. This is the first occasion that 'we' are witness to a ritual taking place somewhere else, not (and here, from one beat to the next, the earth splits between Stravinsky and Scriabin) as participant in the passion of this secret, evoked universe or in the excitement of its discovery.

'"I am the First and I am the Last"—he said/ And thunder echoed a hollow response.'

The King is quoted—just as in the apotheosis of *Les Noces*, where the last remaining singer quotes the words that the bridegroom speaks as he presses his bride's hand to his heart.

The Tradition of the New

In the summers of 1880, 1881, and 1882, Debussy accompanied the widow Nadezhda Filaretovna von Meck and her children on their travels through Russia and Europe. The still very young composer (with unsuspected irony called Petrushka, that is, Parsley, by the Mecks) was in charge of the musical tutorship of the family. Little more can be said with certainty of the musical impressions Debussy brought back with him from Russia than that Glinka and Tchaikovsky were part of them. Even though there are no first-hand accounts that Debussy came in contact with the music of the Mighty Handful in Russia, and even though he was for years apparently indifferent towards the score of *Boris Godunov* presented to him in 1889, there was always Paris—where on the occasion of the world exhibition of 1878 (that is, fifteen years before the ultimate breakthrough of the Mighty Handful gave a musical ratification to the new French–Russian alliance), works of, among others, Rimsky-Korsakov and Dargomyzhsky were performed and where César Antonovich Cui, one of the Mighty Handful, published a series of authoritative articles about music in his country (appearing in book form in 1880 with the title *La Musique en Russie*); and then there are yet the reports of Debussy's friends according to whom the composer returned from Russia well acquainted with Mussorgsky, Borodin, and 'an old opera of Rimsky-Korsakov'.

It is certain that Debussy's musical advances cannot be regarded separately from the harmonic experimentations in the works of particularly Mussorgsky and Rimsky-Korsakov. Rimsky was, in many aspects, exemplary. Though the price of being an example was a worrying irritation: he recommended not listening to Debussy, since 'one runs the risk of getting accustomed to him and one would end by liking him'.

Long before Debussy startled his composition teacher Ernest Guiraud with unresolving ninth chords, Rimsky had already notated passages in his operas and orchestral works, going on for pages, that consisted of little more than successions of major triads, not diatonically, not modulating, but chromatically ascending and decending in relationships of a minor third or a tritone. One characteristic of these passages is that the tonal function always remains the same, or more precisely, that, from *Sadko*, Op. 5 to *Le Coq d'or*, any changes in tonal function are in appearance only. Since the number of tonal functions is reduced to one, they actually cease to exist. The paradoxical consequence of this is that passages which on the surface display the characteristics of a transition period, receive autonomous meaning because of their length. Musical tension becomes disengaged from tonal cadencing and the traditional sequence is replaced with a co-ordinative montage. The effect of 'and then . . . and then . . . and then' is amplified by the block-like orchestration, the homophonic texture, and the repetition of rhythmic motives. The bass, petrified into an ostinato (preferably of a minor third or tritone) or into a single held tone, forms the final confirmation of this musical coagulation.

What formerly was allowed only in the coda, Rimsky does in bar 17. Musical dramatics becomes tableau vivant. No wonder that in the aesthetic of the Mighty Handful, the musical counterpart of literary realism, there was hardly room for the symphony. When, twenty-five years after composing *Antar* (1868)—in which he renewed the traditional symphonic form 'by sending it on a long walk' (Debussy)—Rimsky renamed his second symphony symphonic *suite*, he was doing more than merely replacing one card with another.

The de-dramatization of music occurred paradoxically enough primarily in the theatre. (And subsequently in real life: on the occasion of the twenty-fifth anniversary of the reign of Alexander II in 1880, twelve composers were commissioned to compose music for a series of tableaux vivants in which the apices of a quarter of a century of Russian history would be displayed *pro memoria* and *pro patria*). There is not a single nineteenth-century opera in which the question of 'how does it end' matters as little as it does in *Prince Igor*. The dramatic content of Borodin's opera is hardly greater than that of his thesis *On the Analogy of Arsenical with Phosphoric Acid.* One imagines oneself looking at a substantial living picture book of old Russia. Something is being presented, image by image.

At the exhibition, the Pictures will be replaced by Scenes of Pagan Russia.

Spirit in the Bottle of Cologne

Performance, St. Petersburg, 6 February 1909
For Gentleman with Props
Duration: 16 minutes

Scene One. The Dressing Room

The little man stands in front of the mirror. An ordinary fellow, perhaps somewhat moody and with a look that the unwary observer will interpret either as boredom or self-consciousness. (Of course, the presence of the mirror may cause the more naïve observer to consider narcissism.)

The little man changes his clothes: black slacks of stylish Italian cut, a crimson red jacket according to the latest Moscow fashion, a saffron-yellow vest from a St Petersburg tailor, a top hat imported from South Germany. This outfit is completed by a pair of patent-leather shoes, size 10. The little fellow cuts his nails, paints his lips, powders his cheeks, pomades his hair, showers himself in a cloud of perfume, puts on his white gloves and in conclusion, places six rings with inlaid imitation diamonds on his fingers. On his way to the podium, he inspects his footwear one last time, removes some fluff from his lapel and murmurs a quick prayer in the presence of an icon carried in his mind before going on stage.

Scene Two. On Stage

The little man puffs out his cheeks and bows. Hardly has he finished returning to the upright position than the toy bee (with a barely-visible key attached to its back) on his hat begins to buzz irascibly while attempting fruitlessly to defy gravity, being held captive by a safety pin. The man, feigning fear of an insect sting, chooses to take to his heels. But, alas, he comes not a foot further, paralysed by fright. Still not apprehending the futility of his efforts, the frightened fellow bails out his ballast in the hope of fleeing from his foe: he discharges a dozen doves from his vest pocket, procedes to pull out a profusion of handkerchiefs—the colour combination of which causes in many, or at least in himself, 'toothache'—from his pockets, and, after emptying his back pockets and undoing his cuffs and collar, reveals a samovar, a topee, a Puck, a sorcerer's apprentice, and a sultan.

His sleights-of-hand are dangerously ambitious and stirringly virtuoso. This is the head of the conjuring class, capable of quickly outdoing all and sundry—oops, almost himself as well. So quick, in fact, that he might just well succeed one day in filching his Muse's maidenhead without her being mindful of his deed.

Somewhat out of breath from this much ado about nothing, the fellow suddenly affects sobriety. Serenely, he conjures up a Rhine-maiden—addicted to 'cocaine'—and begins sawing this doomed thing in half. As always, a tedious procedure. After some time, murmuring is heard in the audience (that is seeing this trick for the hundredth time already) which causes him to quickly and skilfully finish his necrophilous task.

As a sign that the finale is at hand, the little man once more puffs out his cheeks. While cursing his impresario under his breath, who, in his omnipotence, grins maliciously while viewing the act from the wings (at that same moment, another impresario, out of breath after having just taken a seat in the twelfth row, reaches enthusiastically for his notebook), the little fellow once again shows off his tricks that (the impresario in the twelfth row is thinking) could make him, the impresario, immortal. Once again, the toy bee attached to his hat attempts to gain freedom, and once again in vain.

The spectacular conclusion that the little illusionist has kept under his hat the entire time hits its mark. Butterflies appear out of his ears and trouser-legs, butterflies in every colour of the rainbow, first ten, than a hundred, finally a thousand until, as if by magic (a leap in the air, a heroic wave of the right arm) the hall turns into one Gigantic Butterfly.

(Even Eric E. Withwalter cannot answer the question, in his epoch-making standard work *Illusion's Disillusion*, whether the butterflies were real or paper.)

Scene Three. Back Stage

During the reception after the performance, everyone wishes the little fellow much good luck. Even the impresario from the twelfth row. He has a look of amazement on his face. 'What a fantastic scherzo', you can see him thinking. 'I can use this man.'

A Photomontage

Every portrait can be replaced by another.

But no portrait can replace who is being portrayed. And yet, every portrait is more honest than the person being portrayed, although less true.

The question is: does the difference between one portrait and ten portraits (between ten and an infinite amount of portraits) result in a difference in the identity of the person being portrayed.

Not only is every portrait merely one of an infinite series of (possible) portraits, it also amounts to the total of them all. The particular portrait is preceded by this series of portraits, just like every word is preceded by an infinite number of words, every sentence by an infinite number of sentences, every book by an infinite number of books, and every piece of music by an infinite number of pieces of music.

Every good portrait makes this visible, just as every good piece of music makes that audible.

The portrait in question: is it animal?

In that case, of an animal that is 'fond of throwing out false scents'. C. Gray thought he recognized the Cheshire Cat. Unfortunately, the colours do not match, since they are, according to the authoritative source *PD*, now green on top and grey underneath, then only grey, with violet underneath, green and even gold. A later Chronicle speaks not of a cat but of a 'pig'; that pig, though, is later 'adopted by a stray kitten'. It is already becoming dizzying, but the going really gets rough where the Boston *Herald* introduces the object of our curiosity as the instigator of 'springfever in a zoo', of 'braying, roaring, chattering, howling, growling', of 'rebellion' and 'escape', and as the chairman during the 'consultation of the beasts' and the brains behind the 'slaying of the keepers'. Perhaps it was this source that triggered K. Schönewolf to apply the word 'Führerfähigkeit' to this instigator. Schönewolf's judgement is more or less confirmed by W. J. Guard who observed that the subject was 'keen of eye, prominent of feature, nervous in movement, quick in observation, rapid in speech'. This rapid speech is hidden behind 'full lips', according to A. Weissman; in the figurative sense of the word, this speech, if we can believe E. Mitchell, seems like 'a donkey's bray'. It is not clear if what is meant is universal braying, the speech of speeches, since what sounds like 'Esperanto' to B. Asagfieff (*sic*), sounds 'not even' like 'Esperanto' to his compatriot V. Gorodinsky. Its laugh, on the other hand, is that of a dog, 'meaningless', 'expressing nothing'; Gray describes it as 'a baring of teeth in a senseless grin'.

Reports on its country of origin are just as confusing. American and English commentators (Saminsky, the *North American*, Lambert) have long been of the opinion that its biological and socio-cultural determinants must be sought in Africa, particularly with the Zulus and the tribes of what was once the Congo. The creature 'is obsessed with mirrors', yet another American writes, who thereby places its roots in the Christianized area of Africa. Lambert, oddly enough, asserts two geographical extremes—Africa and Laos. If the topographical truth lies somewhere in the middle, then Schönewolf's characterological designation ('Asian fanaticism') takes on more than mere metaphorical meaning. Our own trust lies with E. W. White's research, who focuses his attention more to the left of centre, towards Eastern Europe.

As far as White goes, his description of the creature shows similarities to the elf. That is, not to the lovable sprite of books from our youth, but to the little monster, vile and cunning, who lives by means of theft. Only, this elf is said not to be of German, as is usually supposed, but of Polish origin. The race from which he descends can be traced back to the land along the shores of the Strava, a tributary of the River Nieman in eastern Poland. In English, therefore, this elf has become known as the 'straw'. (The word 'strawberry' is the fruit of a misunderstanding. This tasty morsel apparently resembles the straw's olfactory organ. The straw's well-documented dipsomania argues in favour of this etymology, until this etymology in turn is irrefutably contradicted by the half-Persian beauty, Yasmin Howcomely, whose report of the straw—as conveyed by R. Dahl—includes the description of 'a nose like a boiled egg'.) There are at least three expressions in English that emphasize the negative aspects of the straw: 'man of straw', 'the last straw', and 'straws in the wind'.

At this point, we may conclude that we are dealing with an *imaginary creature*, more fantastic, more preposterous, more illusory than the Chimera (after whom it is often called 'Ghima' or 'Guimochka'). But just as to the Chimera—that, according to Plutarch, is a sea captain tending towards piracy—later sources attribute human characteristics to this imaginary creature.

Tschuppik purports the straw as being 'worldly and elegant' and wearing 'a monocle'. Strobel, too, calls it worldly in regard to its 'superiority', its 'grandezza and infallibility'. Our knowledge of Russian is meager, but we are assuming that what the author of the unfinished *Mysterium* called 'minimum tvortshestvo' is identical to what M. Druskin calls 'resourceful imagination'.

And indeed, this creature must have a rich fantasy to be able to, according to the *Magdeburgische Tageszeitung*, convert air vibrations into a 'cigar case and humidor'.

Monocle and cigar case place the straw in the recent past, as does the 'noisy approach of a bombing plane' used by the *Boston Herald* in the continuation of its description of the previously-mentioned instigator of springfever. If there is any truth in the report that the straw was one of the many involuntary donors to Oswald Hendryks Cornelius's sperm bank (Dahl accounts 'fifty straws'), then there must be straw men among us. And yet, the problem of chronology is unresolved. What did E. Schulhoff mean when, in his tract on the straw published in 1924, he includes the remark: 'This pamphlet has been written by me one hundred years ago'? Is that why Lambert includes the straw as part of the mythological race of 'Time Travellers'? Lambert's hypothesis may also provide an explanation for the account given by Carpentier in which two members of the eighteenth century (composers, by the way), sitting on the grave of the straw, consume 'quince preserves', 'angel food cake', and 'hog's head marinated in vinegar, marjoram and sweet peppers'. The contents of the 'casket' that, according to Carpentier, is placed onto a 'hearse-gondola' by 'black figures, wrapped in bobbinet and crepe', is erroneously identified as the mortal remains of our Time Traveller.

Summing up, we can assert that the straw shows resemblance to a tangible creature of God, partly human, partly animal. This latter trait returns in the frequently-made comparison with a chameleon, in which regard its adaptibility (natural mimicry) should be noted. This chameleon is an exceptionally ill-natured animal that craftily outwits its prey; its tongue is a fully-developed trapping device for insects and can be extended to approximately twice its actual body-length.

Certainly, the straw is *not* a chameleon, he merely *resembles* one. The zoology of dreams is not poorer, but richer than the zoology of God.

V

1951—*The Rake's Progress*

1. Northern latitude, eastern longitude

'In Olanda l'ora canta,'

But not only in Holland.

In 1764 Bernard Oortkrass, of Dutch birth, bell-founder by trade, died in St Petersburg, broken-hearted and bankrupt. The Empress Elizabeth, daughter of Peter the Great, in 1756, by way of her ambassador in The Hague, had commissioned him to build a new carillon. The original carillon was destroyed when lightning struck the spire of the Cathedral of the Peter and Paul Fortress. In July 1760 Oortkrass had set sail for St Petersburg, accompanied by five assistants and thirty-eight bells. At the new Russian capital only disappointment awaited the bell-founder: work had yet to begin on the new spire; lodgings had not been arranged; two Germans were to oversee this man of high reputation; four of his five assistants had to be sent back home since the city was only willing to pay for one. When Oortkrass, some years later, demanded to be paid for the work done up to that point, the Senate refused: payment would be forthcoming when the carillon was installed. It was twelve years after the death of Oortkrass before music was once again heard from the spire of the Cathedral of the Peter and Paul Fortress. His carillon is the only carillon in Leningrad. And even though it has recently been restored, the original work has still to be paid for.

The district to the west of the Side Canal and to the north of the Fontanka River used to be known as Kolomna. Pushkin once wrote a story in verse-form about *The Little House in Kolomna.* In that house lives an old friend: Parasha. She is still in love with her neighbour, the handsome hussar Basil, who, disguised as Mavra, is the successor to her mother's recently-deceased cook. 'Kolokolchiki zvenyat', the hussar sings happily. Bells chime—'in memory of Pushkin, Glinka, and Tchaikovsky'.

According to N. L. Oslovianishnikov, the Russian bell originated in the West, not in Byzantium. In which case, the Russian word *kolokol* is derived from the Dutch word *klok*.

And so:

klok	(Dutch)
Glocke	(German)
cloche	(French)
clock	(English)
clochon	(Old High German)
clog	(Gaelic)
klockan	(Tirolean)
klocka	(Swedish)
klokke	(Danish)
klokke	(Norwegian)
glok	(Yiddish)

On the other hand, W. Ellerhorst asserts that the word first appears as *clocca* in a letter from St Boniface to the Abbot Huetberth in Wearmouth.

According to Curt Sachs, the word originated in Eastern Europe:

klakol	(West Slavic)
kello	(Finno-Ugric)
klåkül	(Polab.)

and once again:

kolokol	(Russian)

One argument in favour of N. L. Oslovianishnikov is that the expression *malinovy zvon* (*zvon*: peal) is derived from the word Malines, the Belgian city Mechelen, and not from *malina* (raspberry).

Actually, the city was called by the Dutch name of Sankt Pieter Burkh, popularly known as Pieter and known abroad as Petersburg, with or without the St. In 1914 this name sounded too German and was changed to Petrograd. After 1917, this sounded too tsarist so in 1924 it was redubbed Leningrad. One of the elderly women who guide visitors through the Theatre Museum still calls the city *Pétersbourg* every once in a while.

'The best thing in Leningrad is St Petersburg.'

But this St Petersburg, with its elegant eighteenth-century Italian houses and palaces of ochre, azure, sea-green, and oxblood-red, is the scene of a play that is no longer running.

And yet, on a bitter, snowy December evening, while the squares and avenues are lit up—though God-forsaken and desolate—the stroller can easily imagine that he, a reincarnated Akaky Akakievich, will be robbed of his brand-new overcoat. It is freezing cold. A policeman relates that the ice on the Neva sometimes has a bluish glow.

The noise in the time of Ivan the Terrible must have been enough to wake the dead. At least five thousand bells could be counted in Moscow in his day. They were Russian bells. They differed from the bells of Byzantium, Western Europe, and the Orient both in form and in the way they were played. Sixteenth-century Russia boasted of possessing the largest bell in the world and the largest cannon in the world. The bell was so big that it could not be suspended and the cannon was so big that it could not be fired. Later, in the first half of the nineteenth century, extravagant carillon-playing was curbed. Since the orthodox church softened its ban on musical instruments within its confines, the bell had to relinquish some of its power. But its strength as a symbol remained. Even in 1912, between 1,600 and 2,000 tons of bells were founded in Russia.

The Side Canal is outside the actual centre of Leningrad. Walk along the Nevsky Prospect with your back to the Neva River, turn right at the Stroganov Palace, follow the water of the Moika River until reaching the triangular island, New Holland, and there, running left and right, is the Side Canal. No. 66 is part of a stately block of houses that used to look out on to a prison, the Litovsky Fortress. On 27 February 1917, during the climax of the 'first' revolution, the fortress was burnt to the ground. New housing blocks have since replaced it.

Alexander Herzen called the first, then still illegal, revolutionary magazine, *The Bell.* And when Herzen's contemporary, Prince Odoyevsky, dreamed of free, fifteenth-century Novgorod, he heard 'the ringing bell of the popular assembly'.

No. 66 is a third-floor apartment. An opera singer lived there from 1876 until the year of his death, 1902. He must have had more than just average talent, considering that his earthly remains have the privilege of lying in an exquisite grave at Transgression's Repose.

The deceased singer is accompanied by the deceased writers Dostoyevsky, Zhukovsky, and Krylov, and the deceased composers Glinka, Dargomyzhsky, Rubinstein, Lyadov, Tchaikovsky, and the complete cast of 'Moguchaya Kuchka', the Mighty Handful. One can have a look at all of them for sixty kopeks. An old woman is in charge of keeping the gravestones clear of snow. Transgression's Repose is found at the entrance of the Alexander Nevsky

Monastery. The old, orthodox regulations of the monastery call for three times three religious services daily. Each had its own bell music. 'Blagovest' (on one bell), 'trizvon' (three-peal, on many bells, also called 'krasny zvon', splendid pealing), 'zatravka' (igniter), 'milking the cows' on two bells, 'perezvon' or 'perebor' in which all the bells, beginning with the highest and ending with the lowest, are struck rapidly in succession. In the Alexander Nevsky Monastery, the 'trizvon' is played on seven bells. This 'trizvon' was in three parts and could be repeated three times, just like the *Kosal moya ko . . .* which begins *Les Noces*.

Also, in a corner of the house at 2b Graftio Street, the home of the more famous Chaliapin, the memory of the singer is kept alive. There he poses in nineteenth-century manner in many of his roles, as Mephistopheles in *Faust*, Sparafucile in *Rigoletto*, Sen-bry (Saint-Bris) in *Les Huguenots*. In a glass case lies a musical autograph of Dargomyzhsky, dated 1870, that is, a year after his death. Above the case hangs a portrait of the singer in which he very definitely is the father of his son.

The street closest to the Side Canal just to the north of no. 66 is Decembrists' Street, named after the revolutionary-minded young officers who, in 1825, after the death of Alexander I, attempted a *coup d'état* against his successor, Nicholas I. Before the revolution, it was simply called Officers' Street. The city really has not changed, only its history has become less decipherable.

The dancer Nijinsky, who danced the part of Petrushka and choreographed the *Sacre*, lived on Big Horse-Stall Street, now called Zhelyabova Street, named after one of the members of the 'People's Will', the group that organized the assassination of Alexander II. Even the pre-revolutionary *A Life for the Tsar* and the post-revolutionary *Ivan Susanin* seem like the titles to two different operas. Yet Glinka's notes for both are one and the same.

(One needs to know the code. 'It is not a portrait, but a plan', the Italian customs agent alleged when he discovered a drawing by Picasso in the suitcase of the singer's son. Something similar also occurred to the Petersburg pianist-composer Rubinstein while crossing the border nearly a century earlier. The guard on duty seized his music: not because he was so fond of it, but because he mistook the notes for a revolutionary code.)

The door that permits entry into the part of the block to which No. 66 belongs is no different from all the other doors in the vicinity—except for the closest door to the left. Next to this door, a commemorative plaque has been placed, in remembrance of 'the composer and conductor' Napravnik.

(Far from here, at Place St Louis in the Swiss village of Morges, the wrong statue is still left in the cold.)

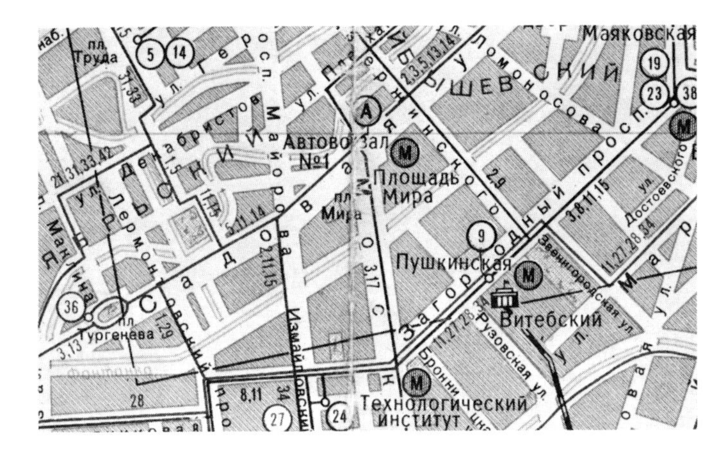

Round the corner from the Side Canal is the conservatoire. Since 1944, it bears the name Rimsky-Korsakov. Rimsky told the son of the singer that the conservatoire was not for him. He was willing, though, to accept him as a private student. That is how it began.

2. *Itinerary*

It does not even take a minute to get to the back of the Mariinsky Theatre. By the way, it is not called the Mariinsky Theatre any more, but the Kirov Theatre. Maria, wife of Tsar Alexander II, has been succeeded by a favourite of Stalin, Kirov—murdered party leader and once the big boss of Leningrad. But Leningraders still talk about the Mariinka, Little Maria.

Are new sets still delivered by boat? It used to be the case that if someone living on the canal looked out of his window, he might see storm clouds passing by. No Golden Cockerel though, that was confiscated by the tsar's censor.

The distance between No. 66 and here is less than the distance between Café Welling and the Concertgebouw.[1] The front of the theatre actually reminds one of the Concertgebouw. At least, at first glance. The sea-green façade is more elegant, though, not to mention what is behind that façade. The refined splendour of the hall and the exuberant opera stagings keep each other in anachronistic balance. No expense or trouble is spared. For one single storm scene from *The Maid of Pskov*, three horses, appearing for a total of six

[1] Café Welling and the Concertgebouw. Café Welling is a bar located diagonally opposite the artists' entrance of the Concertgebouw (trans.).

seconds, are brought from their stables in order to cross the gigantic stage-forest.

Everything has remained intact except the audience, although it still partakes of caviar and champagne during the interval.

In 1874 the first performance of Mussorgsky's *Boris Godunov* took place in the Mariinksy Theatre. During the coronation of Boris, the most famous bells of Russia are sounded. They are not genuine bells though. Genuine bells hang in towers. The orchestra has its own bells. Sometimes they are gongs, with or without piano, sometimes tubular bells or orchestral plates, sometimes strings and winds, and every so often, everything all at once. The coronation bells are grand and imposing. At the end of the opera, when a simpleton bemoans the sorrowful fate of Russia, the same bells become gruesome.

Bells are always pealing in Russian music: in *A Life for the Tsar* by Glinka; in the *1812 Overture* by Tchaikovsky; in 'The Great Gate of Kiev' from Mussorgsky's *Pictures at an Exhibition*; in Rimsky-Korsakov's *Sadko*, in *Kitezh*, in *The Maid of Pskov*, in *Russian Easter*. And later, in Scriabin's sixth and seventh sonatas, in *Prometheus*, in *The Bells* by Rachmaninov, in Prokofiev's *Alexander Nevsky*. The most famous bells that have *never* been sounded are the nearly half-a-million pound Tsar Kolokol, which prematurely collapsed from its wooden framework, and the bells that Scriabin wanted to suspend in the Himalayas in order to signal to the world that the *Prefatory Act* was to begin.

Not all Russian bells are as enormous as Scriabin's, but they are often very large indeed. Yet, they are not true church bells, and they are not anything like Wagner's Grail Bells. They sound more heathen than the bells in Western music.

To the left, a bit further along the Side Canal, an azure-coloured ice-cream cake appears—Nikolsky Cathedral. Russian baroque following an Italian recipe: *Pulcinella* as building. Without its five domes, it could have been mistaken for an eighteenth-century chancellery. The church is surrounded by a park. Closer to the canal, about a hundred and fifty feet from the church, stands a large, four-tiered bell tower. Free-standing bell towers are not exceptional here. The Vladimir Church, for example, around the corner from Dostoyevsky, also has one. This architectonic curiosity must have been imported by the Italian designers of this city.

'The loudest diurnal noises of the city were the cannonade of bells from the Nikolsky Cathedral and the noon signal from the Peter and Paul Fortress.'

According to a Dutch visitor at the time of Boris Godunov, the pealing of bells in Russia was sometimes so loud that 'people cannot hear one another in conversation'. During the nineteenth century it became more bearable. After the revolution, most of the bells have been silenced. A historian wrote: 'The twentieth century . . . the metamorphosis of luminous icons, ringing bells, and consoling incense into lithographs of Lenin, humming machines, and cheap perfume.'

Past the Nikolsky Cathedral, the Side Canal crosses Garden Street. Still further, the canal streams into the waters of the Fontanka. There, to the left. If, making a comparison to Amsterdam, the Neva is the IJ, then the Nevsky Prospect is the Damrak plus Rokin plus the Vijzelgracht, and the Fontanka is the Keizersgracht. Only it is not a genuine canal. The Side Canal is, but the Fontanka is too wide. Only non-Dutch compare Leningrad to Amsterdam because of its canals. It was Peter the Great's intention that even the Dutch would make this comparison, but Mr Wilde, the ambassador of the Republic of the Netherlands, after doing a bit of measuring together with the tsar, came to a disappointing conclusion: the proportions did not match one bit.

Bells are always pealing in Russian music and bells are always pealing in the music of the singer's son.

The bells of *Les Noces.*
The bells of *Requiem Canticles.*
The bells of the *Four Russian Peasant Songs.*
The bells of *Tilimbom.*
The bells of the *Three Songs from William Shakespeare.*
The bells of the *Symphony of Psalms.*
The bells of the *Symphonies of Wind Instruments.*
The bells of the *Concerto in D for Violin.*
The bells of *Perséphone.*
The bells of *The Firebird.*
The bells of the *Serenade in A.*
The bells of *Pribaoutki.*
The bells of the *Sonata for Two Pianos.*
The bells of the *Gorodetzky Songs.*
The bells of the *Concerto for Two Solo Pianos.*
The bells of the *Variations.*
. . .
The bells of *Souvenir de mon enfance.*

The number of churches and cathedrals in Leningrad exceeds even the number of Lenin Houses. There are three merely commemorating the Resurrection, another three for the Annunciation (there used to be four) and the Trinity is triply represented as well. One of them is here, across the Fontanka. And to the left, in the continuation of the last side street before it crosses the Fontanka and Major's Prospect, the St Isaac Cathedral comes into view. The sun is reflected in its enormous gold dome. Actually, everything about the St Isaac Cathedral is enormous. The height, the volume, the colonnades, the estimated weight, the amount (of what, does not matter), the queue of people waiting patiently by the entrance on Sundays, curious about what the travel guide describes as the 'grandeur and vastness' of the interior. The particularly un-Italian squatness of the building is enormous. One cannot be sure from a distance, but closer by, the four bell towers on the roof of the cathedral leave an empty impression.

The last time a large, profundo Russian bell rumbles is in *The Firebird.* After that, the bells will never be the same. A new method of founding is discovered, as well as a new bell-metal alloy and a new mould.

'The bewitchment of the call of the bell as a thing in itself, transcending Psyche and Kronos . . . is uncovered for the first time.'

The bells get smaller and smaller, finally atrophying. Gone are their open sonority, their mighty voice, their dramatic resonance, their formidable dominion. 'BOING' becomes 'ching', or merely 'ting'. Even the bells of the *Symphony of Psalms*—bells consisting of pianos, timpani, and harp—do not sound of sanctity and sexton, if they are even bells at all. Perhaps they are but footsteps, dragging feet of people trudging through the snow. It is a long way still to Venice.

G3 is not the loveliest part of the city, but one is through it pretty quickly. Where the Fontanka crosses the Balkan Highway (formerly: Moscow Boulevard), a gigantic Leader (at present Brezhnev) on the other side of the water keeps a watchful eye on the pedestrians crossing the street. Red letters, as tall as a man, announce a festive event.

Then, turning right, Pea Street (currently Dzerzhinsky Street) which becomes Suburban Avenue. Then a left turn.

In an early description of St Petersburg, mention is made of the first carillon of the Peter and Paul Fortress, the carillon that was destroyed by a bolt of lightning in 1756. It is emphasized that, in order to sound the great bell of this carillon, the bell itself *had to be set in motion*. It is an exception to the Russian rule, which itself is an exception to the general rule.

Carillon playing (chiming or clocking): the carilloneur sounds the fixed bell by setting the clapper of the bell in motion. He uses a rope to do this. He can also strike the bell with a hammer. The timbre of the bell depends on where it has been struck.

Bell-ringing: the bell-ringer sounds the bell by setting it in motion and allowing it to hit against the clapper. Ringing gives signals: there are bells for death, for war, for the mass, for weddings, and to announce the time.

In Russia bells are never rung. Bells are always mounted and played. Fixed bells need less room than swaying bells. Besides, they are less taxing for the belfries. This explains why Russian bells can be so gigantic.

In *Les Noces*, out-of-tune bells are struck very hard.

Suburban Avenue, No. 9: Anton Rubinstein. The theatre of the conservatoire bears his name.

Suburban Avenue, no. 14/25: Tchaikovsky.

In the Rubinstein Hall, a performance is being given of *Eugene Onegin* by the opera class. When Tchaikovsky composed this opera, he had left his house on Suburban Avenue some time before. At that time, Balakirev, on the other hand, was just about to move into a house round the corner.

The Russians are proud of their composers. Wherever there is music, huge

photos hang of Tchaikovsky, Mussorgsky, Glazunov, Prokofiev, Shostakovich, Rimsky-Korsakov. In the museum of the Philharmonic Hall hangs a photo of Rimsky's private student while in his youth. A portrait from 1962 sits on the bureau of the composer D. Proudly he tells about the inscription written on the passe-partout. He has not yet been able, he says, to get hold of a score of *Requiem Canticles*.

And where there are no bells, there are bell-like sounds: the *sforzato-piano*, written-out 'ringing through' ('perezvon'), ricocheting chords. At the least expected moments, it begins.

'The newest music in *Danses Concertantes* occurs between [79] and [83].' It is true, it was the newest, but it had been the newest for at least twenty-five years. Is not the fourth leap of F to B♭ no more than the fourth leap of F to B♭ in the out-of-tune bells that give the starting signal in the *Symphonies of Wind Instruments*? And what is the first and most important chord in these bars (a tower of octaves with an added minor seventh) if not the inversion of the final chord of *Les Noces*?

In *Les Noces*, time is compressed into one endless moment of simultaneous events which finally, when the voices are silent for the first and last time, freeze into a series of bell-like chords. This series of chords is not allowed to complete itself: it is interrupted. There is no conclusion, there is but silence. Though when does this silence actually begin. Does the ringing-through continue infinitely, only inaudible?

Bells can cause people to become disoriented. In Russia they say: 'Hearing the bell, he didn't know where he was'.

At a temperature of 20° F, with six inches of snow on the ground and at the tempo of someone who has to be punctual for his lesson, the walk from Side Canal 66 to Suburban Avenue 28 lasts exactly 34 minutes.

The house is in a courtyard. A shiny brass nameplate on the door of the fourth floor:РИМСКИЙ-КОРСАКОВ.In a glass case on the landing hangs an overcoat and a fur hat. The salon is the salon of someone who holds salons. Once every two weeks, on Wednesday evenings, there is a house concert. If the person playing the grand piano turns his head to the right, he will meet his mirror-image. The glistening-chrome piano lamp must be the latest thing from Better Homes and Garden. On the walls hang the portraits of Mussorgsky, Borodin, Glinka, Rimksy-Korsakov himself and his best friend Glazunov, Tchaikovsky was forbidden.

Each room is described by a notice.

'Nikolai Andreyevich came into the dining-room early in the morning to take a cup of coffee. After this first breakfast he went through the sitting-room, stopped for a moment at the piano, took an accord in the tune he needed and entered his study for work.'

Rimsky-Korsakov: in one hand maybe a second cup of coffee, that accord in the other. Coffee and accord both carefully set down on one of the two bureaux that take up much of the crowded study. One is perpendicular to the wall, the other in front of two windows that look out over the muddy courtyard. Schumann, Lizst, and Wagner keep an eye on things. Flowers are everywhere. Flowers on the wallpaper, flowers in the upholstery. 'Just like my Grandmother's used to be', is what people from good families say while looking at the pictures.

Nothing more.

3. *Southern latitude, western longitude*

June 1914.

'The bells of St Paul's in London.'

On the same piece of paper are three motifs, each consisting of four or five pitches.

'Astonishingly beautiful counterpoint such as I have never heard before in my life.'

So, not in St Petersburg. Not the Vladimir Church, round the corner from Rimsky; not the Cathedral of the Peter and Paul Fortress; not the Nikolsky Cathedral. But at St Paul's in London.

Number 1 in the register of works: *Tarantella* for piano. The piece is not published. It is safely stored in the manuscript collection of the State Public Library in Leningrad. It is written on notebook paper, a scrap really. It's more a rough draft and looks a bit sloppy. The staves are drawn with a ruler. The piece is in C minor. The metre is 6/8. Boom-two-chick, boom-five-chick, thus it begins with open fifths in the bass. The piece is indistinguishable from all the other pieces composed by sixteen-year-olds.

The beginning! The source! The roots!

But the beginning is also the beginning of a thousand others, an entire generation. Of a Russian generation. Of a Russian generation in St Petersburg. They all heard the iron-hooped wheels crackling throughout the city, the sounds of drozhkies on cobblestone, the horse-drawn streetcars gratingly turning the corner, the calls of vendors, and merchants, particularly Tartars.

'*Halaat*, dressing gowns!'

Stored in a collective memory, and not only in that of the former pupil of the Guryevich Gymnasium.

And when the thaw set in, the ice on the Neva cracked so loudly that people could hardly understand one another. 'Nye pozhelayet'l marozhennoyeh' one could hear everywhere. 'Would you like some ice cream?' Today ice cream is still sold on every street corner in the city. Even in the freezing cold. The first thing noticed in Leningrad in the winter is all the gloved hands holding an ice cream and all the fur-hatted heads with tongues sticking out.

And the nose of the generation, filled with the smell of leather, tar, and horses, and, of course, the Mahorka tobacco. 'Men, give us cigarettes', yelled the purple-painted whores on the Nevsky Prospect.

And the retina of a generation.

A Russian generation.

A Russian generation in St Petersburg.

A Russian generation in St Petersburg, born into a good family.

A Russian generation in St Petersburg, born into a good family, destined to study law.

A Russian generation in St Petersburg, born into a good family, destined to study law, brought up on art.

A Russian generation in St Petersburg, born into a good family, destined to study law, brought up on art, gifted with musical talent.

A Russian generation in St Petersburg, born into a good family, destined to study law, brought up on art, gifted with musical talent, living by a canal.

A Russian generation in St Petersburg, of a good family, destined to study law, brought up on art, gifted with musical talent, living by a canal, intimidated by a father.

A Russian generation in St Petersburg, born into a good family, destined to study law, brought up on art, gifted with musical talent, living by a canal, intimidated by a father, fearing a mother.

A Russian generation in St Petersburg, born into a good family, destined to study law, brought up on art, gifted with musical talent, living by a canal, intimidated by a father, fearing a mother, woken up by a Bertha.

A Russian generation in St Petersburg, born into a good family, destined to study law, brought up on art, gifted with musical talent, living by a canal, intimidated by a father, fearing a mother, woken up by a Bertha, helped into his coat by a Simon Ivanovich.

It does not help. The outcome is the result of an anonymous cause.

It is the secret of the onion. The onion-peeler is master of the disappearing act. He peels tunic after tunic. Each tunic causes one to consider the following tunic, and each following tunic causes one to consider the previous tunic. He peels and peels, and wipes his eyes every so often, a little embarrassed. The onion becomes less and less onion, until it even ceases being an onion. The onion-peeler stands there empty-handed. There just is not any secret. Guillaume de Machaut, in the fourteenth century, composed an enigmatic round: 'Ma fin est mon commencement et mon commencement ma fin'. The first mention of a melody played on bells dates from 1463. A certain John

Baret expressed the wish in his testament that the bells of the Parish Church should, at stated times, play the Requiem aeternam in his memory.

There are bells for marriage and bells for death. But they are all played on the same bells. That is why the silence at the end of *Les Noces* is the same as the silence at the end of *Requiem Canticles*.

. . . *there is the same as here, once on a time the same as now, or then; time is drowning in the measureless monotony of space, motion from point to point is no motion more, where uniformity rules; and where motion is no more motion, time is no longer time.*

Bells unsettle the awareness of what they, as clockwork, regulate: time. A bell is also an audible calendar; nowadays merely proclaiming the hour, once also announcing events—birth, death, marriage, fire, war, peace.

. . . *Behind* [Apollon Apollonovich] *the ages stretched into immeasurable expanses. Ahead of him an icy hand revealed immeasurable expanses.*

Immeasurable expanses flew to meet him.

Oh Rus, Rus!

François and Pieter Hemony were the most famous bell-founders of the seventeenth century. They knew what made a good bell. A good bell must be cast such that its sound spectrum includes three octaves, two fifths, a minor third, and a major third. But the minor third should be underneath.

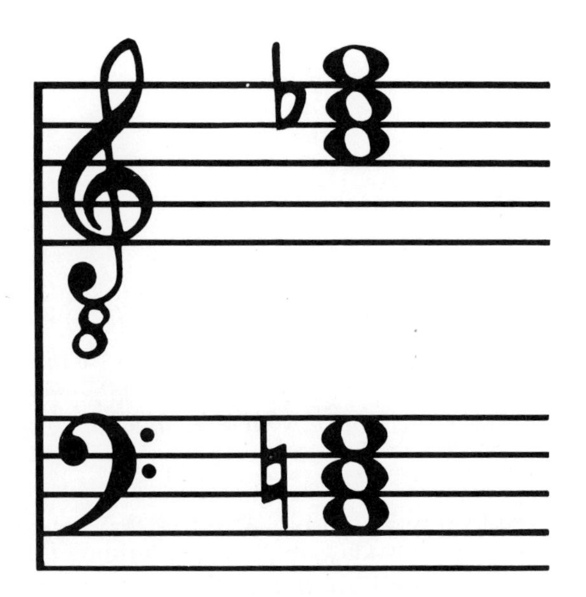

Inverted bell.

Inverted music.

List of Sources

All quotations appearing in this book of which the source can not clearly be deduced from the context are quotations of Stravinsky. General sources (and their abbreviations) are listed below, with details of the edition used in the translation following, where applicable. Please note that parts of *Themes and Conclusions* appeared earlier as *Themes and Episodes* (New York, 1966).

For the chapters 'Stravinsky' and '1951—*The Rake's Progress*' a list of specified sources appears below.

General sources consulted.

Stravinsky, I., *Chroniques de ma vie* (Paris 1935, 1936). [*An Autobiography*, no translator listed, New York, 1962].

—— *Poétique musicale*, ed. J. B. Janin (Paris, 1945, 9th imp.) [*PM*]. [*Poetics of Music*, trans. A. Knodel and I. Dahl, Cambridge, Mass., 1977, 4th imp.].

—— and Craft, R., *Conversations with Igor Stravinsky* (London, 1959) [*Conv*].

—— —— *Memories and Commentaries* (London, 1960) [*Mem*].

—— —— *Expositions and Developments* (London, 1962) [*Exp*].

—— —— *Dialogues and a Diary* (London, 1968) [*DD*].

—— —— *Themes and Conclusions* (London, 1972) [*ThC*].

Craft, R., *Chronicle of a Friendship 1948–1971* (New York, 1972) [*ChFr*].

Stravinsky, V., and Craft, R., *Stravinsky in Pictures and Documents* (London, 1979) [*PD*].

White, E. W., *Stravinsky: The Composer and his Works* (London, 1979, 2nd imp.).

Generally all other sources consulted or mentioned in the text are listed below by chapter in the order in which they appear in the text.

The New Renewed

Gramophone records:

Stravinsky, I., *Chanson russe* (Vera Beths, violin, and Reinbert de Leeuw, piano), BVHaast 039.

Bondt, C. de, *Bint*, Composers' Voice 8101, Donemus, Amsterdam.

America on Sunday

Suvchinsky, P., quoted in *ChFr* pp. 63 ff.

Lissa, Z., *Aufsätze zur Musikästhetik. Eine Auswahl* (Berlin, 1969).

Tansman, A., *Igor Stravinsky* (Paris, 1948).

Markus, W., 'Strawinsky en Adorno. Een verslag', *De Gids* (1/1979), pp. 45–66.

Thomson, V., *Music Reviewed 1940–1954* (New York, 1967).
Thompson, K., *Dictionary of Twentieth Century Composers 1911–1971* (London, 1973).
Lipman, S., *Music after Modernism* (New York, 1979).

Ars Imitatio Artis

Nabokov, V., *The Real Life of Sebastian Knight* (New York, 1977).
Hughes, P., and Brecht, G., *Vicious Circles and Infinity* (London, 1976).
Barthes, R., 'La mort de l'auteur', *Mantéia* 5, 1968; from Dutch trans. J. F. Vogelaar, 'De dood van de auteur', *Raster* (17, 1981).

No Copyright Problem Here

Chekhov, A., see F. Bowers, *Scriabin* (vol. 1, Tokyo, 1969).
Galton, F., *Finger Prints* (London, 1892).
Reese, G., *Music in the Renaissance* (London, 1959, 4th imp.).
Parry, Sir C. H. H., 'Arrangement' in *Grove's Dictionary of Music and Musicians*, 5th edn. (1961, 2nd imp.).
Austin, W. W., *Music in the 20th Century* (New York, 1966).
Dunning, A., *Count Unico Wilhelm van Wassenaer (1692–1766). A Master Unmasked or the Pergolesi–Ricciotti Puzzle Solved* (Buren, 1980).

1919—*La Marseillaise*

Ansermet, E., *Les Fondements de la musique dans la conscience humaine* (Neuchâtel, 1961).
Craft, R., ' "Dear Bob(sky)". Stravinsky's Letters to Robert Craft, 1944–1949', *Musical Quarterly* LXV/3 (1979), pp. 392–439. Also in: Craft, R. (ed.), *Stravinsky: Selected Correspondence* (Vol. 1, New York, 1982).
Onnen, F., 'De waarheid over Summermoon', *Mens en melodie* 3, (1948), pp. 85–7.
Vriesland, V. van, *De Stem van Nederland*, quoted in Onnen, op. cit.
Evans, M., *Soundtrack: The Music of the Movies* (New York, 1975).
Tomek, O. (ed.), *Igor Stravinsky. Eine Sendereihe des WDRs zum 80. Geburtstag* (Köln, 1963).
Prendergast, R., *Film Music: A Neglected Art* (New York, 1977).
Druxman, M., *Paul Muni: His Life and his Films* (London, 1974).
Marill, A., *Samuel Goldwyn Presents* (London, 1976).
Film-Repertorium No. 3 (Projecta-series No. 9) (The Hague, 1960).
Nederlands Katholiek Filmkeuring, see *Film-Repertorium*, op. cit.

A Motto

Babbitt, M., 'Remarks on Recent Stravinsky', in *Perspectives on Schoenberg and Stravinsky*, ed. B. Boretz and E. T. Cone (Princeton, 1968), p. 169.

Ordeals of the Memory

Adorno, Th. W., *Philosophie der neuen Musik* (Tübingen, 1949).
Pascal, B., *Pensées*, quoted in Borges, J. L., 'Pascal's Sphere', in *Borges: A Reader*, trans. Ruth L. C. Simms (New York, 1981).

Forma Formans

Buckle, R., *Diaghilev* (London, 1979).
Noske, F. R., *Forma Formans* (Amsterdam, 1969).
Cage, J., *Silence* (Middletown, Conn., 1961).

Zoonology

Nabokov, N., *Old Friends and New Music* (London, 1951).
Cocteau, J., quoted in Nabokov, N., op. cit.
Tchelitchev, P., quoted in Nabokov, N., op. cit.
Schlœzer, B. de, *Igor Stravinsky* (Paris, 1929).
Messiaen, O., quoted in Leeuw, R. de, 'Rythmicien en ornitholoog', from *Muzikale Anarchie* (Amsterdam, 1973).
Oulibicheff, A., quoted in Slominsky, N., *Lexicon of Musical Invective* (London, 1974, 4th edn.).
Mitchell, E., 'The Stravinsky Theories', *The Musical Times* 63 (1922), pp. 162–4.
Schaeffner, A., *Strawinsky* (Paris, 1931).
Carroll, L., *Alice's Adventures in Wonderland* (London, 1987, 10th imp. Penguin edn.).

1947—*Orpheus*

Cage, J., *Silence* (Middletown, Conn., 1961).
Berger, A., 'Problems of Pitch Organization in Stravinsky', in *Perspectives on Schoenberg and Stravinsky*, ed. B. Boretz and E. T. Cone (Princeton, 1968), pp. 123–54.

Purcell, Pergolesi, and the Others

Newman, W. S., 'Emanuel Bach's Autobiography', *Musical Quarterly*, LI/2 (1965), pp. 363–72.
Zimmerman, F. B., *Henry Purcell 1659–1695: His Life and Times* (London, 1967).
Radiciotti, G., and Cherbuliez, A., *Giovanni Battista Pergolesi: Leben und Werk* (Zurich/Stuttgart, 1954).
Letters of Wolfgang Amadeus Mozart, ed. Hans Mersmann, trans. M. M. Bozman (New York, 1972).

Concocted Reality

Schönberger, E., 'Elektronisch componist Dick Raaijmakers over sinustonen en de grappen met Rachmaninov', *Vrij Nederland*, (24 May 1980).

The Inverted Metaphor

Zamjatin, J., *Teken van leven*, trans. and with an afterword by C. J. Pouw (Amsterdam, 1980).

Zamyatin, Y., *The Dragon and Other Stories*, trans. Mirra Ginsburg (London, 1966).

Prendergast, R., *Film Music: A Neglected Art* (New York, 1977).

Poétique musicale

Ansermet, E., 'L'œuvre d'Igor Strawinsky', *La Revue Musicale* II/9 (1921), pp. 1–27.

Bäcker, U., *Frankreichs Moderne von Claude Debussy bis Pierre Boulez. Zeitgeschichte im Spiegel der Musikkritik*, Kölner Beiträge zur Musikforschung Bd. 21 (Regensburg, 1962).

Cocteau, J., *Lettre à Jacques Maritain* (Paris, 1926, 17th edn).

Cocteau, J., *Le Coq et l'Arlequin* (no place of publication given, 1979, reprint).

Comoedia, see *PD* 249.

Davenson, H., 'Arthur Lourié (1892–1966)', *Perspectives of New Music* V/2 (1967), pp. 166–9.

Gojowy, D., *Neue sowjetische Musik der 20er Jahre* (Regensburg,, 1980).

Honegger, A., 'Strawinsky, homme de métier', *La Revue Musicale* XX/191 (1939), pp. 21–3.

Kœchlin, Ch., 'Le "Retour à Bach" ', *La Revue Musicale* VIII/1 (1929), pp. 1–12.

Lourié, A., 'Leçons de Bach', *La Revue Musicale* XIII/131 (1932), pp. 60–4.

Maritain, J., *Art et Scolastique* (Paris, 1935, 3rd edn.); Dutch trans. C. A. Terburg, *Kunst en Scholastiek* (Amsterdam, 1924); English trans. J. F. Scanlan, *Art and Scholasticism* (London, 1947).

Maritain, J., 'À Propos du Jardin sur l'Oronte', *Les Lettres* (Dec. 1922).

Maritain, J., *Réponse à Jean Cocteau* (Paris, 1926, 17th edn.).

Maritain, J., 'Sur la musique d'Arthur Lourié', *La Revue Musicale* XVII/165 (1936), pp. 266–71.

Maritain, R., *Journal de Raïssa, publié par Jacques Maritain* (Paris, 1963).

Pijper, W., 'Muziek in Amsterdam. Concertgebouw: de feestconcerten', *De muziek* 2 (1927–8), pp. 421–5.

Schoenberg, A., 'Stravinsky's *Oedipus*', in *Style and Idea*, ed. L. Stein, trans. L. Black (New York, 1975).

Smith, B. W., *Jacques Maritain: Antimodern or Ultramodern?* (New York, 1976).

Tannenbaum, E., *The Action Française: Die-hard Reactionaries in Twentieth Century France* (New York, 1962).

Vestdijk, S., 'Strawinsky, de onbetaalbare matrix', in *Keurtroepen van Euterpe* (The Hague, 1957).

On Influence

Copland, A., 'Influence, Problem, Tone', in *Stravinsky in the Theater*, ed. M. Lederman (New York, 1949).

Roussel, A., quoted in Austin, W. W., *Music in the 20th Century* (New York, 1976).

Berger, A., 'Stravinsky and the Younger American Composers', *The Score* (June 1955), pp. 38–46.
Blume, F., *Classic and Romantic Music: A Comprehensive Survey* (article in *Die Musik in Geschichte und Gegenwart*), trans. M. D. Herter Norton (New York, 1970).
Markus, W., 'Strawinsky en Adorno. Een verslag', *De Gids* (1/1979), pp. 45–66.

1952–*Cantata*

Lindlar, H., *Igor Strawinskys sakraler Gesang* (Regensburg, 1957).

Philosophie der neuen Musik

Schlœzer, B. de, *Igor Stravinsky* (Paris, 1929).
Vlad, R., *Stravinsky* (Rome, 1958). (English trans. F. and A. Fuller, London, 1960).
Kirchmeyer, H., *Zu Strawinskys Liedschaffen* (programme notes to gramophone record *Igor Strawinsky—Lieder* sung by Lydia Davydova, Melodiya 200 095–366).
Routh, F., *Stravinsky* (London, 1975).
Siohan, R., *Stravinsky* (Paris, 1959, rev. 1971).
Tierney, N., *The Unknown Country: a Life of Igor Stravinsky* (London, 1977).
Schönberger, E., 'Gesprek met een oud-leerling van Schönberg [Leonard Stein]', *Vrij Nederland* (14 Nov. 1981).
Adorno, Th. W., 'Strawinsky, ein dialektisches Bild', in *Quasi una fantasia* (Frankfurt, 1963).

New York: Robert Craft and Vera Stravinsky

Mandelstam, O., *Selected Poems*, trans. Clarence Brown and W. S. Merwin (New York, 1974), quoted in *PD*.

1943—*Ode*

Bernstein, L., *The Unanswered Question: Six Talks at Harvard*, The Charles Eliot Norton Lectures 1973 (London, 1976).
Tansman, A., *Igor Stravinsky* (Paris, 1948).

Monsieur, le pauvre Satie

Cage, J., 'Defense of Satie', in *John Cage*, ed. R. Kostelanetz (New York, 1970).
Cage, J., *Silence* (Middletown, Conn., 1961).
Leeuw, R. de, 'Monsieur le Pauvre', in *Muzikale anarchie* (Amsterdam, 1973).
Myers, R. H., *Erik Satie* (London, 1948).

Ragtime

Conte, G., 'Les Mitchell's Jazz Kings', *Jazz Hot* 244 (1968).

1917—*Les Noces (Svadebka)*

Stuckenschmidt, H. H., 'Mechanisierung', *Musikblätter des Anbruch* 8 (1926, Hft 8/9, Sonderheft, *Musik und Maschine*).
Krickeberg, D., 'Automatische Musikinstrumente', from: *Für Augen und Ohren. Von der Spieluhr zum akustischen Environment*, exhibition catalogue, Akademie der Künste (Berlin, 1980).
Toch, E., 'Musik für mechanische Instrumente', *Musikblätter des Anbruch* 8 (1929, Hft 8, Sonderheft, *Musik und Maschine*).
Suidman P. (ed.), *Pianolas* (Baarn, 1981).
Strassburg, D. von, 'Offener Brief an H. H. Stuckenschmidt', *Musikblätter des Anbruch* 8 (1926, Hft 2).
Complete Studies for Player Piano. The Music of Conlon Nancarrow. Vols. 1 and 2. 1750 Arch Records S–1768 and 1777.
Satie, E., *Teksten*, ed. Ornella Volta, Dutch trans. Frieda van Tijn-Zwart (Amsterdam, 1976).
Bäcker, U., *Frankreichs Moderne von Claude Debussy bis Pierre Boulez: Zeitgeschichte im Spiegel der Musikkritik*, Kölner Beiträge zur Musikforschung Bd. 21 (Regensburg, 1962).
Nabokov, V., *Glory* (London, 1972).
Nabokov, N., 'The Peasant Marriage (Les Noces) by Igor Stravinsky', *Slavic Studies of the Hebrew University of Jerusalem* III (1978), pp. 272–81.

On Montage Technique

Monaco, J., *How to Read a Film* (New York, 1977).

A Kind of Brecht

Brecht, B., *Gesammelte Werke* vol. 16 (Frankfurt, 1967).
Brecht, B., *Leben des Galilei* (Berlin, 1979, 24th imp.); trans. C. Laughton (New York, 1966).
Brecht, B., *Brecht on Theatre*, trans. J. Willett (London, 1978).

1918—*L'Histoire du soldat*

Borges, J. L., 'The Aleph', in *Borges, A Reader*, trans. N. T. di Giovanni (New York, 1981).

On Authenticating and on Making Current

'Ik vind het pijnlijk dat ik alleen maar herschep' (interview with Gustav Leonhardt), *Haagse Post* (20 Sept. 1980).
Donington, R., *The Interpretation of Early Music* (London, 1963).

A Visit to Lake Geneva

Ansermet, E., *Entretiens sur la musique* (Neuchâtel, 1963).
Field, R. D., *The Art of Walt Disney* (London, 1945).
Ramuz, F., *Souvenirs sur Igor Strawinsky* (Lausanne, 1929).

Schaeffner, A., *Strawinsky* (Paris, 1931).
Stravinsky, T., 'Igor Stravinsky', *Le Figaro* (15 Oct. 1971).
White, E. W., *Stravinsky. The Composer and his Works* (London, 1979, 2nd imp.).

Id est: Hermetic Music

Boileau, C., *La Géométrie secrète des peintres* (Paris, 1963).
Huystee, Th. van, 'Stravinsky's Threni', *Mens en melodie* 34 (1979), pp. 114 ff.
Snijders, C. J., *De gulden snede* (De Driehoek, Amsterdam, no year given).

Stravinsky

The date given after each quotation is generally that of its first English (which may differ from the American) publication. Since some of the books cited are collections of older texts, some of the dates may be somewhat misleading. In a few instances (for example, quotations from Robert Craft's diary) it was possible to give a precise date. The page numbers for references to *Poétique musicale* are first given for the French edition used by the authors (ed. J. B. Janin, Paris, 9th imp.), then in parenthesis for *Poetics of Music*, trans. A. Knodel and I. Dahl (Cambridge, Mass., 1977, 4th imp.) used in this translation. The abbreviations are explained above.

page
204 *ThC* 51, *ThC* 32, *ChFr* 298, *DD* 128, *PD* 200, *PD* 195, *DD* 125–6, *DD* 128.
205 *ChFr* 148, *Mem* 110, *Conv* 26–7, *ChFr* 263, *DD* 129.
206 *DD* 107–8.
207 *Conv* 108, *PM* 120 (79), *ThC* 22, *PD* 372, *ThC* 110, *ThC* 107, *ThC* 24–5, *ThC* 130.
208 *PM* 80 (53), *DD* 26–7, *Exp* 31, *DD* 129, *Exp* 148, *Exp*. 101.

1957—*Agon*

Genet, J., *Journal de Voleur*; trans. B. Fretchman, *The Thief's Journal* (New York, 1964, 2nd imp.).
Mersenne, M., *Harmonie universelle, contenant la théorie et la pratique de la musique* (Paris, 1636); photographic reprint: Éditions du centre national de la recherche scientifique (Paris, 1963).
Arbeau, Th., *Orchésographie*; trans. M. S. Evans, *Orchesography* (New York, 1967, 2nd imp.).
Rabelais, F., *Gargantua and Pantagruel*, trans. J. M. Cohen (Harmondsworth, Middx., 1985, 17th imp.).

The World, A Comedy

Muecke, D. C., *Irony*, The Critical Idiom 13 (London, 1978, 4th imp.).
Mann, Th., see D. C. Muecke, op. cit.
Gogol, N., *The Portrait*, in *The Overcoat and Other Tales of Good and Evil*, trans. D. Magarshack (New York, 1965).
—— *The Overcoat*, in *The Diary of a Madman and Other Stories*, trans. A. R. MacAndrew (New York, 1960, 6th imp.).

Vinogradov, V. V., *Stil Pushkina* [*Pushkin's Style*] (Moscow, 1941), quoted in M. Druskin, *Igor Stravinsky*, trans. M. Cooper (Cambridge, 1982).

Octotony

Rimsky-Korsakov, N. A., *My Musical Life*, trans. J. A. Joffe (London, 1974).

The Firebird as Magpie

Escher, R., 'Ravel in de twintigste eeuw. Notities met het oog op een plaatsbepaling' (conclusion), *Het Residentie Orkest* (The Hague, Nov. 1966), pp. 16–21.
Poulenc, F., *My Friends and Myself*, trans. J. Harding (London, 1978).
Roland-Manuel, A., *Ravel* (Paris, 1948).
Bowers, F., *Scriabin*, vol. 2 (Tokyo, 1969).

1912—*Le Roi des étoiles (Zvezdoliki)*

Schaeffner, A., *Strawinsky* (Paris, 1931).
Le Roi des étoiles trans. George Hessen, CBS Records, 79251/74075.

The Tradition of the New

Debussy, C., 'Au Concert Lamoureux' (*Gil Blas*, 16 mars 1903), in: *Monsieur Croche et autres écrits* (Paris, 1971).
Lockspeiser, E., *Debussy: His Life and Mind* (London, 1962).

A Photomontage

Gray, C., *A Survey of Contemporary Music* (London, 1927), p. 146.
Stravinsky, V., and Craft, R., *Stravinsky in Pictures and Documents* (London, 1979), pp. 619, 611, 386, 607.
Craft, R., *Chronicle of a Friendship 1948–1971* (New York, 1973), pp. 148, 304.
Boston *Herald* (27 Jan. 1924); quoted in Slominsky, *Lexicon of Musical Invective* (London, 1975, 4th imp.), pp. 200–1.
Schönewolf, K., 'Gespräch mit Strawinskij', *Die Musik* XXI/7 (1929), pp. 499–503.
Guard, W. J., *New York Times* (9 Jan. 1916); quoted in *PD* 135.
Weissmann, A., 'Strawinsky spielt sein Klavierkonzert', *Anbruch* VI/10 (1924), p. 407–9; quoted in Kirchmeyer, *Igor Strawinsky: Zeitgeschichte in Persönlichkeitsbild* (Regensburg, 1958), p. 302.
Mitchell, E., 'The Stravinsky Theories', *Musical Times* 63 (1922), pp. 162–4.
Asagfieff [Asafiev], B., 'Über die Art des Einflusses Strawinskys auf zeitgenössische Musik', *Der Auftakt* IX (1929), pp. 106–8.
Gorodinsky, V., *Music of Spiritual Poverty* (Moscow, 1950); quoted in Slominsky, op. cit., p. 204.
Saminsky, L., *Music of Our Day* (New York, 1939); quoted in Slominsky, loc. cit.
Philadelphia North America (4 Mar. 1922); quoted in Slominsky, op. cit., p. 199.
Lambert, C., *Music Ho!* (1934, quoted from the Pelican edition 1948), pp. 137, 47.
White, E. W., *Stravinsky: The Composer and his Works* (London, 1979, 2nd imp.), p. 19.

Dahl, R., *My Uncle Oswald* (Harmondsworth, Middlx, 1987, 8th imp.), p. 137.
Tschuppik, W., 'Gespräch mit Strawinsky', *Der Auftakt* IV/1 (1924), pp. 280–1.
Strobel, H., 'Musiker auf Reisen. Strawinsky privat', *Melos* X/10 (1931), pp. 315–18.
Bowers, F., *Scriabin* (Tokyo, 1969), vol. 2, p. 249.
Druskin, M., *Igor Stravinsky*, trans. M. Cooper (Cambridge, 1982), p. 157.
Magdeburgische Tageszeitung, see 'Unter jeder Kritik', *Anbruch* XI/1 (1929), pp. 39–40; quoted in Kirchmeyer, op. cit., p. 295.
Schulhoff, E., 'Paraphrase übern Herrn Stravinsky', *Der Auftakt* IV/1 (1924), pp. 281–3.
Carpentier, A., *Concierto Barocco*, from Dutch trans. R. Lemm *Barokconcert* (Amsterdam, 1978), pp. 59–64.

1951—*The Rake's Progress*

Price, P., 'The Carillons of the Cathedral of Peter and Paul in the Fortress of Leningrad', *The Galpin Society Journal* XVII (1964), pp. 64–76.
Schilling, F. P., 'Das russische Glockengeläut', *Musik und Kirche* XXXI (1961), pp. 107–15.
Ellerhorst, W., *Handbuch der Glockenkunde* (Weingarten, 1957).
Sachs, C., *Handbuch der Musikinstrumentenkunde* (Leipzig, 1930, 2nd imp.).
Billington, J. H., *The Icon and the Axe. An Interpretive History of Russian Culture* (New York, 1966).
Blue Guide: Moscow and Leningrad, ed. Evan and Margaret Mawdsley (London, 1980).
Nabokov, N., 'The Peasant Marriage (Les Noces) by Igor Stravinsky', *Slavic Studies of the Hebrew University of Jerusalem* III (1978), pp. 272–81.
St Petersburg. A Travellers' Companion, selected and introduced by L. Kelly (London, 1981).
Lehr, A., *Van paardebel tot speelklok* (Zaltbommel, 1967).
Starmer, W. W., 'Chimes', in *Groves' Dictionary of Music and Musicians*, vol. 2 C–E, (London, 1954, 5th imp.).

Quotations

page

257, line 2: Rice, W. G., *Beiaarden in de Nederlanden* (Amsterdam, 1927), p. 20.
258, line 31: Stravinsky from *ChFr* 205.
265, line 18: Stravinsky from *Exp* 30.
265, line 24: Billington, J. H., op. cit., p. 474.
266, line 38: Lindlar, H., *Igor Strawinskys sakraler Gesang* (Regensburg, 1957), p. 23.
273, line 6: Mann, Th., *Der Zauberberg*; trans. H. T. Lowe-Porter *The Magic Mountain*, (New York, 1969, 4th imp.), p. 547.
273, line 12: Bely, A., *Petersburg*, trans. R. A. Macguire and J. E. Malmstad (Harmondsworth, Middx., 1978) p. 53.

Index

Page numbers in italics indicate musical examples